ADVANCE PRAISE FOR *HARVARD 1914*

"A delicious, well-crafted historical novel set at Harvard and in Europe during World War I. Harvard men and women will be enchanted by Allegra Jordan's re-creation of the moving story behind those German soldiers' names inscribed on the walls of Memorial Church."

—Daniel Klein (H '61), NYT best-selling co-author of
Plato and a Platypus Walk into a Bar

"What makes reconciliation possible? How can we shift our ground and make room for forgiveness? In this carefully crafted novel Allegra Jordan explores these questions and shows that the power of writing itself, the stored and accumulating power of poetry, and most of all the immense reserves of redemptive energy locked up in the narratives of scripture can be released into our lives, take us out of entrenched positions, and set us free."

—Malcolm Guite, Cambridge University chaplain,
singer-songwriter, and author of *Faith, Hope, and Poetry*

"A marvelous story of people a century ago struggling with issues of love, war, prejudice, and change that are as relevant today as they were in 1914. Filled with interesting, complex characters. Allegra Jordan writes with grace, understanding, and a fine subtle humor."

—Julius Getman (H LLB '58, LLM '63), prize-winning author
of *In the Company of Scholars* and *The Betrayal of Local 14,* and the
Earl E. Sheffield Regents Professor of Law, University of Texas

*"Downton Abbey has found a brilliant successor in this spellbinding tale of love, death, and war.
The finest war fiction to be published in many years."*

—Jonathan W. Jordan, best-selling author of *Brothers, Rivals, Victors: Eisenhower,
Patton, Bradley and the Partnership that Drove the Conquest of Europe*

HARVARD 1914

A War Romance

by Allegra Jordan

GOLD
GABLE
PRESS

Harvard 1914 is a work of historical fiction. Apart from the well-known actual people, events, quotes (especially from C. Copeland and A. Lowell), and locales that figure in the narrative, all names, characters, places, and incidents are the products of the author's imagination or are used fictitiously. Any resemblance to current events or locales, or to living persons, is entirely coincidental. The author is grateful for permission from the Harvard University Library Archives to use actual student letters in chapters 16 and 34. The author expresses gratitude to the *Times* (London) for use of the brief excerpt in chapter 5.

Permissions
Gold Gable Press
105 Pebble Springs
Chapel Hill, NC 27514
www.harvard1914.com

Library of Congress Cataloging-in-Publication Data

Jordan, Allegra.
Harvard 1914: A War Romance/Allegra Jordan – 1st ed.
     p. cm.
ISBN-13: 978-0988203105 (Gold Gable Press)

2012948378

COVER AND BOOK DESIGN: Nancy McMillen, Nancy McMillen Design, Austin, Texas
FRONT COVER PHOTOGRAPH: Radius Images/Corbis
BACK COVER PHOTOGRAPH: Hulton-Deutsch Collection/Corbis
AUTHOR PHOTOGRAPH: Rex Miller

To

THEODORE,

ALEXANDER,

and

MICHAEL

———◦◦◦———

and in memory of

REX COPELAND, 1969–1989

THE MENIN ROAD

Belgium, December 1, 1914

B urial did not come easy for the dead of Ypres.
The broken men lay where they fell, their bodies strewn in the
fields of southern Belgium: in Wytschaete and Hollobeke, Gheluvelt
and Polygon Wood, Messines and Menin. The German soldiers interred
the dead they could drag behind their firing lines during the waning
days of battle. But in late November, after a massive, month-long
assault gave no rational hope of victory, high command curtailed recovery. Moving soldiers into no-man's-land was suicide. Rescue and burial,
out of the question.

Instead the wind, snow, and rain absolved the field of its bitter
crop in one sloppy storm. Rain soaked the ground and churned a vis-
cous mud. The mud dislodged sandbagged walls, snapped telegraph
wires, sucked boots off, and swallowed the bodies mired in the sodden
terrain. As the rain turned to snow, the north wind scattered it across
the graveyard, creating a new, uneven field. It was an imperfect burial.

During the early-dawn hours of December 1, a young German signal corps soldier stood at the corner of two adjoining trenches. His
short blond hair was uncovered; his helmet, the heavy and ornate cover
of the uhlan's, rested on the ground. The rain had soaked through his
gray overcoat and dampened his tall leather boots. His thin nose
dripped constantly, irritated by the smell of wet wool.

Lieutenant Wilhelm von Lützow Brandl, 21, held in his hands a
wire and a transmitter, but he had stopped working with them. Instead,

he stood transfixed, looking over the wooden parapet at the snow blanketing the field.

All gone, he thought: builders, farmers, teachers, students. Is this how we end? he wondered. Jumbled parts in a mass grave, swept under a clean white carpet.

The wind bit into his neck. It burned his bruised ear, and the quick-falling snow piled around his boots. But the question repeated ceaselessly in his mind, like a record's needle turning after the song is through, the machine's energy not yet spent.

It seemed like such a short time ago when one single death—Max von Steiger's—brought his world to a halt. Mere months ago he'd been a student in America, at Harvard, when Max had died. Now there were too many dead, too many to mourn just one.

"Lieutenant Brandl!" barked a voice from around the corner. He reflexively reached for his helmet.

"Herr Captain, there's no signal." He fumbled with the strap. "These wires—"

"Brandl, you idiot!" Captain Grimber interrupted. Wils felt Grimber's hand pull his arm around. He cringed at the sight of the thin man's yellowed teeth and the smell of his stale breath. "Work without a helmet again and I'll court-martial you. Heinsel, mark him down. Half rations for Brandl." Wils scowled as the short, barrel-chested Lieutenant von Heinsel scratched his name in a small notebook.

The captain took the transmitter and crouched on the duck boarding, his canvas-covered helmet bobbing as he examined the equipment with a skill that completely eluded Wils.

The captain, like so many career officers in the Prussian army, thought that war brought out the best in people. His dull, cold eyes brightened when he spoke of a promised post in Paris. To get back there—for the German army had been close in October—the cables had to transmit.

Wils shivered as he looked at the captain's hollow cheeks. Grimber looked up. "Sit down. Heinsel will pull a new line and you will bury it. The weight of the snow will snap it by noon if you don't." Grimber stood up and left for the barracks with Heinsel in tow.

As Wils waited for the new line, a thin, square-faced sentry passed by, stepping quickly over Wils' snow-encrusted boots. The sentry craned his neck over the edge of the parapet, looking into the brightening gray horizon, and then he left. Two replacements rushed into the trench from the field carrying a large spool of barbed wire. They disappeared around the corner of the L-shaped trench toward the bunker. A group of soldiers with short spades and pickaxes slogged by next, blurry-eyed and muddied from the tops of their spiked helmets to the soles of their knee boots. One slipped on an icy patch of duck boarding, barely catching himself on the edge of the sandbagged wall.

An hour passed and von Heinsel did not return. The snow had stopped, but the cold became worse. Wils pulled his knees up and wrapped his arms around his legs, trying to conserve heat. The acrid fumes around him hurt his lungs. His toes and fingers were numb. His eyes fluttered as he fought sleep.

He began to recall a place where a light wind would rustle the ivy's brilliantly colored leaves to its dictate, fanning them down one red-brick building, across Harvard Yard, and back up the tall columns of another.

October would turn the Yard into walls of gold and red and orange. Smoke from fireplaces, dormant from a summer's rest, curled into the clear blue sky. He sat beside her on the steps, bathed in the sun. Lilac perfumed her dark curls. He lifted a ringlet and brushed it across his lips. Helen's eyes were royal blue and clear—bluebells on her light skin, like those in the fields behind his house. He laughed as she told him about her latest poem. He took her hands, and her face moved closer to his. Her breath felt warm against his cheek as she spoke, and her eyes looked steadily into his. He took her in his arms, felt her sweater, her breast against him. He could taste her kiss—soft and warm. The touch of her lips soothed him. It relieved the pain in his stomach and the hurt in his chest.

Suddenly, a flare shrieked into the air, close to his position. His body went rigid, and he looked furtively around his trench, expecting a shell. He waited and heard a distant explosion.

He shook his head. The corridor of that part of the trench had not changed. Muddy sandbags were still piled in front of him. The gray mist remained in the air.

He put his hands over his face and closed his red, irritated eyes. He was hungry for her voice, her touch. He pulled out a ring on a chain around his throat and kissed it. He tried, but he couldn't summon her back.

The mud of Flanders had absorbed his dream.

PART I: 1914

Harvard

———◦∞◦———

Cambridge, Massachusetts

And this is Old Boston
Home of the bean and the cod.
Where the Lowells talk to the Cabots,
And the Cabots talk only to God.
—John Bossidy, 1910

[CHAPTER ONE]

HARVARD YARD

Wednesday, August 26, 1914

I t was said that heroic architects didn't fare well in Harvard Yard. If you wanted *haute monde,* move past the Johnston Gate, preferably to New York. The Yard was Boston's: energetic, spare, solid.

The Yard had evolved as a collection of buildings, each with its own oddities, interspersed among large elm trees and tracts of grass. The rich red brickwork of Sever Hall stood apart from the austere gray of University Hall. Appleton Chapel's romanesque curves differed from the gabled turrets of Weld and the sharp peaks of Matthews. Holworthy, Hollis, and Stoughton were as plain as the Pilgrims. Holden Chapel, tucked away as it was, looked like a young girl's playhouse. The red walls of Harvard and Massachusetts Halls, many agreed, could be called honest but not much more. The massive new library had been named for a young man who went down on the *Titanic* two years before. There were those who would've had the architect trade tickets with the young lad. At least the squat form, dour roofline, and grate of Corinthian columns did indeed look like a library.

The Yard had become not a single building demanding the attention of all around it, like the overwrought and triumphal Memorial Hall just outside its boundaries. The Yard was the sum of its parts: its many irregular halls filled with many irregular people. Taken together over the course of nearly three hundred years, this endeavor of the Puritans was judged a resounding success by most. In fact, none were inclined to think higher of it than those forced to leave it, such as the bespectacled Wilhelm von Lützow Brandl, a senior and the only son of a Prussian countess, at that hour recalled to Germany.

A soft rain fell in the Yard that day, but Wils seemed not to notice. His hands were stuffed in his trouser pockets; his gait slowed as the drops dampened his crested jacket, spotted his glasses, and wilted his starched collar. The dying elms provided meager cover.

He looked out to the Yard. Men in shirtsleeves and bowler hats carried old furniture and stacks of secondhand books into their dormitories. This was where the poor students lived. But the place had a motion, an energy. These Americans found no man above them except that he prove it on merit, and no man beneath them except by his own faults. They believed that the son of a fishmonger could match the son of a count, and proved it with such regularity that Wils feared for the future of the wealthy class.

He sighed, looking over the many faces he would never know. I believe it too, he thought. *Mein Gott.* He ran his hands through his short blond hair. I'll miss this.

His mother had just wired demanding his return to Germany. He pulled out the order from his pocket and re-read it. The rain had started while he was collecting it in University Hall. She insisted that for his own safety he return home as soon as possible. She argued that Boston had been a hotbed of intolerance for more than three hundred years, and now news had reached Berlin that the American patriots conspired to send the German conductor of the Boston Symphony to a detention camp in Georgia. That city was no place for her son.

She had her points, although he was certain the reports in Germany made the situation sound worse than it was. The papers there would miss that Harvard was welcoming. If the front door at Harvard was closed to a student due to his race, class, or nationality, inevitably a side door opened and a friend or professor would haul you back inside by your collar. Once a member of the club, you stuck together.

But Boston was a different matter. Proud, parochial, and hostile, Boston was suspicious of anything not Yankee shabby. It was planned even in pre-Republic times to convey—down to the last missing signpost—"If you don't know where you are in Boston, what business do you have being here?" And they meant it. From Boston Wils kept his distance.

Wils crumpled the note in his hand and stuffed it into his pocket, then walked slowly to his seminar room in Harvard Hall, opened the door, and took an empty seat at the table just as the campus bell tolled.

By the time he arrived, the room was populated with twenty young men, their books, and a smattering of their sports equipment piled on the floor behind their chairs. Wils recognized the arrogant mien of Thomas Althorp and the easy confidence of John Eliot, the captain of the football team. Three were in Wils' final club, the Spee. Another student was a Swede, and two were from England.

The tiny, bespectacled Professor Charles Townsend Copeland walked to the head of the table. He wore a tweed suit, checked tie, and carried a bowler hat in his hand along with his notes. He cast a weary look over them as he placed his notes on the oak lectern.

The lectern was new, something which seemed to give Copeland pause. The new crest was carved onto the wood and painted in bright gold, different from those now-dulled ones painted on the backs of the black chairs in which they sat. The old crest spoke of reason and revelation: two books turned up, one turned down. The latest version had all three books upturned. Apparently you could know everything and were expected to by the time you left Harvard, although it was said the alumni office insisted that one never really "left Harvard."

It would take some time before the crest found its way into all of the classrooms and halls. Yankees were not ones to throw anything out. Wils had been told that two presidents and three generals had used this room and the chairs in which they sat. It wasn't easy to forget such lineage, as the former occupants had a way of becoming portraits on the walls above, staring down with questioning glares. They were worthy—were you? Their faces seemed to imply the answer was inevitably no.

Professor Copeland called the class to order with a rap at the podium. "You are in Advanced Composition. If you intend to compose at a beginning or intermediate level, I recommend you leave." He then ran through the drier details of the class.

"In conclusion," he said, looking up from his notes, "what wasn't explained in the syllabus is a specific point of order with which Harvard has not dealt in some time. This seminar started with thirty-two students. As you see, enrollment is now down to twenty. The registrar has already moved us to a smaller room." His eyes looked somber, as if the night had come in mid-afternoon.

"If you do remain in this class and on this continent, I expect you to write with honesty and clarity. Organize your thoughts, avoid the bombastic, and shun things you cannot possibly know about.

"Mr. Eliot, I can ward off sleep for only so long when you describe the ocean's tide. Mr. Brandl, you will move me beyond the comfort of tears if you write yet another essay about something obscure in Plato. Althorp, your poems last semester sounded like the scrapings of a novice violinist. And Goodwin, no more discourses on Milton's metaphors. It provokes waves of acid in my stomach that my doctor says I can no longer tolerate."

Wils had now heard the same tirade for three years and the barbs no longer stung. What had lasted was the fact that Copeland spoke to him when passing in the Yard.

As Copeland rambled, Wils felt himself wishing to argue against his mother, against duty, against, Heaven forbid, the philosophy of Kant. The situation was not as intolerable as his mother believed. These were his classmates. He had good work to accomplish. The anti-German activity would abate if the war was short—and everyone said it would be. His return to Germany would be useless.

He thought of the Fogg Museum—a new selection of American paintings had just been installed. And he'd yet to visit those glass flowers made in Dresden. Professor Francke wouldn't think too much of him, either. The new Germanic Museum would have to open without more of the Brandl money.

"Brandl!"

"Sir?"

"Don't be a toad. Pay attention." Copeland was standing over him.

"Yes sir."

"Come to Hollis 15 after class, Mr. Brandl."

Thomas sniggered, "German rat." Wils cast a cold stare back.

When the Yard's bell tolled the hour, Professor Copeland closed his book and looked up at the class. "Before you go—I know some of you may leave this very day to fight in Europe or to work with the Red Cross. Give me one last word."

His face, stern for the past hour of lecturing, softened. He cleared his throat. "As we have heard before and will hear again, there is loss in this world, and we shall feel it if not today, then tomorrow, or the week after that. That is the way of things. But there is also something equal to loss that you must not forget. There is an irrepressible renewal of life that we can no more stop than blot out the sun. This is a good and encouraging thought.

"Write me if you go to war and tell me what you see. That's all for today." And with that the class was dismissed.

WILS OPENED the heavy green door of Hollis Hall and dutifully walked up four flights of steps to Professor Copeland's suite. He knocked on a door that still bore the arms of King George III. Copeland, his necktie loosened at the collar, opened the door.

"Brandl. Glad I saw you in class. We need to talk."

"Yes, Herr Professor. And I need your advice."

"Most students do." The professor ushered Wils inside.

Wils detected the smell of stale ash that permeated the room. The clouds outside cast shadows into the sitting area around the fireplace. Rings on the ceiling above the glass oil lamps testified to Copeland's refusal of electricity. The furniture—a worn sofa and chairs—bore the marks of years of students' visits. A pitcher of water and a scotch decanter stood on a low table, an empty glass beside them.

Across the room by the corner windows, Copeland had placed a large desk and two wooden chairs. The windows were open and a breeze caused the threadbare curtains to threaten one of the lamps on the desk.

Copeland walked behind the desk, which was piled high with news articles, books, and folders. He pointed Wils to a particularly weathered chair in front of him, in which rested a stack of yellowing papers, weighted by a human skull. Copeland had walked by it as if it were a used coffee cup.

"One of ours?" asked Brandl, as he moved the skull and papers respectfully to the desk.

The severe exterior of Copeland's face cracked into a smile. "No. I'm researching Puritans. They kept skulls around. Reminded them to get on with it. Not dawdle. Fleeting life and all."

"Oh yes. 'Why grin, you hollow skull—'"

"Keep your *Faust* to yourself, Wils. But I do need to speak to you on that subject."

"Faust?"

"No, death," said Copeland. His lips tightened as he seemed to be weighing his words carefully. His face lacked any color or warmth and the wrinkles around his eyes made him look like an old elephant. "Well, more about life before death."

"Mine?" asked Wils.

"No. Maximilian von Steiger's life before his death."

"What the devil? Max—he, he just left for the war. He's dead?"

Copeland leaned toward him across the desk. "Yes, Maximilian von Steiger. And no, he didn't leave. Not in the corporeal sense. All ocean liners bound for Germany have been temporarily held, pending the end of the conflict in Europe."

Wils' eyes met Copeland's. "What do you mean?"

"Steiger was found dead in his room."

"Fever?"

"Noose."

Wils' eyes stung. His lips parted, but no sound came out. "You are sure?"

As Copeland nodded, Wils suddenly felt nauseous, his collar too tight. He loosened his tie. The two sat in silence for some length.

"May I have some water, please, Herr Professor?" Wils finally asked in a raspy voice. As Copeland turned his back to him, Wils took a deep breath, pulled out a linen handkerchief, and cleaned the fog from his spectacles.

The professor walked over to a nearby table and poured a glass of water. "How well did you know Max?" he asked, handing the glass to Wils.

He took the tumbler and held it tight, trying to still his shaking hand. "We met in confirmation class in Prussia and we shared the same mathematics tutor. But I've known him forever."

"Did you know anything about any gaming debts that he'd incurred?"

Debts? "No."

"Do you think that gaming debts were the cause of his beating last week?" asked Copeland, sitting back in his desk chair.

Wils moved to the edge of his seat. The *prügel*? Last Wednesday's fight flashed into his mind. There had been a heated argument between Max and a very drunk Arnold Archer after dinner at the Spee Club. Max had called him a coward for supporting the British but not being willing to fight for them. It wasn't the most sensible thing to do, and on Thursday at the boathouse Max had received the worst of a fight with Archer's gang.

"It was a schoolboys' fight. They were drunk. Max was beaten because Arnold Archer was mad about the Germans beating the British in Belgium. Archer couldn't fight because America's neutral, so he hit a German who wouldn't renounce his country. These fights break out all the time over politics when too much brandy gets in the way. People get over their arguments."

"Didn't Max make some nationalistic speech at the Spee Club?"

Wils' back stiffened. "If he'd been British it would have gone unnoticed. But because he was German, Archer beat him." He paused. "Max was going to tell the truth as he knew it, and thugs like Archer weren't going to stop him."

Copeland tapped a pencil against his knee. "How well do you think his strategy worked?"

Wils' eyes widened. "Being beaten wasn't Max's fault, Professor. It was the fault of the person who used his fists."

"Wils, Arnold Archer's father is coming to see me this evening to discuss the case. His son is under suspicion for Max's death."

"I hope Arnold goes to jail."

"Arnold may not have been involved."

Wils set the glass down on the wooden desk and stood up. "He's a pig."

"Wils, according to Arnold, Max tried to send sensitive information about the Charlestown naval yard to Germany." A faint tinge of pink briefly colored the professor's cheeks. "Arnold said he knew about this and was going to go to the police. Max may have thought that he would go to jail for endangering the lives of Americans and British citizens. And if what Arnold said was right, then Max may have faced some very serious consequences."

"America's not at war."

The professor didn't respond.

"Why would Max do such a thing?" asked Wils curtly.

"Arnold says he was blackmailed because of his gaming debts."

"What could Max possibly have found? He's incapable of remembering to brush his hair on most days."

Copeland threw up his hands, nearly tipping over a stack of books. "I have no idea. Maybe America's building ships for England. Maybe we've captured a German ship. Apparently he found something. Some time later, Max was found by his maid, hung with a noose fashioned from his own necktie. His room was a wreck." Copeland looked at him intently. "And now the police don't know if it was suicide or murder. Arnold might have wanted to take matters into his own hands—as he did the other night after the Spee Club incident."

Wils ran his hands through his hair. "Arnold a murderer? It just doesn't make sense. It was a schoolboys' fight. And Arnold's a fool, but much more of a village idiot than a schemer."

"Don't underestimate him, Wils. He's not an idiot. He's the son of a very powerful local politician who wants to run for higher office. His father holds City Hall in his pocket."

"Are you speaking of Boston City Hall?"

"Yes."

"I could care less about some martinet from Boston. I'm related to half the monarchs in Europe."

"City Hall has more power over you right now than some king in a faraway land," said Copeland. "Arresting another German, maybe stopping a German spy ring—that would be exactly the thing that could get a man like Charles Archer elected to Congress. I'd recommend you cooperate with him."

"If Arnold killed Max—" He stopped, barely able to breathe. Max was dead? Unthinkable.

"It could've been suicide," said Copeland.

"Was there a note?"

"Nothing. That's why the Boston police may arrest Archer even if his father does run City Hall. Either it was a suicide and it won't happen again, or perhaps we need to warn our German students about a problem." Copeland's fingers brushed the edge of his desk. "The police want to talk with you before innocent people are accused, and I'd recommend you do it."

"Innocent people? Arnold Archer? Is this a joke?" asked Wils.

"He may not be guilty."

Wils paused. "I'm not sure how much money his father's giving Harvard, but it had better be a lot."

"That's most uncharitable!"

"And so is murder of a decent human! Where's Professor Francke?"

"The police questioned him this morning and he is cooperating. His ties to the Kaiser have brought him under suspicion. City Hall thinks he could be a ringleader. The dean of students asked me to speak with you and a few others prior to your discussions with the police. They should contact you shortly regarding this unpleasantness."

"If that is all—" Wils bowed his head to leave, anger rising in his throat.

"Wils, you had said you wished to ask me about something."

Wils thought back to his mother's telegram. Perhaps she'd been right to demand his return after all. He looked up at Copeland, sitting under an image of an old Spanish peasant. He seemed to have shrunk in his large desk chair.

"No, Herr Professor. Nothing at all. Good day."

Copeland didn't rise as Wils turned to enter the dimly lit hallway. As his eyes adjusted, a poem from Copeland's class came to him. Wils turned back to his teacher and said:

> *"For the world, which seems*
> *To lie before us like a land of dreams,*
> *So various, so beautiful, so new,*
> *Hath really neither joy, nor love, nor light,*
> *Nor certitude, nor peace, nor help for pain*
> *And we are here as on a darkling plain—"*

Copeland brightened. "Swept with confused alarms of struggle and flight, where ignorant armies clash by night," they finished together. Wils nodded, unable to speak further.

"Matthew Arnold has his moments. Please close the door from the outside." Copeland looked down again, and the interview was over.

THE RAIN had driven the students inside their dormitories and flooded the walkways in Harvard Yard. As Wils left Hollis Hall, he removed his tie and pushed it into his pocket. The damned Americans talk brotherhood, he thought, but if you're from the wrong side of Europe you're no brother to them.

Max dead. Arnold Archer under suspicion. And what was all of that ridiculous nonsense about the Charlestown naval yard, he wondered, nearly walking into a large blue mailbox. He crossed the busy street and went toward his rooms in Beck Hall.

In his mind, he saw Max trading barbs at the dinner table and laughing at the jests of Wils' roommate, Riley, an inveterate prankster. And how happy Max had been when Felicity had agreed to go with him to a dance. But he'd been utterly heartbroken when she deserted him last year for a senior. This past summer they'd walked along the banks of the Baltic. He said he would never get over her. He never really had. What had happened?

Anger welled up inside Wils as he opened the arched door of Beck Hall and walked quickly past Mr. Burton's desk. The housemaster didn't look up from his reading. Wils shut the door to his room behind him. His breath was short. His hands hadn't stopped trembling. He had to find Riley and discuss what to do about Arnold.

Wils picked up a porcelain vase and threw it against the brick fireplace. It crashed and shattered, the blue and white shards falling over the crimson rug.

[CHAPTER TWO]

BERTRAM HALL

CONCORD, MASSACHUSETTS
Saturday, August 29, 1914

C olonel William Buttrick Darlington, Harvard Class of 1863, was a tall, thin man in his early seventies. He had a shock of thin gray hair brushed across his forehead, and a fine nose—one that Cleopatra herself would have envied. He had never been known to voice a single immoderate sentiment in his entire life. In fact, since he married the talkative Mrs. Darlington, he'd not managed to be heard on many subjects at all.

But his money spoke for him. He owned the largest estate on the banks of the Concord River, which stretched for more than a thousand acres on either side of the water and encompassed several hills, a greenhouse, a gazebo, a park, a garage filled with elegant cars, a boathouse, and a large red-brick mansion. The manse, Bertram Hall, had been built in the grand Federal style. A bright polished weathervane shaped like a clipper ship capped its white cupola. Its golden gleam could be seen for miles, standing higher than the maples, Scotch pines, and birch trees that wooded the property. The ship's crow's nest stood a rumored six inches higher than the Congregational church's thin white spire.

The family had built its fortune in shipping during the Napoleonic wars. One hundred years later, they remained one of the richest families of Boston society, the trust having survived a century of bankers, teachers, preachers, gadabouts, spendthrifts, and Harvard graduates.

Boston, however, had not reached its final verdict on the Darlingtons. Rumors of Tory sympathies lingered. They had the temerity to marry a lost branch of Concord's famed Buttrick family, whose forefathers' known contempt for the likes of the Darlingtons shone true on April 19, 1775. Major John Buttrick had stood at the forefront of battle at the Old North Bridge and helped turn the Redcoats, *and those who sympathized with their tyrannical plans,* back to Boston. No marriage could change history, society felt.

The family had countered by placing a bronze statue of George Washington on their front lawn back in 1840, and the colonel had served with some distinction in the Union army, unlike many of his neighbors who hired men to go in their place. These acts did little to mollify the neighbors. The Puritans had been able to pick out a Tory in their midst several generations before the upstart Darlingtons had even landed.

Thus, when the ladies of the Equal Suffrage Society asked the Darlingtons to support the 1914 women's voting rights movement with a dance at the estate, the family accepted with alacrity. It was widely believed that they were in no position to refuse, especially after their disgraceful conduct during the War of 1812.

As a result, on the last Saturday in August, Colonel Darlington and his wife opened their home to raise money for women's suffrage at the last dance of the summer. The banks were bursting with money, real estate values had risen with the outbreak of war in Europe, and farmers predicted a bountiful harvest. The burghers of Boston were rich, and the ladies of the Equal Suffrage Society knew it. It was time to fleece the flock.

The dance that night was an elegant affair, as was anything the Darlington money touched. Japanese lanterns glowed a mellow orange all along the driveway to the mansion. Servants assembled trays of delicacies on the closely cropped grounds by the kitchen. Smoke from spits roasting lamb and beef drifted lazily in the air. Boys cranked ice cream machines under bunting-hung windows. Young women in white pinafores carried silver trays stacked with pastries into the house. Children ran across the lawn in a pack, carrying sparklers toward the bright white lattice gazebo, which stood at the edge of the Concord

River. All of Boston's top society had turned out this evening, crowding the receiving line by the time seventeen-year-old Helen Windship Brooks and her parents reached their hosts.

Helen was a thin girl with a pretty smile, large blue eyes, and a sharp tongue. Boston attributed her spirited opinions to her mother's side, which had produced generations of unflinchingly frank women who lived forever, or at least they seemed to. Her charm and steadfastness were attributed to her father's family, which had produced generations of men bred to withstand the onslaught of Windship women. Brooks men tended to live only into their late sixties.

On that cool August evening, Helen stood prettily by both of her parents in the receiving line at the Darlington mansion. Like most of the unmarried girls there, she wore a simple dress of white silk. Her adornment was a matching white silk purse and a white satin ribbon wrapped around her dark hair, worn tonight in a severe knot. Mr. Brooks insisted that Boston encouraged and approved of this temperate style. She thought it made her look like George Washington and that Boston approved because Boston didn't change, not even for war.

And there was little hope of Boston changing now. She looked down the receiving line. No one seemed to even notice there was a war going on. Men in black or white jackets and two-quart hats stood talking in a circle. The ladies were dressed in immaculate silk gowns in the colors of the Boston season: white and gray, brown and black—the colors for every season, at least as far back as Helen could remember. It was as it always had been and always would be, Boston without end, Amen. And if anyone wished to peacock, she could expatriate to New York. That was how they'd lost Aunt Adèle.

Colonel Darlington stood erect on the red-carpet dais at the top of a set of wide, polished steps, his eyes smiling as he greeted them. Standing beside him was his wife, Bertha, dressed in reliable Boston brown. She was a good Christian woman, prone to gossip, and when she smiled, her penciled eyebrows nearly reached her hairline. Above her was a sign that read, "Rights for Women, Boston's other poor, downtrodden majority."

The colonel kissed her mother's gloved hand. "Enchanted, Mrs. Brooks—"

"Merriam Brooks! Have you heard the good news?" interrupted Mrs. Darlington. "Frank Adams and Caroline Peabody are to marry!"

Helen stiffened as her mother nodded.

"And I see you've brought Helen!" Mrs. Darlington's eyebrows cocked. She placed her fleshy hand on Helen's upper arm. "Helen, I won't mention the fact that you're not engaged, but Robert Brown is here and available to dance." Her pink cheeks looked like tiny polished crab apples. Helen turned to see that her mother and father had been accosted by another couple, abandoning her in the receiving line.

Helen felt her face go hot. "Thank you," she said, looking down at the edge of her white slippers.

Mrs. Darlington's hand tightened on Helen's arm. "I hope you'll return for the Harvest Festival next Saturday. We'll have an event to raise money for voting rights. We're having young ladies get in a motor-car and race, and your mother said you'd volunteer to drive."

Helen blanched. "I'm not sure I'd like to do that, Mrs. Darlington."

"Nonsense, Helen," Bertha Darlington replied. "I'm surprised she didn't tell you herself. It will be good for you," she said, nodding and elaborating on this plan and others that might be of use in procuring a husband under circumstances which were, she sighed, not ideal. If the newspapers had not made such a fuss over her mother's arrest last week, and if her mother would stop talking about—Mrs. Darlington blushed—"you-know-what," she whispered, then things could return to normal and Helen could once again look for a husband.

During the brief time between Mrs. Darlington's first confidence and her last, the innuendo of her speech, charity-laced as it was with concern for her upbringing (or lack thereof), Helen felt that her walk to the mahogany-paneled ballroom was much in the fashion of the Puritan adulteress Hester Prynne, and the dance floor her three-hour scaffold. Because if Mrs. Darlington greeted her at the door with such forward ideas, Helen had a notion of what the rest of the room was thinking, and felt her heart on display under the gilt ceiling, along with so many dandified duck quarters and spun sugar fruits. Behind the arched eyebrows and bored faces were her judges, magistrates, and governors, all knowing the same thing. That her mother, recently jailed for distributing information and actual devices for family limitation by mail, was too busy solving the world's problems to properly raise her daughter. That it was understandable, given the circumstances, that Frank Adams would choose Caroline instead of her. And no news of war halfway around the world would change the fact that here, in Middlesex County, Helen's future was bleak.

Helen sniffed. Things must be better in more sensible areas of the country—maybe Nebraska or Iowa, she thought.

Athens on a hill. Indeed.

HELEN WATCHED her mother, a humorless woman with a hawklike nose, walk over to the head table to help count the contributions. They hadn't discussed next week's festival, whom Helen was to marry, or Helen's general state of mind. And they'd most certainly not spoken of the unpleasantness during the past week.

Helen had barely seen her mother since March. Mrs. Brooks had spent the summer with Margaret Sanger in New York in order to learn how to care for the women of the tenements. There she wrote, published, and distributed information about preventing pregnancy, tracts intended for the poor of New York's Lower East Side. The federal government had recently indicted both women and several of their friends under the Comstock Law for violating postal obscenity laws. This had prompted Helen's father to demand his wife's return to Boston while she awaited trial. But as soon as Merriam returned to Boston she began to mail this type of information from their parlor, leading to a second arrest on the steps of Boston City Hall for violation of the state's postal obscenity laws. This time the news made the pages of the *Boston Evening Transcript*. Only the eruption of war in Europe had been able to push it off the front pages.

Helen wished they could just leave the dance. She watched her mother, clad in a gray silk dress that nearly matched her lips, stand at the contributions table with the proud air of a woman used to carrying the weight of the world on her shoulders.

Helen's father, Mr. Jonathan Brooks, on the other hand, who rarely carried more than the weight of a good history book in his hands, looked longingly in a different direction, toward a group of his friends standing by the drinks. He shifted restlessly in his starched collar and black jacket and looked as if he were a bit embarrassed by the entire evening. He had made the case just that morning that he preferred to sit in his study with a new book, *The Mechanics of the Horseless Carriage.*

It wasn't, Helen knew, that her father was against merriment. It was just that he had all the friends he needed and didn't think he'd like anyone he'd not yet met. She, on the other hand, liked very few of the people she'd met and looked forward to meeting new ones at college.

Caroline and Frank stood nearby in a circle of admirers close to the musicians. Not far away, in the corner, was the broad-shouldered, dark-eyed Robert Brown, nodding while escorting a great-aunt to a seat near the window. He could not stand dances, she knew, and he had told her he'd been mortified by his mother's interference regarding their future prospects together. Not that his protests mattered.

"Father," asked Helen, standing beside him at the margin of the ballroom, "don't you think it's a bit untoward to have a celebration like this when the world is in such peril? The British are being blown up and here we are at a party."

Her father opened his mouth, only to shut it quickly. His eyes seemed to go dull. "Helen, try to imagine yourself having a good time. That's what I am doing."

"Perhaps we could leave?"

"I tried to negotiate that into the agreement I made with your mother this morning. We must stay. The ties that bind and all." But his large face, with its widening whiskers and graying hair, spoke what he wouldn't say aloud.

They stood in bored silence for a good ten minutes, watching the events and pretending to be entertained. When a person came by to greet them, Mr. Brooks would give a nice smile and engage in brief small talk about the weather or the Harvard football season, and in those short exchanges Helen would dutifully nod, feeling each time as if she were a hypocrite. None of these people had paid a call on their family since her mother's arrest, and several had been too busy with other things to even inquire as to their state of mind. She especially had a hard time even choking out words of greeting to Mrs. Peabody, who had been exceptionally vocal at church in her concern for community decency standards.

About the time Helen had become convinced that all hope was lost, Robert Brown walked to her side. He'd been dismissed by the aunt, who was now talking with Caroline Peabody and Frank Adams.

As Mr. Brooks hailed a waiter with a tray of scotch whiskies, Robert bowed to Helen. Except for their eyes, they could have been cousins. Outsiders had, at times, mistaken them for brother and sister, given their similar coloring, height, and demeanor. He would have been a much better brother than her own, she often felt, as Peter seldom did a thing she told him to do.

"Your mother made you come tonight?" she asked.

"I asked if I could work on the new car instead, but she'd have none of it. She said I was to get married and that this dance might be my last chance."

"She shouldn't despair just yet, Robert."

"She's probably justified in my case. I brought a book to horrify her," he said, with a slight smile. "I intend to start reading after I ask if you are indeed leaving to Radcliffe tomorrow."

"If only it could have been tonight."

He swallowed to keep from smiling again, and, as he did, his white bow tie bobbed at his throat.

He looked so awkward dressed in his white tie and black tails, she thought. He belonged on a train to Colorado, to ride horses in the valleys, or to hike among shimmering aspens. He'd always talked of big skies and wide spaces when they were children; dances to him were forced labor. But he had always been dutiful, and this she respected.

He leaned toward her and, while looking out to the crowd, whispered, "Caroline is always at her worst when she thinks she's at her best."

"Her best? I'm not certain that state exists."

"Come now. Christian charity—"

"Begins at home? With our mothers?" she asked with a wicked smile.

He gave a cough. "They may have too much charity," he said in a tone that turned as exasperated as she'd heard it in some time. "Mine has just taken in a young girl from Vermont to live with us while she studies. And then I'm to marry you while your mother, meanwhile, has vowed to save the world. It's a sickness of some sort. Some days I pray that God will save us from Boston women as they rule the world—"

"That would give them too much credit," she interrupted coldly. He nodded sympathetically and they fell into silence again.

"Jonathan!" A man's deep voice called from across the hall. Helen and Robert looked up to see Colonel R.E. Harris walking over to them, seemingly embarrassed by the number of his well-wishers and hangers-on. A military doctor, Harris was built like a bulldog and topped with curly dark hair surrounding a rapidly balding pate. He'd always been kind to Helen since she was a young girl, and she was delighted to see a real military man. He'd not been around to witness the news of her mother's fall from grace.

"Harris! Good to see you!" exclaimed Brooks, clapping him on his shoulder, as Robert Brown excused himself at the insistence of the aunt, who motioned to him from across the room, her teacup apparently empty.

Dr. Harris bowed slightly to Brooks and Helen. "Jonathan, your latest book is just the thing. I finished the chapter on the Battle of Pharsalus while on the train from Washington. I loved it! Losing Pompey was quite the tragedy for Rome," he said, shaking his head. "Helen, how much of that book did you write?"

Helen blushed at the praise. "I was only the proofreader."

Her father shook his head. "She's my right hand and I'm sorry to lose her to college."

"Or worse—to one of these ruffians at this dance tonight!"

Dr. Harris gave a hearty laugh.

"Let's discuss something else. Harris, is there a new dreadnought in the Charlestown naval shipyard?"

"Yes! She's a great new ship! What guns, my friend," he said, his eyes lighting. "The Secretary of War is considering naming it *Pennsylvania.*"

"Damn!" said her father. "I had money on the *Massachusetts*. Why the *Pennsylvania* if we're doing all the work?"

"You know how political these things can become." Harris looked around and leaned closer. "You wouldn't believe its guns' range."

"Pennsylvania could use some innovation," said Brooks with a sour look. "I'm glad the country has bought them a boat. Any other news?"

"Well, I read that the opera company is stranded over in Europe and won't be back for the start of the season. Everyone seems to be stranded somewhere, with the shipping lanes a mess as they are. And yes, I almost forgot! Sir Artemis Horn will be speaking at the Geographic Society in Harvard Hall next Tuesday. And Wigglesworth didn't invite us! Claimed limited seating."

"What?" asked Mr. Brooks.

"Positive. We're sans billet."

"This requires liquid," said Brooks decisively. "Helen, Harris and I need to repair to the bar to discuss this matter. Why don't you go congratulate Miss Peabody? You know, Harris, she's marrying Frank Adams."

"You don't say. Now that *is* news!"

"Yes, I do. Come, Harris, let's commence and not hold Helen up further." And off they went to the large mahogany bar to continue their discussion.

Helen felt chuffed as she walked over to a small gilt chair by the wall—abandoned and exposed. She certainly would not congratulate Caroline.

Even before her mother had been arrested for distributing contraception through the mail, Caroline had come first in Boston society. Her family had houses on both Beacon Hill and Chestnut Hill, a building at Harvard, and a founding stake in the Boston Athenaeum. Should a Peabody adopt a rabid dog that insulted the State House carpets, opinion held that the dog would make the Boston Four Hundred list in the high thirties, above the Brookses but below the Lodges. Helen felt Thoreau had been quite right about trading his neighbors for a shanty in the woods. If they were at all like Caroline, she'd welcome the solitude.

As the evening wore on, the room grew hotter and so did Helen's temper. Didn't her mother realize how the arrest affected her daughter? Did she care? While the rest of the ballroom performed a reel, she simmered about how unfair it was for society to treat her family as it had—she'd not done anything wrong. And yet they'd been vilified with this one small misstep—a lynching most likely led by Caroline's mother. Mrs. Peabody had lived through her daughter's accomplishments for years, not that there were that many, Caroline usually losing out to Helen or her good friend Ann Lowell. But now Mrs. Peabody had her shot at their family and she, with guns ready and powder dry, wasn't wasting any time. Frank had been Helen's. At least she'd thought she had a chance this summer.

Helen thought that Mrs. Peabody and the Kaiser could perhaps be the same people, except, she had to acknowledge, that Mrs. Peabody's damage was only social. And so it was that by the time Caroline Peabody actually presented herself to Helen, Helen felt she could have snubbed Caroline just for saying good evening.

Helen stiffened in her seat as Frank and Caroline greeted her. Frank's blond hair was immaculately groomed, his starched smile as crisp as his collar. Caroline was four feet eight inches of sunshine, her waist cinched into a tiny dress that fell to the floor in half a dozen satin layers. She resembled a doll of fine porcelain, with the same vacant stare.

"I understand that congratulations are in order," said Helen, trying to keep up appearances.

Frank thanked her, nodding uncomfortably and looking away, mumbling that they would send out engagement notices shortly.

Caroline giggled. "I know that the post office is quite busy with your mother's business—sending all of those packages. I hope you don't miss our invitation," she said with a cherubic smile.

At that moment, during a long pause, all Helen could think to say was "I think you are a horse," but that lacked any sort of elegance.

Frank turned a bright pink. "Caroline—"

"I was only teasing," said Caroline. "Helen knows that. How is your mother?"

"My mother's at the contributions table," said Helen, recovering. "Do you wish to contribute?"

"I was just telling Frank, we hope she's recovered from her excitement."

"She's fine, thank you. Frank, I'm sorry to hear that your uncle died."

Frank bowed his head and thanked her for the condolences. After a few moments of silence, he spoke again. "Miss Brooks, I regret that we must leave, but Admiral Wilson said that he wished to meet Caroline. We'll speak later?" he asked, nodding again to Helen as he whisked his fiancée away.

Helen felt the tight boning of her dress cut into her side as she swallowed her anger on an empty breath. She looked at the clock to see she still had two hours of torture left to stand in the shadow of Frank Adams, a gallant and handsome young man who could, she very well knew, make her happy. She knew she wouldn't see him later and hated that she wanted to. It was so humiliating.

Oh, Frank, she thought, why did you have to choose now?

As she sat back in the tiny chair and arranged her white skirts, she felt the full weight of the Brooks side of her family clucking, tut-tutting, and being overall put out about her mother's outspokenness exhibited in such a public manner. It was one thing to read Thoreau's *Civil Disobedience.* He was a former neighbor and it would have been inhospitable to ignore the work. But it was entirely another thing to actually abandon your family for a summer in order to put your disconcerting, immodest plans into practice. And if her mother just had to rebel, why couldn't she do it by becoming a rogue census-taker and not a sex merchant? Helen fancied herself rather better off in the killing fields of Belgium hunting for the Kaiser's butchers. There no one would know about her mother's embarrassing darker side.

"Say, are you Peter's sister?" The voice startled her. The accent was British.

She looked up to see a handsome young man with dark hair and bright green, intelligent eyes who introduced himself as Rhyland Cabot Spencer, from her brother's crew team at Harvard. He lifted her silk-tasseled dance card.

"May I claim this dance?" he said, writing his name in very large letters across the top half of the card.

"You've just claimed three, Mr. Spencer."

"Why, so I have, but please call me Riley. It sounds Irish, and my very British father hates it," he said with a conspiratorial smile as he took her gloved hand and lifted it close to his lips. "Dancing with you keeps me out of the clutches of your brother, my crew captain and, if I might say so, a homely fellow to have such a lovely sister. He'd have me rowing tonight if I weren't otherwise occupied. So since the fairest lady here is seated right before me, I thought I'd make a bold move and ask her to dance."

She gave a light laugh, almost involuntarily. What a charming young man—tall, his skin fair, and British. His cheekbones were high and delicate. And when he grinned his entire face lit up. His teeth were small, straight, and bright.

Suddenly a flash of recognition came upon her. "Aren't you the one who called my brother a 'dim-witted fright of a bink' in front of hundreds at the Princeton race?"

"Miss Brooks, such language!" he said as she stood. "Peter threw me in the Charles River for that one. It was absolute hell getting that smell out of my hair. I paid dearly for such disrespect, and it hasn't happened again. I'd prefer to be known as the one who offered his assistance helping you move into Radcliffe tomorrow."

"How did you know I'm moving tomorrow?"

"You didn't think Peter was going to move those boxes, did you? He acts like royalty now that he's the crew team captain."

"He wore that crown long before he got to Harvard," she said with a wide smile as she set her purse on the table, abandoning it for the dance.

Those poor British boys fighting in Belgium, she thought, as he placed his arm firmly around her waist.

This was the very least she could do for the war effort.

WILS SQUINTED at his cousin Riley from across the dance floor. He'd lent Riley one of his formal suits for the evening, as his cousin's other white jacket had been smeared with a woman's rouge. Riley looked absolutely terrible in the borrowed clothes, but it hadn't impeded his typical progress—he was already asking a pretty young woman to dance. Women never learned.

Wils shook his head and walked over to a small table in the corner of the dance hall. The orchestra launched into a reel and all that silk and lace began spinning around the room.

He adjusted his spectacles as a service boy came by with a tray holding several flutes of champagne. He took one and sipped it. Quite refreshing. It was probably the only thing to work off last night's champagne headache. *Gesundheit,* he thought glumly and drained it.

Wils sat back in the little gilt chair as his headache was slowly dulled by the champagne. He, in contrast to his cousin, had no one to dance with despite being dressed impeccably in his own white jacket and white tie that he had brought from Berlin. His dark pants were perfectly tailored and his short blond hair neatly cropped. With his long fingers he drew a *W* in the condensation on the empty flute. Even more unlike his cousin Riley, he wished he were far away from the dance and from all people.

Why Aunt Frieda married an Englishman he had never understood. And why he looked after Riley, he often forgot. Habit, he guessed.

He gazed out into the whirl of dancers, twirling against a backdrop of velvet curtains and gold tassels. They looked so pleasant, these Bostonians. Until they fingered you for a German spy. Then the whole lot would up and have you in stocks. He secured another flute and tossed it back.

He should be, in fact, with Riley at Beck Hall, waiting for news from the field. But then he frowned and thought better of that idea. If he were at home he'd be hounded by his mother. He'd telegrammed her about having to wait to leave until after the police interview. Her pain upon learning of Max's death stuttered in telegraphed notes across the Atlantic until neither he (Wils) nor Western Union could read anymore. The day's last two notes remained unopened as Wils left for the dance.

Another waiter came by, and Wils took his fourth flute of champagne. It had become stuffy in the room and the liquid, so cool on his throat, felt even better when belted back quickly. He was dreadfully tired and his shoulders ached. Terribly tired, in fact.

His hand brushed a silk purse as he put down his glass. The purse tumbled to the floor and spilled open. As he reached to pick up the contents, he sniffed. The paper smelled of lilac, he thought. He stared slightly groggily at the page and then turned it over.

FALL COMES IN SHADES OF RED
by Helen Windship Brooks

Fall comes in shades of red
And leaves in shrouds of white
But crisp, silver snow
can't consecrate fields
Burned while God slept at night.

Night rests in shades of gray
To hide the sun's sacrist,
And gravel grayed beasties
from shadows emerge
Turn dreams to dust, mem'ry to mist.

Mist comes in all its despair
And won't lift until
It chills fair maids who longed for love
in rubble abed.
Their voices silent, still.

He put it down and sat back, a dark look on his face. He didn't like it. Not one whit. Did this Miss Brooks think she was Emily Dickinson? He tugged at his starched collar. I mean, this mist chills us all, dear girl, not just fair maids who longed for love. What about all of those dead men?

After a few moments he re-read it. Perhaps it was the champagne talking, but he did like the part about the chill and the rubble. He frowned. The gray clearly represented Germany. He shook his head and tossed the paper onto the table by the silk purse.

What presumption. Some pinch-nosed, brown-draped, Boston spinster writing this patriotic nonsense. They should stick to telling people how right they were about abolition. They could go on about that for hours and hours. But give them something else to be self-righteous about and off they'd go again, putting their pens to paper and telling everyone how right they felt about their own actions.

He wished the whole unpleasantness in Europe were over. Max's death had been such a shock. The anger against Germany was palpable. He gave an involuntary shiver. Support the British and you're a hero; support the Germans and you might as well hang.

He looked through the crowd, tired and bleary-eyed. It wasn't as if things were better in Germany. If he went home he'd probably arrive just in time for the Russians to invade. Such a mess.

And so he put his head down on the table, wishing once again to be back in his room in Beck Hall. But even better, to close his eyes and have done with all of them.

In what seemed to Wils to be an instant, he felt a tug on his shoulder. He opened his eyes. There was no music anymore, just the dull clink of dessert plates being stacked on trays by kitchen boys. He turned to see a young woman in white pulling at his arm.

"The dance is over?" He blinked, his eyes blurred. It was the pretty girl who'd been dancing with Riley. What did she want?

"Sir, do you know what happened to my purse?"

He looked at the tiny purse, which had wicked the condensation of four champagne glasses into its silk. It was a soggy, dripping mess. Her poem was also damp.

"My purse, sir."

He seemed to vaguely recall a poem. Brooks, it was. "Are you Helen Brooks?" he asked. She didn't look like a pinch-nosed spinster.

"Yes."

"Are you related to Peter Brooks?"

"He's my brother," she said, looking perplexed at the wet silk. "Did you see what happened?"

Wils' mouth felt like cotton. He needed some fresh air and wished she'd leave. "Oh, sorry about your purse. I put it over there to be out of the way. Won't it dry?"

"Silk spots."

"Oh. Terribly sorry." He blinked again, reaching for her poem. "Couldn't your mother have kept it for you while you danced?"

Her eyebrows arched. "My mother is too busy to hold my purse."

"Oh," he said, still groggy. "This fell out too," he said, picking up her poem. "I'm Wilhelm von Lützow Brandl, a friend of your brother's. I row on his crew team."

"You read my poem? Did you like it?" Her eyes softened.

"It fell open and caught my eye. Sorry about the ink," he said, handing it to her. "I must have placed it too close to one of these glasses. Do you have another copy?"

"No."

"Well, it's still fairly legible. I do like poetry and, even though our countries would disagree about the war, you made a decent start of it," he said, trying to cheer her up.

The kindness in her face vanished. "You're German?"

"Yes."

"And you thought this poem good?"

Had he said it was good? He hoped not. "It has its moments," was the best he could say about it. He winced as her ears reddened. "Really, Miss Brooks, it's a good start. But death is a hard subject to do well. My professor says that death brings out the bad poet in us all. Perhaps you should have started with the moon over the water or some such."

"The bad poet in us all?" She squared her shoulders. "First the Germans invade Belgium and then my purse!"

His eyes narrowed. "I couldn't have invaded Belgium because I've been at Harvard rowing on your brother's crew team. You might consider that some Germans still love America."

"As much as they love Belgium?"

He shrugged. There was no hope of rational discussion with this young woman. He berated himself for even opening his mouth.

"Good evening," she said, abruptly turning on her heel and heading toward an older, stocky man who was motioning to her that he was leaving.

As she walked away, Wils felt a keen urge to flick some water on her matching silk skirt. How ridiculous this young lady was, turning on him because of a comment on her poetry! How many times had he been told to use others' poetry as a model—to reduce excess verbiage, or to consider a more subtle approach, and to avoid death in poetry completely? You didn't see him getting upset. Yet one word to this young lady and she intentionally misunderstood him. *Unvernünftig!*

He stood up and stalked outside. Good thing Harvard didn't admit them. They were intolerable enough at a dance—their own territory.

A chill ran up his spine as he passed a group of women cackling by the ice cream tables. The memory of a class with some Radcliffe girls flooded back to him. They had sat in the back tittering about the squirrels in the Yard while the professor had tried to teach Plato. No one got any work done.

If he were to meet a woman with any sense it would probably be because the poor lady was on her deathbed and had to get serious with the few words she had left.

Wils picked up his pace along the gravel path to the gazebo, stuffing his hands in his pockets. The women of the Equal Suffrage Society had made every mistake in the book. They arrogantly insisted that they could do a better job with government, as if changing human behavior were like changing a pair of silk shoes. Humility, a necessity for understanding, had run screaming in the opposite direction.

If you told them they made no sense, they would say that men had invented logic to oppress them. If you told them current problems were complicated, they would tell you how difficult it was to match silver sets from one generation to the next. And if you told them they would have to work hard, they would go on and on about pain in childbirth. Indeed. A few hours of suffering that every man had to hear about for the rest of his life.

He stopped. Yet what about the pain they inflicted on men? Look what Felicity Chatsworth had done to Max.

He stood in the vast yard and looked up at the clear sky. The moon was large and bright, each star brilliant. It was hard to fathom that soldiers now abed, in rubble, saw the same sky.

Wils walked slowly down the rest of the path to the river, where he found Peter Brooks alone in the gazebo, his tall, spare frame resting uncomfortably against one of the wrought-iron supports. He stood in shirtsleeves, smoking an Egyptian cigarette. Its scent mixed with the fragrant blossoms of a white alder bush. Water flowed quietly, reflecting the full moon on its surface.

"I met your sister, Peter. I don't think she's that fond of Germans." The wooden swing creaked loudly as he sat down on it.

"But the British are a different story," said Peter in a brisk tone. "Her friend Ann said she danced exclusively with Riley tonight." He skipped a small rock in the river. "Wils, your cousin is irresponsible, a philanderer, and, as far as I can tell, completely incapable of being serious about anything except rowing."

"Come now, Peter. That's unfair even by my standards. Riley was just dancing. No harm in that."

"I'm sure that's what Lily thought. And Isobel and Grace too."

"I'll give you Lily and Isobel, but Grace, and Rose, and, well, Edith and Lucia—" Wils broke off awkwardly. "Those weren't entirely Riley's doing."

"Is he still engaged to Edith?"

"No," Wils said quickly. He frowned. Was that right? "Actually, I'm not sure, come to think of it."

Peter looked at him intently. "Keep an eye on your cousin for me, Wils. Spencer needs to stay away from Helen."

"You're not her father, Peter."

"And she's not your sister," Peter said drily. He flicked his cigarette into the water, picked up his jacket, and walked away along the gravel path.

Wils shrugged as he heard the steps recede. Perhaps if he had a sister who danced with Riley he'd be angry too.

He sat back in the swing and pushed his hands through his hair. A dull ache from the champagne he'd drunk had returned. And still all of his cares were with him. He'd irrigated his troubles, but not washed them away.

The water lapped at the banks of the river, a soft swish and murmur. There was a distant splash—perhaps a mink or a muskrat—and the evening cry of a few migrating birds. But that was it.

It was so different here, he thought. So wild. The world beyond the gazebo, across the river, was untamed. It hadn't been manicured into submission for four centuries like his lawn in Prussia.

Perhaps this was what the earth looked like when it was new. Trees, and rocks, water, the leaves. Before Arnold Archer, before Riley Spencer, before Max, before war.

Wils looked out into the depths of the wood.

It was the America Goethe wrote about—reclaimed from the wilderness by honest toil. A community bound together by the demands of the frontier. Yoked to work but free of tyrants. Free of the burden of history. Without the blood of the past draining in every walled city's gutter. The blood his own Kaiser shed in Belgium. Of Napoleon before that. Cromwell. The Romanovs, Hapsburgs, Tudors, Angevins, Guelph, Ghibelline, Visigoths, Bosnians, Serbians, and countless others.

Perhaps the wood had been a playground for young girls and boys for the past thousand years. He smiled, thinking of how much fun he'd had as an eight-year-old, when he'd run through the trees with his dog, Perg, under a ceiling of yellow leaves—a child playing with a simple, rich abandon through the shortening afternoon hours. Before the end. Before the misery of adult life dawned on him. Before Max disappeared into the night.

Those before me rest in shadow, he thought. Those yet to be born will never know me. Yet we are immortals, marching in columns before God; millions of us, moving from the light of life into eternity. He stopped the swing.

Mein Gott, why did you let Max die?

His heart sank as he looked into the sky. The stars were so clear. And so uncaring.

[CHAPTER THREE]

MERRIMACK HILL

LEXINGTON, MASSACHUSETTS
Sunday, August 30, 1914

The maze of paths leading to Merrimack Hill from other fields was now abandoned and private, covered in years of pine straw and flanked by brambles, disappearing in the ever-thickening forest gathering around the Brooks family home. Piles of fieldstone littered the property in odd lines, fossils of old stone fences now unrecognizable to the yeomen farmers who had once worked the land. The great fields of Lexington, once cleared for farming, now sprang with sugar maple and aspen, catalpa, ironwood, and oak. Buckthorn gathered around stone walls, its roots and branches toppling the rock in places, making it difficult to pass.

The fields were much older than the house on Merrimack Hill, which had been built well after the last of the Mohicans, the last shot of the Revolution, and the last of the age of gentlemen farming. Helen's grandfather had built it to be at one with nature and at complete odds with his neighbors, who, at that time, had been overcome by the craze of Thoreau's famous experiment in simple living at Walden Pond.

Helen's grandfather was one of the few who resisted a simple life, maintaining that if one really wanted to understand life, plenty of people had written books on the subject and those books could be read from the bounty of one's well-tended and elaborately carved hearth. As the family's shipping interests provided more income than they could ever spend, Brooks Senior built a large house in which to raise his only child, Jonathan Edwards Brooks, outside of the clutches of the brain trust on Beacon Hill in Boston. For added security, should Boston society wish to visit him in Lexington, he purchased two additional estates, in Maine and New Hampshire, to which they could escape.

By the dawn of the twentieth century, the Brooks estate sat on seven hundred acres at the southern edge of the Merrimack River Valley. The house had been built a half mile from the same road on which the Colonial militia escorted the British back to Boston and, as was the wont of Brooks men, traditional: a red-brick Federal with three floors and a basement, two central chimneys, and white-painted windows outlined by black shutters. Gas lanterns lit the bright red front door, and by the wide slate steps at the front visitors found an iron boot wipe bolted into a moss-covered stone.

The interior of the house, given the disposition of its inhabitants, was slightly less bucolic. Some maintained that a house divided against itself could not stand, but the new Mr. and Mrs. Brooks found just the opposite to be true. Over the decades of their marriage they found that the more divided their house, the more secure the peace.

And thus, in the first room off the main hallway, the parlor, Helen's mother, a Windship from Boston, established her territory. Before she'd married Jonathan, the Brooks family had stuffed its statues and paintings, chairs, and books in the room. The day after the wedding, Merriam donated the overage of books to the Boston Public Library, an act which, according to friends, had sent her fragile father-in-law to an early grave. He was not against charity, but giving his books away was his equivalent of letting blood.

Her parlor was then transformed into a room decidedly different from the rest of the house. It was distinctly feminine, with stuffed floral chairs and white walls set with borders of silver silk damask. White tasseled lamps lit the ceilings and alcoves where various carved owls and ancient goddesses sat looking stately. On one wall hung a large sepia portrait of Merriam Brooks as Athena, and on another, a picture of Seneca Falls. Mailing supplies overflowed the room's central table, including boxes of *Family Limitation,* the dreaded sixteen-page tract (illustrated) on how not to have children. Carved into the mantel were the words of Saint Paul: "Love Bears All Things." Each Brooks family member was convinced it spoke of his or her own martyrdom.

This had been a silent room over the summer. In March, Mrs. Brooks had left for an extended visit with Margaret Sanger, a nurse she had met at the 1912 Industrial Workers of the World strike in Lawrence, Massachusetts. But ever since her return in early August, Merriam had rarely been around. She now spent her time in the winding corridors of the Boston tenements or with her lawyers. City Hall had been particularly stubborn about her repeated violations of the decency laws by mailing *Family Limitation* to local women. The state and federal authorities had sought to compromise. Unfortunately for Mrs. Brooks, it was an election year for several city bosses who wished to run on morality and decency platforms.

Helen viewed these activities in an entirely different light from her neighbors, but one even more damning. Her mother's cause was ostensibly to provide better health care for the women and children of Boston's slums, but Helen had noticed over the past few years that if her mother's hands were idle, she'd find a new problem to solve that would remove her further from her hearth at Merrimack Hill. Two years ago it was workers' rights. This year she worked for family limitation and equal voting rights, both of which, Mrs. Brooks felt, would contribute to better health for women. Next year, as day followed night, it would be something else.

And so Helen, who was not a worker, neither Irish nor Italian, not poor, and in good health, knew she was of little interest to her mother. Her father had raised her. The two of them rarely spent much time in the parlor but worked in a study positioned in the Brooks home as far from the parlor in their minds as the east was from the west.

The library was a very different sort of room: leather-covered chairs; books carefully catalogued by author and subject; wine-red walls hung with family portraits (of relatives other than themselves); and a bust of Edmund Burke in a dark alcove. On the mantel of the red-brick fireplace sat models of three clipper ships. A large bank of windows overlooked the east garden full of Russian blue sage, lavender hydrangeas, and four trellises of climbing wild roses. Her father, Helen felt, had been right to refuse the red velvet curtains her mother had installed when he'd gone on a fishing trip to Maine. But perhaps he'd been precipitous when he'd called the Boston Animal Hospital to haul them away to be used as bedding for orphaned dogs.

It was in this study where on an early Sunday morning Helen sat across from her father, fidgeting in her chair. Her shirtwaist's high lace collar prickled her throat. She shifted, pulling her feet under her long white skirt as she tried again to concentrate on her reading.

Mr. Brooks, across from her, lay back in his chair dozing off, his chin on his chest and his newspaper dangling over his large stomach. He was still in his dressing gown and slippers. His hair, once dark, was now peppered with gray. He was stouter; he was grumpier. And that morning so was she, finding it impossible to think of anything that would make her happy, despite the promise of a handsome young man coming to move her things that afternoon.

The grandfather clock in the corner chimed the half hour in a low, sonorous tone. Helen looked up from the manuscript she was reviewing. It was on the history of clipper ships and she'd promised her father she would read it before she left that afternoon for college. A breeze from the windows fluttered his paper and rustled the flowers outside. He twitched in his chair, and his breathing became more stubborn, lapsing into a series of occasional snores.

Helen glared at her spotted purse beside the green banker's lamp on the reading table, recalling the remarks of the young German. In her mind she could see him lifting his eyes, his vision blurred through excessive drink. A fair face and rich clothes could not disguise the brutishness of the Hun that lay just beneath the surface of their happy talk of Schopenhauer.

Her poem was quite good, she grumbled. True, a burning field didn't exactly evoke man-made terror, and gray beasties could refer to large rodents, she guessed, but her poem wasn't about going to sleep on a farm and that young man knew it!

She looked out the window to the bright day, hoping to go back to better thoughts. Perhaps she'd write a poem about a man asleep at a dance who wakes to find himself trampled. She brightened at the prospect.

"I didn't know that I was writing a comedy."

She had not realized her father was awake. "Not a comedy, Father."

"A tragedy?" her father asked.

"Of sorts," she said.

"What is the subject of this most recent drama? The great clipper race I allude to on page thirty-five?"

"Father, I admit I was thinking about something other than this draft."

"Impossible."

She thought she caught a smile and gave one back. "I've a question about that poem I wrote last week. I was quite proud of it. Did you think it too emotional?"

"I don't recall," he said. "Why do you ask?"

"Because a young man at the dance last night told me to avoid death in poetry completely until I could do it better."

His eyebrows shot up. "He said that?"

"Yes."

"Well, without trying how does this ruffian think one is expected to learn?"

"My point exactly."

"Helen, his comment makes little sense. He sounds daft."

"I agree," she echoed.

"Not, Helen, that one can't learn wisdom without experimentation. We don't start from scratch. I'd never suggest that. It would be an insult to Edmund Burke. I'd never insult his memory."

"I never thought you would," she said, settling back into her chair.

Her father roused himself and stretched. "Let me see your poem again," he said with a yawn. She went over to her purse and brought it to him, watching closely as he looked at the paper.

"This appears smudged."

"He put it beside his *four* glasses of champagne. Or whisky. Or some type of alcohol."

"He sounds intemperate to me."

"He's German."

"He is? Well, that explains it. Germans are an intemperate sort. You know, Visigoths and all. Nietzsche, Feuerbach, and Marx returned them to their hopeless roots," he said softly. "All the wrong conclusions from Napoleon's conquest." He sighed and his voice trailed off as he read through her work again. "Yes, yes, yes. Helen, I think this is a good start, and very fine in many places, but in all candor I have seen you write better. The torched fields are a little strong." He shook his head. "And the part about the women is self-pitying."

Helen was taken aback. This was what the German had said. "But father, men start wars, they die, and women are sad."

"Well," he said, then halted and cleared his throat. "You mustn't tell your mother I feel this way because she'd take it as an attack on her sex and not as a matter of my opinion about a poem. In my experience, women have a way of helping a government send men off to war to die once the men, as you say, start the war. But you might consider that war is often forced upon men who don't wish to go at all. Men are inherently peace-loving animals. And then women say they'll never forget; how glorious it all is—and then men have a way of dying brutally and the women then do forget, which ranks only slightly less problematic than when women don't forget and cause the next generation to wish to avenge their deaths."

Helen looked intently at him. "Father, perhaps Mother would take what you said as an attack on our sex because it seems to be an attack on our sex and not a criticism of my poem. My maid feels sad and it's not because she's guilt-ridden about sending men off to war."

"Dear child, men have been beaten about the head and shoulders by women's feelings for generations, not to mention eons. You have been exceptional in that you're more like a son to me than I'd expect any daughter to be. The mist chills us all, Helen. Not just women. Maybe your German drunk has a point."

"But it's all right to be sad when you are the victim of things beyond your control. These are not shrill Prussian mothers thrusting their sons into Belgium."

She saw his lower lip curl.

"You think he has a point."

"A bit of one," he said.

"You think my poem is the most silly chuff you've read?" Her face reddened.

"That's not what I said." He looked pained. "Perhaps the young man's point wasn't made in a polite manner, but at college you'll have to listen for the merits of the argument and not the way in which it's been presented. Sometimes we learn from those we disagree with."

Helen sighed. "I will think on it," she said, returning to her chair, and to a tedious discussion of sail rigging on the clipper ship *Flying Cloud*. Only twenty-three pages left. She put a large *X* over a perfectly decent paragraph and in the margin urged him to rewrite it for clarity.

Ten minutes passed before she heard the Sunday paper rustle again. Her father peered from the other side of the editorial section.

"You know, Helen, I received a note yesterday which I'd meant to give you." He sat up and walked over to his desk, picked up a bright white envelope, and brought it to her.

"What's this?" she asked.

Her father began to fill his pipe, not looking at her.

HARVARD UNIVERSITY

Dear Jonathan,

Have your daughter come to my seminar "Editing for Editors," starting this Monday. Harvard and Radcliffe do not have the same calendar, and my other classes have already started, but this one doesn't start until Monday, and given her work for you, I've made an exception. I hear she's a good writer. Enrollment is down, as some of the boys have left to seek their glory before the war's end, which we all hope will be imminent. I could use a good editor and wouldn't want to fill the space with a dunce when a tried-and-true Brooks was available. However this is a senior-level course, meets on Mondays and Tuesdays, and demands a copious amount of creative writing. She needs to be prepared to work. Last item: class meets in Harvard Yard. I would not expect any trouble for her in such a small class. I know these boys and they seem to be of the good sort.

Sessions start at three o'clock this Monday, *punct.*

> Yrs as ever,
> C. T. Copeland

A class with Copeland! The note took her breath away. What a gift! She stood up hastily, her papers falling at her feet. "Thank you!"

"You must promise to learn all you can in order to revise my manuscript over the Christmas break," he said, pulling on a long white churchwarden and emitting a large puff of smoke.

"Of course," she said elatedly as she reached down to gather the pages. She was delighted. Her heart felt light again. Tut-tut, Mr. Brandl—my father has given me Copeland! We'll see who leaves Harvard the better for it.

At that moment Patrick, a squat servant with thick, curly white hair, came to the door, wiping his hands on a cloth. "Mrs. Brooks' lawyer is going to be meeting you in twenty minutes and she's sent me down to say you are needing to be getting ready now. I'm to drive the missus to Radcliffe in a half hour."

"Patrick, do you like this lawyer better than the last one?" Brooks asked.

"I'll give him the toss if he canna help Mrs. Brooks. She's a good woman."

Her father rolled his eyes. "Excuse me, Helen. Must get dressed to attend to your mother's business. City Hall is not budging on this one and thus we must talk to the lawyers today and every day, it seems. Patrick, after you return we'll need to visit the Adamses in Quincy. We won't make the funeral, but we should at least make an appearance at their house."

"Helen," he said, reaching into his pocket. "One more thing." His eyes avoided hers as he took out a small black velvet box, put it on her reading table, and turned to go. She opened it to find a ring with a pearl, small and barely pink, set in a delicate lattice of gold.

"Oh, thank you," she said, surprised. She took it out and slipped it on her finger. It was beautiful.

"It is not to be confused with the pearl of great price," he said, walking to the door. "That is you. I've paid dearly for you, and you have turned out marvelously, even if you indulge in romantic poetry." He left abruptly, before she could say anything else.

She flushed at the high praise. Perhaps he had realized that she was his daughter and not a book after all.

[CHAPTER FOUR]

RADCLIFFE COLLEGE

CAMBRIDGE, MASSACHUSETTS
Sunday, August 30, 1914

The distance from Lexington to Boston and Cambridge was not far—the British had jogged it quickly in 1776. What was different was the frantic pace, as if the Earth's rotation required Boston and Cambridge people to move at a lightning speed or, God forbid, it would stop spinning. Fumes from cars, smokestacks, and smells from animals in the street markets poured into the Brooks family car when Patrick, her driver, and Helen stopped suddenly for a bewildering assortment of carts and children in the teeming, narrow streets.

When Helen had inquired about how anyone could think in such an environment, her father answered that they didn't, they just parroted what they read on the opinion page of the New York newspaper. Helen hoped it meant that they were too busy to comment on her mother's activities and would focus on important things, such as stopping the Kaiser in Europe. Or, failing that, the works of Milton.

And there was reason to hope on this front. Professor Copeland mentioned nothing of her mother's behavior in his letter to her father.

But what had begun as divine elation at the new challenge of being in Copeland's class slowly transformed into fear as they neared the Harvard-Radcliffe campus. She'd not prepared nearly enough. It had only been a random occurrence that she'd learned that death brought out the bad poet in us all. Yet that was one of the most basic tenets of writing, according to that young man at the party.

How could her tutor not have told her?

She took a deep breath to calm herself. She needed to apply herself, just as Professor Copeland urged her to do. She could do that. One step at a time.

A truck filled with produce suddenly pulled in front of them and began to turn in the street. Patrick pulled the brake lever hard, sending the car bucking.

"The curse of Mary Malone chase you to Halifax!" yelled Patrick, his fist menacing the other driver. He turned back to Helen, his face pink. "Don't you be telling your father that I taught you new, er, proverbs." The car lurched forward in the traffic again.

"Will your friend Miss Ann live with you?" Patrick asked, shifting in his seat uncomfortably. "I hear your brother is sweet on her."

"Yes," she said. "They will probably be engaged by Christmas, unless Mother's actions drive Ann away."

"Now, Miss Helen, you canna be hard on your mother. She's helped women who have it very hard—with their men out working or drinking or in jail. They've more children than sense and she's helping them. No one else is looking out for them, God help them." He stuck his head out of his open window at a stopped peddler's cart. "Canna you move your cart, sir?" he called over the engine's noise. "The Devil with him," he muttered. "Stopping in the middle of the road when decent people have places to be."

"Some would say my mother is out to help herself, not them."

"I'd put my boot to their throat should they talk like that around me. True, I always get suspicious myself when I see the rich running to help us out. Makes me want to run the other way most times. But this is different. You're too hard on her, Miss Helen."

"She should stay out of trouble with the police."

"She needs not to be cursing the officers, that's for certain," he said with a laugh. "But they had it coming. Rifling through her things, looking for those . . ." Helen saw his curls become stark white against the embarrassed pink of his thick neck.

Contraception. She knew. An embarrassing business if there ever was one, not that her mother cared what she thought. Helen looked out the window and Patrick went on muttering about how if there were a friend in need Mrs. Brooks would see to it that those needs were met. But this charity had been exacted at a great price.

At the edge of the Radcliffe campus their black touring car waded into a sea of other such cars, engines sputtering and backfiring, each overflowing with trunks, quilts, hatboxes, and furniture. By the time they neared Longworth Hall, Patrick seemed to be cursing exclusively in Gaelic.

Helen's eyes lit up as they turned the corner and the building came in sight. Here was her home for the next few years, and she was to be a student not only at Radcliffe but in Harvard Yard, studying under the famous Copeland. She would read, and study, and write, and when all was said and done, she could be anything she wished. An author, a poetess. She'd give readings at the public library and talk with school-children. A car would drive her to New York City to read her works before crowds. She'd take a train to speak in lecture halls in St. Louis and San Francisco. In her mind's eye, and modesty often prevented her from admitting this even to herself, she hoped that if she were truly diligent and careful and terribly lucky, she'd end up with a bust in the Boston Athenaeum.

This, today, would be her first step toward that marble quarry, if she didn't stumble over fundamentals that her hit-and-miss education forgot to inform her about.

Longworth Hall was a tall red-brick building with bright marble trim and a granite foundation. Its entryway and sidewalks were filled with young women in summer hats talking in groups of threes and fours. Matrons stood by their cars directing the unloading, and haggard men walked in and out of the building carrying hefty trunks and boxes of books.

They spotted Peter sitting by the steps, in his straw boater, navy jacket, and starched brown trousers, surrounded by women.

"Peter," Patrick called from the car, "hurry it up! Your father says I'm to return and drive him to the Adams funeral."

Peter nodded and waved to the three thin, sallow-faced youths who started unloading Helen's bags. "Helen, get your key from Miss Sullivan in the foyer. They'll take your things to your room."

"Is Riley Spencer here?" she asked, looking for the young man from the night before.

"No. Just get your key and we'll meet you inside."

She frowned as she walked into the foyer. Riley had said he'd be there.

The entryway was stifling hot and packed with people for its entire length. The din—women calling to each other, girls fumbling with keys, fathers with maps—made it nearly impossible to locate the front desk at the other end of the hall. Helen waded through the crowd to the desk and met a large woman with a wide face, bright cheeks, and a mop of curls. The stout housemistress, Miss Maureen Sullivan, was a formidable woman with some reputation of prosecuting offenders, according to Ann, who had heard about her from a friend.

"Good afternoon, Miss Brooks," Miss Sullivan said, turning to retrieve a key from the boxes behind her. "Please sign for your key," she said, presenting her with three forms. Sweat beaded Miss Sullivan's upper lip, but she stood there without fanning herself. "Do you know the rules?"

"Your letter said to keep telephone calls to a minimum, curfew is at eleven, and—" Helen was jostled by a parent.

"Mrs. Jameson, I'll be right there," called Miss Sullivan in a loud voice. "No fussing with the portraits and no men in your room after tomorrow. We don't want any problems." Miss Sullivan furrowed her brow as she looked past Helen again. "I see your brother by the steps. He'll be knowing the rules," she said, narrowing her eyes. "Captain of the crew team or no. Now, call if you have trouble, but don't expect me to come running. It's moving day and we're busy. Next!" And with a wave of her hand, Miss Sullivan dismissed her.

"Your room is this way," Peter called. "I scoped it out." He picked up a box and started up the steps.

"Miss Sullivan seems to know you," she called.

"I can't hear you," he said in a loud voice as they walked up the steps. As they turned the corner, a young boy with a heavy stack of newspapers nearly crashed into them.

"Sorry," the boy said, juggling his papers. His face was smudged with ink.

"What's the rush?" Peter asked.

"Special edition of the *Crimson* for the upstairs parlor," he said.

Peter's eyes widened as he looked at the headline. The young man gave him a copy and was off.

"Maximilian von Steiger murdered and Arnold Archer arrested!" he read aloud. The color drained from his face

"What is it?" asked Helen. "Who is von Steiger?"

He shook his head and waved to the young men who were holding Helen's boxes.

Helen unlocked the door to her room. Peter walked right past her into the dark room, and he seemed to know exactly where everything was. He opened the heavy curtains, pushed open the window, and ignoring the rest of the crew, began to read his paper. "Insanity," she heard him whisper.

He didn't even look up as the young porters walked in with her bags.

Helen directed the young men to put the boxes in the middle of the floor. As they dropped her boxes on the braided rug, a puff of dust billowed out. Helen wrinkled her nose.

Peter looked up from the paper. "Thanks, men. I'll see you in an hour at the boathouse." They left.

Peter didn't move to help her, so Helen walked over to him and craned her neck to read the details of the story.

She had never heard of the young man who'd died, and the details were difficult to puzzle through. Archer, the son of a powerful city boss in Boston, had said von Steiger was German and a spy who had hung himself when confronted with his infamy. Yet Archer had been found with a gold watch belonging to the victim's friend. There was no suicide note. And Archer had been in a public fight where he'd threatened to kill the young man for not renouncing Germany.

A frustration crept under Helen's skin. She felt sorry for the dead young man, but if he was a spy, it was better to lose him than a thousand men at sea. Max was now one more victim of the Kaiser, just like so many Belgian children. And if he was going to be a willing soldier, then that was one more soldier the Belgians wouldn't have to fight at the front. But if he were innocent, the death was awful—a life cut short for terrible reasons. It was irritating. Death made her irritable even if it was richly deserved.

The walls' cheerful white molding lost some of its gloss. The two desks, bookshelves, and red-brick fireplace, she decided, were a bit shabby for such a new building but acceptable. The large braided rug would have to go, however. She gave it a stamp and more dust puffed out. Miss Sullivan would definitely have to call for a maid.

Peter shook his head, put down the paper. After a few moments he said, "An outrage."

"Did you know the victim?" she asked, setting a stack of books on her desk shelf.

He shook his head. "Not well, but I do know Archer. He's a smooth sort, the kind I stay well clear of. He's always licking President Lowell's boots and cozying up to professors and the like. It's said he gets whatever he wants because his father is quite powerful. You know Arnold's father, Charles Archer, is the one giving Mother a hard time."

"Really?"

"Yes. Charles Archer wants to show he's fit for public office. I'm surprised that his son could even be arrested. They must have powerful evidence."

"So the police must think Archer killed the German?"

"I'm not sure at all," Peter said as he walked to a box, opened it up, and pulled out a few books for Helen. "It only says that yesterday they found a watch on Archer that belonged to Wils Brandl."

She frowned. "Wils? The young man at the dance?"

"Oh, yes, I forgot you'd met him."

"I have," she said. "Churlish and German and—"

He held up his hands. "Stop right there. I'll not hear it about Wils. He is ten times the man his cousin is—who you were quite keen on dancing with. Wils is a gentleman of the finest sort. But as for Max, except for the watch it could have been a suicide. He was quite upset about a girl who left him. Max and another crew mate of ours, Jackson

Vaughn, have been in some sick contest about who was more suicidal over losing their girl. Max seems to have won."

"Max loved a girl enough to kill himself?"

"Possibly," said Peter testily. "He is, after all, dead. Something killed him."

She waved him off. "Really, Peter. Do you see Mother or Father killing themselves if one of them walked away? I would rather think that they'd enjoy the time apart."

"Good night, Helen! What is the matter with you? You've never been in love like he was. His girl left him and he was inconsolable. Wils told me he could barely get out of bed after it happened."

"What happened?" came a voice from the door. Ann Lowell stood at the door carrying a round toile-covered hatbox tied with a white organza bow. Helen and Peter turned swiftly.

"Miss Lowell!" said Peter, his countenance completely changed. He walked past Helen quickly and took the box from Ann's arms. "I thought you were at the Adams funeral," he said gently.

She smiled prettily back at him. Her golden hair was tied up with a black bow and fell in ringlets over her shoulders. Her skin was perfectly white, and contrasted with the black lace on her formal Sunday dress. As she smiled, she lifted her almond-shaped eyes and gazed adoringly at Peter. The look helped remind Helen that it was now her Christian duty to be happy about being a distant second in her best friend's affections. "The funeral was quickly over and my parents wanted to leave for Maine for a week. So I came early," said Ann.

She turned to Helen and her eyes suddenly widened. "Is that a new ring?" she asked.

"Yes," said Helen, walking over and showing Ann her hand. "Father gave it to me this morning." Peter hadn't even noticed. What Ann saw in him was completely beyond Helen. Now that she and Ann lived together, perhaps they could be as close as they used to be, before Peter decided Helen's best friend should be his.

"I wish I'd kept my men to help move you, Ann," interrupted Peter.

"Thank you, Peter," she said, her cheeks dimpling. "I thought I would need more help, but I met a member of your crew team outside."

"Cheers!" came a British accent from the hallway, and it was Helen's turn to smile. Riley Spencer walked in, carrying a large steamer trunk that he set down by one of the stuffed chairs. She noticed he was pale and his tie was loose. He looked harried. "Sorry I'm late. I must have written down the wrong time," he said with a glare at Peter. "Jackson Vaughn said he was given a different time than you told me this morning."

"Jackson didn't show up either. He's all right, is he?" asked Peter.

"No, he's not. Jackson is still despondent. He's having nightmares. But he's not as bad as Wils today. Or Max," said Riley quietly.

"What's wrong with Wils?"

"Terrible headache." He lowered his voice. "Too much champagne."

Peter winced. "Champagne headaches are the worst. Terrible business, all." The two men nodded.

"Would you help Ann?" Peter asked after a respectful pause.

"Of course," said Riley. "But I just need to catch my breath after bringing up this heavy steamer trunk. Be down in a second."

Peter offered Ann his arm, and turned to give Helen a concerned look before he shut the door. The pair sat in silence for a minute as Riley caught his breath. Helen noticed he had little of the cheer he'd brought to the dance.

"Riley, I'm sorry about the loss of von Steiger," said Helen after some length. "Did you know him well?"

He shook his head. "My cousin, Wils, was his friend back in Germany. Von Steiger's father acted as Wils' father after Wils' own father had died. Wils' father had been a great poet and a good man. My cousin felt his loss keenly."

Helen was confused. "How are you cousins with Mr. Brandl? I thought you were British."

"My mother is German. Her formidable sister is Wils' mother."

"How is Wils dealing with the news?"

"I don't know. Things have been nasty since we came back from summer holiday, but we thought it would pass. And now I'm not certain. I'm a bit concerned, not least because I live with Wils and a murderer is on the loose." He set his jaw and shook his head. "Damned unpleasant business." Riley peered into an open box on the table beside him. "What is this?" he asked, lifting out a volume. "*Little Women.* What's that about?"

"A family of sisters whose father is at war."

"Do you like it?"

"Every woman does."

"Should every man?"

"I don't know any man who has read it," she said, watching him fidget with the book.

"Perhaps the girls find their peace," Riley said, then shivered as if shaking off a bad thought. He put the book back and paced nervously. "We all are called to find our own peace when war intrudes so on our lives." He walked over to her window seat and looked out. "An excellent window," he said, his eyes suddenly lighting up. "You could put a ladder up here and escape anytime you needed to."

She felt her cheeks go pink. "There will be no ladders of any kind put under that window."

He gave a soft laugh and looked back. "Miss Brooks, from the looks of it I've arrived too late to be of use in hauling your boxes, and I've no interest in Miss Lowell's—"

Before he could finish his sentence, they heard steps pounding in the hallway. Into the room burst Miss Sullivan, her large face red, her curls untamed and hostile.

"Riley Spencer!"

"Miss Sullivan."

The woman's small dark eyes darted around the room. "I heard you were in the building."

"I was just leaving."

"I'll not have you here, not even for moving day." She gave Helen a stern look. "Miss Brooks, your grandmother and mother would probably prefer you kept your moving to your own family."

Helen's face went bright red. "He's doing me a great favor, Miss

Sullivan. I've a problem returning rudeness for kindness."

"I'm sure you do, Miss Brooks," she said, her hands on her ample hips. "But you don't know his history. After today, no men are allowed in Longworth Hall." She poked a meaty finger at him and glared. "Especially not you. Do you understand me?"

"Perfectly," said Riley. He returned her contemptuous glare. "Miss Brooks, perhaps we will continue our conversation at a different time."

"Wait, Riley—"

"Let him go," said Miss Sullivan, standing in front of Helen as Riley walked out the door. "You'll not be seen with that young man as long as I have something to say about what goes on under this roof. If I see him back here, I'll be obliged to write your father. He's no good for a woman like yourself." She turned on her heel and left the room.

Helen was aghast. How rude! How could someone do such a thing in polite company? He'd done nothing wrong, and yet he'd been treated abominably. Her frustration—the carpets, her fear of class, the murder—erupted into fury.

She ran to her window and saw Riley below, walking to the curb.

"Riley, wait!" she called. "Riley!"

He looked up and around, then waved. "Miss Brooks? Do you need a ladder?"

She laughed. "Would you like to come to the Harvest Festival this Saturday in Concord?"

"Is it any fun?" he asked.

"There's a car race and I've been asked to be one of the drivers."

"A race?" He beamed. "I'd be delighted to come. We'll take my cousin's car."

"Will we have to take your cousin?"

"Most certainly! I promise you'll like him. See you then." He waved, turned, and walked down the street.

She brought her head back inside.

"Good God, Helen!" said Peter from the doorway. He strode over to the window and shut it. "Have you none of the sense the good Lord gave you? Riley Spencer's an engaged man."

[CHAPTER FIVE]

BECK HALL

CAMBRIDGE, MASSACHUSETTS
Sunday Afternoon

The news of von Steiger's death and Arnold Archer's arrest electrified the campus, spreading throughout residence hall lounges, from student to student, and in quiet murmurs among the staff. Wils had found a fresh broadsheet in the foyer of Beck Hall. He was shocked to find that the evidence that had forced the police to arrest Archer was his (Wils') very own gold watch, one that he'd lent to Max. But he frowned as he read the rest of the *Crimson*'s report, filled as it was with innuendo and anti-German accusations.

He felt sick to see that Archer's family was launching something called a Patriots' League in order to help the government identify other German spies. He hoped the police wouldn't fall for such a ruse.

He opened the door to his apartments and walked straight to his room. He threw the newspaper in the waste bin. Max—a German spy, indeed! What filth.

At least Arnold had been arrested. For despite Copeland's protests about all of Arnold Archer's family's power, it seemed that the privileged were not above the law. Some justice might prevail in New England after all was said and done.

Wils shook his head, sat down at a thick oak table opposite his bed and under a tall arched window. He opened his books to get to work. If he were forced to leave classes due to the war, he preferred to withdraw with high marks. He didn't want his classmates sniggering about the stupid German amongst them. Most of his assignments were not difficult, they just required doing. The only one that really required thought was a poem for Professor Copeland's seminar on advanced editing, and he'd found his topic.

For this poem he had decided to write about fate: cruel, cold-hearted, absolutely rotten, callous fate. Three blind women in the stars chopping up people's lives with their nasty scissors. Kaiser Bill with his stupid war gulping down Belgium, scraping for France—demanding power in exchange for men's red blood. Prussian mothers throwing their sons into harm's way for some hysterical and ill-founded mission.

What was it with his own government? The war wouldn't create freedom to pursue the noblest instincts of anyone's soul. Germany above all? And what if they accomplished that? What good would it do for humanity?

Free will, my Aunt Frieda's big bottom, he thought, whipping out a piece of paper and beginning to write.

It had been easy at first, as he wrote, his anger fueling his art. But as his mind relaxed, as he spent his anger, the ditty from the girl's poem last night crept into his mind and replayed itself over and over.

> *Fall comes in shades of red*
> *And leaves in shrouds of white*

He recalled her looking down at him, startled. He laughed as he thought back to her cheeks' reddening when she had detected the slightest whiff of criticism. Her raven hair looked so severe against those flushed cheeks.

Yet it set off to perfection the white skin of her throat.

He found several minutes had passed by the time he got back to work again. Such insecurity for one so beautiful—that was his final judgment as he picked up his pen again.

This time he was interrupted by a loud noise in the hallway. An irksome young man standing outside his door was spewing angry words about Germans.

Ignore it, thought Wils, pushing his ink pen hard to the page. He was almost finished, and then he'd leave for the club.

But the lunatic kept at it. He threatened to confront any German he saw and then broke into sobs. Wils stiffened in his chair and put down his pen. He heard the muffled voice of Mr. Burton, his beefy hall master, trying to calm the young man down, arguing house rules, but the man kept at it.

Wils could hear every last caustic remark about his nation. Enough was enough. He was not a coward, and there came a time when one had to stand up to a bully.

A loud crash shook his door, sending the brass knocker rumbling. Wils rushed to the living room fireplace and picked up the poker as Mr. Burton shouted and a door slammed. Wils ran to the hall but found it empty except for Mr. Burton, and at his feet the remains of a shattered chair on the wide floorboards. Burton's balding head was covered in sweat.

"Go back, Wils," said Burton. "There's nothing here."

Wils turned to see a large scar across his door.

Burton continued. "The boy's cousin was just killed in Belgium. Have a little mercy, for God's sake," said Burton, collecting the broken bits. "And put that poker back unless you want them to grab it and use it on you."

"I'm not going to be threatened."

In a heavy motion, Burton raised himself up. He stood shoulder height to Wils but was three times as thick. Perspiration dripped from his nose.

"Don't you be getting into this trouble, Wils," Burton said in a low tone. "Some people are looking for a fight and they'd just as soon fight you as not. And don't think you can take them. The police aren't going to be helping you after what's just happened to Arnold Archer. They protect their own over at City Hall."

"They didn't protect Arnold from his crime," Wils replied hotly. "That means the Archers have enemies at City Hall too. I'm talking with the police tomorrow."

Burton didn't reply as he sat back down to write a report.

Wils was livid. It was time to leave.

He locked his scarred door and walked to Burton's desk.

"Burton. My door."

"I'm preparing the paperwork as we speak."

"Then good day."

"Where are you going, Wils?"

"Dinner," he said, pushing open the heavy entryway door.

"I'd stay away from the Spee."

Stay away from the Spee? Hardly. He'd had enough of this non-sense. "Good evening, Mr. Burton," he said, not answering his request.

"Good evening, Mr. Brandl."

Wils defiantly walked to the club's mansion, becoming angrier with every step.

Damn Max! Archer was looking for fire and Max had lit the fuse. Maybe he was a gambler. Maybe he did have debts. Wils took a deep breath. He just didn't know.

Wils caught the face of Ronald Chudley in the window looking down at him with a haughty mien. The young man walked away, and then the window was empty.

To hell with them all, Wils thought, turning on his heel. Burton was right. Why would he even want to go to the club? Thinking on it, he most emphatically didn't. He'd eat at the Harvard Union, where Morris Rabin would see that he was left in peace.

SINCE EARLY AUGUST, as the war in Europe escalated, anti-German sentiment flared through Boston, and beyond all reason. It had become spectacle and sport. People didn't want to entertain serious debate. German professors were being watched by their fellow Cantabridg-ians—their neighbors and friends. German books were being burned. The Spee Club, a place of privilege, was now a place of anonymous elbows in his back. Ink had been spilled on his books. A chair had been pulled out from under him. Since early August he'd been met with glares and quiet taunts at crew practice. Jackson Vaughn's mother in

Alabama had even warned her son not to fraternize with "the enemy." (And Mrs. Vaughn was only one generation removed from the Southern Rebellion!)

It couldn't last. Everyone was saying that the conflict was so massive it couldn't be sustained. Everyone would be ruined if this war didn't stop—that there had to be some emergency brake. He hoped so. But he was unsure that would happen. They'd learned after Napoleon to believe that power was the ultimate expression. That idea had no emergency brake.

As Wils entered the Harvard Union, the pungent fumes of lye reminded him why he seldom dined there. Not only were the environs less than luxurious—wood chairs against scarred tables scattered around a cavernous room—but he knew no one. Eating at the Union was an anonymous experience where food went into a body without any of the nourishment one found when eating with a friend before a warm fire. There would be no laughter here, only food. But there would also be no recrimination. That was a victory of sorts.

He heaped a tray with lamb pie and roasted potatoes, then sat down, placing his notebook on one side of his tray to create a barrier to anyone of manners wishing to speak with him, and for a quarter hour was left in peace.

"Brandl!" came a voice from across the room. Wils looked up to see Morris Rabin walking toward him with a paper tucked under his arm.

Rabin was dark and short, from a rough neighborhood in New York. Despite working part-time in the Union kitchens to earn money for school, he'd outranked Wils in nearly every class they'd taken together.

"Brandl? What are you doing here?" he said, moving Wils' notebook and sitting down.

"Avoiding patriots."

Rabin nodded. "I heard about Archer, may he hang higher than Haman. Did ya know about this?"

"Copeland told me Wednesday. The police want to talk with me tomorrow."

Rabin leaned back. "Your watch. I heard they found it on Archer yesterday when they searched his room."

"Yes. I gave that watch to Max when his broke."

"I'm surprised Max didn't pawn it. I mean, it doesn't look good. Even if Arnold did go take the watch, these gambling debts—"

"Don't say it," said Wils, his stomach tightening. For a man from a rough neighborhood, Rabin was always interested in upper-class intrigue. Perhaps that was the way of the world. A man is jilted, it's his pain to deal with. But die and it's everyone's business.

"Oh no," said Morris. "I'm on your side in this. I liked Max. We were friends before he became such a sad case," he said, shaking his head. "I'm sorry he's gone."

"How is Jackson taking the news?"

A look of weariness crossed Morris' face. "Not well. His nightmares about Jenny have been getting worse. He kept me up all night last night and now with the news about Max—well, he had better pull it together. Enough of this love, I say!"

"I'll drink to that," said Wils, raising his glass.

They sat in silence for a moment. Morris had brought little of his usual cheer, and Wils wondered if he should risk the rest of his lamb pie getting cold.

"Wils, I did find something that I think will interest you," Morris said, offering a newspaper. "I was going to show you tomorrow in class. It's about the war."

"Save it," said Wils glumly. "I'll find out soon enough. My mother just recalled me."

"No, mate, I'm serious," he said, his eyes intense. "You can't go." As Morris pulled out the *London Times* from the crook of his arm, Wils held up his hands in protest.

"Morris, I've seen one too many nasty articles on how insecure we Germans are. You know, it's not like America hasn't been in its share of wars during the past century with its own natives, or the Mexicans and the Spanish. And America's not been between an angry France and Russia before, has it?"

"Are we on trial here? You have this wrong. The London papers say the Germans are winning." Morris pointed to the middle column. "Mons and Cambrai: Losses of the British Army."

"What? Where'd you get this?" he asked, surprised to hear such news. "I'd heard about Namûr, but—"

"Exactly!" said Morris. "It's bad for the British and French and frankly I hate the Kaiser, so I'm not too happy about the news myself. We shouldn't reward tyranny. But the Kaiser's plan is working. Your ma isn't going to be sending for you after this. The *Times* would never print this news if it weren't really bad for England."

Wils read down the column:

> The German commanders in the north advance their men as if they had an inexhaustible supply. Of the bravery of the men it is not necessary to speak. They advance in deep sections, so slightly extended as to be almost in close order, with little regard for cover, rushing forward as soon as their own artillery has opened fire behind them on our position. Our artillery mows long lanes down the centres of the sections, so that frequently there is nothing left of it but its outsides. But no sooner is this done than more men double up, rushing over the heaps of dead, and remake the section. Last week so great was their superiority in numbers that they could no more be stopped than the waves of the sea. Their shrapnel is markedly bad, though their gunners are excellent at finding the range. On the other hand their machine guns are of the most deadly efficacy, and are very numerous. Their rifle shooting is described as not first-class, but their numbers bring on the infantry till frequently they and the Allied troops meet finally in bayonet tussles. Superiority of numbers in men and guns, especially in machine guns; a most successfully organized system of scouting by aeroplanes and Zeppelins; motors carrying machine guns, cavalry;

and extreme mobility are the elements of their
present success.

To sum up, the first great German effort has succeeded.
We have to face the fact that the British Expeditionary
Force, which bore the great weight of the blow, has
suffered terrible losses and requires immediate and
immense reinforcement. The British Expeditionary
Force has won indeed imperishable glory, but it
needs men, men, and yet more men.

Wils looked over at Morris, shocked at what he had read. "The
Times is saying—"

"Yes, Wils. It could be over. Just not as they—or I—wished."

Wils shook his head in disbelief. "Thank God," he mumbled.
"Mother wanted me to leave this week after I spoke to the police."

Morris clapped him on the shoulder. "Well, now you won't have to
go to war. Riley—he may be going. But not you. The war is almost over,
it seems. Keep the paper, Wils. I've got to go back to work."

Wils thanked him and re-read the story again, his heart beating
faster as the reporter spoke of German victories. The tightness rolled
back in his chest, and he thanked Morris silently for bringing such
news. Morris was solid. He was always there to lend a hand in crisis. He
certainly had bailed Jackson out when Jenny McGee had broken his
heart. And Morris was a working-class man, tried-and-true. He'd listen
to both sides, you'd see him cogitate, and then he'd say something typically measured and moderate and be done with it. He wasn't ideologi-
cal. He wasn't rich but he certainly wasn't rabble. Morris Rabin was
what was good about America. Solid.

Wils finished his food in a much better mood, picked up his paper
and books, and walked back in the twilight to Beck Hall. He bade a
stiff but cordial good evening to Burton and opened the scarred door
to his flat.

Riley glared from the settee. His shirt was wrinkled, his tie
undone.

"Where have you been?" Riley demanded. He picked up a copy of the *Harvard Crimson* and waved it high. "You are completely irresponsible. I saw that door and thought you'd gone and done something dreadful. I can't believe how unfeeling it is of you to leave without a note."

"Is complaining still the national pastime of England?" asked Wils irritably, walking past the brick fireplace. He sat down in a leather chair opposite the settee. Beside him was a table with several telegrams in a jumbled pile.

Riley scowled. "From the look of the telegrams, your German mother bests me complaining by far."

"Let's not talk about it."

"Wils, I know how bad this must be for you. You are in the pit of despair. I offer you a rope but you seem to want a lid."

Wils looked above the mantel at the large portrait of his mother and Riley's mother, Aunt Frieda, with Aunt Gertrude as young girls. The three looked mildly amused at his predicament. He took off his glasses and put them down on the table but said nothing.

Riley went on. "I know that Max is dead and that the murderers may be coming after you next."

Wils' face went white. "What? Me? Copeland said nothing of the sort to me." Good night, he thought, opening his collar.

"It's what the papers report: Americans are taking justice into their own hands," said Riley.

"We don't know that. Archer killed Max, but we don't know if he's going to kill other Germans. I rang the *Crimson* to investigate."

Riley blanched. "You rang the *Crimson*?"

"Yes. Arnold's a murderer."

Riley rubbed his eyes. "Dear Lord! Don't you know that Arnold's father runs this city? Why didn't you stay out of it, Wils? Max might still be alive if he'd stayed out of all of these politics."

"*Es ist nicht möglich!*" said Wils. He shook his head and took a deep breath. "It's not Max's fault he was murdered, no matter what he did. I don't want to fight with you, Riley."

"He knew better and so do you. No more phone calls. No more going out by yourself without saying where you're going. And your mother is going to post a security guard tomorrow outside of our door. We're not going to have our door broken down. Webster Potter's cousin was killed in Belgium and Webster is big enough to break the door and us. I'm surprised he didn't." Riley's frustration seemed to grow with every order he gave. "Good night, Brandl! Don't you realize that by going to the paper you've made us both targets of Arnold's new 'Patriots' League'?"

"That league is a sham."

"For now. But things can change. One ship sunk, one country falls, and we will have a full-fledged witch hunt on our hands. And don't tell me these people don't know their business on that score. The Salem witches had it bad."

"Riley, this will blow over in the next few weeks. Every year there's some protest. If it's not for labor, then it will be patriotism, and if not patriotism, then something else. Remember how angry they were about planting oaks in the Yard? That's what they do around here. Protest and rallies are sport."

"Blood sport, it looks to me. And they're after your blood. We're going to take some precautions about your safety," said Riley, getting up from his seat. "I've had enough of this. Have you eaten?"

"Yes."

Riley frowned. "And yet you still act like an idiot, leaving without notice as to where you are. I've not eaten and I'm terrible about dealing with problems on an empty stomach."

Wils watched as Riley left for the adjoining room's pantry. He stretched his legs and rested his head against the back of the sofa. He noticed that Aunt Frieda had Riley's smile.

"How long does foie gras last?" called Riley.

"I don't know. Smell it." There was a pause in the kitchen.

"Smells like it always does. Let's give it a shot. Wils, would you like to come with me to a festival in Concord this weekend?"

"With whom?"

"Helen Brooks."

"The woman from the dance last night?"

"Yes," called Riley.

"No, Riley, I don't wish to go. And if you go, you'll be playing with fire. Peter suspects."

"He should," said Riley. "I wish to court his sister. She's a beauty."

"I'll give you that, but she'll make you take the brunt of her sharp tongue. And there is the problem that you're engaged."

"I am not."

"Edith thinks you are," Wils replied.

"That is not my fault. I didn't ask her to marry me."

"Then why did she say you were engaged?"

Riley stepped out from the pantry and his face grew hard. "I hate to sound unchivalrous, but I never asked her to marry me and I've no intention of doing so. A man knows if he's proposed."

"Peter heard differently," said Wils.

"Really, Wils," said Riley indignantly. "Now I need your car, and even more I would like you to drive so I can fix all my attention on Miss Brooks. I hear she's smarter than you were when you entered Harvard."

"It's what you do with intelligence that matters, not that you have it," said Wils in a careless tone as he flipped through telegrams.

"That's quite enough. Helen is champagne without the headache. She may be the one for me. You and Peter will have to get accustomed to it." He returned to the pantry.

"I've heard that at least a hundred times," muttered Wils. But arguing with Riley was a lost cause. He'd end up driving the pair. Riley would insist on it and not rest until he'd given in from some mix of duty, guilt that his family was richer than Riley's, and desire to protect his car from his cousin's depredations.

"Have you heard how Jackson is doing?" called Riley.

"Nightmares," replied Wils.

"Sounds like progress."

He turned over the paper at the bottom.

LORD KITCHENER HAS CALLED FOR MORE TROOPS.
RILEY, YOU MUST COME HOME. FATHER.

The color left Wils' face. He put it back, as if its touch were poison.

[CHAPTER SIX]

RADCLIFFE AND
HARVARD YARDS

Monday, August 31, 1914

H elen had prepared for bed Sunday night as usual, writing out her prayers in longhand. She told God that she wished to do well that term; that He should help her mother find a more productive use of her time and help Riley Spencer figure out if he was engaged or not. And that God, in His infinite mercy, should blow up the Kaiser.

Such prayers provided cold comfort, though, the next morning. Helen did not sleep well, and on Monday morning she awoke even before the first bell, nervous about the first day of class. She dressed quickly, carefully buttoning her crisp white shirtwaist, hooking the back of her navy skirt, and wrapping her long dark hair into a tight knot secured with a dark silk ribbon.

Ann's mother had left a box of pastries for their first day, and as Ann was still asleep, Helen breakfasted quietly with the news reports from the morning newspaper. She read with gloom the story about the terrible British defeat. There were rumors of a new offensive in France, of the new German empire swallowing Europe as a whole, and hard talk of how the student Arnold Archer, son of a powerful politician in Boston, had actually done America a real service in alerting authorities to a spy in their midst.

Questions were raised about a German professor feeding pigeons—whether or not those pigeons were messenger pigeons—and an announcement was made by Professor Kuno Francke that his plans for the new Germanic museum at Harvard were put on hold. Three students withdrew over the weekend to go to war, and yet class continued, the professors insistent on the careful observance of the academic year. At least the topic was no longer family limitation among the poor, she thought, grateful that God had answered at least a bit of her prayer.

She brushed the crumbs from her skirt and left for class, careful not to wake Ann as she shut the door. It was an indecorous and unexciting beginning to things. This was not how she'd imagined her first day of college, she thought, walking outside. She had no idea what she'd planned for that day, but walking by herself into a room full of women she didn't know wasn't the experience of which she'd dreamt.

Her first class, mathematics, went well, taught in the Radcliffe Quadrangle by Miss Parcher, a quiet lady with white hair and skin so thin it was nearly translucent. Her voice warbled as she spoke and Helen, who had read ahead to chapter three, had no problem keeping up.

For her next two classes—modern literature and world history—she sat at rapt attention only to find that both were lecture classes in which no student opinion was sought nor was it to be offered. Her teachers, a balding young man for literature and a dour matron for world history, were terribly boring. She hoped class would become more exciting and challenging and reminded herself that the past was not always a predictor of the future, although, as her father pointed out, it typically was.

Helen returned to her dormitory at noon and ate lunch with Ann. Ann's morning had been as uninteresting as hers, with the exception that Ann had received an offer to read the scripture at Radcliffe's Opening of Term Sunday service on behalf of the Lowell family. After Ann had left to audition for the choir, Helen packed her books and made her way over to Harvard Yard for her final class of the day.

Professor Copeland's "Editing for Editors" seminar was held in a small room in Boylston Hall, a building now hidden by the construction surrounding the completion of the mammoth new Widener Library. The walkways leading around the workers had become a labyrinth of wooden planks and temporary railings. With some difficulty Helen made it to the rough granite hall.

She walked into room 14. She was ten minutes early and all the desks were empty. Every move she made seemed to echo off the bare walls and scuffed floorboards.

In each chair she saw a note.

> "I saw some Belgian children last trip. Their hands had
> been cut off by the Germans and they were starving.
> We have to help them. If we don't they will die."
>
> —Captain Joe Stubbs of the steamship *Essex*
>
> ***Stop the Kaiser's terror in Belgium!***
> ***Join the Patriots' League!***
> ***Rally by the College Pump tonight at 8:00 to find out more!***

Helen shook her head at it and put it in the trash bin. She hoped the Kaiser would pay for what he'd done.

Precisely on the hour, a rush of men flooded the room, pushing past her to sit at the back of the class. As they streamed in she thought that they looked nearly identical with their short hair, starched shirts, and dark suits. Some wore glasses and others jackets with various crests on them. One young man looked particularly wan. A debauched life, she supposed. They all seemed to push the notes from their seats onto the floor.

Professor Copeland, in a bowler hat and brown checkered suit, strolled in by the time the third bell sounded. He seemed not to notice that his class, with the exception of Helen, sat as far from him as possible, but instead put his hat by the lectern and opened a notebook to call roll.

"Amory."

There was no sound. Professor Copeland cleared his throat. "Amory," he repeated.

Silence.

"Does anyone know where Herbert Cincinnatus Amory might be?" Copeland asked.

Helen saw a young man raise his hand. "Amory withdrew this morning."

Copeland pulled out a pencil. "Thank you," he said, marking his notebook. He asked for no explanation and began again. As he read, his eyes were magnified by his thick glasses.

"Brandl, Breckenridge, Brooks, Elken, Ferguson, Hoyt, Iselin, Kingman, Meltzer, Porter, Rabin, Reycroft, Shepherd, Simpson, Stone, Tibbetts, Vaughn, Wharton, and Zilgitt."

He looked up and surveyed the class. "Greetings to our first meeting of 'Editing for Editors,' a class where you will write and then we will critique your work as we would if we were publishers. As you know, Harvard relies on you to refresh this ancient fellowship and hopes you will add luster, and not tarnish, to our ranks.

"Let's commence. I assume you all have done the assignment. Please pull out your work and we will begin editing, starting in alphabetical order. We were to start with Amory, but as he is not here—"

Helen's stomach lurched as the students rustled their papers. She'd received no assignment. She thought back to the note her father had given her. She felt her face flush as the men behind her quieted down.

"Brandl, please read your work and then, class, we shall see what we think of it."

Brandl? She turned with horror and recognized the young man from the dance. She'd not made him out at first, there in his street clothes. His blond hair had fallen over his eyes. His crisp navy jacket, white shirt, and striped tie made him look much like the others.

He pulled out a sheet of paper and began to read.

WHAT LACHESIS, THE FATE, SAW
by Wilhelm von Lützow Brandl

Lachesis shifted her silv'ry robe
Of stars across her maiden's breast
As Agamemnon brought an eagle
Atalanta, a spear and chest.

Under the brooding eye of the fates
Kings and heroes chose their lives
While the three sisters laughed
At what true soul liberty gives.

Then she saw Odysseus search
The valley of dry bones
And take a simple bowler hat
As crown for his next home.
Her heart flickered with hope
As he drank from Lethe's measure
And vanished from her sight again
To live in simple pleasure.

When he was finished the class was silent, and Helen was thoroughly confused. She had no idea what he'd just recited.

"Mr. Rabin," said Copeland, "you are the editor at a magazine called *Editing Virtues and the Learned Man*. What have you to say about this work?"

Helen heard Rabin clear his throat. "It's quite lofty, as is the style of our Mr. Brandl, but it's also obscure. I didn't understand it at our study group and I don't understand it now," responded the young man in a heavy New York accent. "But it's perfectly pompous enough for Harvard."

Helen would have felt sorry for Brandl, but she felt it just deserts for the other night.

"Mr. Brandl, this from your good friend Rabin? Why did you inflict obscure poetry on our class?"

"As ever," said Wils in a voice that sounded bored, "Mr. Rabin aims for the gutter and hits his mark. This poem is straight from Plato's *Republic*. Men have little choice in their circumstances, and then use what choice they do have to solve their last problems, not the ones that confront them. I wrote about how Odysseus outwits the fates by renouncing materialism and power—his crown that brought him all of the problems of war and voyage. It's appropriate for our world today, where power and material goods—not striving for excellence found in each soul—are seen as the best use of a man's time."

There was silence as Morris Rabin shook his head but refused further comment. Copeland looked around the class. "Mr. Shepherd." A fair boy with a dimpled chin spoke.

"Would Plato know Ezekiel?"

"Good catch. Mr. Brandl, Harold Shepherd points out that the valley of dry bones is Hebraic. Why are you mixing your Greek and Hebraic theology in my class?"

"The reader would know it. I only intended it to sound familiar," protested Brandl.

Copeland looked around the room again. "Any more comments? Iselin, have you something to say?"

Dane Iselin, a thin boy with red hair and freckles, spoke. "Wils, why would you write about Plato when your country is at war? Why not just write about how hard it is to be German in America? I thought we were to write about what we know—to trust ourselves."

Helen saw Wils' face flush to the roots of his blond hair. "Because writing about Plato in Boston won't get you killed." A chilled silence filled the room. Embarrassed for him, Helen looked down at her blank notebook paper. He must have been referring to von Steiger.

After a pause Copeland spoke. "Mr. Brandl, I have a few comments. First, Mr. Iselin is right—a poem about how things are right now from your perspective would be a good idea, even if you don't share it with the class. You must write about what you know and trust your instincts. You are a good man who thirsts for knowledge, and the world needs this. Remember who you are, Mr. Brandl. Second, please don't write any more Plato. My doctor tells me I can't handle it at my age. It will provoke—"

"SPELLS OF BLACK DEPRESSION," chanted the students in unison. All except Helen. She looked around, feeling vaguely uncomfortable, as if she were sitting in on someone else's conversation.

"Yes, yes, quiet down," said Copeland to the class. "Consider my health when you write, Mr. Brandl." Copeland looked down to his notebook again.

"Breckenridge, you're next. Please read your work for the class."

Helen's stomach turned as she realized where this was going. Philip Breckenridge, a ruddy boy with dark brown curls, then read a poem about the death of his dog. He was firmly ridiculed by the class for writing on the passions of death. Helen, who had no poem for the day, looked through her purse while they talked. She saw her poem, stained with moisture from the other day, and blushed to remember what Wils had said about it. It was freakishly bad, she thought. She folded it and then put it away.

"Brooks, please read what you've brought us," called Copeland.

There was silence as Helen felt the eyes of all in the class bore into her. It took her a bit, but then she said, "I don't have a work, sir."

"Nothing to read?" he asked with a frown. "You've edited three books for your father. How can you have nothing?"

Wils looked over at the frightened young woman. He had been surprised to see her when he'd walked into the room. She was the pretty girl from the dance, albeit the one with the temper. Riley had said she was smart, but Wils hadn't realized that she was smart in a way that would get her in Copeland's seminar.

But as she stiffened in her seat under Copeland's questioning, he stifled a smile. She probably didn't know how to take Copeland's comments. She seemed just the type to let him get under her skin. Perhaps she'd learn to take criticism. They'd all been baptized under Copeland's withering stare and she should be no different.

"I didn't receive the assignment," she said. "Your note to my father told me what time to arrive but that was it. I thought on the first day I'd learn what we were to do."

Copeland frowned. "Could you recite anything for us?"

"I'd be happy to provide something tomorrow," she answered.

"You have nothing for us?"

"No."

"No elegy or sonnet? A ballad, perhaps?" asked the professor.

"No," she said, flushing deeply.

"Could you recite a limerick?" Several men snickered, but she just sat straight, looking ahead. Copeland gave a curt wave to the rest of the class. "Miss Brooks, please get a copy of the schedule after the bell rings. Tomorrow I expect you to come to class with a work of yours that we shall critique as if we were professional editors. Also, you will need to join a study group. Next week we'll have a group writing project." He looked back down at his notebook.

"Marvin Elken, would you—"

Helen's hand shot up.

"Yes, Miss Brooks?"

"How will I find a study group?"

He nodded. "Gentlemen, Miss Brooks needs to join a study group. Please raise your hands if you have an opening."

Wils looked over at her and felt a little sorry for her. No man raised his hand, nor did he. He was already in a group with Jackson and Morris. If they were to add a person, they'd need to discuss it first, especially as the person in question was a woman with a known temper.

But Copeland didn't seem to wish to let the class off easily on this score. As he allowed the silence to become painful, Wils felt a begrudging admiration for the young woman. There she sat, frightened and nervous, but she didn't burst into tears. And she didn't protest. In fact, she seemed to bear it well. As he knew far too well, being the only one of your kind in a room changed you. When isolated, he tended to see things differently, as if things were blurry even though you knew your eyes worked just fine. And you knew that if the people shaking your chair would just stop, your eyesight, your pulse, and your overall temperament would return to normal.

"Professor," Helen said, "I'll work on the assignment alone for now."

Copeland gave a thin-lipped frown. "Gentlemen, I've never seen a room of men cower so in the presence of a young woman. I hope you reconsider this evening. I expect by the next time I see you here in this class one of you will have a space for her in your study group. Now, Marvin Elken, please recite your work."

Helen sat as in a fog for the duration of the class. She'd rather be with her mother stuffing family limitation pamphlets into envelopes than to produce a poem by the next day and join a study group. Copeland continued the class recitations in alphabetical order until they reached Hoyt. The bell then tolled, signaling the end of class. He announced a public reading to be held the next week as they gathered their books.

As Helen collected her notes, the men rushed by to leave. Wils Brandl walked to Copeland's lectern, picked up the class schedule, and went back to her desk.

"Miss Brooks, I'm Wilhelm Brandl. We met at the Saturday—"

"Yes, I remember," she said curtly. He frowned and then seemed to regroup.

"Here is the assignment page," he said, handing it to her. He stood there for a moment as she packed her things.

"Miss Brooks, may I ask you something? You had a good poem from the other night. Why didn't you recite it for class today?"

"You weren't so kind to it on Saturday."

"This is a class of patriots and I assure you they'd have loved your poem. And did you hear what Morris said about mine?" His eyes smiled from behind his spectacles. "I'd be hard put to find a more derisive review."

She looked at him, puzzled as to his intention. "I'll write something tonight."

"It's just—" he continued earnestly, "it was a fine poem and in Copeland's class it's usually better to present something, even if you think it's not your best work, than to say you're empty-handed."

"Don't make her worry," said a young man standing behind Wils. "She did just fine." He introduced himself as Jackson Vaughn, the pale boy in the back. His accent was slow and melodic, that of a southerner. A short young man beside Jackson introduced himself as Morris Rabin. He smelled of kitchen soap but his manners were polished. He opened the door for her as they left the room.

As they walked into the hall, they were surprised by two policemen in blue suits with bright shiny gold buttons, standing up from a bench, as if they'd been waiting for them for some time. One officer was tall and lanky, his face rough with pockmarks. The other was stout and bald, his bug eyes taking them in. As they approached, Helen's heart began to race. What was this?

"Wilhelm Brandl?" said the tall man. "I'm Inspector Walter Gordon of the Boston Police," he said, extending his hand, "and this is Officer Kim O'Hara. I'd like to ask you a few questions if you don't mind."

"Here?" asked Wils, flushing. "I thought we were meeting at four thirty at my flat. My attorney is scheduled to attend."

The short officer shook his head. "Can you come with us? This will only take a few minutes." He reached for Wils' arm.

"Why?" asked Wils, pulling his arm back.

Helen saw the muscles twitch in Gordon's jaw. But Wils drew himself up to full height. He was tall and his chest was broad from rowing. "My attorney made an appointment, which I intend to keep. I insist on having counsel."

"We want to talk with you, not your attorney. As a foreigner, you have no right to one."

Morris walked closer to the officer and spoke softly. "This man has more friends than just his attorney."

"I'm not talking to you."

"Perhaps you'll talk to President Lowell," offered Helen. The officer looked down at her. "He's a relative." It was only a half lie, she thought. It would be true after Ann and Peter were engaged. She would discuss that matter of timing with God later that evening.

"President Lowell, you say."

"I do," said Helen.

Morris clenched his fists and refused to move. The short officer put his thumbs in his belt and glared at Morris. Gordon set his jaw, stepped back, and nodded.

"I'll see you in a half hour then," he said. O'Hara and Gordon walked off, the hall crowd parting for them.

"Thank you, Miss Brooks," said Wils with a nod. "I should go now. But thank you," he said quietly. He seemed less sure of himself as they looked at each other. His eyes, behind his glasses, seemed to wish to smile.

Helen caught herself wishing to comfort him.

Perhaps this was yet another price that country's citizens paid for their king's hubris. She shook her head as she walked along the wooden

planks outside of Boylston. Halfway back to Longworth Hall she
stopped to adjust the books in her arms. She looked back in the direction of Wils Brandl, puzzled by a man who would choose to live in a
hostile country.

⧓

WILS WAS NOT REASSURED by the presence of his mother's choice of a
lawyer to confront the police officers he'd just met. Robert Goodman
was a slight, bespectacled attorney from old New England stock. Could
he stand up to City Hall?

The two met at Wils' flat, and were talking when a knock sounded
at the door. Wils turned to see the two detectives he'd met only a quarter hour earlier standing on his threshold.

"Walter Gordon and Kim O'Hara here. May we come in?"

"Please," said Goodman, offering seats at the living room table,
which O'Hara and Gordon claimed.

"Mr. Goodman, a few questions for your client." Wils took a chair
beside Goodman and folded his arms across his chest.

"Mr. Brandl, why did you call the *Harvard Crimson* about Arnold
Archer's alleged involvement in the von Steiger suicide?"

Goodman said, "He called because—"

"Let the boy speak," said O'Hara in a wheezy tone.

"People should know that a murderer is in their midst," declared
Wils.

"You told them he may have killed von Steiger."

"He may have," said Wils. "That's why your department arrested
him, isn't it?"

"Our chief gave the order, and we follow orders. And when the
chief told us to let him go back to his family, we unlocked the door and
let him out."

"He's out?"

"On bail. He was released this morning to his family. Did you tell
the *Crimson* anything else?"

"No."

Gordon leaned forward. "Archer says Max gave him your watch to pay a gambling debt."

"I have no knowledge of debts."

"Were there reasons for the fight between Archer and von Steiger at the Spee other than politics?"

"I have no idea."

"Mr. Brandl, did you gamble with Mr. von Steiger?"

"No."

"Why did you go with him to Plymouth? I understand you drove by the Charlestown navy yard on your way down there."

"Plymouth? How did you know about that?" asked Wils curtly.

The officer sat back, stone-faced.

"Max wanted to see the USS *Constitution*," said Wils. "He likes old ships. And he also needed to send a package home from one of the civilian wharves."

"What was in the package?" asked Gordon.

"I didn't rummage through it. Books, clothes. The usual things. At least that's my guess."

"Why did you choose that day to go?"

Wils couldn't recall the details. "I don't know. Let me get my diary," he said, walking back to his bedroom to collect a small leather notebook from his desk. "It says here we went because Max was down. We shipped a crate home for him as well as looked at an old ship."

"Who paid for the shipment?" asked Gordon.

"I did. Max was short on cash and I ended up paying. But it seems silly to try to bill him for it now."

The officers exchanged looks.

"Is there anything else?" asked Goodman tersely.

"No, except the diary," said O'Hara. "We'll take it."

"No." Wils resisted the order.

Goodman leaned toward him. "Your diary is part of an investigation now. Please turn it over."

"It's mine."

"Let me see it," said Goodman. Wils handed it to him, open at the August entry.

Plymouth with Max. Stopped over at the Charlestown
navy yard to see the USS *Constitution*—pathetic sight,
all leaks right now. Dropped off Max's crate at Long
wharf; mother must transfer 50 to my account to cover
shipping draft. The naval yard was an ugly place, full of
concrete and shabby buildings and with three new
hulking gray ships. The letters *Pennsylvania* were being
painted on the largest. Plymouth harbor, in contrast, is
open and has beautiful sailboats skimming along it.
The Pilgrims knew what they were doing when they
landed here. Terribly sad history. Even the natives took
pity on the settlers. Fabled Plymouth Rock is small.
Stone church and cemetery are impressive in their
foreboding qualities—and the stones tell tales of such
sorrow—children died in horrendous numbers. These
Pilgrims were grim. Almost as grim as Max, who is still
distraught about Felicity. I wish to God that woman
had never met my friend! But the Pilgrims had tenacity
which saw them through. These Americans are an
impressive lot. Just a few bad apples (Felicity).

"That's hardly anything of use," said Goodman with a frown.
"The ship—"

"The notation about that ship doesn't mean a damn thing, and you
know it. You'd have to have a lot more on my client to make any kind of
case. Wils needs a few moments to copy down his assignments."

Wils glared at the trio, jotted some notes, then handed the diary
over. He felt ill as Gordon pocketed it.

"Did you know Archer's mother was German?" Gordon said.

"No," said Wils coldly.

"A barmaid from Bavaria who married a rich politician. She hates
the Kaiser."

That explains a lot, thought Wils. Bavarians did often hate Prussians. They were Catholic, Prussians were Protestant. Beer festivals
instead of manufacturing. How Wils' own Bavarian father ever fell in

love with his Prussian mother, he never could fathom. Rebellion? Forgiveness? Whatever it was had probably not reached Mrs. Archer or her offspring.

"The world is a prejudiced place," said Wils, happy to see them leaving.

"When will Wils see his diary back?" asked Goodman.

"It will be a while," said O'Hara. "You'll be around?"

"Of course he will."

When they were gone, Goodman turned to him and instructed him in a brisk tone. "Stay put until this is resolved, but once it is, my sincere advice to you is to return to Germany."

"They think that Max is a spy."

"Yes, they do."

"And they think I am involved?"

"Your diary is incriminating. If you had wanted to, you could have told the German military that new ships—and just how many— were in the shipyard. It could give the Kaiser some kind of military advantage."

"But I didn't! And Arnold is the one who committed—"

"And Arnold was arrested. Apparently the Archers have enemies in City Hall too. Now Arnold's provided enough information on you that they're investigating you for helping your friend spy on a U.S. shipyard. You are not to go around *any* shipyards until you walk up the gangplank to board a civilian ship for Germany. Am I clear?"

"How did he know what was in my diary?"

"I don't know. Does anyone besides Riley have a key?"

"Harvard's entire housing office."

"Burton?"

"Of course. As well as my Irish maid and French laundress."

"And now your Italian security guard. You employ most of Europe here, it would seem," Goodman said with a thin smile. "My office will contact your mother, Wils. This is a serious matter. It may take a few weeks to sort out," he said.

"Weeks?"

"Yes."

"Why?"

"To clear your name."

Wils swallowed hard.

"Wils," said the dour lawyer, "I cannot stress to you how serious this matter is. They're not deporting Germans, they're sending them to internment camps down south in Georgia—and not the part you'd wish to be in. I'm going to try to find you a boat and get you on it, but it's going to take some time. They're not letting many ships go in and out right now. Once your name is clear it would be best for you, until the war is over, to return to Germany."

"I'll miss my final year," Wils protested.

Goodman nodded. "Do seniors even attend class at Harvard?"

Wils shrugged.

"Well, that settles it, Wils. I need your word of honor if I'm going to negotiate these terms. The minute you are cleared to leave and I find a ship, you will be on it. Do I have your word?"

Wils nodded. "You think it is the best course?"

"It's the only course. Boston is not where I'd wish to be right now if I were German. Your mother's right."

"Then I give you my word to leave when you call."

"I'll get to work on it," said Goodman, putting his notes into a scarred leather briefcase.

"How exactly will you negotiate this?" Wils asked as Goodman walked to the door.

"These issues have a legal side and a political side to them. I'll have a few members of the City Council call the police chief."

"I thought the Archers had the City Council's support."

"My wife is the governor's daughter. We're not without friends."

"Oh," said Wils. A bit of the tension left his shoulders. Perhaps his mother knew what kind of lawyer to hire after all.

Wils closed the door behind the lawyer. He tugged at his tie and sat down on the settee across from the fireplace. He felt restless and angry.

He was no threat. All he wanted to do was finish his studies. After that, who knew what the world had in store for him?

He'd thought of starting a school on the Baltic Sea where he summered. He'd work with the fishermen's children, teaching them and recording their stories. In his mind he saw laughing children pulling a bell with a thick length of rope, dismissing school for the day and running off to the harbor. He saw his dog, Perg, chasing after seagulls as he walked along the beach in warm wool sweaters in the autumn twilight.

Instead of this dream he'd found himself entangled in a friend's debts, and under suspicion from local burghers. He shook his head. It felt as if a vise were wrapped around his temples.

He walked over to his bedroom window and opened it. He looked out mutely, staring for a long while at the street, hoping for a gust of fresh air to pour through. He felt like a prisoner, with a guard at his door and the angry mob of Cambridge outside his window ready to strike.

Just like Helen. When they'd first talked, she had been all prickles and sharp edges as soon as she figured out he was German. Perhaps he could have lied about her poetry, flattering her with false words to woo her. But certainly she would see through that. She'd seemed more intelligent than that.

He smiled. Intelligent—she'd placed in Copeland's class. And then she'd stood up for him today to a police officer. Not many these days would have done so.

And for the next few moments, try as he might, he couldn't concentrate on revenge or assignments, or Max, or even leaving for Germany. He instead found it impossible to shake the image of Helen Brooks sitting in class looking terrified.

Poor girl, he thought, stepping back from the window. This is how we learn humility.

[CHAPTER SEVEN]

LONGWORTH HALL

RADCLIFFE COLLEGE

"Did you say Jackson Vaughn is in your class?" asked Ann, setting her knitting needles on the parlor table. "Are you sure?"

Helen looked up from her desk, where she'd been staring at a white page for the better part of an hour.

"Yes. He, Wils Brandl, and Morris Rabin tried to give me advice after class. Do you know Mr. Vaughn?"

"Oh yes," said Ann, moving aside a skein of thick yarn on the sofa where she sat. "He's a very romantic figure. He's been at death's door since being jilted."

"He did look pale," offered Helen.

"Death's door," Ann repeated. "His family is in shipping down in Alabama."

"Alabama?"

"Yes, from the same plantation that Uncle Tom was supposed to have been killed at."

"I thought that was in Louisiana," said Helen.

"No. Alabama. I'm sure of it."

Helen shrugged. "The sins of the fathers. But Peter said Jackson actually tried to kill himself."

"Oh yes. He got very drunk and swam out to sea. But he'd left a note and when Morris and Wils found it, they took a boat out and fished him out of the water."

Good night, thought Helen, turning back to her work. Her father had often warned her about southerners and their extreme views on passion.

"Helen, you could write your poem about Jackson."

"I don't think that Mr. Vaughn would appreciate that, as dramatic as it might be." She put down her pen. "This poem has to be about something I know about and I'm finding out that I know nothing about anything."

"That's nonsense, Helen. What are others writing about?"

"One wrote of his dog, and one wrote about something so obscure I couldn't be expected to tell you what it was. That was Wils Brandl, Riley Spencer's cousin."

"And do you like this Mr. Spencer?"

"Perhaps," Helen said weakly. "But did Peter tell you that he thinks Riley is engaged?"

"Really? After he danced with you? I'd be surprised if it were true. You know how protective Peter is of you. He didn't like Frank Adams either."

"He shouldn't have worried," said Helen. "I apparently had no chance with Frank even before Mother's arrest."

"Did Riley say or do anything that would make you think he was attached?"

"Nothing."

"Well, perhaps he's not. Maybe Peter was wrong."

"I will ask Riley about it."

"Please don't," Ann said quickly.

"Why ever not?"

Ann started to speak and then stopped, several times. "Helen, men do not like being asked to consider that they may have done something wrong. I think it would make Riley angry if you were so forthright."

"Some might say that an engaged man who doesn't act engaged with another party should have his integrity questioned and perhaps even get it in the neck."

"Is that the lesson you learned from your dealings with Frank Adams?"

Helen winced. "But men speak plainly! Wils Brandl told me to my face he didn't like something I'd written and Father said that even though we don't like what is said we must listen for the content of the message."

"And how did you receive that news?" asked Ann.

Helen nodded slowly. "I see your point."

"You are just like your brother," said Ann with a warm smile.

"What do you mean?"

"Impulsive. You remember that day in July when we saw the Jewish wedding on the Maine beach?"

"Yes."

"Well, late that afternoon Peter said he would row me over to my uncle's new cabin, and instead he rowed to the cove. As he was about to declare himself, the sky turned dark. Peter thought he would row back, get the automobile, and come for me. So intent was he—the captain of the Harvard crew team—on speeding back to get me to safety that at the edge of the cove he turned the wrong way. That was the last I saw of any human for three hours."

"Another victim of a Brooks family member's impulses. I hardly see that as a good lesson."

"Helen, being in love is completely lost on you. I adore your brother's impulsiveness. Now I am off to bed. Good luck with your assignment."

Helen watched Ann as she stood up and carried her knitting back to her bedroom. Her long blond hair flowed down her back in soft curls over the white lace of her dressing gown. Ann never looked unkempt.

As the door closed, Helen picked up her pen, reinvigorated by this new line of thinking.

That image of the summer day in Maine had stuck with her. The man on the beach had dark hair and was laughing. He seemed so happy. As if he'd seen what Jackson and Max had seen. A joy born of a love that poured out of him, impossible to contain inside. He had laughter in his heart.

She wished for that, she thought with a sigh. That man on the beach had seemed to be filled with a joy as deep as he was tall. An ample portion, indeed. Perhaps joy could replenish itself again and again in the human heart. Perhaps for eternity. And perhaps that's why if you had it and lost it, you would react as Jackson or Max had.

She recalled it had been a beautiful morning in Maine. Raphael couldn't have painted the sky any bluer. There was a crowd of dark-haired men with their caps, all smiling and clapping each other on the back. A tiny girl with the veil who let out a laugh when they lifted her up in the chair. The man was seated on a chair across from her. Some danced in circles around the lifted chairs while others clapped. A few children kept running to the water, their nursemaids chasing after them.

After Helen looked at the clear white of her empty page for several minutes more, it occurred to her that her father's criticism might have missed the point of someone like Jackson Vaughn entirely. What if a few moments of love changed your life completely? It had happened to Heloise and Abelard, she thought. And to Lord Nelson and Lady Hamilton, although that was hardly the morality lesson one should emulate.

A few moments of pleasure—why would it be worth such torment? She thought again of the Jews at the wedding in Maine, and the laughter in the man's throat. That wedding seemed like such a joyful affair, not at all like the wedding she envisioned for Caroline Peabody and Frank Adams of Lexington, Massachusetts.

As she looked at her paper, the image of the seashore came back to her, beckoning her to write. She shuddered, thinking of what Mr. Brandl would say.

[CHAPTER EIGHT]

BECK HALL

HARVARD COLLEGE

Riley's women no longer made much of an impression on his friends. They came in such succession, and with so many varying types of dress and accents and hairstyles, that his friends had long ago found it best to remove themselves from the scene entirely. The chase was between the new young woman and Riley, not Riley's friends. When they became involved in the drama, they often found themselves placed like pawns around the board to reflect glory upon their prince, or to take a fall in some horribly dramatic way that intensified the lovers' sensations of danger but did nothing except get the friends banged up. They found themselves to be second thoughts to Riley when he was so engaged, and worse, expendable pieces, until Riley or the young lady came to their senses and moved on.

It was often best just to ignore the both of them during these times, even though it could, at a dinner or dance, seem cruel to ignore the young woman of the moment. Morris, Jackson, and Wils had all made the mistake of befriending one of Riley's girls. They ended up with a person who inevitably asked them to pry out information about his goings-on, or wished to talk of his ill use of her, or wished to use them to make Riley jealous, until the young woman finally realized there was no future in this for her and dropped them all. This pattern had played itself out enough times that Morris, Jackson, and Wils were quite wary, no matter how titled or beautiful the lady in question was.

And they'd also decided, for the most part, that it was the young woman's fault. There were enough warning signs all around Riley that conveyed news she did not wish to hear. If she was intelligent, she would listen to the voices on the winds telling her to flee. If a woman was with Riley, it was because she was ripe for a chase and a passion, something best shared by only two.

Knowing this, and understanding how the situation would inevitably play out, Wils was kicking himself that he'd given a second thought to Helen Brooks.

But he had.

He wished to hear her out. To move beyond her bigotry and see what fueled her mind, what inflamed the insecurity behind her blue eyes, and what gave her such shocking brashness. Despite her obvious flaws, there seemed elements of brilliance in her, he sensed. Unformed and scattered, but it was there.

Her passion for Riley would burn out—it always did (usually because of something Riley did). And if she didn't dissolve in the conflagration—perhaps there would be a space for a quiet poet.

"Wils! I asked you if you were coming," demanded Morris.

"What?" he asked, pulled from his reverie. He looked across the table at Morris and Jackson, who were still eating lunch. "I was thinking about later today—"

"That bare-knuckle prizefight at the docks. You're coming, right?" asked Morris excitedly. "Jackson is."

Jackson nodded in between bites of an apple. "If there's drink."

"There'll be plenty," said Morris. "Are you going to eat that oyster pie?" Jackson pushed his plate over to Morris without a word. "What about you, Wils? You coming?" Morris eagerly sliced into the pastry.

"I was thinking of something else," said Wils. "What would you think if we were to invite that girl from class to join us?"

Morris' mouth opened. "Riley's new girl? Helen?"

Jackson shook his head. "Have you lost your mind? She'd just sit around asking us about Riley."

"Really, Wils," said Morris. "I learned my lesson after Lucia."

"And I after Antoinette," said Jackson. "I've performed all the public service I care to on behalf of Riley Spencer."

"I'd forgotten about Antoinette," said Wils, wrinkling his nose.

"Screechy voice," said Morris, raising his hand to mime finger-nails against a chalkboard.

Wils shuddered. It all came back now. The ears too. "But I was thinking that Miss Brooks is different. She did get into Copeland's class."

"She's a first-year," said Morris disdainfully.

"But she's capable of senior-level work," countered Wils.

They both looked at him as if he'd lost his mind. Perhaps he had. But Wils didn't relent, and Morris, after a few more minutes of haggling, finally broke the impasse.

"I'll hear her out. If she does good work we can let her in. But"—he put his hands on the table with a thump—"the first time she says the word 'Riley' she is out."

Wils agreed this was a fair deal.

"Now," said Jackson, "are you going to the fight with us?"

Wils shook his head. "No. Dockworkers tend to be a patriotic lot."

"Against patriots, are we?" asked Morris.

"I am for the rule of law. Patriots, and their League, don't seem to care about the law, and I think I'm right to stay away from gatherings where the purpose is to fight. I'm staying away from most Harvard things as well."

"That's not fair," protested Morris. "You saw that President Lowell is returning ten million dollars of a donor's money because the donation requires that a German professor be fired. Harvard's not for sale."

"If Harvard were safe, Max would be alive."

"What if Max committed suicide?" asked Morris gruffly.

"And what if it's murder?" replied Wils coldly. "I had once thought that Harvard played fair, or at least fair enough. Now I don't believe they do if you're German."

"Some would say that Kaiser Bill isn't terribly interested in being fair," retorted Jackson.

Wils looked angrily at him. "If you'd stop thinking about yourself for once, you'd notice that the Kaiser's actions have caused me more than a slight inconvenience as well."

"I want to fight for England," said Jackson.

Wils rolled his eyes. "You're American. What time is it?"

Jackson took out a pocket watch and looked at it. "Twelve fifteen. You didn't really lend your watch to Max, did you?"

"Yes, I did. How was I supposed to know he'd pawn it or give it to Archer or who knows what? I told Riley I'd take him to a doctor's appointment at one."

"Is Riley sick?"

"No. Army physical. His father is making him take it."

"Let me come with you," said Jackson. "I want to fight. I'm sick of school."

Wils waved Jackson off.

"I heard Riley's having a little trouble with a girl in England," injected Morris.

"Who told you that?" asked Wils, surprised.

Morris shrugged. "When you work in the student union you hear things."

"Good God! That's very fast. Edith just telegrammed last week!" said Wils.

"What do the union workers say happened to Max?" asked Jackson.

"They know, my friend," said Morris. "That's why we're not down at Archer's beating him up right now. Everyone knew Max was in debt and that he tried to get money by telling the Germans what was in the shipyards and now the police think Wils is in on it too. Personally," he said, pointing his fork at Wils, "I think naval power is the wrong way to go. To those who think naval supremacy is the future, I say—"

"You knew this?" said Wils, flustered. He felt hot. "How?"

"People talk."

"Why didn't you tell me?" asked Wils, putting his finger in Morris' face. "You knew Max was my friend!"

"I didn't hold back," retorted Morris. "You never asked. But now that it's all official with the police, I'm telling you."

"What else hasn't come up?" demanded Wils.

Morris shrugged. "I've never told you that Copeland has it bad for Mrs. Jack Gardner."

"Everyone knows that," said Wils, with a sour feeling in the pit of his stomach. He shut his notebook.

"And everyone knew about Max gambling," said Morris indignantly. "They think that Archer was doing his duty—"

"*Fahr zur Hölle!*" shouted Wils. "Since when is murder a person's duty?"

"Look, I miss Max just as much as the next fellow, but what he was doing was wrong."

"I think that news about Max is just skulduggery and vicious rumor to hide the fact that Arnold killed a classmate," Wils shot back. "I've got to leave soon. Jackson, let's have it."

"Fine," said Jackson. He opened his paper and began to read.

MY FRIEND
by Jackson Marion Vaughn

Excuse my boots on your table.
No, I don't want water,
But whiskey, yes, well, that's in season.
Don't mind that look in your lover's eyes.
The fear's there for good reason.

There are many pressures I'm under
I wouldn't mind putting asunder
A few that won't make a difference
Like him. So I brought
A friend, here, a pistol-friend
To help me out.

"Stop, stop, stop!" said Morris.

Jackson shot him an angry look. "I'm just getting to the good part, where I shoot Marvin and Jenny realizes she was wrong."

"Why would she realize she was wrong if you murder her lover in front of her?" asked Wils.

"Snap out of it, Jackson!" said Morris furiously. "Jenny McGee is gone and I refuse to pull your clogged, stinking soul out of another polluted river. You're wasting your life."

"Take that back!" snapped Jackson, pounding his fists on the table.

"I will not! I've had it with her and I've had it with you! You would never, ever make it in my faith! My God! Philip Breckenridge's poem about his dead dog was better. I mean, tell me—what were you going to say when Copeland told you he hated this?"

Jackson's face was white with rage. "I'd break his face with my fists." The table rocked as he pushed back from it. "I'm going to war."

"What?" asked Wils, as Jackson opened his satchel and started stuffing papers into it. Jackson said nothing.

"You don't understand. She is the only thing that made my life better and nothing will ever get her back!"

"Why don't you go to her?" Wils offered.

Jackson's face contorted, and Wils thought he'd start to cry. "Because she won't have me, you idiot!" he yelled. "What the hell am I doing in this place?" He started walking to the door.

Wils stood up. "Jackson, we're all under a lot of pressure—"

"Get away, you sonofabitch! I quit!" he yelled. "I'll be in the Yard." He slammed the door as he left the room.

"Morris, go after him. I've got to take Riley to the doctor."

Morris jumped up from the table and ran out the door.

Wils shook his head. These southerners were worse than the French when it came to matters of the heart.

DURING Dr. Parcher's warbling monologue on Euclidean geometry, Helen rewrote her poem for Copeland's class. She eliminated the second verse entirely during Dr. Gibbs' recitation of the history of the 1848 rebellions in Europe, and rewrote it during Dr. Mathilda Pembert's deadly dull description of social hierarchy in Ur of the Chaldees. By the time Helen sat down in Boylston Hall for her advanced editing class, she'd decided her poem was a good as she could make it.

Copeland walked in wearing his usual bowler hat and typical three-piece suit. The last bell rang, he doffed the hat, and called roll.

"Brandl."

"Here."

"Breckenridge." There was no answer.

"Philip Breckenridge," he said again. "Does he have a cough? Is he ill?"

"No sir," said Roland Tibbets. "Left this morning for the war."

"Did he take his dog?" asked Wharton.

Copeland shook his head, made a notation, and completed the roll, ending once again with Zillgitt.

"Miss Brooks, what is your work on today?"

"Excuse me," said a voice. Helen turned to see Wils Brandl with his hand in the air. "You didn't call Jackson Vaughn."

Everyone look at Copeland.

"Vaughn withdrew just before class."

"Did he say why?" asked Morris Rabin.

"I do not discuss personal matters, Mr. Rabin," said the professor. Helen saw Morris' face darken. "Miss Brooks, your topic?"

"A Jewish wedding I saw this summer in Maine."

"Are you certain of your selection? You know we are not that kind on the topic of love poems."

"It's a different type of love poem." He shrugged. Fairly warned, she proceeded.

AYD (THE WITNESS)
by Helen W. Brooks

They wore gray suits and brown ties
To the wedding by the shore.
Their covered heads and laughing eyes
Crackled with wit not given in halves.

I didn't know them,
But I laughed in their mirth.

I didn't see your love
But I felt it in my heart.
I didn't hold the chair
But my hands clapped in time.
I didn't sing
But my heart did. And loudly.

I never touched the water that day
But a bit ran down my face
That such grace had bloomed
In a garden of sand.

Wils glanced up. What had she just read?

Copeland looked around the room, beyond her. "Mr. Rabin, you seem like you wish to chat today. This is a poem about your culture. What do you think of it?"

"How can I feel this good at a wedding when my shoes are too tight and I'm being chased by an aunt who kisses me on my lips?" Dane Iselin laughed out loud and Morris continued. "Jewish weddings have been great for centuries—"

"Makes up for the food—" said George Wharton.

"Enough already!" said Morris with a hostile look.

A murmur began in the class.

"Quiet," said Copeland. "Yes, Mr. Wharton. Do you have something to add about the New English writing about Jewish weddings?"

"I do indeed. Miss Brooks thinks we should all be overcome by a wedding? She doesn't give me a reason to care about them—whatever their religion. This, I'm sorry to say, is the problem with a culture immersed in Thoreau. They think they know it all just because they thought about something once or twice. They think their experience replaces knowledge and science. And they think that nature actually cares when it could care less."

"I do not," she said hotly.

"I found it extraordinary," interrupted a voice from the back. Helen turned to see Wils. "Professor, I'd like to hear it again."

Copeland's bushy brows rose. "Mr. Wharton would say that once is enough."

"I disagree with him. I thought she had some well-turned phrases and I wanted to hear that bit about touching the water."

Copeland's head bobbed a bit as if he were weighing whether to walk to the Boston Common or hire a car. "Miss Brooks, let us hear it again, and then Mr. Brandl, I expect you to explain yourself, and not ask Miss Brooks to the dance." Several men broke out in laughter. But her confidence was bolstered at Wils' compliment and she ignored them, reciting again clearly for all to hear.

"George," said Wils, when she finished, "what I think you missed, and what makes this a nice work, is that she's an outsider looking at something beautiful. It's critical that they're not like she is. I know you're from Philadelphia and you fancy yourself different from those in Boston, but you're not. This young woman is very different from the Jews. She shows how being outside changes you. You see people differently and sometimes," he said, his voice softening, "you like what you see. In fact, George, I think her poem shows just how bad your last love poem actually was. Perhaps her example will help you improve your own work."

Helen looked down, folded her hands, and tried to control her smile.

"Brandl, your prose is purpling," said Copeland, cutting him off. "Miss Brooks, this is a good poem. Gentlemen, take note—it's the best one yet. You need this woman in your study group." Then Helen flushed, feeling the giddiness that typically accompanied flattery.

"Next! Iselin. Present your work."

And then the world moved on past her. She sat a bit stunned as the next man read, her adrenaline receding. No longer the center of attention, no longer being called on, Helen felt relieved that the presentation was over, excited by the fact that her work was found to have merit—and by Wils Brandl, a person many, including her brother, considered a real poet. She also felt the odd desire to have the attention of those around her focused on her work again. Perhaps she should go into teaching, she thought, as she listened to Dane read.

At the end of the hour, Copeland reminded the class of next Monday's public reading, required their attendance, and left.

As Helen gathered her books, she looked up to see Wils Brandl standing once again beside her desk. A smile rose to her lips. "You liked it?" she asked. "You weren't just being kind?" His eyes were bright and friendly.

"There was no kindness involved," said Wils, as he helped her with her books. "I tried to tell you yesterday that I thought you had me wrong about our first meeting. Blunt words for a person's work do not mean blunt words for a person. My cousin said that you were, well, not my equal at present, but quite intelligent."

Her eyebrows arched. "Not your equal?"

He took a quick breath. "I've been harassed by professors for three years now. After you've faced the scorn I have, then I'll talk to you about being my equal."

She gave a laugh completely uncalled for in the situation and perhaps terribly improper under the circumstances. "Such bravado," she said, trying to stifle her smile as Morris Rabin appeared, the pungent scent of lye still on him. "I admire it."

"You do?" said Wils with a smile. "I have more."

"Did you ask her?" Morris said.

"About what?" asked Wils, wishing Morris would leave immediately.

Morris frowned at him. "Jackson left our study group and we've come to ask you to join us. We can meet in the Harvard Union at lunch to review assignments."

"Study with you two?"

"Yes," said Wils, a bit too quickly for his taste.

She hesitated. "I'm afraid our views may be too divergent—"

Morris interrupted. "Nonsense, Helen. Wils and I never agree on anything. If we were only friends with those with whom we agreed, we'd have no friends. We'll see you Monday, then." And with that he nodded and left the room for work. The two were now alone.

"That Morris," said Wils. He turned and looked at Helen. "Tomorrow?" he asked, holding the door for her.

"Mr. Brandl?"

"Yes?"

"You know I'm to go to a festival in Concord this weekend with your cousin Riley Spencer."

His face fell, and his smile disappeared. "Yes, I know," he said after a pause. "I'm to drive."

"Really?"

"Is there something you need to know about Riley?" he asked in a bored voice.

"Wils, I don't know how to put this. But do you know if there is another woman? Is he indeed engaged?"

He bit his lip and turned to examine the door casing. "I'm sorry, Miss Brooks, I try not to get entangled in my cousin's affairs."

She felt her own blush. "I didn't mean to impose. I just thought you would know if it's true."

He looked back at her, angry with himself. He should have listened to Morris and Jackson. It had begun—the questioning, the prying, the "but doesn't he love me?" protestations.

"Would you like me to tell Riley you asked of him?"

"No thank you," she said, aware that all was now wrong. The easiness of before was gone and they were again strangers. "I will be my own messenger."

They walked a few steps in silence down the hall to the point where they would part, she returning to Radcliffe, he to Beck Hall.

"Miss Brooks, Morris and I would be honored if you'd come to our group. You're a woman of talent who can hold her own and is not afraid to speak her mind. But Riley isn't part of that group."

She nodded. "I'll meet you and Mr. Rabin at the Harvard Union on Monday."

He gave her a half smile. "You know, this is a good thing, or at least it can be." He walked down the hall toward Beck and out, the glass doors swinging behind him. She watched him as he made his way down the crowded path.

[CHAPTER NINE]

HOTEL SOMERSET

BOSTON, MASSACHUSETTS

R iley Spencer felt tired as he walked with Jackson Vaughn to Hotel Somerset on Commonwealth Avenue. After the day at the doctor he wished to go into Boston for a quiet bit of anonymous drinking, and it was only blind luck to find that Jackson wanted to come too. As Jackson was filthy rich, he could pick up the tab. Riley would indulge in a large steak dinner to soak up the vast quantities of scotch he was about to consume.

Edith's telegrams hounded him from overseas, and he was not at all happy about it. He had been given the terrible news from his doctor at the day's physical that the things he'd done with Edith could, under some narrow circumstances, give rise to children. The thought displeased him greatly. Edith was seldom dissuaded by things like probability, logic, common sense, or plain facts. Should there actually be a child, he'd put money on it belonging to another man in London.

But that was not the only source of melancholia for him. He could not stop thinking of his Saturday night with that lovely Miss Helen Brooks. Completely unlike Edith or the other women he'd— well, courted was perhaps too rigid a concept. Miss Brooks was wifely material. There was something different about her—but what, he'd no idea.

He stifled a smile. Her brother, Peter, absolutely despised him, which made thinking of her all the more pleasurable. In one fell swoop he'd have a beautiful girl to squire to dances and her brother would be furious.

And, who knew? he thought, as Jackson, walking beside him, droned on about his miserable day. Perhaps Helen and he would make a life together in London.

He was so tired of women like Edith. They made such empty-headed demands on his time. Really, would Helen Brooks ever ask a man to compliment her shoes or earbobs? Did any man really care about those things? Except to purchase a chance at a night's toss, of course.

If only Edith would go away, life could be perfect. He was resourceful and good, capable of much, he felt. But he needed direction, Wils had said. Helen could most certainly help him there.

They entered the ornate hotel lobby. Electric lights from crystal chandeliers lit baroque paintings on the walls and made the gold leaf shimmer on the high ceilings. Riley saw Jackson's reflection in the great gilt mirror on the far wall. His friend looked terrible, even for him. Clothes hung off his skeletal frame and his skin was pale. Alcohol on his breath would be a positive improvement to the way it smelled right now.

Riley requested a table despite the look of utter incredulity from the host that Jackson wished to be seated. The host seemed to regard Jackson as some type of foreign object to be disgorged from his dining establishment as quickly as possible. He was placated only after Jackson's shipping business had been mentioned and after Jackson agreed to wear one of the restaurant's jackets. The two young men were finally seated, near the kitchen.

"Jackson, you need to eat," said Riley. But Jackson glumly shook his head.

"No amount of food will bring her back. I want to go to the war," he said, his voice cracking.

"War? That will kill you."

The waiter came and Riley ordered a basket of hot popovers, filet mignons with Stilton cheese, boiled potatoes in a burgundy reduction, and, to start, shots of single-malt scotch.

"Will you join the Red Cross?" he asked Jackson, dismissing the waiter with a turn of his head.

"I'm a field-ready marksman."

"But you're not British," blurted Riley. "Or French, for that matter. Why not fly an airplane? It would be brilliant to see what the clouds look like from on high. And I hear they're not picky about the nationality of the volunteer corps."

Riley saw a flicker in his eyes—the first sign of hope he'd seen in his friend since that ghastly breakup with Jenny. Jackson reached for the bread. "Would they let me?"

"Of course," Riley said, pushing the butter toward him.

"Could your father get me in? He's in Parliament, right?"

"I'll cable him tomorrow."

Riley broke open a popover. He took a deep breath as the steam rose from it. How good to be out of Cambridge, he thought, buttering it and eating it slowly. He stretched his legs under the table. Sitting here with Jackson was so much better than being at the doctor's office today getting his army physical. And the talk of war made Jackson seem almost happy. Perhaps it was what he needed to get over Jenny.

"Can I go when you go?" asked Jackson after a few minutes.

"What? I'm not going for a while. I hope the fighting's over by then."

"That's hardly patriotic!"

"You don't know the British like I do. And besides, my father said I was to get Wils through this rough patch first, what with Max and all dying and everyone looking at him as if he were a spy, and now I've also got a horrible woman problem. If I left now to join Lord Kitchener's army, Lord Kinnaird would have me hung." The scotch burned a little less this time.

"Who?"

"Edith Kinnaird's father."

"The girl with the teeth? From Scotland?" asked Jackson.

Riley made a face and nodded. "She says I'm the father of her child."

"Are you?"

"What a question. I am not!" Riley leaned closer. "But can you believe that the Western world has not determined how to accurately tell if a woman is having a baby until it can be seen?"

"So she's lying? Damned woman."

Riley threw up his hands in exasperation. "I'm not an expert on how these things work. The doctor said what we did could, under some very long chances, create a child."

"What type of chances?" asked Jackson in a low voice. "These things are quite a mystery to me."

"To everyone. Apparently you can only conceive a child when the moon is full and mimsy are the borogroves or some such nonsense."

"A baby would change things."

"It's not mine. And besides, I've met a new girl—Helen Brooks."

"No," said Jackson emphatically. "She is bad news for you. Or, at least her brother is. You shouldn't get involved with her."

"That makes it all the more fun," said Riley with a broad grin. "She and I danced all the dances on Saturday night. It was amazing," he said, pushing back from the table. The liquor was starting to work, relaxing his shoulders. He felt like an Irishman after supper—ready to talk about a fair lass from across the heather. Ready to hold forth. Ready to issue statements. Hell, a few drinks more and he'd be ready to send a statement to the Spee Club's social secretary. Helen had blue eyes, dark hair, white shoulders, and, thank God, her teeth were straight.

"I'm in love with her."

"How do you know that?"

"I've no idea. I just know."

"Peter is protective. He won't be happy," Jackson said with a severe look on his face.

"Don't be a scold," Riley said. "Helen's invited me to a local festival on Saturday. I think she's made her decision."

"But what about Edith?" asked Jackson, just as two elegant waiters arrived with silver-domed platters.

"There is nothing to say about Edith. A man should know if he's engaged, and I'm not. What about you? When are you resuming class?"

"There's nothing to say about that either. I've paid for my dorm room and can stay there until I take the post your father secures for me. But no more classes for me. I'm done."

"Well, then, let's forget our troubles and eat," said Riley as the white-gloved waiter whisked away the domes to reveal two large filet mignons. The juices collected around the edges of the potatoes and steamed carrots. Riley inhaled deeply.

"Come, Jackson. The British don't let scarecrows fly their planes. You need to put some meat on your bones."

[CHAPTER TEN]

THE HARVEST FESTIVAL

CONCORD, MASSACHUSETTS

Since 1714 the centerpiece event of the Middlesex County Harvest Festival had been the reenactment of the marriage of the Pilgrims John Alden and Priscilla Mullins. The townspeople dressed in costume and met around an arbor covered in wild roses to celebrate the happy time. An artist "of the first-class" was hired each year to paint the scene, and the painting was donated to the young woman who played Priscilla.

The roles rotated between townships, except for the coveted role of Priscilla. The festival's charter required that the committee "scour the county" for "a maid of seventeen yrs who was the fayrest in mynde and heart and soul and face, whose price would be set beyonde rubies." It was a requirement that every young maid in each Middlesex township knew by heart, no matter how rich or poor, infirm or hale, bluestocking or unlearned.

All the young girls had at one point dreamt of holding hands under the golden September sun with John Alden—including Helen. This was to be her year. She had been told as much in January. But that was before her mother's fall from grace.

When the actual day of the Harvest Festival arrived, Helen had more than a suspicion she was to be snubbed, and how badly, Ann explained that morning, was no longer in doubt. Her community work, writing honors, and careful conduct had been all wiped away, Ann said, when Mrs. Brooks decided to start mailing *Family Limitation* (illustrated). Caroline was to be named the Priscilla that year. Helen would stand in as a Wampanoag native.

"What? Not even a Pilgrim?" protested Helen.

"I'm as bewildered as you," said Ann, red-faced in sympathy at her friend's humiliation.

"But what community service has Caroline done to be a Priscilla?"

"She's marrying Frank Adams, an extraordinary community service for both families."

Helen winced. "But—but—why shouldn't you preside? Why are they not honoring you?"

Ann swallowed hard. "They asked me to be John Alden's sister."

Helen burst into tears.

"I told them it should be you," said Ann softly as she reached for her best friend to embrace her. "I'm so sorry, Helen. If it were me I'd have made you Priscilla."

"And if I were them I would have picked me too," said Helen in a muffled voice on Ann's shoulder. Ann's blouse smelled like fresh lilies.

At length Helen rose and wiped her eyes on the back of her gloves as the clock chimed from the mantel.

"Helen, I've got to leave and meet Mother. Are you coming out with Riley?"

"Yes, my possibly engaged escort."

"You're not going to ask him about it, are you?"

"No. You've convinced me not to. So instead, we will race cars to further embarrass ourselves."

"You'll win that race," said Ann, smoothing her friend's hair. "Caroline has no idea what she's up against. You'll be proud at the end of the day, I promise. Now, I have to leave. Will you be all right?"

Helen sniffed as Ann picked up her purse, walked out, and closed the door. There was no more time for tears. Riley would be here in a moment and she didn't want to greet him with a swollen nose and red-rimmed eyes.

As she finished dressing, she admonished herself with words of

Thoreau: "However mean your life is, meet it and live it; do not shun it and call it hard names." She tucked her light wool butternut sweater neatly into her slender skirt and captured a loose tendril to go back under her tawny straw hat. Satisfied, she picked up the bag of red, white, and blue ribbons her mother had asked her to bring to the festival and went downstairs to the foyer.

"Miss Brooks! A letter!" called Miss Sullivan from her corner. Helen cringed as the woman's voice rang out through the room. Everyone looked up at her as she went to retrieve the note.

"From Mr. Archer. The other girls have already picked theirs up." Helen opened the envelope and found a typed page.

> Dear Miss Brooks,
>
> I am forming the Harvard and Radcliffe Chapters of the Patriots' League. The League was started by my father, City Councilman Charles Archer, when I was unfairly jailed (and quickly released) for bringing to light the activities of a German spy. My father is running for the U.S. Congress and knows how to stop the flow of damaging information across the Atlantic, to prevent vice in our city, and to help our country!
>
> The first rally in Harvard Yard was a success, and we have plans for five more. But we need your help.
>
> I understand your mother and my father are currently at odds. I believe they might be persuaded to work out their differences should you help protect the City of Boston from the German spy you so recently defended in Harvard's halls. News of this has scandalized many good folk, and I know that you must have been misled to have done such in the first place. I am offering you a chance to demonstrate your patriotism.
>
> As you know, dark forces are at work. We have reason to believe that some of the very people who enjoy the

freedoms of our country are using those freedoms to wound the children of France, Belgium, Russia, and Britain. These people live among us, even here at Harvard. The newspapers stated this week that the foreign worker population of Boston stands at nearly twice the population of native-born men. We are outnumbered, and where we do know of perfidy we must act.

We ask you as a patriot and as a fellow sufferer in the war against the Kaiser to join us in our cause.

> Sincerely,
> Arnold Archer

A chill ran through her as she read the note. How self-serving. She balled up the paper, threw it in the trash, and walked outside to greet the day.

ANOTHER LETTER had arrived that morning across Harvard Yard, but it was written in German.

Riley had noticed a general upswing in Wils' mood that week, and took advantage of it to persuade Wils to drive him to the Harvard Festival. He needed to concentrate on Helen exclusively and not on driving, and he'd run out of money for the month so he couldn't hire a taxi.

As they were leaving the wood-paneled foyer of Beck Hall, Mr. Burton gave a slight cough.

"Need something, Burton?" asked Riley.

The plump headmaster looked up over a thick book. "Are you gone for the day?"

"That's my business," said Riley.

"Wils, does your mother know you're out for the entire day?"

"I'll return her telegrams on Monday."

"I'll notify her."

"You will not!"

"I will indeed," said Burton gruffly. "You're not the only one she's cabling. She told me that if the steamship traffic opens and you're not on the boat she would hold me responsible."

"Sorry for the inconvenience, Burton. She's worried."

"No problem," he said with a phlegmatic cough. "We all have mothers. But yours is formidable. Where there's her will, there's her way."

"Then you know what we face," called Riley as he opened the door to leave.

"Oh, and Wils—" Burton flipped through a sheaf of papers. "A letter came this morning by courier. It had German writing on it. Do you wish me to hold it?"

Burton reached for a thin envelope from a pile of mail and held it out to Wils.

Wils backed up to the desk and looked at it. The seal was old-fashioned—the von Steiger family's crest. He frowned and mumbled quick thanks, stuffing it in his jacket pocket. This was the last thing he wished to deal with today—some official notice of duties from the von Steiger family.

"What's that?" asked Riley.

"Nothing," said Wils, hoping to ignore it. Today he'd spend in the company of Helen Brooks. Not with the dead.

RILEY, his navy jacket limp, tie bright blue, and his khaki pants borrowed, held open the door of Wils' touring car for Helen as Miss Sullivan stood on the porch of Longworth Hall and gave a snort. Riley swallowed a self-satisfied grin as Helen tucked her long skirts inside. He stepped in, closed the door behind them, and let Wils drive them out Garden Street.

"Fine day for a festival," offered Riley, noting the bag of ribbons between him and Helen on the seat.

Helen frowned and looked out the window. Wils gave a quick look back at her from where he sat in the front seat.

"Helen, is something wrong?"

She pursed her lips and waited a moment. "Yes. Yes, it is. I received some bad news right before I came."

"What is it?" asked Riley.

"It will sound silly."

"Nonsense," both men said in unison.

"It really is," she said. "I was passed over for an honor at today's fair."

"An outrage!" said Riley.

Helen looked at him, bewildered. "How can you think it an outrage if you don't know why it happened? Obviously some people think it's quite justified."

"But, Helen, if you thought you deserved it then you probably did. That's all I meant."

"What are the facts?" asked Wils.

Helen leaned forward to speak over the engine's noise. "Priscilla Mullins was a famous Mayflower maiden whom both Myles Standish and John Alden wished to marry. John Alden won her, and at each year's festival there's a painting made of the marriage where we all dress in costume. I was to play Priscilla, but the part was given to a woman in town named Caroline Peabody. I've been demoted to playing one of the minor characters."

"Which one?" asked Riley, moving closer. Helen had fire and he liked that, even when it was directed at him. Edith was so very bland.

"A Wampanoag native."

"A native?" Wils laughed.

"That's a fine role," protested Riley. "Those natives were important to the survival of the Pilgrims. They are the heroes, in my book."

"You think so?" asked Helen.

"Oh yes," said Riley, putting his arm against the back of the seat. Suddenly the car swerved and Riley was thrown back to his side.

"Sorry," said Wils. "An errant squirrel."

Riley shot a deprecatory scowl at Wils.

"What's the problem with your mother, Helen?" asked Wils.

"She's ruined my life."

"With the pamphlets she's mailing out?" asked Wils.

"You know about them?"

"I've been trying to get on her mailing list," said Wils. "I hear they're illustrated."

She burst into a laugh. "This is serious!"

"I apologize for my cousin," injected Riley seriously.

"If it helps, Helen," continued Wils, "I know what it's like to have an embarrassing relative. The Kaiser invades Belgium and all my plans of a quiet life evaporate."

"But it's not like that at all, Wils."

"You just said your mother ruined your life."

"My life is not ruined like yours. Boston's mad at our family. Not all of Europe."

She saw Wils bristle. "Helen, my point is that they're still family. They're wrong but they're still ours. And you shouldn't go around saying that your mother ruined your life. It's not becoming."

"Helen doesn't need a lecture from a total stranger," said Riley.

"Wils is not a total stranger," she said.

"Since when? You hardly know this man."

"We're in class together."

"Helen," said Wils, "what will you do about this slight?"

"I have no idea."

"I'll tell you what you're going to do," interrupted Riley. "You're going to win the race with me, a future war hero. Then they'll know who's the better—"

"You could run Caroline Peabody off the road in the race," offered Wils.

Is that justice? she wondered, sitting back and looking out the window again. The smell of the city began to recede and the cool air of the country sharpened. The avenues were once again lined with tall trees and stone fences, hemming in the rolling hills and farmland— away from factories and science and into a world where the weather still mattered.

WHEN THEY ALIGHTED from the car, the Harvest Festival was in full swing. The sky was a bright blue with white billowing clouds lazily drifting in the crisp September air. Packs of young boys in white shirts, black breeches, and tricornered hats ran laughing through the tents, their toy guns popping at each other. A clique of young girls congregated at the corner of the tent, talking animatedly to each other, occasionally looking around to see what, if any, boys might be looking their way. The smallest children stood by a fruit press, wincing as they drank cranberry juice on dares.

Tables were laden with food for sale. Irishmen called out, hawking bowls of clam chowder, blueberry pies, and apple tarts. Steam rose from plates of corn on the cob, half a dozen ears for two cents. An Italian man stood behind a table with a fresh bowl of whipped cream chilled on ice beside bowls of raspberries and blueberries, one scoop for a penny. The Trinitarian Congregationalists sold bread puddings, lemon cakes, and maple syrup from their tables, while the Unitarian Universalists, who churched across the town common, sold pickled herrings, bottled oyster sauce, and poached salmon on plates with slices of lemon and dill. Jars of lavender honey and tins of apple butter were spread out on tables decorated with gourds, squash, and dried Indian corn, tied together at their tops with twine.

The people in the costumes changed, but the festival would not. Helen's father had said that it served the memory for Middlesex County, recalling the gratitude of another year of survival: against disease and cold in the early days; the brutality of the Indian Wars; and the valiant shots of rebellion fired by humble farmers. He also thought it served as an excellent berth from which his generation could make a pompous ass of itself.

FOUR BRIGHT RED Bugatti race cars sat at the entrance to the festival, bathed in the early-autumn sunlight. Each car looked like a glossy red bullet placed on its side. Shiny silver pipes protruded from the engine. The two black leather seats at the far end were framed by large wheels that looked as if they could have been stolen from any passing bicycle. Beside the race cars stood Colonel Darlington's Rolls-Royce Silver Ghost and a sign that read:

THE PETITION DRIVE

Raising Money for Lady Liberty!

RULES:

Women drivers only.
One man may ride along, but he mustn't touch the wheel.
Two laps around; first to finish wins.

GRAND PRIZE:
The use of the Darlington Rolls-Royce for one week.

BET ON YOUR FAVORITE!

WE CAN'T FUND THE VOTE IF YOU STAND THERE
WITH YOUR HANDS IN YOUR POCKETS!

This event was approved by Reverend Ames.

"Helen, you didn't tell me there was a prize," said Riley. "I have an excellent plan for the use of the Rolls-Royce once you and I do win."

"Miss Brooks! The ribbons!" came a commanding voice from the inside of the tent.

The smile on Helen's lips evaporated. "Bertha Darlington!" She whispered to Riley and Wils. "If I'm not back in five minutes, please come and get me."

Riley shielded his eyes from the brightness of the September sun. "Command me as you wish."

"Miss Brooks!" insisted Mrs. Darlington.

"We'll meet back by the cars," offered Riley as Helen turned to face Mrs. Darlington at the Petition Drive booth.

"Were those young men bothering you, Helen?" she asked, taking the ribbons Helen had brought from Cambridge.

"Not at all. Have you seen my mother?"

"She left. There was an emergency with some factory woman in Boston."

"She isn't here to watch me race?" Helen exclaimed hotly. "She signed me up for this!"

"Bertha Darlington!" Mrs. Belinda Peabody, Caroline's mother, was suddenly with them. Her face was pale, her thin lips pursed, and her eyebrows cocked for battle.

"Is there a problem?" Bertha asked.

"A reporter," declared Mrs. Peabody. Her hatband, which vaguely resembled a ferret, quivered on her head, radiating waves of anger. Mrs. Peabody turned to Helen. "Did your mother invite him?"

"Of course not," Helen returned, not knowing if it were true. She noticed that Mrs. Peabody's hat was indeed a former ferret. It had the unfortunate effect of making her look somewhat ferret-like herself.

"If your cousin Phillips Brooks were still alive, he might be able to counsel her on the appropriate use of reporters."

"Perhaps Charles Archer did," offered Mrs. Darlington. "He's here today with his son to speak about their new Patriots' League."

"Councilman Archer is here? That is all, Miss Brooks," said Mrs. Peabody with a terse smile. She turned her back to Helen and began to discuss the matter with Mrs. Darlington.

Helen fumed as she spun on her heel. Mrs. Peabody had no sense of grace in victory, no nobility. That's what happened when you weren't the main branch of the family.

Helen searched the crowd for Riley and Wils. She didn't even want to be in the Peabodys' silly town anymore, she fumed. They could have Lexington and Concord, Frank, Caroline, and all of the other members of their bullying, arrogant gang.

She was going to win this race and then she'd act perplexed as to why Caroline hadn't been able to do better on the track.

Helen walked to the edge of the tent and looked across the field to where the cars were being moved. A gust of wind sprang up and blew hard against her hat, lifting it and flinging it into the green expanse. As she chased it, a group of children dressed in colonial garb rushed in front of her, following a wooden hoop. Another burst of wind carried the hat past a group of young troubadours. One stepped back on the hat with the heel of an old-fashioned shoe and slipped, crushing it.

A large young man suddenly dashed over and helped the young lad up. He picked up her flattened hat and returned it to her.

"Thank you," she said, as her long hair flew around her face. He was tall and clean-shaven, with a square jaw and closely cropped brown hair. His gray suit made him look like a newly minted lawyer.

"I only wish I could have been quicker." When she put it on her head, the crown fell out and they both laughed.

"I'll be fine," she said, trying to be heard above the noise of the children. She extended her hand. "Mr.—"

"Arnold Archer, at your service."

[CHAPTER ELEVEN]

ARNOLD ARCHER

CONCORD, MASSACHUSETTS

Helen's eyes widened at the name.

"And you're Miss Helen Brooks, right? Peter's sister?"

"How do you know me?"

"Everyone has heard about you defending Wils to the police the other day," Arnold said. "And you were in the newspaper, standing behind your mother when she was arrested. That was you, right? I mean, I read the papers, just like you, I assume."

"We both read the papers. One does when their mother is arrested, at the urging of your father, I believe." He did not move back to let her pass.

An announcement came from across the field: "All racers to the field."

"I have a favor to ask of you, Miss Brooks."

"A favor? What? You wish me to help you?"

"I wish you to help your country."

"Mr. Archer, I will not join your Patriots' League. I've heard you've been making speeches in the Yard and that they have a nasty habit of turning into brawls."

"Hear me out. My father and I have put two and two together— your mother's problems with my proposed solutions to our German spy problem. My father's received word that the Kaiser is doing every-thing he can to ask Germans in this country to get that information to

Germany—to spy on the country that has given them safe harbor and home. He also will take advantage of his subjects' weaknesses—like he did with Max von Steiger. And no, I didn't have anything to do with that poor young man's death, despite what you may have read in the papers. I was as horrified as you.

"But," Archer continued, edging closer, "we live in an open society—any German national can wire Berlin right this very minute. And we have evidence that many are."

"You can stop your lecture," she said, puzzled as to what he thought she knew.

"Helen, German informants may destroy us all."

"Are you speaking of Wils Brandl?" she asked.

"Yes. We need you to let us know what he's up to."

"I'll not be involved in something as awful as spying on a poor poet."

"He's not just anyone. He's the only son of Bavaria's favorite poet and a Prussian countess."

A national poet? Wils hadn't told her.

"If you intend to defend your friend Wils, as you did to the police," Archer said in a stern voice, "and ignore the needs of the innocents here, perhaps there are other common interests."

"I hate the Kaiser's warmongering and will protest to any man who says differently. But that doesn't mean I share interests with people like you."

His face hardened. "Quite right. We don't share all interests. My mother doesn't send obscene materials through the mail. She's ruining your life."

"And your witch hunt is ruining yours," said Helen hotly. She tried to step around him, but he cut her off.

"My father can make your mother's trouble go away. That's why I thought you might help him out with Wils."

"Her lawyers will save her."

His face darkened. "Have it your way. But don't be surprised if suspicious minds take matters into their own hands. Many have lost relatives to the Kaiser's army already and are angry." He towered over her. "If you simply say Wils has been in contact with the Kaiser or the German army, he'll be held safely in detention—"

"In jail?" she spluttered. She threw her hat down on the ground in disgust. "I can't help you. In fact, I'll tell my father."

His lips curled in a sneer. "You'll say what exactly? That you refuse to help America against a danger on our doorstep? If you love this German—this snake—you can save him."

"I'll not send an innocent man to jail," she stormed. She stepped around him and walked straight across the field to the cars. Halfway there she turned to look back, but Archer had already disappeared.

Love Wils Brandl?

She had no time for this nonsense. She picked up her pace, tying her hair back in a tight bun as she marched toward the cars, bewildered that Archer thought she loved a German.

[CHAPTER TWELVE]

THE RACE

CONCORD, MASSACHUSETTS

There were times when the Brooks family was at its best. This was not one of them, thought Mr. Jonathan Brooks glumly as he sat atop his perch in one of two announcer chairs. His wife had been arrested and now awaited trial; his son was talking of running off to fight for the British; his daughter had been jilted by Frank Adams; and now there she sat, in a car beside a young man of unknown origin.

He took out his pocket watch and checked the time. Colonel Harris, in his white fisherman's sweater and a straw boater, sat beside him, practically oozing good cheer, waving the checkered flag to the rhythm of the wind.

Brooks lifted his megaphone. "Fifteen minutes! The race will commence in fifteen minutes!" But his voice had little life in it.

His brow furrowed as he regarded Caroline Peabody and Frank Adams smiling beside their car for the society reporter's camera. Frank Adams wasn't the best catch, but he was preferable to what could well be an aspiring Jack the Ripper signed up to drive with Helen. He didn't know this man, but he looked like a salesman.

"They could move a little faster," Harris clucked.

Car number two's volunteer, Mr. Brooks explained, was Robert Brown of Boston, driving with one Jane Billings, a friend of the Brown family. Jane was the pretty blond daughter of a railroad fortune, in Boston to study music at a local conservatory. Her father was

Frederick Billings of the Northern Pacific Railroad Company—a Vermonter who'd made his fortune in California and for which a town in Montana had been named. Brooks sniffed as he looked at Helen and her escort in their car talking to a mechanic, who was pointing to different levers. Peter and Ann sat in their car talking intently to each other.

"At least your family will ship off on time," said Harris. "You know, Brooks, I hope those tires are on tight. I saw a race last year where one just popped off in the middle of the track. Bounced into another driver and nearly took his head off. And then the brakes on the first car failed—"

"That could be Helen you're talking about!"

The colonel shifted in his chair. "Oh, not at all. Now everyone knows to tighten tires."

"Her mother shouldn't have allowed her out there. It's wrong to put these women in such peril."

"Why aren't you in the car with her?" asked Harris.

"Merriam forced me to announce the race."

"A woman's fondest desire is to see a man work. That's why I'm a bachelor."

"Spot on," said Brooks and then looked down glumly at his shoes. And now Merriam wasn't even there, having been called to an emergency in Boston. Some Labor Day weekend festivity had gone awry.

He hated this race. He hated festivity. He hated Boston society. And today he even hated his shoes. They were so awful. New and shiny. He'd misplaced his old black leather ones, and these had been his only option. They pinched his bunions and flopped like a pair of sandals on his ankles. His damnable hat felt too tight at the temples, and Harris knew he'd not fit in any race car currently on the market.

"Brooks, you're in a deuce of a bad mood."

"Helen's going to get hurt."

"I'll fix her," said Harris.

"Repairing my daughter once that unknown young man sitting beside her gets her thrown out of the car shouldn't be something a man my age should have to worry about. He looks like he has eyes for Helen."

Dr. Harris frowned. "I thought you said you didn't know the boy."

"Just look at him."

"He looks nice enough."

"That's my point: a little too nice. He's up to no good."

"Right," said Dr. Harris. He lowered his voice. "If anything happens, we'll put arsenic in that young man's drink."

"Painful?"

"Exceedingly," said Harris.

"A tracheotomy with a penknife," offered Brooks. "What about that?"

Harris shook his head. "Too noticeable. Stick with arsenic. I'll diagnose it as a liver ailment."

Brooks thought for a moment. "Right, then."

"Right," said Harris, waving his flag again, trying to get the attention of the drivers.

Amidst the ostentation of the trees, Brooks sat back with his megaphone and straightened his wool vest. His chest felt a little less tight, and the breeze felt cool and comforting.

He liked this Harris fellow. He might even invite him to join his book club.

❧

"WHERE'S WILS?" Helen asked Riley, as she looked quickly around the field. "He's—"

"Wils?" said Riley, shaking his head. "Forget Wils. You've got to learn to drive. This is a serious business now."

"Wils needs to know that Archer is trying to have him deported for espionage."

"Oh, that," said Riley nonchalantly. "He knows. Don't worry about Wils. His mother takes good care of him. You needn't."

"But—"

"Is that Caroline?" he asked, pointing to a young blond woman who was smiling for a reporter as she put on her driving goggles.

"Yes."

"Let's win this race, Helen." A broad grin swept over his face.

[CHAPTER THIRTEEN]

THE LETTER

CONCORD, MASSACHUSETTS

The wooden stands were new and sturdy, slowly filling with towns-folk and children, eager to see what these women would do with the race cars. The wide arena in which they sat afforded warm sun and plenty of open sky. The rolling hills in the background created a natural amphitheater for the day's race, one that, should Wils have been there just with Helen, he would have enjoyed enormously.

He shook his head. If Helen had had any sense she would have asked her brother to race with her.

He hated to feel this way. His cousin Riley was a rake if there ever was one. But Wils had promised his aunt he'd look after him. And honor demanded that he push Helen from the furthest reaches of his mind. But just as soon as he thrust the thoughts of her into some dark corner and fled to the narrow path of the righteous, he'd catch a sent of lilac in a tree or think of a phrase she might like and then—

Madness lay that way. Had Goethe taught him nothing about the pain of mortal love? Why would he want that? He tried to think of Faust's mistress, struggling as she died to put aside the promises of flesh and to reach for the divine. That he might find such strength. He put his hand to his chest, his heart physically aching.

There he felt the letter marked "von Steiger." He'd forgotten about it from earlier that morning. Duty beckoned.

Wils opened the parchment and was jolted when he saw Max's

wobbly cursive. Dear God, he thought. It's from Max.

> Wils,
>
> Please don't despise me for my actions. I've no courage
> or strength to continue on, and I've no way out. My
> debts stand too high to pay. My parents cut me off
> several months ago because of them.
>
> I had an agreement with a German agent to pass along
> information about the navy's shipyard, for which he
> canceled some of my debts. I botched that job, as I
> botch everything I touch.
>
> I was told they'd recommend me for a treason trial.
> I've no idea of how that law stands in America, but it
> didn't seem good. I only counted ships in the
> shipyard—anyone could do that, it would seem.
> Perhaps I counted the wrong ones.
>
> I'm paying with my life. No one can make more of an
> admission of failure than that. But I've thought long
> and hard about it. After Felicity left, much of my life's
> joy went with her. This is the only honorable exit for
> me. Please forgive me for turning to dust my fortune
> and my friendships.
>
> I'm sorry to burden you with this letter. I felt I owed
> you an explanation. And that, at least, was a debt I
> could pay. My family will have enough pain. My hope is
> that in Germany they'll think I've perished at war,
> except for my mother, for whom I ask you to pray.
> They won't understand around Boston and they'll get
> it all wrong. They always were such gossips.
>
> The Church says we're immortal. If that is the case,
> then pray my soul finds peace. If it's not, my troubles
> are through.

Fare thee well, friend. You were always kind to me
both here and at home. I beg you for your kindness in
death's final duties.

Max

Wils put his head down in his hands. *Gott im Himmel.* Max was a
suicide.

He looked up, into the colors beyond the amphitheater, the sky
and the hills. He'd had such a peaceful life here. It had none of the trap-
pings of Berlin or Vienna, and none of their burdens. But Max's suicide, Jackson's attempt, Riley's demands, their women, their deaths—
all came into his world with their chaos and their noise.

He looked up and saw from across the stands Arnold Archer on
the field, his arms crossed before his chest, watching him intently. He
pocketed the letter and hoped the race would be over quickly. He needed
to return to Cambridge and speak with his lawyer.

[CHAPTER FOURTEEN]

THE KISS

CONCORD, MASSACHUSETTS

"Trust me," said Riley loudly, over the noise of the idling engine. "You'll not have to say anything to her after you win. And to make her jealous, I'll kiss you when we win."

Helen nearly choked. "You will not."

"Yes, I will, and you'll like it. Now try turning the wheel."

"You won't," she mumbled. Her cheeks turned slightly pink as she wondered about whether or not she'd like his kiss. She shook off the thought and put both hands on the wheel. It felt as if she were lifting an entire trunk of clothes. She needed to concentrate, but it was difficult. The engine noise had been so loud she'd not been able to make much of the directions offered by the mechanic about a new brake system.

But by the time she decided she'd not want a kiss under any circumstance, she heard Caroline's voice erupt in anger over the cars' loud engines. To Helen's surprise, Caroline exited her car and gave Frank a cold glance.

She couldn't hear a thing being said, but suddenly Mrs. Darlington appeared. Helen thought she looked like what Martin Luther must have pictured when he wrote "a bulwark never failing."

She turned back and swallowed a smile as Caroline got back in her car. All the engines were rumbling when Dr. Harris gave the signal.

"On your marks! Get set!"

Reverend Ames fired the signal gun.

"Go!" boomed Brooks. The race was on.

Ann's and Jane's cars purred off smoothly down the uneven dirt road. Dust blew in a small cloud behind each of them. Helen released her brakes, her car gave a little sputter, and then it stalled, jerking both her and Riley back and forth. The crowd laughed as the mechanics ran out to help start the car again.

"The car, Helen. Don't worry about them, Helen," said Riley.

Caroline's car hadn't moved either, and Frank looked miserable.

"Give it a lot of fuel this time," offered Riley. She tried it. The car lurched a few feet and over to one side and died again—in the path of lane number one, and the mechanic, who'd not left, cranked the engine again.

Caroline's car came roaring to life in that lane behind them as Riley looked up in horror. "We are going to die!"

"Not today!" said Helen, setting the car back into second gear and pulling hard on the wheel as fast as she could. Her car shot off like a bullet, to the cheers of the crowd she left behind.

"How did you do that?" he asked.

"Force of will," she said with her eyes fixed on the road ahead. They rounded the first turn by the river, and there, beside a trove of golden-leaved trees, they passed car number three.

"Do Ann and Peter have a problem?"

Riley turned. "Peter's inspecting Ann's hand."

"Hope she is all right," said Helen. "But we have to catch Miss Billings."

"Helen, I'm not sure the car can handle more speed on this uneven road."

"Peter said that this car could go more than seventy miles per hour."

"Rubbish. Not on a dirt road. Too dangerous."

"But we have to go faster to win," she said, speeding up while rounding the next turn, trying to close the distance with Miss Billings. "How will we get to the finish line if we don't drive?"

Riley grasped the back of her seat more firmly.

"Mr. Spencer!"

"No intimacy intended, Miss Brooks, but there's no door handle for me to hold on to and I must say I fear for my life right now more so than at any other times past."

"Or times future?" she asked. "Are you enlisting in the British army?"

"I got my physical this week. I'm to go in a few weeks if things continue. Watch for the trees."

The last stretch of the first lap was fairly straight. Miss Billings looked to be only two lengths ahead.

Helen sped up. Twenty, twenty-five, thirty miles per hour. The car began to shift in the grooves of the soft dirt.

Suddenly a loud pop came from Miss Billings' car ahead as a tire blew out. The car swerved directly in front of them. Helen pulled the steering wheel sharply and they ran off the track into the soft grass. The car immediately stalled out. Helen usesd all her strength to turn the steering wheel back to a neutral position.

But Riley jumped out and ran back to Jane's car. "Are you two all right?"

The passengers nodded. "We'll walk back," called Robert.

"Not at all! We'll signal for help at the end of the race," yelled Riley, running back to Helen's car.

Just then Caroline's car flew swiftly by. She passed the two stopped cars without a moment's hesitation.

"Riley, she didn't even stop!" Riley cranked the engine again and they sped off. "That's damned uncharitable. We stopped."

"We stopped because we were run off the road. Just catch up with her and watch your language."

Helen bucked her car into a higher gear. The car began to hurtle toward Caroline and the distance began to close.

"Do you remember what the mechanic said about braking at high speeds?" said Riley.

"Did he say something about that? I've never driven a car before. I thought you were aware of that," she said. Thirty-seven, thirty-eight, forty miles per hour. Once again the car was starting to weave from side to side as dirt and rocks were kicked up behind them. But they were gaining on Caroline—just one length behind now.

"H-Helen, the car is going out of control!" he stammered as she sped even faster.

"Out of control but across the line first!"

"You must slow down!" he yelled as she jerked the car out of the grooves in the middle of the road and onto the wide arc of the grassy shoulder.

"If I slow, I won't win," she said exuberantly as she swept cleanly past Caroline's car. She grimaced as she pulled the wheel hard to get back into the grooves in the middle of the track. Their car lunged forward through the tape.

The applause was audible over the engine's roar and Helen pulled the steering wheel hard to avoid running into the spindly chair legs of the announcers' seats.

"I won!" she said, amazed at the result.

But unfortunately, the car had not stopped. It bobbled over onto the green, where a servant was setting up the quilt auction.

"That woman!" said Riley.

Helen spied her not thirty yards ahead, bending down to pull quilts out of a trunk.

Helen quickly pulled the hand brake, but the car continued to coast.

"How does the car stop?" she cried.

"The brake! The brake!"

"I'm pulling it!" she said, starting to panic as the lever did nothing. "It's broken!"

"Stop the car! The other pedal!"

"There's another one?" she said, feeling around the floor with her foot.

"Yes! That's what the mechanic said! The car was fitted for this race with another one!"

"Where?" she asked.

"On the floor!" yelled Riley.

She looked up. Fifteen yards to the table. She started stepping on everything on the floor. The car jerked forward.

"I can't get anything to work!" Closer and closer they came.

"Helen, pull any lever you can find!"

The hood cover launched up. "That isn't it, Riley!"

Riley put his foot over on her side, where the pedals were covered with the lengths of her skirt. "This is going to hurt," he said as he pounded his foot down.

"Ouch!" she squealed.

The car stopped abruptly, shaking Helen and Riley in their tiny seats.

Riley looked up. "I'm so sorry, Helen."

"I won, Riley!" she said, taking in a deep breath. Her cheeks were pink, and her hair was half fallen from its knot.

"Yes, you did!" he cheered.

"Helen! Helen! Hurrah!" called Peter as a large crowd ran out to the car. Dr. Harris squeezed through the group, holding a gleaming trophy overhead. A crowd rushed past Caroline toward her.

"A picture! A picture for the *Boston Evening Transcript*!" yelled a reporter.

"Wait, Helen!" said Riley. He jumped out of the red car, ran around to her side, and swept her from her seat into his arms.

Overcome with the joy of winning a race, of flying through the air faster than ever before on such a beautiful September day—she felt she would burst. But just as she wished he would put her down, he kissed her fully on her lips as the reporters' cameras flashed. She blushed deeply as he looked up from the embrace and gave an exuberant smile to a crowd that cheered them with many huzzahs.

And Helen, in the middle of all of the attention, understood that she had just won something she did not want at all.

As the crowd dispersed, Wils approached the pair. His face was pale.

"Riley, something has come up. I need to return to Cambridge."

"Is something wrong" asked Helen quickly. "Arnold Archer—"

His cold look silenced her. "Riley, I've got to go."

"How will Helen get back?" asked Riley.

"I'll take her," said a large man. Helen withered under her father's angry glare.

She took his arm silently. The pair walked off in subdued silence as Riley glowered at Wils.

[CHAPTER FIFTEEN]

THE HARVARD UNION

HARVARD COLLEGE

Helen's Great-aunt Longworth's portrait, hung in the main foyer of Longworth Hall, scowled at her. The thin-beaked Great-aunt Longworth, dressed in a white ruffled cap, did not kiss men. In her day, when she had helped negotiate an agreement for Radcliffe College, it was said that one man required an attending physician and another wept openly.

As for the rest of the residents of Longworth Hall, much was made of the photograph published by the *Boston Evening Transcript*. Such lack of reserve was certainly not Boston (perhaps not even Hartford). It hadn't helped that Riley had come by and left a conspicuous flower arrangement. Even Ann had treated her with distance, greeting her after the race with stoic reserve. Helen tried to explain later in private that she'd not wanted the kiss, but felt it stupid as she spoke. She had, after all, brazenly asked Mr. Spencer to join her.

One act of charity gone completely awry!

She had a hard time pinning down her feelings for this young man. He was handsome and rich, and he had made her laugh. But his words—what had he actually said? Nothing of depth. Nothing stirring. She had the sense that he would say anything to avoid a disappointed look. He'd spoil her rather than speak honestly. Riley was genial and that was it. He left little of himself.

It was much harder than she had expected to fall in love with a man who was constantly followed by others who insisted that you hear how terrible he was. And it was even worse if he were rumored to be engaged, and even worse if you weren't supposed to ask him about it. He'd been nothing but kind to her, and she didn't want to return the gift of such kindness with a cold shoulder. She could hear Ann scolding her now: "What if he wanted to give you the gift of the Plague? Would you accept Plague out of politeness?"

How stupid she'd been to kiss him! She wasn't in love with him and that was terribly, horribly, unconscionably, and mystifyingly unfortunate given what had publicly transpired. Best to avoid Mr. Spencer for the next few weeks.

The next morning Helen left for class early, avoiding the newspaper, angrily pulling on her gloves, and affixing to her head a wide-brimmed hat in hopes that it would shield her from prying eyes as she walked to the Harvard Union to study.

As HELEN OPENED the large wooden door to the dining hall, she was hit by the caustic smell of soap and the heat of the room, which clung to the heavy wooden tables, despite the tall Gothic ceilings rising above. Her face broke into perspiration and tendrils of her hair, fallen from under the hat, clung to her skin as she looked around for Morris and Wils. It was still early and she felt a fine mess, jumpy and irritable as she walked to the far side of the nearly deserted dining hall. She placed her hat on a table by a window and pulled her hair back into place, pinning it tightly.

She opened the latch on the window and pushed it open, sticking her face over its sill. The window looked into a small garden, a sad bramble of roses and spindly ivy growing along a shaded brick wall. For several minutes she let the crisp outside air pour over her. Compared to the kitchens, even this city air filled with factory dust smelled better. And at least the vines' troubles were their own.

After a few minutes, she felt someone's eyes on her, an odd sensation. Turning, she saw Wils standing at her table, as polished as an apple. His blond hair was in place, his blue crested jacket immaculate, white shirt starched. Even his shoes gleamed. How long he had been standing there she did not know.

"Wils, you left so quickly yesterday," she said, looking toward her hat. He'd placed his notebook beside it. "Is everything all right?"

"Yes. In fact," he said, with a kind smile, "better than all right. I've solved a riddle."

"A riddle?" she asked, as he pulled out a chair and offered it to her.

"Do know about the death of my friend Max von Steiger?"

"Everyone does, I'm afraid," she said as they both sat down.

He gave a half smile. "I guess that's so. I've been devastated by it. I've not felt this terrible since my father died when I was ten. But Max sent me a letter that I just received, and that note has done me more good than any judgment that could be brought down upon Arnold Archer. I turned it over to my lawyer on Saturday and have a feeling things are going to get back on track."

"But Max is—he's not coming back. How is it better?"

He gave a soft laugh. "Right. You're right about that. But I thought I could have done something about it. That I had failed him in some way. And I learned that I didn't. He actually wished me well."

"So he wasn't a spy for the Kaiser?"

"Max had problems. But the fact that he wrote me was important. He wished me to have peace. I, Wils Brandl, was important enough to him for one of his final acts to—" He broke off his words. "Well, he wished to reach out and comfort me. It's quite nice coming at such a difficult time for Germans living in America."

Her tendrils curled around her throat in such beauty, he thought as he looked at her. "I felt at peace with my friend because he said that he would be all right and that I'd not failed him. His blessing—it apparently meant a great deal to me," he said with a cough. "Where is that Morris Rabin anyway?" he said as his blue eyes glistened. "Morris is another good friend, but one with a penchant for being late." He sat back in his chair and said nothing else.

"You have courage, Wils."

"Courage?" he asked with a half smile. "I've done nothing but tried to keep my head, and that none too successfully. Perhaps I should have seen more about what Max was up to. I will never again let my heart deceive my eyes like this. It was all before me, but I just didn't want to acknowledge it."

His tone had fallen to a whisper and he looked away. She was certain he was talking of the kiss and not of Max. Suddenly the conversation halted and became difficult. And yet he needed to know that his trouble was not over.

"I have some bad news, Wils, and I don't know how to say this, so I'm just going to tell you. Arnold Archer asked me to say that you were a German spy."

Wils closed his eyes and took a deep breath.

"Wils—"

"You're President Lowell's relative," he said in a voice that was suddenly irritable. "You can fix Arnold, can't you?"

She looked down at her hands in her lap. "I don't know why I said that. It was a mistake. I was trying to protect you."

"You told Archer you wouldn't help him, right?"

"That's right."

"I am not America's enemy," he said, and, as he spoke, she raised her finger to his lips, stopping them with her touch.

Her touch. Her fingers were warm and tender and sent a shock through his body. His skin felt on fire as she sat before him, her hair loose in a low knot, her long skirts so close to him that he could feel the heat of her body.

She pulled back and looked down at her books. The silence between them accentuated the clink of plates and the scraping of wooden chairs being rearranged around them as the union began to fill.

"Will you be at the reading tonight?" he asked.

"Of course," she said, looking across the hall. "Where is Morris? I thought he was joining us for this study group."

"He's unusually late." They were silent again.

"Wils, why did you leave yesterday so quickly?"

"I had to get Max's letter to my lawyer."

"But what—?"

"Yes?"

She drew a deep breath. "What if today I kissed someone on Saturday and on Sunday I wished I had not?"

A smile appeared at the corners of his lips. "That kiss was a mistake?"

"Yes," she whispered back.

A curious look came to his eyes. "I could have told you that."

"You can't torment me about it any more than I have myself."

"I'm creative."

"Wils Brandl!"

His smile seared her heart as he spoke. It was spring again, and she could smell the honeysuckle blooms, even in the caustic fumes of the Harvard Union.

"Wils! Helen! Sorry to have been so late!" came Morris' voice from the doors of the kitchens. "Not only are the Germans marching on Paris but the crooks who run this place scheduled me to work tonight during Copeland's reading!"

Wils spoke casually as Morris pulled up a chair, and Helen put on an outward show of being happy to see him. The talk was no more that day about Arnold Archer or a kiss in the newspaper, but about schoolwork and assignments and the hundreds of details that no longer mattered to either Wils or Helen.

[CHAPTER SIXTEEN]

SEVER HALL

HARVARD COLLEGE

ANNOUNCEMENT FOR A READING

by Professor Charles T. Copeland, Class of 1882

Selections from *Candide* by Voltaire

Candide Is a Man Without a Plan,
And Serves as a *Morality Tale for All*,
Especially Seniors Without Plans Post-College

Monday, 6:00 P.M. Upstairs in Sever Hall 11

Hackett Hopkins ran out of the afternoon downpour and into Hollis Hall. He barely stopped to wipe the mud from his boots before hustling up the four ancient flights of steps. Letter in hand, he rounded the corner to find room 15.

"Professor Copeland! Are you in there?" He pounded on the door. The thin young man's face was red with exertion. He unbuttoned his rain slicker to cool down while catching his breath. Footsteps approached.

"Damnation! What can you possibly want from me before a reading?" came a muffled voice from behind the closed door.

The slight, balding man in tweeds opened the door and then broke into a smile.

"It's you, Hackett. Why on earth didn't you say that it was you?"

"Lettah from the president's house," the boy replied in a thick New Hampshire accent. He held up a damp envelope. "The president said it's from the Simpsons."

"Ah! Let me see it!" he said, taking it quickly out of the young man's hand. He walked a few steps back into the room in search of his letter opener. "Come in," he called behind him.

Hackett stepped into the apartment and looked around, waiting for his eyes to adjust. Copeland's suite was dark that afternoon. The large window framed a dull sky pouring down rain outside. It was open at a slight angle, dripping water onto a stack of students' papers. Oil lamps cast shadows upon the exposed wooden beams in the ceiling.

"Have some food if you wish," Copeland directed. He motioned to a small tray of apples, cheese, and crackers on the coffee table.

Hackett picked up an apple and rubbed it on his shirt as Copeland opened the letter.

> The Simpsons
> 34 King Edward Street
> London, England
>
> President A. L. Lowell
> Harvard University
> Cambridge, Massachusetts, U.S.A.
>
> Dear President Lowell:
>
> I have your kind letter of yesterday. I have not yet learned the exact facts about Deighton's departure from Harvard and can only surmise that it was due to an unwarranted inference upon his part. He is an exceedingly sensitive young man and wrote to his mother that the German professor had pilloried him before the class in refusing to allow him to alter the hour of his German section and had immediately after granted several members of the class the privilege for which he had asked. Deighton's long residence at Eton

College has made him quite the Englishman with all the bitter prejudice against Germans, of whom he doubtless assumed the professor to be one although I understand the fact is otherwise. However that may be, the next communication from the boy was a letter from the *Campania,* advising us that he was sailing in the steerage to join the British army and his mother is hot on his trail to bring him back. This, I fancy, she will be able to do, so that I look forward to having him back in Harvard within two or three weeks. The whole thing is really laughable, a tempest in a tea-pot.

Professor White and Mr. Cram were good enough to assure me that there would be no obstacle placed in the way of Deighton's return to Cambridge, after consulting some of the powers other than themselves. It is therefore quite probably that I shall have the pleasure of a personal conference with you shortly.

I trust that it will not be necessary to mention the matter to the German instructor; it is quite too childish.

> Very sincerely yours,
> H. W. Simpson

Copeland grimaced as he tossed the note onto the desk. Pleasure, indeed. Parents seldom took pleasure when their boys disappeared from the campus.

"Anything I need to report to the president, sir?" Hackett asked.

Copeland's eyes narrowed. The tray was clean, and the apple gone—core and all.

"Tell him I'll hold Deighton's space in class and make any other adjustments necessary," he said gruffly. The messenger stood up and brushed the crumbs from his slicker onto the carpet.

"Hackett, please get me a list of all the British students on campus. If they follow Deighton's lead, then I will have fifty more Mrs.

Simpsons to deal with." The professor shuddered at the thought.

And with that task, Hackett thanked him for the food, bade him good afternoon, and closed the door quietly behind him.

As Copeland shut his window, he stopped to watch the young man pick his way across the soggy expanse of Harvard Yard. The boy's hands were stuffed in his pockets and his rain hat pulled down around his ears. Water filled his fresh tracks as soon as he made them.

Copeland stroked his mustache in thought as he leaned his head against the cool wall. What I wouldn't give to trade places with Hackett. It would be good to once again be adrift.

He looked back at the stacks of papers on his desk. Students rarely challenged him anymore. They always seemed stuck. Different faces, same problems, year after year. This war was interesting. Different, at least. Very different.

The boy could be anywhere, he thought: Belgium, where the Germans had invaded. England, where training camps were. Or France. Probably not Russia, he thought in silence. Too unstable.

Copeland shivered, thinking of Deighton's mother. I would hate to be Deighton, he sighed. His mother would set him straight—if she didn't shoot him first.

He rummaged around the desk for a folder and created a new file marked "Simpson," then set it in a pile on his desk.

The clock chimed five thirty. He walked to a pile of jackets draped on a chair and pulled on his overcoat. He was putting on his bowler hat when a knock came at the door.

"Hackett, come in," he called. The door opened, and he looked up to see Arnold Archer towering over him.

This was a young man he wished was at war already. Brick walls had more finesse.

"Yes?" asked Copeland in a flat tone. The clock in his corner chimed the half hour.

"Sorry to bother you, Professor. I just need a moment. May I sit?"

"Now?"

"Please, sir."

Copeland sighed and ushered him in.

"Professor, my father told me that I should talk to you about that first class assignment. He said if I did, you could make it right."

Copeland furrowed his brow as he removed his jacket. "That depends. Did you actually turn in your assignment?"

Archer shook his head. "I haven't had much time, with all that's been going on. I've been helping my father run for Congress."

"I've heard."

"He thought you would understand and make things all right on that front. I can't pass if you give me a zero. I need this class to graduate in the spring." He gave a crooked smile. "My father wants me to work in Washington with him if he gets elected."

"Have you done the reading?"

"President Lowell told my father you'd understand."

"What am I to understand?"

"That I've got a lot going on right now," said Archer. He gave an agitated snort.

"Let's make this clear. I am Copeland. President Lowell is not, and your father is not. I have no need of their assistance in my class-room. That assignment was given to you last spring and you were entirely capable of doing it. Your work for the past three years, while it tends to the purple and is often poorly spelled, shows some signs of moderate promise. And if you want a political career, as you seem to, I suggest you learn the mechanics of the English language."

The young man's face drew up in a scowl. Copeland pursed his lips. Let him marinate for a few more seconds, he thought.

Archer stood up.

"I haven't dismissed you, Mr. Archer. You came here without an appointment demanding my time and I trust you'll not wish to cause me further *a-gi-ta*. Here is what I'll give you. Come to the reading tonight and write about what you hear. Fifteen pages, minimum. I'll mark what you turn in as twenty-five percent of your grade and the rest you'll have to prove on your final examination."

"Tonight?"

"Yes, and if you are going to lead your rally tonight as the flyers you've posted suggest, then I suggest you take care of your grade first. You'll be lucky to pull a passing grade, but it can be done."

After he spoke, the young man got up from his chair and left.

THERE WAS A TIME he would have been harder on the young man— actually make the boy complete the assignment. It wasn't hard. It only required a minimal amount of effort.

But there were bigger problems now. Let the world sort the Arnold Archers. He didn't need to be the one to administer that lesson when the world would do it for him. He took a deep breath, picked up his book, and put on his overcoat again.

The rain had stopped by the time Copeland walked on the path through the Yard, stepping carefully around the puddles that had grown by the sidewalk. He felt a few drops of rain fall onto the back of his neck, and looked up. A squirrel chastised him from the tree's branches. The professor shivered, turned up his collar, and picked up his step, passing the gray blocks of University Hall and into the shadow of Appleton Chapel. He saw a crowd gathering at the foot of Sever Hall, there for his reading.

He stopped to take it in. It pleased him that they came, and even more so that they came to Sever. It was the appropriate theater for his reading. He knew it and they knew it too, in part because he told the dullards.

Sever was not one of those lesser buildings around it, trimmed in ephemera and dancing for attention. This was a Mesopotamian potentate brooding in shadow, dark and foreboding. Not one speck of white paint offset its blood-red bricks, and precious little sandstone whimsy lightened its mood. More than one alumnus had complained of the hall's recessed archway, its semi-turrets, and the unusual fenestration. The massive hall, for many, was not what an educational building in Harvard Yard should look like.

They, of course, were wrong. As Copeland told his students time and time again, Sever Hall spoke more of people than of brick.

Brickwork leaves and vines, flowers and sprigs, curled along the side of the hall and up its walls, filling inlaid brick flower boxes. The bricks were cut into sixty different variations, from which emanated an irrepressible life.

This building needed no ivy. Its life burst from the city's own clay and from the students within the classrooms and hallways inside. And he—a man Harvard had denied promotion to for more than twenty years—filled it time and time again with his readings. He entertained students, he investigated their quarrels for the college, and he listened to their troubles. And what could be more important now, at a time when boys were running off to war?

Or were having war forced upon them. He caught a glimpse of Wils Brandl walking across the Yard to the hall.

His face fell. Wils was a wonderful student and would have gone far as a writer. But he'd be absolutely useless as a soldier, probably dead at the first volley. He wasn't made of the same stuff as Jackson Vaughn or Philip Breckenridge.

Thank God the Brandl lawyer had the good sense to drag out his time in Boston. The boy's only hope was that the war should end quickly. Wils could never shell a cathedral. Professor Kuno Francke said the Germans were fair, but after this past month's reports Copeland believed his colleagues and a few students were exceptions. And, in fairness, they were also exceptional.

A few loose raindrops fell from the cut-brick flower boxes, some glancing off his coat as he waded through the throng. Yes, he thought, let the other buildings cry out from painted doorways and columned porticos. Sever Hall knew that students, like so many variations on red brick, were the college's ever-present life, unique and abundant. They looked the same only if one stood too far back or was too caught up in the flash of columns to notice.

[CHAPTER SEVENTEEN]

CANDIDE

SEVER HALL

The rain had tapered to a mist as Helen walked to Sever Hall that evening. It ushered in a cold that chilled her despite her dark shawl and brown woolen dress.

She found the wide hallway filled to capacity and people flowing up the central staircase. She found an opening near the left entrance and climbed the few steps to the first hall level, then wriggled her way through the students into the center of the main hallway. It was warm there.

A man called from the upstairs hall: "The doors will open in five minutes. No pushing on the steps!" The crowd lurched forward. Helen was jostled.

"Excuse me, sir," she said with a sharp look. The young man who had pushed her had a red face and stout shoulders. On his arm was tied a black ribbon.

"Are you lost?" he asked, beads of sweat on his upper lip. "This is a Harvard event. Men only."

"I have an invitation from Copeland himself."

The lumbering giant laughed in her face, his breath sour. She pulled out her perfumed handkerchief, held it to her nose, and tried to think of Milton.

"Bill, do you see any other women at this reading?"

A man called back from down the crowd, "No, Kurt. Did one escape from Radcliffe?"

"My God, yes."

Helen turned her back to Kurt and crossed her arms in front of her. As she looked around to find Wils, it seemed that Kurt was right. She seemed to be the sole woman in attendance.

The crowd surged again suddenly, causing Kurt to stumble against her and step on the hem of her skirt. A card dropped out of his pocket.

"Sir, my skirt," she said indignantly.

"I have no idea what you are talking about," he said in a loud voice. "If you can't handle walking up a few steps, it is not my concern." She heard snickers among bystanders.

When he picked up the card she saw that it announced a rally that evening at the College Pump in support of the British, French, and Belgians. "Wear black armbands," it said.

As the queue moved forward, a tall young man stopped suddenly in front of her and pushed back. Helen stepped back to regain her balance. It had become a game.

"Did the lady have too much tea today?" asked Kurt. A burst of laughter came from the crowd. She felt her chest tighten. They were doing this on purpose. She saw more with black armbands.

"Miss Brooks!" called a voice from above.

Wils Brandl waved at her from the upper stair banister, a wide smile on his face. "Professor Copeland will be glad to see you as well. He's right here—would you like me to have him escort you?"

She smiled and waved up to him. "It's the German," she heard one behind her whisper.

"I'll be all right," she called. Now I will be, she thought with renewed confidence. She gave Kurt a look of moral opprobrium as the line began to move again. There were no further problems.

Wils met her at the top of the steps and offered his arm.

"Is Copeland really waiting for me?" she asked.

"He should have been, and that's the point. He knew better than to send an unescorted woman in among these types."

They entered the crowded auditorium and sat by the closed bank of windows against the far wall. The wooden seats were well worn and tightly packed. Wils' long legs didn't quite fit, and his knees hit the back of the chair in front of him. He moved them over to make room for her skirt, but in doing so, found himself even closer to her.

"I'm sorry about this," he said, shifting.

"It's all right," she offered. "I'm not certain who they expected to fit."

"Then I give up," he said as his knees pressed against her skirt.

"Wils!" called Dane Iselin from two rows behind.

"Yes?" he said, looking back.

"—he'll be dead just like von Steiger," came a whisper.

"Brandl's next—"

Helen's blood went cold. Her ears pricked up. Brandl? It was hard to hear over the noise of Wils calling back an assignment note to Dane.

"—doesn't matter. The more dead here, the less over there—"

"—going to die anyway—"

"—a lot more Germans than Brandl to be had, Arnold," said a whisper.

"Shut up, Kurt!" a voice hissed.

"It's now time to begin," called Professor Copeland as she looked over to see Kurt out of the corner of her eye. Sitting with him was Arnold Archer. Her face drained of color. They'd been watching her.

She felt rivulets of perspiration begin to trickle down her back. "Archer," she whispered, sitting up.

Professor Copeland demanded silence.

Wils shrugged. "Forget him."

"But he's—"

"And he'll always try," he said, leaning closer. His breath tickled her ear. "Let him."

"Open the windows!" called Copeland, and she turned, hearing laughter from the front rows. She craned her head to see a young man's face appear at the large window by the lectern.

"Mr. Cabot," said Copeland, "resting on a ladder cannot possibly be comfortable. I intend to read this book for a very long time."

"And I intend to escape shortly," said the young man.

"Very well," said Copeland in a dry tone, turning to face the class. "But I selected the passage about beating a young man for you in hopes that it may set a good example."

"A completely hopeless exercise, Professor," said Cabot with a grin that stretched from ear to ear. He refused to budge.

Copeland gave a dramatic shrug, then began to speak. "As some of the less befuddled of you know, there is a war going on in Europe and some current nastiness here in Boston. My friend Owen Wister, Class of 1882, and my colleague Kuno Francke share my sentiments on the matter and have been quite vocal about where things have taken a bad turn for Germany.

"Gentlemen, I bid you a most humble and hearty welcome tonight, and I beseech your patience as we listen to an old tale. There is something in young men that causes them to lose themselves growing up. And there's something more basic that helps them recover their way. For some it's the teachings of the Great Creator. For others it's a strong sense of right and wrong. For some it's dumb luck. But many regain their path, and for this we are unfeignedly thankful." Copeland paused.

Helen looked sideways at Wils, a young man intent on the speaker. He was such a good sort, she thought. He caught her looking and gave her a grin.

"Let us return to the Germany of old—before Nietzsche and before Marx," said Copeland, "What Professor Francke calls 'the true German.' *Candide* is a story about a young man expelled from Germany— the castle of the most noble baron of Thunder-ten-tronckh—and how he found his way."

And with that Copeland began to read. Silence came over the audience as the tale began, laughter erupting at various points, the pages turning slowly.

She found herself forgetting Archer, and Kurt, and just falling into the rhythms of Copeland's voice. It felt right to be there, she thought, with Wils, listening to a reading. This was the theater she loved.

If she could have stopped time, she later thought, it would have been then.

AFTER AN HOUR of reading, when the audience had seen Candide through numerous tribulations, Copeland announced that he was finished and that they could find the book in the library. He dimmed the light at his table and walked out with a dramatic flourish.

The students stood up and began to shuffle out of the auditorium through tall oak doors. As Wils and Helen neared, Marvin Elken clapped Wils on the shoulder and launched into talk of crew practice, oblivious to whether or not Wils was interested. Marvin was a wiry young man, whose bright blond hair radiated from his small head as he energetically told of the strategy to beat Princeton that he'd just thought of while Copeland read. Helen stood at Wils' shoulder while the two men talked.

Helen felt a jostling as the students filed out. "Tonight we'll have a German expulsion," came a whisper in her ear. She turned to see Arnold Archer. Wils was suddenly pushed. He ignored it and continued to talk with Marvin.

"Coming to the rally, Brandl?" asked Kurt as he lumbered by. Arnold looked coldly at Helen as the crowd pressed in on them.

"Leave him alone," said Arnold, walking past them. "He's German trash."

"Who let that young man out of jail?" asked Helen to no one in particular. The room suddenly quieted as students began filing out more swiftly.

"I took your mother's lead on the incarceration bit," said Arnold.

"Helen," interrupted Wils, "he is not worth your time," as the gang left.

Wils offered her his arm as they turned to descend the steps.

"Wils, does this happen often?"

"More often than I'd like. That's why my mother posted a guard at my apartment."

"Should your guard be here to escort you home?"

"Helen, if he were here, who would guard the room? No, I'm not going to be a prisoner outside of my room too. But it is nice to have an ally in the room. Now, do you have someone to walk you home?"

She nodded. "Peter is meeting me at Appleton Chapel."

"Well, I am going the other way. I'll see you tomorrow?"

She nodded.

It was painful to watch her walk away. He walked out onto the moonlit path that would take him back to Beck Hall. The air was chilled from the rain but the sky clear. He didn't wish to walk it. He had no idea what he'd do with himself back at home. He wished to be at Radcliffe, looking up at her window, softly calling her name, and speaking up to her in quiet whispers.

Could it be?

The flicker of her eyes. Dear God, it ate into him. Her touch on his lips that afternoon promised so much. Her fingers—they promised eternity. But they didn't sate. It was not peace, but teased and promised more.

What did he need with his books, his room, a reading? All he wished for was a patch of riverbank, the sun, and her. An eternity to be with her.

He closed his eyes. Who was this woman? He longed to pull her to him. To have her. He wished to run to Radcliffe yard and kiss every stone on which she had stepped. It felt a glimpse—even the barest glimpse—of heaven.

He was still musing on that thought—or perhaps it was the line of her throat—when he felt a blow from behind. He fell silently onto the broad sidewalk along Harvard Yard, fading quickly into darkness.

[CHAPTER EIGHTEEN]

BEDSIDE

HARVARD COLLEGE

H elen and Ann were sitting at their morning breakfast in dressing
gowns and braids when a knock came on their door.

"Miss Brooks," called Miss Sullivan from the other side. "Morris
Rabin is on the telephone for you downstairs."

Helen met Ann's glance with surprise.

"Be there in a moment," called Helen. She stood up and unraveled
her braids as she walked to her bedroom, pulling on a navy dress and
calling for Ann's help with the tiny buttons up the back. While Ann
assisted, Helen tamed the dark waves of her hair into a deft twist and
tied it with a white ribbon. She went downstairs to Miss Sullivan's desk,
where she was handed the telephone receiver and speaker.

The short cable did not stretch far beyond the scarred counter at
which Miss Sullivan sat, in a purple dress with her hair in a pompa-
dour. The hall mistress at least made the pretense of reviewing the
day's schedules for the college maids.

Helen leaned close to the speaker. "This is Helen Brooks."

"Helen, it's Morris. No study group today. Wils has been hurt."

"What? Is he—"

"He's not good. Riley found him unconscious on the sidewalk.
Someone hit him after the reading," said Morris.

"Archer?"

"No idea. He is in his bed for a couple days and I'm taking care of—"

"I'm coming over," she interrupted.

"Women aren't allowed in Beck Hall," said Morris.

"But if he's been hurt, surely they would allow a visit."

There was another pause. "Helen, I don't know how to say this. But if you're looking for a way to get closer to Riley this isn't the time."

Helen felt her cheeks turn bright red. "I understand," she said, swallowing hard and hanging up the phone. She returned it to Miss Sullivan.

Helen walked slowly up the steps, chastened. Ann looked up.

"Horrid news, Ann. After the reading Wils Brandl was attacked."

"No," said Ann.

"It's terrible," Helen said, standing on the carpet, her arms crossed in frustration.

"There's a basket of cookies my mother brought to me, over on my desk. You should take them to him and see how he's doing," said Ann.

"Riley Spencer lives with him and I can't bear to face him."

"Good citizens are good despite obstacles."

"I'd not thought of that," Helen said, walking to the coatrack. She pulled out a thin wool shawl and wrapped it around her shoulders, then picked up the cookies and walked out the door.

THE SKY WAS BLUE and cloudless, and filled with such a warm sun that it threatened even the darkest thought. The weathervane atop Harvard Hall gleamed gold, nearly matching the leaves in the trees of the Yard— the canopies of some newly planted elms and the reds of a few oaks.

At Beck Hall, Burton made no attempt to stop her visit. He ushered her into Wils' rooms along with the other visitors. He informed her Riley was gone for the day and Wils was asleep.

Helen was greeted by Professor Copeland, a police officer, and another man—tall and Germanic, introduced as Professor Kuno Francke. They stood in the middle of the room, nodding at the hushed tones of the police officer's report. The officer was a large man in girth and stature, his florid face animated by the conversation. Professor Francke, on the other hand, was reserved, tall and thin. On his nose sat a pair of round spectacles that seemed too small for his face. Perhaps it was that his gray hair was pushed back from his forehead; perhaps it was the short bristly mustache that didn't look like it belonged. He looked like a young boy wearing a disguise.

Copeland welcomed her. "Miss Brooks, I'm glad you came. Wils was calling for you."

"Really?"

Copeland looked at her askance.

"How is he?" she said, attempting to frown disinterestedly.

"Not terrible," said Copeland in a low voice. "A knock to the head, some bruises. A scrape on the face. Riley Spencer was escorting two ladies home when—" The police officer gave a pointed look at Copeland.

"What, Sean? They are ladies until proved otherwise. He was escorting some ladies home when he found Wils on the sidewalk. He talked to the police, then left about an hour ago to take care of some of Wils' business."

She swallowed hard at the news of the women but ignored it. "May I see Wils?"

"Of course. Please come with me." He put his hand on the glass doorknob and turned to Helen. "You're not going to faint on me, are you?"

"No," she said as they went into the room.

Wils' room was dark and cool, its curtains pulled. She saw him resting on his bed, across from a large writing table. A young nurse in a starched white uniform sat in the corner in a stuffed chair, reading by the light of a small night lamp. She looked up but didn't move.

Neither did Wils. Helen saw his face was scraped—perhaps where he'd fallen. A small roll of bandage and powders cluttered a nightstand. The room smelled like camphor. He seemed to be breathing easily.

"He'll wake soon," said Copeland in a whisper. "Have a seat." He sat on a stool by Wils' bed, offering her a large leather chair.

"Spencer said Wils called your name as they were carrying him to his room. I've been asked to investigate for the college on a related matter." Copeland put his hands on his balding pate. "Could you tell me what you know?"

"I know a lot," she said quietly, but with confidence. "Arnold Archer did this. I don't know if that is what the college wishes to hear."

"We've no interest in sullying a three-hundred-year-old reputation for someone who can't behave properly," returned Copeland. He leaned toward her. "We don't want the likes of Wils to be hurt for political matters. He's a talented young man, Miss Brooks, although you mustn't ever tell him I said so. It may corrupt him." He sat back and rubbed his hands over his face. He no longer seemed the confident professor of last night. Instead he kept looking nervously over at Wils, as if he didn't know what to do. He leaned toward her again. "But I am concerned. Wils doesn't choose his friends well."

Professor Francke entered and Copeland rose to speak to him.

"Charles," said Francke, "I'm going to resign if Archer isn't expelled. He must be made an example. Count Brandl is from a high-ranking German family. First von Steiger, now Brandl."

"You've threatened to resign just about every week since the war broke out."

"These aren't manufactured grievances—"

Wils suddenly gave a moan. "Helen?"

Copeland and Francke abruptly halted their conversation. Copeland gave a slight cough. "Kuno and I will notify the nurse. We'll be outside."

The door closed quietly behind them.

"I should have listened to you. It's not safe here," he said in a hoarse voice.

"Is Europe at war safer?" she whispered back.

He shook his head and winced. "Perhaps safer than sitting in the presence of a sharp-tongued Boston bluestocking."

She smiled. "Would another knock on your head civilize your speech?"

"No chance," he said with a slight smile. She caught the sparkle of his eyes before he closed them. "Thank you for coming." He lapsed into peaceful silence again.

She looked at him sleeping: his blond hair mussed, his cheeks pale against the dark pillow. His shoulders—wide and muscled from rowing —twitched now and then, and his arm was carelessly draped over the side of the bed.

She was struck by its beauty, as if she were looking at him for the first time.

She reached for his hand to arrange it by his side. His hand was large, easily able to encompass hers. She held it for a moment.

The door opened behind her.

"What are you doing, Helen?" came a clipped British accent.

[CHAPTER NINETEEN]

RILEY SPENCER

BECK HALL

Helen turned and saw Riley standing in the doorway, his hand cradling a badly bruised eye. His forearm was bandaged with gauze, and dark spatters stained his white shirt. His tie was loose at the collar, his dark hair was uncombed. He looked like he'd not slept. She didn't know how long he had been there or what he'd seen.

"What happened, Riley?"

He shook his head. "Not in front of Wils."

She stepped quickly outside and Riley closed the door behind them.

"I took care of some things."

"Archer?"

"They'll have a deuce of a time cleaning him up."

She swallowed.

"It seems we both were taking care of Wils," he said irritably. "Only I have an obligation to do so, seeing as Wils belongs to my family."

She said nothing in reply.

"Do you know that Wils and I are leaving for war?"

"When?"

"Soon." He shrugged. His jaw tensed as he looked over to one side. She caught a lipstick mark on his collar.

"Miss Brooks, I understand some news has reached you," he said in a quiet voice. "Some news that may have made you think less of me these past couple of days. May I speak plainly?" She nodded.

"There is a woman who has told many of my friends that she is to be married to me. Peter believes I'm engaged."

"Are you?" she asked, but she felt like a fraud as soon as she spoke. Even if he had no fiancée, she wouldn't love him.

He shook his head. "The truth is that I am not. I've made it clear to this woman that I never asked her to marry me and don't intend to marry her. I think a young man named Lawrence is really the person she will end up marrying. I needed you to hear and to know this."

Riley stepped over to her, sat down, and took her hands. His felt rough and cold, his touch profane after sitting by Wils.

"Helen, I'd like to talk with you about our future. I'm going—"

"I don't wish to hurt your feelings," she interrupted. "I'm grateful for your kindness. But we have no future."

His face darkened as she pulled her hands back. "Oh come now. What do you mean? You kissed me."

"I made a mistake, Riley."

"You don't kiss someone if you're not serious about your intentions."

Her back straightened. "I am sorry, but I'm not in love with you."

"Nonsense. I know it may take some time, Helen. I'm not an easy man to live with, although I assure that that will change. I had—I just— I mean, between now and the time I leave, I'd hoped I could continue my friendship with a most remarkable young woman. I had counted on it, in fact."

"Mr. Spencer—"

"You haven't tried to love me! Please," he said, with an angry look. "You felt something at the dance. Tell me you didn't and I'd call it a lie. You were happy then, Helen. What's different now? A piece of mistaken information?"

"No," she said. "I'm just—just—" She searched for the right word.

His smile evaporated. "Don't lie to me," he said, his voice crackling with anger.

"I shouldn't have kissed you."

"Well, you did, and here I am." He stood up and paced before her, the belligerent air of victimhood pinned to his chest.

"Riley, I'm sorry to hurt you, but I cannot return your love. I-I'm so sorry," she stammered, standing up. "I wish I had been candid. I didn't mean to—"

He held his hands up to stop her from talking.

How had she been able to wound him? Nothing she had ever said would have so much as touched Frank Adams' heart. She had been as ineffective as a pop gun. Yet Riley looked hurt. Isn't this what he did all the time? Wasn't he the one who littered the dance halls with broken hearts? "Riley, I don't think that—"

"I am at the very least honest about who I am. I'm not engaged. I don't go kissing people by accident. And I thought I would at least make that plain."

As she struggled for words, she saw that his emotions, so evident a few seconds ago in his eyes, suddenly became hidden by a careless look. He turned away. There was nothing further to say.

"It's best if you just leave," he said, almost bored.

She turned on her heel and walked out, through the hall, past Mr. Burton, and out the door, fighting back tears.

"Miss Brooks!" she heard Burton call. "You forgot your shawl!"

She swallowed, thanked the hall master quietly, turned, and left, inquiring no further about the young men in Beck Hall. She didn't know which was worse: causing the pain or living with it. She assumed the former, but, in truth, preferred neither.

Wils would hear of this, she was certain. Riley would tell him and that would be the end of their friendship.

She closed her eyes and took a deep breath. Then the pain would dull in time. Soon—perhaps very soon—they would all be gone: Riley and Wils. They would leave for war and she'd have to live without them.

As she began to walk home she burst into tears. She couldn't bring herself to return to Longworth Hall. Wiping her eyes with the back of her glove, she turned and walked toward the Charles River. It was quiet along that path. A vigorous walk in nature might clear her head and she didn't care a whit if it smacked of Thoreau. Her father would just have to understand.

THE CHARLES was a notoriously slow river, its water brown from steeping in the wetlands surrounding it. While carriages and cars busied themselves on either side of the banks, the river itself seemed to absorb and swallow the sound from the roads. Its dirt paths were wide enough for the myriad of daily visitors: wandering students, nurses pushing prams, young boys bicycling, and the beggars who slept on carpet bits under the graceful Georgian bridges that arched from the banks of Cambridge into the wilds of Allston. Squirrels ran up the large elm and oak trees, which at the river's narrowest parts stretched their limbs out to gossip with their counterparts across the river. Under their spreading branches sprang rushes and daylilies, and an occasional spot of beach to dock a boat or to watch the fours and eights as they skimmed past to the rhythm of the coxswain's call.

But Helen barely looked at the trees or the water as she marched around the Charles River that day or the next. Instead of watching the autumn sun glisten on the water or the fours and eights gliding by, or listening to the wind whisper through the leaves, she thought of Riley. On the third day it came to her. The problem wasn't Riley; it was really Wils.

She liked him: the poetry, the reading, advice regarding her mother. Wils—the caustic, blunt young man—he knew her.

But he'd not call on her anymore. He'd be gone. Whatever Riley told his cousin about the incident could hardly be flattering.

That night she confided her troubles to Ann. Her friend had no words of comfort. Ann advised her to keep the revelation away from her overly protective brother. In this Helen needed no instruction. She wished to leave all public professions of faith to her mother.

[CHAPTER TWENTY]

THE CHARLES RIVER

Late September

Wils walked into Copeland's Bolyston Hall classroom a week after the attack. His face was pale and drawn and when he turned to sit in his wooden chair, he turned slowly, as if the pain had not left him. He gruffly nodded to Helen as he walked in, amidst the murmurs of his classmates.

Classroom numbers had dwindled again, such that Copeland gave everyone ample time to discuss the (de)merits of modern verse. But when it came time for Wils to speak, he waved the professor off. In a rare act of charity, Copeland assented and moved on.

At the end of class young men crowded around Wils to speak to him. Helen looked at the group of intent faces, peppering Wils with questions, then picked up her things to quietly leave. As she walked to the door, she heard chairs shuffle behind her and Wils called out her name.

"Miss Brooks! Wait," he said in a hoarse voice, untangling himself from the crowd and walking to her. He seemed thin, his dark jacket hanging loose across his shoulders. Yet his eyes gleamed, and without a hint of distance.

"I wanted to thank you for visiting."

She looked away from him. "The ensuing argument with your cousin was hardly a reason for thanks."

They lapsed into silence.

"Are you all right?" he asked at length.

"Wils, do you want to come watch the practice?" called Dane, walking with Marvin Elken.

Wils shook his head. "A few other things going on, Dane."

"Does it involve a pretty skirt?" called Marvin, laughing and walking out the door.

"Why, yes it does," called Wils back as Helen turned a bright pink.

"Miss Brooks," he said as Marvin left the classroom, "I hear you've taken to walking down by the river. I was hoping to join you this afternoon." His tired eyes smiled at her.

She looked at him and smiled. "You feel up to a walk?"

"My doctor said some fresh air would be good," he said as they walked out the classroom door.

They left the construction of Harvard Yard, passed the congestion of the shops and private dormitories in Harvard Square, and made their way to the banks of the Charles, walking north along the river. They spoke of events of the day—of Wils leaving the crew team, the fury of Copeland's edicts about Archer's rally, the battle raging at the Marne—while they strolled down a path and onto one of the river's bridges. At its crest, he stopped and rested against the wall.

"Would you like to know how Riley's doing?" he said, looking at the people walking along the far shore.

"How is he?" she asked.

Wils shook his head. "He's spent most of the past week in despair."

She looked away. "I'm terribly sorry to be the cause of it."

"The Dudevant twins are helping him recover."

"Twins?"

"We each handle grief in our own way," he said, turning to her with a half smile. "But take some comfort. In this case it's not disloyalty. I know that because he's often on the couch moaning about how you were the angel who was going to convert him from a wastrel into a good man."

"That's God's job," she said with a look of exasperation.

"Who will help God?"

They both laughed. She looked at him, and shook her head. "I made a mistake."

"As did I." He shook his blond hair from his eyes as he looked at her intently.

"Wils, what mistake did you make?"

"I listened to him tell me about how wonderful you are. And now I can't get you out of my mind," he said softly. "I don't mean to startle you, but time is short for me here. I have tried, and tried, and tried to forget you, but I've failed. And in truth, Helen, I don't want to just think of you. I don't wish to walk with you just today, but tomorrow, and the next, and the day after that. I know I have no right to ask this, but I had to find out if I might at least hope before I left, that, if I return, you might hear me out."

Her lips parted in surprise as he continued.

"I'm so sorry. Honor should prevent me from asking you, but I had to know," he said, his eyes fixed on hers as he spoke.

"Yes," she said, a smile springing to her lips. "A thousand times yes."

He closed his eyes and whispered, "Thank you." In a moment he opened them and, seeing her still there gave a joy-filled laugh. "Come, Helen," he said, offering his arm. "Come with me. Let's walk a bit farther. It gets dark so early these days."

She put her hand on his arm, and as he covered it with his own, she looked away, unable to contain her smile.

Each afternoon they walked together, at times arm in arm, and at times at a distance. Some days they spoke of Wils' home in Prussia and his duty to his country. Other days, of her ideas for a poem or the latest reading of Copeland. And others about nothing in particular. It was those times that their laughter was most easy and their hearts at peace. But the days grew short. As Wils' strength increased, the call of home grew more difficult to honorably resist.

THE NEXT WEEK Wils told Helen that Robert Goodman, Esq., had called with the terms of truce by which the city would drop its investigation into Wils' shipyard visit. He was to leave within a fortnight, on a privately chartered boat, he said, as he watched her face darken.

As they walked around the Charles, he promised that he would return to her as soon as he possibly could.

She met his glance, and, after a pause, asked if there was something she could do to help him.

"—Like throw you in the river so you'll be too sick to leave."

As she said the words, he looked down at her, his eyes filled with sadness and admiration, but he said nothing.

"Wils, how is it that you're so unlike other Prussians? You don't long for war or Belgium—"

"I did steal my cousin's girl," he offered.

"There is that, but you're different from the Germans I read about in the papers today. Professor Francke is different. But there are so few of you who are different, I fear for your country."

He shook his head. "I do too. The Prussians believe the laws are different for them—that they're stronger, and can use that power to make Germany rank above all other countries."

"To what end?" she asked in an exasperated tone. "That's what I want to know. What could possibly be worth all of this carnage?"

He shook his head as he looked out to the water. "Things," he said dully. "Others' things. Power. Pride."

"And you? What made you different?"

He gave a deprecatory laugh. "My father was a poet—a man who could pluck beauty from the air. He saw the unseen and wrote that there was more to life than what we could measure. I believe he was a great man. At least I thought he was." He looked away from her down the bank to a group of young men launching a small boat into the water. One threw a rock at a pair of bickering squirrels. The animals turned and fled up a tall elm.

Wils extended his arm to her, and the pair began to walk again.

"Was he not a great man?" she asked, after a pause.

"I can't tell," he said, his voice suddenly wavering. "You see, he died when I was young. And soon after, I began to forget him. It's terrible. I can't see him anymore in my mind—he has no form, no smell, no voice. He's a portrait on a wall, not my father. Helen, it's a terrible thing to forget the dead. It's as if he really did die then, only I'm the one who was disloyal by leaving him." He turned to her suddenly and held her arm tightly.

"I won't forget you Wils," she promised rashly.

"You can't mean that. I didn't mean to forget my father."

"Don't tell me what I can and can't promise. Doesn't your mother remember your father?"

"No man could stand in his shadow," he said bitterly. "There is no one for her to re-marry. Men like my father have vanished, except for a few." His voice trailed off as he, suddenly conscious of the grip on her arm, removed his hand. "They've been replaced by the Prussian war machine. It's all power and things. There has to be something higher than that to live for."

"Do you think there is?"

He nearly laughed. "Helen, of course I do. I'm my father's son. But I've stopped reading philosophy for now. All I think of these days is you."

"Come now," she said, a smile flickering in her eyes.

"It's true." He said, turning back to her. "Helen, do you know what happens when I think of you?"

"What?" she asked.

"Music. I hear music."

"The sound of a cuckoo clock?"

"A psalm," he said, in a tone that silenced her mirth. "I'm serious. It's something about waiting patiently and finding—no, that's not exactly right. It's vague. It's something about time and joy meeting."

"Is it everlasting?" she asked as he reached for both of her hands.

"It feels like it must be. But I don't know," he said with a shrug. "Do you think of music?"

"I think of color," she offered.

A glint of mischief appeared in his eyes. "Reliable Boston brown?"

"No," she said, laughing. "I see yellow, blue, and white."

He wrinkled his nose. "A French kitchen? What about red?"

"The color of sin? Not at all. My colors are crisp and vibrant: your hair, your eyes, your skin."

"Oh," he said as his eyes widened in hope. He said nothing further, but knelt before her and covered her hand in kisses there at the river's edge.

Late that evening Ann looked at Helen from across the room at Longworth Hall. Her friend sat before a mirror combing her hair. She looked radiant in her white lace gown—the young woman she'd not seen in many months. Ann told her that she too would take up walking. It seemed to have done Helen's spirits a world of good. She'd never seen her friend so happy.

Helen smiled as she brushed out her long, dark hair, but she kept her secret.

THE TENTH OF OCTOBER was breezy and cool; the sky was gray, threatening storms. Helen suggested they not walk that day. Wils, noting that she was well dressed for such an outing with her wool shawl and long skirts, suggested a different path. Helen pulled her shawl tight around her shoulders and followed reluctantly.

He led her down to the banks of the river to a small wooden boat.

"What is this?" she asked as the wind breezed up again.

"A boat ride."

"On a day like this? Are you mad? You'll exhaust yourself rowing."

"Won't you help row?"

"You expect me to row?"

"Such little faith in my manners," he clucked and held her hand while she stepped into the craft and sat at one end.

"I have faith in the wind," she replied.

"Helen, I did pick up a thing or two from rowing all those years with your brother," he said wearily, pushing them away from the bank with the edge of an oar. "A little faith, please." With strong strokes he pulled to the middle of the river. His face reddened as he struggled. Helen thought him mad. The Charles River was slow, but the wind was not, and Wils had only recently recovered.

In the middle of the river, the wind coursing above them, Wils suddenly pulled his oars in. "Rowing is hard work," he said. "You're right. Your shawl, please," he said.

"You're not going to dry that oar with my shawl, are you?" she said as she handed it to him.

"Does wool spot like silk?"

"Don't change the subject."

"Which is what?"

"You're trying to drown us—"

"To stop your chatter?" Wils asked.

"To silence words and ideas you don't like to hear."

"Helen," he said with a broad smile, "you sound just like me! And as you know, rough words for an idea don't mean rough thoughts for a person. Now move to the middle."

"Whatever for?"

"To balance the boat. You're the ballast we move around to get the right weight-bearing load in the—"

"You're calling me ballast?" she spluttered as the winds howled.

"Other way. Sit with your back to the wind," he said, as she menaced him with a stern look before she turned away from him. He ignored her and pulled a piece of twine from his pocket, knotting the top of the oar to her shawl. He shifted behind her, putting his arms around her.

"My shawl?"

"Hold this," he said, giving her the oar, and pulling the shawl around her. "Lean back now," he said, pulling her toward him.

"Mr. Brandl!"

Wils pulled her back as the makeshift sail became taut. She leaned back into his arms and the sail carried them swiftly through the water. They laughed all the way down the river, gliding quickly, whereas before it had been a struggle.

"Look at the banks," said Wils as they flew by nurses and cyclists.

"If I never row another stroke I'll be perfectly happy," he said, leaning up and kissing her cheek. "You'll make an excellent ship's mate."

"I'm better at mutiny," she said, dipping her hand into the cold water and splashing him for good measure.

After a good distance they came to a barren spot, where the buildings and cars were far away from the river's edge. There he stepped out and splashed over to the bank, pulling the boat to dry land. He offered his hand and helped her out.

"Come," he said, taking her hand and leading her to a small embankment.

She caught her breath. On the ground was a richly embroidered cloth dusted in rose petals. She looked at the fabric, so different from the brown of her shawl, and turned to him.

"What's this?"

He cleared his throat. "The shipping lanes have cleared. I've three days."

She walked to the cloth, pulled off her shoes, and stepped on it in her stocking feet. It was intricately patterned, with hues of greens and reds and blues bursting from it. In the center were two vines embroidered in gold, each wrapped around the other, their tendrils overlaying the letter *W* with an *H*.

"I can't hold you to a promise when I don't know the future," he said as she took in the tapestry. "It's not honorable. But when I return I will ask you to marry me."

"They say the war will be over by Christmas," she said, examining the gold thread. "You'll arrive just in time to return. This is true?"

Wils nodded. "That's what they say, but no one knows if it's true. Helen, dearest—I would trade the world to marry you."

She looked back at him and smiled. "Then what should stop us?"

"Your father, for one. Helen, I'm serious. He might prefer a long engagement."

"You should marry him, then."

They both laughed as Wils shook his head, unable to contain his smile.

"You'll marry me?" he asked, standing close to her.

"I will. And I don't need to wait three months for you to return to know it either."

He knelt before her again, taking her hands in his and looking up into her eyes.

"Oh, Helen,
Die Liebe welche Gott geweiht,
Die belibet bis in Ewigkeit.
The love which God consecrates abides for eternity," he said tenderly as he kissed the hands in his. They were soft and small, and smelled of fresh flowers.

She knelt beside him and, leaning toward him, kissed his forehead gently.

"The love which God consecrates abides for eternity," she repeated. "I marry you, Wils." She closed her eyes, and in a moment his lips met hers. They were warm and kind.

"In Prussia I have a ring for you," he murmured. "A sapphire as blue as your eyes."

"And a coronet?"

"Well, yes, actually."

She gave a slight laugh. "I've no need of one. But—" She thought, then stopped. She reached for the satin ribbon in her hair. Taking the pearl ring from her finger, she threaded it through the satin, knotting one end. She kissed the pearl and draped the ribbon around his neck, tucking it in his shirt. "Keep this until you return from the war," she said.

"When I return," he repeated softly, taking her in with his eyes.

"My promise is binding," she said, with breathtaking confidence. "I'm your wife if you will have me. This war will not change that or me."

"I will have you," he said wrapping his arms around her waist and pulling her closer to him. "My love for you is—"

"An ever-fixed mark?" she interrupted. He gave a soft laugh as he leaned down to kiss her lips.

"What an unsentimental lot you are for a wife," he said with a deprecatory sigh.

"*Your* wife?"

"Indeed." He nodded. "*My* wife. As of this day forth, Mrs. Brandl, church wedding or not."

It was settled. It had been as natural as breathing, she thought as she knelt in the warmth of his arms.

A COLD RAIN began to fall as Wils walked Helen from his car up to the steps of Longworth Hall. He promised to call on her father that weekend. Not caring a whit for the rain, she glided into the building. Ann would be astonished at the news!

"Miss Brooks! Your father—" Miss Sullivan called out.

"Does he know?" Helen asked, surprised.

"Know what?" the large woman said with a snort. "Don't interrupt. Your father called to take you home. Your mother's been arrested, *again*"—she emphasized the word in her ham-handed manner—"for giving safe haven to criminals. Your driver is picking you up in five minutes to meet your brother, who is already at City Hall. He said to pack for a few nights and meet him at the corner." Sullivan seemed delighted at the news.

Helen walked upstairs, the color draining from her face. As she closed the door behind her she burst into tears. They flowed freely as she swiftly gathered her things into an evening bag—a notebook, brushes, a change of clothes.

Not now. Wils was leaving. She couldn't go.

She took a deep breath, drying her tears on the back of her hand and dashing off a quick note to let Ann know where she was.

She should be glad to be free of Radcliffe for now. The place felt too small for her, with Miss Sullivan below as her juvenile jailer, and not an assistant of any useful type she could think of.

She was no longer a child to be moved by her mother's or Miss Sullivan's caprice. She was Wils Brandl's wife.

[CHAPTER TWENTY-ONE]

MERRIMACK HILL

J onathan Edwards Brooks ordered his breakfast in the study that next morning. He was in no mood to talk. His back was turned to the miracle of color that the east garden had become, his lights were dimmed, and he seethed in his dark red lounging jacket in front of his study's warm fire. He had a headache, and his headache had a name: Merriam Windship Brooks.

An hour into his morning regimen he was still simmering, the peppery scent of his third cup of tea no balm for his troubled soul. He finally gathered the strength to look at the morning papers to read what shocks were in store for him today: war, wife, or other calamities.

The top headline, as usual, was that the Europeans were killing each other in all sorts of brutal fashions. Why European killing each other still made headlines was unclear to him. For hundreds of years this had been going on: the Hundred Years War, the French Revolution, Napoleon. Every time you turned around, these people were killing each other, typically in the name of enlightenment, pride, or some God-given right to another man's wine cellar.

His eyes scanned the paper—the mayor's son had run off to war to fight for the British. At least that news pushed Merriam's story off the front page. Although she would probably complain about that too. He could just hear her now. The Civil War delayed women's suffrage and here men were, trumping up another war in order to delay a vote on women's issues yet again.

And so it went that the sun had climbed a fair way into the sky by the time Mr. Brooks actually cracked the shell of his hard-boiled egg. Just as he added a judicious pinch of pepper and opened his mouth to pop it in whole, he stopped, adjusted his pince-nez, and shook his head at a news story at the bottom of the page.

HARVARD REITERATES REGULATIONS
REGARDING RALLIES

Harvard University has reiterated its restrictions against discussions of contentious political issues after this last month's rally in Harvard Yard, led by Arnold Archer, son of influential congressional candidate Charles Archer (see related story, page 1). It was the third rally of this type since the Kaiser invaded Belgium. Given that the rally fell immediately after a reading by Harvard's Assistant Professor Charles Copeland, there was considerably less mayhem and drinking than accompanied the previous two rallies. However, many had copies of *Candide*, Copeland's text that evening, and these they threw into a bonfire. Other books burned were by the German professors Kuno Francke and Karl Munsterberg.

The authorities immediately put out the fire, citing the hazardous combination of exuberance, spirits, fire, and political opinion.

After an angry complaint from Professor Copeland, the Harvard Corporation reissued its 1912 regulation which states, "The halls of the University shall not be open for persistent and systematic propaganda on contentious questions of contemporary social, economic, political, or religious interests."

The topic inflames passion on the campus. Harvard has seen almost as much attrition this fall as it did

during the entire War Between the States. Officials
have attributed the exodus of students to the ready
availability of news reports regarding how the British
are now engaged in some of the most exciting,
honorable soldiering to have been available to
students since Theodore Roosevelt, Class of 1880,
charged up San Juan Hill. (For related story, see front
page: "Late-Breaking News: Son of Mayor Leaves for
War; Sets Example for Youth of Today.")

At that moment Brooks pondered enlisting. Perhaps he could
shed a few pounds and fit into one of those dashing aeroplanes. He
looked sullenly down at his paunch. Maybe a zeppelin, he thought with
disgust.

But before he could finish his self-flagellation, he heard steps on
the gravel of the driveway.

It had better be his lawyer, Ronald Choate, and Choate had better
have some answers, or Choate would be choked. His mustache twitched
in rage.

"Father?"

His walrus mustache perked up. Helen was better than Choate.

"Yes?" he replied, looking at her in the doorway. The frown
returned.

Helen had come from a walk. Her hair was unbound, her cheeks
reddened by the wind. Mud clung to the hem of her wool skirt. Ophelia
in the moated grange looked better, he thought.

"Dear child, why did you go out in this mess?"

"How could I sleep after the police searched our house last night?
The house felt like it was caving in on me. I went for a walk."

"Yes, the police," he sighed. "A most humiliating business. At least
they didn't find any additional people hiding out or doling out family
limitation booklets by the gross. Please, come in."

"There could have been more women hiding at our house?"

"Who knows who your mother met in New York?" said Mr.
Brooks.

Helen's heart sank. "Are we safe for now?"

"Of course not!" he said brusquely. "This has permanently affected our standing in the community. We'll be outcasts just like the Darlingtons." He looked sadly up at a portrait of his father in military uniform. "In some ways, Helen, it's quite liberating, but in others it's not, especially for my unmarried daughter."

She decided now was not the time to discuss Wils. "Then if there's no danger here, may I just return to my studies? I could be of use in Cambridge."

He moved over on the settee, and motioned her to sit down. "Then both you and Peter would have deserted me. I need you here, Helen." He suddenly looked older, she thought. Much older. And she understood that for today there would be no talk at all of Wils or of returning to Cambridge.

"Helen, your mother really wishes to help this cause but—but—" He caught himself, holding his hands up in protest. "Let me remember myself," he said, catching his breath. "We've had too much emoting around this house as it is. I'll start over.

"While I cannot take credit for what others choose to do, I did marry your mother and I knew that the apple wouldn't fall far from the tree. Your grandmother was at Seneca Falls and raised a fighter. They believe that reasonable people work with the world, unreasonable people change it, and that"—he sighed—"is why we have the house in New Hampshire—to get away from unreasonable people! To flee such slings and arrows of outrageous fortune when the police come for the occasional odd duck in our family."

"But Father, Mother has been entirely unreasonable. And she looks down on us as conventional."

His beetling eyebrows met in the center of his forehead as he thought. He seemed to wish to agree, and as he pondered the question the bushy brows seemed to war with each other. After an interval he began again.

"Hiding those women from the police was a bad idea. This is not the Underground Railroad. Your mother is now in serious trouble. Apparently Ms. Margaret Sanger and her friend jumped bail and fled to avoid defending their principles in a court of law. I hope they are posted on a ship to England."

"Why did the shipping lanes clear, Father?" Wils had said the same thing.

"They're not clear. But they're also no match for the likes of your mother or her friends. And the truth be told, anyone with connections can get through—probably the Kaiser himself—if they have the will to do so. Apparently these ladies possess that in spades."

"Leaving Mother here to face the charges—"

"Leaving your mother here. Yes. It's good they did."

"But she'll be blamed!"

He sat up and looked at her blankly. "I need her here, Helen. I mean, at least she'll be here in Boston. And I'll—I'll—" His shoulders slumped. "Well, you know I'll be there beside her, writing the checks to the lawyers and making sure that no one lays a hand on my wife."

Helen gave his plump hand a sad pat. "That's the spirit, Father."

"I'm so gullible when I'm in love," he grumped. Helen winced. So was she.

"Why did Mother decide that changing the world was worth all of this?"

He sniffed. His mustache drooped past his thick neck onto his velvet collar. "You haven't figured that out?"

"I'm mystified by her energy."

He gave a slight laugh, his chest rumbling. "She is a reformer. That's what she wants to be—to help people who can't help themselves. It can be a noble calling, and her heart's in the right place."

"But what of us?"

He looked down to her. "You don't feel compelled to distribute family limitation devices, do you?"

"Not in the least."

He took a refreshing breath. "Neither do I. It's her calling and her constitution. It doesn't have to be ours."

"And you love her for it? After she abandoned us?"

"Nonsense, Helen. She says I took you from her and alienated your affection so that you'd prefer me to her. But that is of course nonsense, and I dismiss it every time she brings it up. I love her. But I don't love her helping a person evade the law. I don't love that at all. But she is a fierce competitor and has a fine mind. Under all of that *Sturm und Drang* lies a soft heart, albeit one that tends toward taking in all the strays of the world. I have no need of a meek wife, and I hope I've not raised a meek daughter."

Helen rested her head on her father's sleeve. "But I hear the meek shall inherit the earth."

"I certainly hope not," he said with a sigh. "I had my money on you and your mother."

They sat together in silence, her head on his arm, each unwilling to part from the other, as they stared at the fire, waiting for the lawyer Choate to arrive. Orange and gold flickered in the shadows, their warmth reaching out to take the chill from the air and to rest troubled hearts. The scent of the leather and tobacco of the study, the tall cases crammed with familiar books, the soft sound of the fire—it felt like home again. It felt like old times: before her mother's arrest; before the coming of Wils Brandl; before Frank and Caroline and Riley; before her mother left for New York and she for college—when it was just Helen and her father working together in the study, and there was no trouble so big that they couldn't solve it together.

[CHAPTER TWENTY-TWO]

THE LAWYER, THE COOK, AND THE MECHANIC

MERRIMACK HILL

The glow of the vespers light through the rain could not sustain the even-tempered facade that Helen's father attempted to project to the world. He had been curt with Mr. Choate, Esq., whose news had not been kind. Charles Archer would not allow Mrs. Merriam Brooks to come home. Archer was in an ill temper himself, his son having been expelled just that morning from Harvard. Beat another student all you want, but do not cross Copeland, was the lesson Harvard administered. Charles Archer, whose consent was necessary for a bail agreement for Mrs. Brooks, was in the process of attempting to find a Red Cross post in the Mediterranean for his son and could not be bothered with the likes of Mrs. Merriam Brooks today, or any other official business.

Her father had made Patrick apoplectic when he yelled at the chauffeur for not having the car ready to take him to City Hall that morning. The ride had been canceled later due to Choate's advice that the presence of angry husbands would only reduce the likelihood that cooler heads would prevail in the delicate negotiations required to get Mrs. Brooks back to her house. Patrick, in a fit of Irish pique, developed a pain in his back of unknown origin and indeterminate duration. He retired to his quarters at midday and refused to leave.

Finally, Mr. Brooks thundered at the new cook, who had changed dinner menus at the last minute. The metal skewers of venison had a sesame sauce to which he was allergic, and he fumed that any Boston cook should know brown sauce, not sesame sauce, belonged on venison. Helen tried to mediate after her father took a cold leg of duck into the study. But the cook was a temperamental man whose food had, he insisted, brought life to the dead, made lame men walk, and the blind see. The cook would have none of it, and, his temper getting the best of him, refused to work again until his honor had been satisfied. He walked out the front door. He stood sulking under a side awning as the rain dripped overhead, a cigarette his only comfort.

Helen looked around the empty entry hall, its wide polished pine floors and ornate moldings. It felt antiseptic and cold from its thick Turkish carpets to its landscapes hung precisely just so. No dust collected in any of the corners, around the feet of the grand staircase, under the marble hall table, or even around the brass umbrella bucket. The cut glass around the front door was shined and even the padlock on the white painted oak doors of her mother's parlor gleamed with new brass.

There was no comfort here. She sighed and closed her eyes. She wished she could be in Cambridge with Wils, talking about anything. Well, almost anything. But Father had been on the telephone the entire day and there had been no chance to call him.

She looked around and then walked upstairs, deciding that the time had come for her to exchange her wool dress for a cotton nightgown. She would escape to her soft bed with a book about a queen of England or France or Italy—someone with more problems than she. She loosed the navy ribbon, letting her hair fall to her shoulders, and walked up the steps, defeated.

And so, with the cook angry, Mr. Brooks frustrated, Patrick with the vapors, and Helen retiring, it was perhaps not the most propitious of times for Mr. Wils Brandl to make his first call upon Merrimack Hill. He would not, at later times, think of it as his finest moment, and those present who remembered the day in later years would confirm his assessment.

The rumble of a car in the drive at that hour was not Helen's concern. A knock on the door came as she reached the top step. She looked down into the foyer. The cut glass around the large door obscured her view of the visitor. There being no servant about that her father had not angered, she sighed, turned back down the steps, walked to the door, and opened it.

Wils Brandl looked up at her from the top of her granite steps, under the cover of a dark umbrella. His spectacles were spattered with rain and his blond hair damp. Rain dripped all around him.

"My love," she said, stunned.

"I heard just today about your mother," he said quickly. "I went to your hall and they said you were gone. I called Peter at the crew club. He gave me directions to your house," he said. "I came in the rain."

"Peter gave you directions?" she asked.

"He knows," he said. "And approves," he said as she laughed in delight. He walked into the hallway and took one of her hands in his.

"*Mein Gott,* Helen, I can't leave without seeing you again. My lawyer's called. Two days from now I must sail."

"No!" she said defiantly. "I won't let you!"

A smile burst forth upon his lips. "My love commands me to stay?" He pulled her into his arms and kissed her, still in his wet raincoat. "Then I wasn't dreaming?" he said softly, as he felt her shiver under layers of white silk.

"Your wife?" she said.

Heavy steps came into the hall. "You there!" came a gruff voice.

"Father, it's—"

"Another young man from Harvard? How many are there, Helen?"

Wils stepped back. "I'm Wilhelm von Lützow Brandl."

"Helen, this is not the boy from the Harvest Festival."

"He was a mistake," she offered promptly.

Mr. Brooks glowered at Wils Brandl from the top of his blond hair to the laced brown leather shoes. "And how do we know Mr. Brandl is not a mistake?"

"I'm going to marry him."

"Treason!" he spluttered. He turned to Wils. "Sir, I regret that I must ask you to leave this very minute."

"Your daughter, sir, I have asked her to marry me." Helen's face brightened as he spoke, sending her father into paroxysms. "And I can't leave before I see her again."

"You're German?" he demanded.

"Yes sir."

"Then aren't you about to leave for war? What business have you to ask anyone to marry you?"

"Father, he said all of this to me, but I love him and I wish to marry him."

He turned to his daughter and pursed his lips. He took a deep breath and closed his eyes. When he opened his eyes after a moment he attempted a controlled tone.

"Mr. Brandl, this is a very difficult time for our family. So I don't care if you're Otto von Bismarck himself, you must leave this minute. I have a wife in jail and I'll have you know I would not be averse to joining her by taking desperate actions against suitors who do not know when to leave!"

"Father!"

Wils drew himself up and gave a quick nod. "I am sorry about your wife's problems. I would gladly render any service to your family for the sake of your daughter. That's one reason I drove here."

"You help me?" said Mr. Brooks with a sneer. "How could you possibly help me?"

"I have a lawyer, Robert Goodman."

"Goodman?"

Wils nodded. "That's a thought," her father replied in a softer tone. "I hear he may be more helpful than Choate, who is more a banking man."

The three stood there in silence for a moment, neither man turning to leave or backing down. After some time Wils said, "I apologize for the lateness of the call. May I call on Helen tomorrow?"

"You may call on her when Helen's mother is back in the house. But not tonight, son. There are too many things going on."

"Father, please let him stay," she begged, fear in her eyes as he turned to go. "He's leaving for the war."

"You love me, Helen," said Wils. "And that is enough for now." He looked up with a bow of his head at Mr. Brooks. "Sir, may I return tomorrow?"

"If her mother is at the house."

Wils bowed his head slightly to both of them, picked up his umbrella, and left.

"Wils!" she called, following him out the door past her father. She caught him at the bottom of the steps and encircled him with her arms. He embraced her, his slender girl who smelled of lilac. No father, no matter how angry, could reach inside him and pry this hope from him. Mr. Brooks rolled his eyes at them from the top step.

"Helen, come in from the rain," he called.

"Wils, come back and see me before you leave," she said.

He smiled broadly and spun her around. Then he put her down carefully on a step and held his umbrella aloft over the two of them. "Your father will—" he said, looking up to the towering figure of Mr. Brooks, silhouetted by the hall lights. "Talk to him tonight." He gave her the umbrella and ran to the front of his car to crank the engine. It gave a few coughs and started.

"Father!" she pleaded. "Please!" The engine started outside.

"Tomorrow," her father said. "Let us return to this in the harsh light of day."

Wils stepped up to the driver's seat. "Miss Brooks, you'll see me again at first light," he said. She stepped back from the car, the rain pouring around her, as he began to drive off. The taste of his lips was still on hers, the heat of their touch still warm.

She would take tomorrow, and whatever he could give her, she thought. She wished only for him.

"Come in, Helen," called her father as the car rumbled toward the front gate. But she stood watching Wils as if she were a sentinel.

The car suddenly stopped and its lights went dim in the distance. Helen squinted and saw Wils running back through the rain.

"Sir, two of my four tires have been punctured."

"What?" asked Mr. Brooks. "How?"

"I have no idea. Do you sprinkle nails in your driveway?"

"I do not. Was the steering off when you drove out here?"

"Not at all. My car is of the finest make. It drove well all the way here."

"Mr. Brandl, you drove in on two flat ties and didn't notice anything?"

"Mr. Brooks, the tires were of the finest caliber and in perfect order. May I use your telephone to call the mechanic?"

"The mechanic shops are closed," said Brooks. "We'll call Patrick."

"He's ill," said Helen, her eyes lighting up.

"There are spares in the barn."

"Patrick has the key," she countered.

Mr. Brooks frowned, shrugged, then finally seemed to give up. "I can't fight both City Hall and my own household. Come in, son. Have you had supper?"

"No, sir," he said.

"Ah, right. Well, I'll call the cook. He made a venison with a sesame sauce—a spice that feels like a pebble in your teeth and tastes like paper. If you can stomach it, it's all yours. Other than that, there's a bit of roast duck left from lunch." He reached his hand down to shake. "Jonathan Brooks, Helen's father. Pleased to meet you," he said begrudgingly.

Helen smiled at her father, who was attempting to rebuild a genial facade, act the role of host.

"Yes sir," Wils said, accepting her father's proffered hand. Her father stopped.

"There's to be none of this looking at Helen this evening, Mr. Brandl. I know that Harvard gave up compulsory prayer, but that does not mean we've abandoned our morals altogether at the Brooks house. Helen is retiring and will not be down the rest of the evening."

"Father—"

"Good night, Helen."

Wils looked up, his eyes smiling at her. He nodded. "Good night," he said quietly. He turned to Mr. Brooks. "You were saying, sir." And without another look at Helen, Mr. Brooks led Wils down the hall to the study.

As they turned to the library, she heard her father ask, "Would you say you were a Goethe German, or say more of the Nietzsche type?"

"Goethe, definitely Goethe."

"Bach?" asked Mr. Brooks, eyeing him closely.

"Beethoven too."

"Not that the German romantics didn't have their own problems," came her father's reply. "Well, that makes a deuce of a difference. So how is Robert Goodman these days?"

Helen heard the door close to the study. Euphoria ran from the tips of her toes to the far reaches of her fingers. She glided up the steps, spun around on the landing, and practically floated to the soft bed in her room.

He came to her!

While armies clashed in faraway lands, her mother was in jail, and her father railed at cruel fate, he had come! The world turned, too uncaring to stop for the love of one young girl, but he had stopped. He stopped for her.

This was what Jackson and Max had felt, she thought, holding a pillow tight to her breast.

She got up and danced over to the window to close her curtains for the night, thinking that love was color and music and all that was wonderful. As she looked out to the lawn she caught a glimpse of a figure walking in the rain. Of this she would never be certain.

It seemed, for a moment, to be the cook, and he was carrying what looked to be a skewer and a mallet in his hands. Implements that might puncture a young man's tire.

[CHAPTER TWENTY-THREE]

THE FIELDS OF LEXINGTON

Helen dressed quickly the next morning, pulling on a soft sweater and hooking the buttons along her dark skirt. She gathered up her hair with an ebony comb, put on her short calfskin boots, grabbed a shawl and went downstairs, eager to see Wils.

The foyer was quiet, the parlor locked. She stepped up to the front door and opened it. The rain had stopped and the sky was now clear and chilled. Wils' car remained at the drive near the gate.

She closed the door quietly and walked to the study to find him.

The morning newspaper lay on a table, illumined by a warm blaze from the brick fireplace. Its headline brought ill news of the war. Earlier in the month, the tide of the war had seemed to hang in the balance, the Germans now desperate in northern France. Two million men in France pushed them back from Paris, past the Marne and then to the Aisne. The numbers of dead were incomprehensible.

The reports were now of a reckoning in Antwerp, and a new call came from the British army for recruits. The Rheims cathedral had been shelled, Lille was under siege, but Louvain looked to fall. The muddied, flooded plains of Belgium had begun to pull hundreds of thousands of men toward it—British, Irish, French, Indian, German, Moroccan, Austrian—like the undertow of an ominous wave.

But that was not all. She looked with disgust at the picture on the front page. Standing in Scollay Square was the golden-tongued Charles Archer, rallying a crowd of angry men in hats and coats to send more supplies to Europe. The story said that if elected to Congress, Archer promised to crack down on German spies in Boston—working in hotels, driving taxis, teaching and studying at colleges. Army reports, the government said, were now to be written in code, and government censors would be ever more diligent about sifting through the mail. Archer said that an intelligence failure could lead to a disaster that would wipe out the male population of areas of town like Roxbury and Dorchester. He urged them to join the Patriots' League; to conserve sugar and wheat, which could be exported to troops overseas; to volunteer for the ambulance corps; and above all, as distasteful as it might be, to keep a close eye on anyone who might be sending information to the Kaiser. It was their duty now. And anyone who wasn't with them— the unions, the suffragists, anyone who put themselves above others— those people represented a danger to the fabric of society which could not be ignored.

Such ill tidings, she thought, shaking her head.

She turned the page and found the news: "Mrs. Merriam Brooks to be arraigned today, again." The picture showed Mrs. Merriam Brooks waving an actual contraceptive device above her head in protest. Archer was quoted as saying that he found her work repugnant and that he'd urge, if elected, that people like Merriam Brooks should be put in jail no matter what rank they held in society. The caption of the picture said that Brooks was now considered a flight risk and that she would be incarcerated until she stood trial.

Helen heard footsteps from the garden and looked up to see Wils walking outside beyond the study's windows, under the canopy of late-blooming wild roses. She put the paper down and ran out to him. He wore a dark sweater of Peter's and his wrinkled trousers from the night before, the hems damp with dew.

"You survived my father?" she asked. He nodded silently, his eyes intent on hers.

A telephone rang. They looked guiltily into the study.

"I asked him last night for your hand," he said.

The ringing stopped.

"What did he say?"

"He said you'd do what you want. Will you be my wife, Helen?" His eyes would not let her go.

"Yes," she said in a breath, taking his hands in hers. He smiled as she reached up to him on her tiptoes to give him a brief kiss. His hands still held hers when she asked what exactly her father seemed to think of her choice.

"Another kiss first," he said. She obliged.

"Yes, well, I think he was impressed by the title. And he seems to think that it doesn't matter what he says, but that you will take your own counsel. Oh, and he really liked the idea that our library has a whole section on naval warfare, and we have translators nearby at the university who will help him read through any book in a language he can't read."

She looked askance. "Were the books for him a fair trade or some type of consolation prize?"

Wils looked puzzled. "The latter, of course."

"Did he say that? I've wondered before if he'd trade me for a first edition of Burke or—"

"Take the victory, Helen—"

The telephone rang again in the hall and heavy footsteps pounded on the stairs. "My father—" she said, pushing away from him. She stepped back into the study, and partly hidden by its heavy oak door, saw her father standing in the main hallway at the foot of the steps.

His suit was his most serious charcoal gray, and his was face turned up toward the top step. "Helen, I'm leaving. Choate says the deal's back on. Patrick's driving me to City Hall to pick up your mother. I'll be back this afternoon and we'll fix Count von Lützow's tires. Make sure he gets something to eat, would you?" And without waiting for a response he rumbled out the front door, closing it behind him.

The house was still again, its silence heavy as she went out into the garden again.

"Father will return this evening."

"I'll be gone by then," he said, looking away. He was examining the roses on the trellis.

"Not if—"

He turned to her swiftly and she stopped, silent. She nodded as he offered her his arm, and they walked together, past the garden and into the wood. He didn't care where. Anywhere—it didn't really matter.

They followed a path deep into the property, beyond a grove of sugar maples that stretched out across an entire meadow. Their path was covered in the confetti of leaves and the ground was damp from the prior day's rain. The moisture wicked into their shoes and clung to the hem of Helen's dark skirt. In quiet conversation they passed the edge of the old stone wall with its piles of red and orange leaves gathering along its base, and went to a place where they could not be seen or heard by another mortal, or found by the world, until they wished to be.

The canopy above was filled with the bright leaves of aspens and birch trees waving gently and floating downward like ticker tape from a parade. Raindrops still clung to the silvery threads of spiderwebs stretched across crooks in trees, which glistened in the morning sun. She pulled her shawl tighter as they walked to an old bridge, under which rolled a stream, swollen with rain. Occasionally her foot would stumble and he would reach his arm around her, touching her, if only for an instant, to help set her right again.

He stopped in a grove of golden birch trees, tall and slender, their branches creaking in the soft wind, the bark slashed and peeling. One of their fellowship, fallen along the path many years ago, now provided a shelter and seat for myriad seedlings and other travelers in these woods, both great and small.

"Here," she said softly. "Here."

"Shh," he whispered, stopping her talk with a kiss.

The wool wrap fell to the ground as he stepped to her. She gave a nervous laugh, and, as she did, he pulled her closer, seeking to find her there—Helen the woman, leaving Helen the young girl behind. He wished to push back the barriers created by others—the faces she felt looking in at them through the skies and branches of an abandoned wood. It was only the two of them now, and he hoped to find her there too—just her.

His tongue parted her lips and touched hers—a flicker, a caress. A moist touch. The desire her mother preached against.

But she was no longer a child. She closed her eyes, and moved in her mind to the perimeter of the speckled wood, looking at herself from behind the gold leaves of an autumn tree. As he kissed her, she felt she belonged in the body of the woman she had watched, and that even God would discreetly leave them these few hours to themselves.

It was Wils' touch she desired—so rich and complex and deep. She no longer thought a child's thoughts of kisses, but an adult's. She reached her arms around his neck, her breast pressed to his chest.

He swung her into his arms and lifted her against the fallen tree. There he ran his hands through her hair and he kissed her temples, her chin; he pressed his lips against the white of her throat.

She brought her eyes to his, searching—for what, he did not know —then kissed him again. Her tongue flickered in his ear, her warm breath inflaming him. It was an unbearable sensation of desire and hope.

He stopped suddenly. "Your mother will kill us—"

She shook her head and he stopped talking. There was no hint of the young girl now. "I will not live without you in my world. I am your wife," she said, pushing her hair over her shoulder. He slid his hands under her sweater as she fumbled at the buttons of her skirt. His clothes and hers fell to the ground. He felt her shiver, as he laid her down, their bodies wrestling beneath a bower of golden leaves and white-barked trees.

Her body rose to him as he reveled in the soft flesh of her breast. He whispered her name, kissing her, as he shifted his weight onto her.

They clung to each other under a blue sky, on a bed of sweater and shawl, until they were spent, and the shadows of midday clouds fell upon them.

For the lovers there were no angels, no songs, no stars, no melodies. It was only the two of them, and the calm understanding that they were no longer alone. They had been transformed by something bigger than themselves, which had smothered their own hearts and claimed them for its own.

◈

HELEN AND WILS returned to the house slowly, lingering in the woods as the sun began to recede. Occasionally he would stop along the wooded path and raise her hand to his lips. She'd return his smile or press his hand.

The house was empty and they went straight to the kitchen, ravenously hungry. There was no cook but they found a pot of soup and a round of wheat bread. They sat at a thick wooden table, laughing and talking about anything and nothing at all.

It was near mid-afternoon when the telephone rang. Wils watched the flow of her skirts against her legs as she crossed the room to answer it.

A look of pain shot across her face.

"Helen," he said, standing up. Her lips trembled as she handed him the phone.

"Your lawyer. You are to come to the harbor right away." She smoothed a lock of his hair away from his forehead as he spoke to Mr. Goodman. He hung up the phone and pulled Helen to him.

"We've no car. You can't go," she protested.

He shook his head. "I gave my word. Jackson's family has struck a deal involving their cargo ships. All of the clearances have gone through. I don't know when the next one might be allowed out. It's part of the agreement for clearing my name with the local authorities."

"But you did nothing wrong."

"They'll let me leave and, well, dearest Helen, don't cry now."

He touched her face. A tear fell on his hand, and he put it to his lips and kissed it.

"The war will be over before I get there."

"That's a lie," she said.

"Pray it's not. And then I'll return and we will have a proper ceremony."

"I don't need one."

He smiled kindly. "My mother needs a ceremony, and I suspect so does yours. We'll have a gold carriage draw you to our chapel."

"A chapel?"

"Yes."

"You'll return?"

"All the king's men couldn't stop me."

They stood in silence, clinging to each other. Suddenly the clock tolled three.

"I know of a car we could use," she said in a mournful tone.

[CHAPTER TWENTY-FOUR]

BOSTON HARBOR

It was late in the afternoon when the Darlington Rolls-Royce purred out of the long drive from Merrimack Hill. Seamus, Colonel Darlington's driver, drove while Helen and Riley sat in the back talking to each other. For Helen, it felt like a ride in a tumbrel.

The woods of Lexington gave way much too quickly to the bricks of Boston, a city bustling about its business that late fall afternoon. Trucks, horse carts, and cars cluttered the roads. Ornate homes and soaring church spires became punctuated less frequently by the three-story lofts of the working class as they neared the town's center. A few blocks more and there were no more houses to be seen. They'd been replaced by the granite facades of banks, department stores, and government buildings. The city's clock tower cast its long shadows over the road below. Only occasionally did a smaller building spring up— the vestige of the Colonial era. The car drove by the Boston Common, where tourists gathered, and past the old burying yards and churches. As they neared the ocean, the air became wet and carried with it the smell of tanneries and of fish stored in large metal warehouses. The sun had been bright at the start of the journey, but now it had begun to fade into the west.

Helen and Wils made plans, talking of inanities such as what to do with his car (his lawyer's associates would come for it), and class room assignments (Goodman had also made arrangements there). The words they used came out paltry, useless, and false when compared to the emotions that engulfed them both. A touch, a word, a look could not possibly convey the despair that they felt.

THE SS *ELIZA* was a mid-sized cargo ship, up from Charleston. It was one of the two dozen owned by Jackson Vaughn's family. Dark gray and hulking, a smokestack rose from her middle, and from the lone mast at the front, four small flags flapped in the rising wind. Few port-holes punctuated its hulk. The cabin quarters above the deck seemed small from the pier, but would provide ample room for the three additional passengers journeying to London.

The Vaughn family had offered the ship to the British government on four conditions: safe passage across the Atlantic; authorization to sell a boat full of military stores to the British army; a position for Jackson in the new experimental aeroplane division; and authorization to return Wils Brandl to Germany. The paperwork had been drawn up immediately and the shipping lanes opened, as if by magic.

The wheels of the car rumbled onto the cobblestones of the Long Wharf as Seamus pulled into the harbor. Helen heard bells toll, but she could not tell which ship's departure they signaled.

The mood of the harbor in the setting light was rushed and noisy. Fishermen in thick sweaters steered their boats to dock and called out for the scales to weigh their daily catch of cod or flounder or mackerel. Grain elevator operators shouted over the din, hurrying their men to complete the day's work before dark. Burly stevedores in coveralls shouted orders to a crane operator unloading steel beams from a towering cargo ship. Port authorities in dark uniforms walked along the pier with clipboards, stopping to speak to captains or bursars about their paperwork, and there was a long line at the customshouse to be dispatched before the lights could be turned out. Passengers jostled through the gangways, laden with suitcases and boxes, searching for their ships. And workers on break sat at the edge of the pier, their legs dangling over the side. They ate hot slices of bread and drank from bottles. Occasionally one swatted at the seagull and pigeon beggars who came too close.

As Helen and Wils alighted from the car, Jackson ran over and began to talk of luggage and papers. Helen turned to see that Riley was at the dock with Morris, loading a steamer trunk into a crate. He waved convivially and she walked to him. Morris went to call for a sailor to help nail the crate's lid shut.

Suddenly she was there, alone with Riley.

He looked down at her. The wound around his eye was completely healed. "Glad you came, Helen. Wils would have been in a lot of trouble if we left without him."

"I want to wish you well," she offered.

He gave a slight laugh. "Will you congratulate me on my upcoming marriage?"

"What?" she asked, puzzled. "Marriage? To whom?"

"Edith."

"But—"

"But what?"

She was confused. "I didn't know you were engaged."

"And I thought—well, it turns out that thinking will do you no good. Sometimes our choices are made for us."

"But you don't love Edith. You said so."

"Helen," he said good-naturedly, "please don't put impediments before my fragile will. I have only belatedly found my honor, and even if belatedly, I would think that you of all people would applaud. Do you love him?" he asked, gesturing toward Wils.

"With all my heart."

She saw the muscles in his cheek tighten. "Why?"

"He knows who I am. And I'm better for it."

His face became an impenetrable mask, but for only a moment. "My cousin has been a prince to me, even though God knows I've never deserved him."

"You saved him from Archer."

"No. I avenged him. If I had saved him it would have been to my credit." He picked up her hand and kissed it. "Until we meet again?" he offered.

"Godspeed, Riley," she said with a nod of her head. He turned away.

"Riley," said Helen suddenly, "be careful. France is about to fall."

"Such lack of confidence!" he said. "I'll straighten them out." She laughed as he turned and walked up the gangplank into the ship.

The boat's bell sounded. "Hurry!" called Jackson to Wils, stopping to shake her hand. He bade her a swift good-bye and disappeared into the ship's cabin.

Wils was suddenly at her side.

"Now?" she asked.

He gave her a kiss on her forehead. "I can make it until Christmas, Helen. Can't you?"

She nodded mutely.

"Wils! We've got to leave!" called Jackson. Morris walked out, waving at the men. As he passed Helen and Wils on his way back to the dock, his eyes widened in surprise.

"You're with Helen?" he asked, incredulous. He shook his head as he walked away. "Women," they heard him mutter.

They both laughed. "I love you," he said. An errant curl tickled his nose. "Oh, and I have something for you." He released her and handed her an envelope. "Read it after I go." She gave a brave smile. Then he took one last look at her: her cheeks were ruddy, her eyes bright. But behind them he saw a look of bewilderment.

He understood. He kissed her once more, gently, then suddenly pulled away and walked to the ship. "Stay there," he urged.

Inside the cargo hold he found a cold, cavernous room, lined with steel beams and fitted with dozen of crates for shipment.

"Wils, there's something to eat in the main cabin," said Riley, who was making his way to the upper deck. But Wils rushed past him to the steep steps. He held on to the thick ropes alongside the staircase and ran to the upper deck railing. There he turned and searched, and burst into a smile, seeing that she was still there.

The sun was fading; the sky striated in purple and navy and pink. Workmen lowered the flag over the government's inspection office. The cloth flapped furiously in the wind as they wrestled with it. The motion of the pier—the travelers, the crates, the stevedores, the fishermen—began to slowly recede.

He stood silently on the deck looking out to where he'd left his heart. He could make her out to the very last. Her skirts blew around her legs, her hair in the wind. She held to the dock's railing as if it were an anchor.

Oh God, he thought. Don't let this happen. Not now. Let the war stop, he prayed with open eyes.

It was a slow motion that pulled him away. Little by little the distance grew, until he could no longer see her.

All that was beautiful was going. Like a garden that falls asleep before a very long winter.

IT WAS ONLY TIME, she thought as the ship left her view. She had lived for years without him. Waiting a bit more could be endured. She had no choice.

She closed her eyes. Someday—someday—they'd sit idly in the same room, only a few feet apart from each other, knowing that they had forever together. She'd look up from a book and see him writing notes in the margins of his own. He would read for a bit, then come over and kiss her, eventually resuming his reading beside her. They would go to the symphony, and sit together at dinners, and drive to Maine along the rocky coast, stopping for picnics or for kisses that were no longer hurried, and no longer stolen.

They would talk of all the things under the sky and still have ever more time. But for this they would have to wait.

Helen walked back along the pier, barely noticing those pushing by her, with suitcases and worried looks, arriving from a long journey, or eager to start again. She was numb. He was gone.

A young boy ran by and bumped her hand. The envelope fell to the ground. She quickly reached down and grabbed it.

"One moment," she called to Seamus, still at his employer's car.

She went into the waiting room of the inspection office and sat down in an old wooden chair under the dull light of an electric lamp. She opened the envelope and found a single piece of paper.

THE WATCH
by Wils
for Helen

Without so much as a "By your leave" you
Changed my perfectly calibrated watch
For one that stops when you leave a room and
Won't resume until your return. The watch
You could have kept, but you stole my breath too
And that I needed to say: "My heart was
In that watch. Keep it 'til the God of peace
Stills its motion at eternity's edge,
And a river spirits my soul away
To the source of your smile
And the place of God's laughter."

Across the river, through the Square, in the Yard, and up the stairs of Hollis Hall, Professors Kuno Francke and Charles Copeland were working well into the night. They had come together once again to review the next edition of the *Harvard Illustrated Magazine,* a student monthly, for grammar and good judgment, of which there was little to be found between the ears of these young sops.

Francke sat on the faded divan before a warm fire in his three-piece suit, shirt still buttoned at the collar. He drank Copeland's scotch and laughed occasionally with his friend. It was one of those rare moments in his schedule that afforded a respite from talk of war and defending his German heritage. Copeland was not one he need explain himself to. Such people were in rare supply these days.

For such friendship, he'd come to the squalid room each month to work. He understood why Copeland didn't move out of Hollis. The place brimmed with vigor. Yet the quarters had never been acceptable for a professor. The ceiling was too low, the bookshelves too few, the smoke stains on the ceiling from the oil lamps untenable. But his friend could not be pried from Harvard Yard with a crowbar.

Kuno, in his less generous moments, thought it was because his friend fancied himself the heir of Ralph Waldo Emerson, who had once occupied that room. Even so, Copeland could keep Emerson's books and not his plumbing, paint, or settee. Modernization could make life better. But such arguments fell on deaf ears.

Copeland sat comfortably in his chair at his desk. His tweed jacket and glasses fit him perfectly. The only things out of place were the ends of his mustache, which he twisted as he read through the pages.

"Balderdash! I'm not sure why we don't just give up on these students," he mourned. "I can't understand how any man could make such a fool of himself on one piece of paper."

"Who is the writer?" asked Francke, looking up.

"Peter Brooks. He writes only in the passive voice!"

"Strange," said Francke. "I have sometimes—on rare occasions—found young Brooks to be talented—almost gifted. Obviously not in this case, though. Did he get the facts right?"

"They seem to be in order," responded Copeland. "But you know, a broken clock—"

"Yes, yes, Charles. Right twice a day," Francke mumbled, returning to his proofreading.

Progress was slow. A number of freshman writers had joined, and little was satisfying. They saw the same mistakes year after year, Copeland thought with ill humor. "I'm too old for this!"

"How old are you, Charles?"

"Fifty-five."

"Bah! There have been several people as old as that."

Copeland's scowl at his colleague was interrupted by a knock at his door.

"What do you want?" he called in an angry tone.

"Message from President Lowell," came a high voice.

Copeland frowned, straightened up, and answered the door. A young boy handed him an envelope and left.

The professor picked up a silver knife on his desk and opened the letter.

"Brandl has left us, Kuno."

The German professor looked up and pursed his lips. "Prejudice begets all sorts of horrible things, many unintended and unforeseen."

Copeland sat back down in his chair and shook his head. "Wilhelm Brandl, Godspeed," he said quietly.

"I'll miss Wils," answered Francke. "Do you think he'll return?"

Copeland looked over and shook his head. "I don't know. I don't know if Harvard will change too much for him. Or how he will be changed by the war."

"You know, Charles, I got the impression you didn't even mind him being German."

"Humbug! He was a gifted young man," Copeland said, turning to his next page as he dipped his fountain pen in a well of red ink. "His last poem was a tolerable piece of work." He began to mark up the page proof, but then stopped and looked over at the German professor. "Kuno, in Hollis 15 there is no north or south, nor east or west. He will always be welcome at my door."

PART II: 1914

War

Flanders

When I tread the verge of Jordan,
Bid my anxious fears subside;
Death of deaths, and hell's destruction,
Land me safe on Canaan's side.

—WILLIAM WILLIAMS, 1745
Guide Me, O Thou Great Jehovah

[CHAPTER TWENTY-FIVE]

THE ROAD TO YPRES

December 14, 1914
NOON

The quick-falling snow held no beauty for the soldiers of the newly formed Second Wiltshire Regiment. It fell from a gray sky, stuck to their boots, and clung to their coats as they marched along the crowded supply road.

The snow had fallen since dawn. A thin crust barely covered the mud of the Belgian fields leading to the front. But there was enough snow to gum the wheels of trucks moving south stuffed with ammunition and food. Empty vehicles clattered back along the same narrow path, creating a magnificent traffic jam that stretched twenty miles back to the North Sea.

Soldiers trudged alongside the clogged roads. The mud in the ruts and ditches was cold liquid, mixed with snow and stirred by the marching of a thousand fresh men. The uneven terrain twisted ankles. And when they slipped they often cut themselves on road debris, or the sharp end of a spade. Riley had cut his ear three miles back when he fell, banging his head against a pallet of metal ammunition boxes that were being offloaded from a truck. The frigid air made it throb.

Lieutenant Rhyland Cabot Spencer marched south with his platoon. He was bespattered, cold, and quiet. A broken lorry had forced them to dismount and walk along the crowded road starting five miles back. Although an officer, he had chosen to do as his captain did, and carry the same burden as the enlisted men: sixty-one pounds of shovel, bayonet, compass, mess tin, canteen, maps, flashlight, rations, clothing, ammunition, pack, pistol, and rifle. He wished his captain had not been so egalitarian. The weight ground him even farther into the mud—in places it came up well over his knees. It was rare that the mud would reach a man's hat, he'd heard, but it wasn't out of the question. The soft ear covers from their cloth hats would just not suffice in these conditions.

The troops did not march with light hearts. They didn't sing and they didn't laugh. They stared in horror at the state of the men on the other side of the road, returning from duty in Ypres.

Spencer was one of the thousand men of the Duke of Edinburgh's Second Wiltshire Regiment, formed west of London. His father had obtained an officer's post for him near Salisbury. He traveled to Devizes and provisioned at the supply depot before encamping at Weymouth for basic officer training. He was a good shot, friendly with the men, and, as his father saw it, a natural for the PBI—the Poor Bloody Infantry.

The Second Wiltshires replaced soldiers in the army's Seventh Division. When the assignment had been made, it looked as if Riley would be training at Weymouth for the duration of the war. The Seventh—the Immortal Seventh—had no need for green recruits. They had assembled eighteen thousand professional soldiers from the corners of the British Empire.

But that changed in mid-October, when nearly ten thousand Immortals fell in fierce fighting before the weight of two full German armies. They'd been outnumbered in places ten to one and had nearly been encircled by the Kaiser's onslaught. That they had courage and skill was indisputable. They had also been better trained and stood their ground. But now half were wounded, missing, or dead. Green recruits could not make up for the experience found in the minds and hearts of the men who'd recently been blown to bits. But they'd have to make do.

When Riley decamped from Dunkirk that day, the sporadic battle lines ran from the North Sea coast of Belgium, south past the city of

Ypres, and into northern France. For the past two months the carnage had been breathtaking, even for the most battle-hardened. It was said that the bodies of men and animals around Ypres lay so thick that God's quartermaster used the city for spare parts.

No white covering of snow could paint this a new heaven and a new earth, thought Riley, so God might just save the white stuff and spare them the pain of wearing it as they walked.

The thousand Wiltshires knew where they were going. They walked to meet the five—maybe six—German armies not twenty miles away. Some said that it was possible they'd return. A few actually had. You just needed to keep your head and not have the bad luck to get shelled by a Black Maria or Fat Bertha.

And luck might very well favor them. The new captain of Riley's company was a lucky man indeed. Twenty-five-year-old Aubrey Tomkins was from the old Seventh, and his careful manner inspired confidence. He had been in the army, it was said, since he was sixteen, and his knowledge and skill were unquestioned. You wouldn't find him putting on airs. Despite the fact that he was walking in a full pack, his tunic, tie, and breeches showed him as the officer he was. His short blond hair defied military orders to stay down. The enlisted men said Saint George himself had guided the captain's shots in the last battle. That he had the vision of a prophet. And that his natural father was most certainly Irish, as his luck was uncommonly good. Well, good for one with the misfortune to have been at Ypres.

The captain had introduced himself to his four lieutenants upon their arrival at Dunkirk, and had set them on a course for the front lines, their company at the front of the new regiment. Tomkins marched alongside the column, keeping an eye on them. Occasionally an orderly would rush to him and he'd call the line to a halt. During these respites Riley would turn to his sergeant and discuss the latest issue of *Punch* magazine or the most recent Christmas package of tobacco and chocolate from Princess Mary to the troops. They'd talk about anything but the mud, which they were all to ignore. Every man had to step in it and complaining would only make things worse. Tomkins would call out to a few men and give them orders. These soldiers would leave to pursue their mission, and the rest would resume their march under the gray sky in the falling snow.

"Step aside!" called Captain Tomkins for a sixth time.

"Aside!" echoed Riley. Four platoons moved back, almost all in good formation. The men made way for an ambulance to push around a rations lorry. Riley looked at the back of the truck as it rattled past. It was packed full of men, on a day the battle lines were quiet. They fell back into place and marched again.

Riley surveyed the wet fields. An old farm, he thought—a crop of death for now. A hundred years at least had passed since the world had given a care about the towns surrounding Ypres. He certainly hadn't. It had existed for centuries without his help, and he'd prefer it go back to that state.

He'd been told a medieval cathedral stood in the city's center, a monument to the cloth trade in the times of King Canute or Charlemagne or some such. When the cloth markets moved, the city slipped into obscurity. He supposed children had played around the town's crumbling walls. Their fathers and uncles farmed in the surrounding villages of Wytschaete, Hollobeke, and Gheluvelt. They made tiles at Zillebeke and bricks at Zonnebeke. They poached in the king's woods near Passcheaendale and Ploegsteert.

Their lives, like his, had been upended by that Prussian lunatic, the Kaiser. That man, without a doubt, was even more annoying than Edith at her worst. At least Edith had only caused him heartache. But the Germans! They had marched half their army into France, half into Russia, and the third half—for it was very large—somewhere around the world, blowing up ships and oil tanks and causing all sorts of misery.

In September, the French, Belgian, and British Empire forces gained in France, pushing the Germans back past the Marne River and the Aisne. The Germans could no longer move west, so they raced north. Behind the French and British armies were the supply ports along the North Sea. If the supplies were gone, the British and French armies would soon be too. That seemed to be the German thought on the matter.

The British and French forces, for their part, thought they were pushing the final remnant of the German army back to the fatherland the Hun thought so highly of. In this they were mistaken, and their miscalculation gave way to terrible bloodshed.

The Kaiser had thrust six German armies into the western battle-front, pressing on the Belgians in the north, the British in Belgium's center, and the French and British forces to the south. The Germans had superior munitions, better supply lines, and tens of thousands of fresh troops.

The British commander-in-chief had been in France at the time. He hurried north to Belgium with his main corps, pulling his tired armies north toward Ypres, fighting bitterly at La Bassée, Neuve Chapelle, and Armentières. He'd had no idea how hopelessly outnumbered his troops were. Their intelligence had been poor, and they had few artillery shells to use.

But they didn't know the odds, and that made much of the difference as the battle line seesawed back and forth during late October and into November. They should have despaired, but, ignorant of their condition, they did not let their hearts fail.

In the north, a few ragged divisions of the Belgian army bitterly engaged twelve fresh German divisions—more than two hundred thousand men. No matter their courage, they could not hold against such a force. The Belgians began to falter, and, sensing a breakthrough, the Germans pushed harder. Within two days the Kaiser's armies had advanced over the choppy terrain of dikes and canals to capture outposts near the Yser River, almost to the British supply port of Dunkirk.

Dispatches Riley had read back at Weymouth showed that the Belgian king's army was nearly surrounded. The king's men threw themselves again and again at the Germans, but despite inflicting frightening casualties on their enemy—more than one hundred thousand—the Kaiser's men came back in overwhelming numbers. The Belgian army was about to be lost, along with the ports of Dunkirk, Calais, and Boulougne.

Then, on October 24, Albert, king of the Belgians, turned the North Sea's salt water against his own country. He ordered the Yser River's floodgates opened and bombed dikes to flood the fields and canals, forming an impassable lake in front of the German army. His country was now Carthage—its fields sown with salt water, rendering them unusable. But he'd saved sixty thousand lives and every man, woman, and child in England heard of the feat. Riley heard the story read to him from the front page of the *London Times* twice the same day while at training camp, once at breakfast and another time at supper. It was a message of cheer to buck up heavy hearts.

The Germans, thwarted, had sent their remaining seventy-five thousand men south to fight the British along the center and southern battlefronts. Their casualties had been horrific, but their fury not spent.

And the news for Riley had been exceedingly grim. Nearly one thousand Wiltshires had been slaughtered in heavy fighting northeast of Ypres, triggering the Second Wiltshire's call into duty.

Riley had heard the tale with a heavy heart. Britain's Seventh Division was at Ypres, sandwiched between the battles raging north at the Yser River and south at La Bassée. The orderly carrying their field plans had been captured and their positions were known. Even worse, at the last minute British ground intelligence rushed back with news: the Germans had been reinforced with three full army divisions. Actually, they'd found out later, there had been five.

The fighting began in earnest in mid-October on the Passchendaele Ridge, where the British weathered a fierce German artillery barrage. But the British were more experienced than their German counterparts and despite being outnumbered, held their ground for nearly a week.

The cost of the stalemate was tremendous. The Germans killed the Wiltshires stationed due east of Ypres in a wood. Suddenly finding a clear path to Ypres, the Kaiser's men moved on the city. But the British rallied by calling into action every able man they could find: officers, the wounded, typists, cooks, engineers, secretaries, groomsmen, orderlies. The meager band beat back the German soldiers with anything they had—rifles, pistols, knives, fists, clubs, rifle butts, even a cooking ladle, Riley had heard. The Germans were pushed back in bloody hand-to-hand combat until bodies lay stacked on each other, the unburied choking the paths such that even the message runners could barely pass.

Five days later, six German divisions burst forward in a new offensive at Gheluvelt, a village southeast of Ypres. The British knew the attack was coming but were unable to stop it. The Germans had artillery, munitions, and men, and British supplies of all three were low. The spike-helmeted soldiers raked them with gunfire at close range. In one sector the Germans wiped out a thousand Royal Welsh Fusiliers, and then sent a battalion to capture a château nearby.

Having secured the plateau and the Gheluvelt château, twelve hundred Germans now had a clear path to take Ypres and the ports. But they stopped and waited for orders, during which time they took to looting the mansion and eating a full meal, savoring the hard-won victory within their grasp.

Riley's captain, Aubrey Tomkins, was one of the five hundred British soldiers who stormed back through the woods and across an open plain, all while under constant fire. Two hundred fifty made it to the château and opened fire on the twelve hundred. The Germans panicked and fled, and the British, once again, closed the road to Ypres. Tomkins was promoted to captain and given command of two hundred fifty soldiers of the Second Wiltshire Battalion, the Twenty-first Brigade, Seventh Division. His command included four platoons of fifty each and four subalterns, one being Lieutenant Riley Spencer. Their orders were to reconnect with the old Seventh, then commence south to La Boutellerie, a few miles south of Ypres, in France.

The battle continued for another two weeks. At Wytschaete on the Messines Ridge, the Germans rebounded. Scottish reserve troops, armed with outmoded rifles, were heavily shelled and finally withdrew, their retreat obscured by the smoke of burning buildings and haystacks.

On the morning of November 11, a thick fog rolled over the land. The German force to the north was on the move, shelling everything in front of them. It was said that entire trenches of British soldiers were blown up by the German shells, burying men alive. It created both a grave for the soldiers and a footpath for the German army. The British fought back that day to a stalemate, firing into the dreary fog.

When the sky cleared, the British found a graveyard in front of them. The shadows before them were actually corpses. They had killed every German, breaking their enemy's spirit, at least for the day.

The Germans pushed no farther and the British scrambled for reinforcements. The Seventh had lost nine thousand five hundred men—more than two entire brigades. Exhausted, both sides began digging in at points along the emerging Western Front, knowing they would once again have to face each other.

Britain held, but at a great price. The Kaiser had killed their leaders: the junior officers and sergeants who had constituted the best-trained army in the world. Their muddy boots were filled by lawyers and bankers, students and bus drivers. Riley had been hustled from his training camp into duty within a mere four weeks. Unfortunately, so had most of the soldiers who wore the simple emblem of the Seventh on their sleeve: a white dot on a black field.

And the jewel that had been Ypres—a medieval city where garments were once woven in gold and silver—was now a gutted shell. Cloth Hall lay in ruins, he heard, its slippery floor now used as a makeshift hospital. It had caught fire during the battle. Stained-glass fragments coated in smoke dangled outside of their window cases, hanging from ligaments of tattered lead caning. The lights—reds, yellows, blues—no longer shone in the windows. Instead it was the moans of the dying that wafted through, floating upward and dissolving in the noxious night air. You could hear them, it was said, in between the shelling.

It was now almost winter solstice. Riley was thankful the days were not long—less time to see the damage done to the men and the terrain.

The snow was not beautiful to him, no matter what the poets said. Beauty was a pile of sandbags already in place. It was food that didn't require you to take a bottle of bismuth soda pills with it. Water that didn't smell like sewage. It was a drink of spirits to still the pain in his shoulders and back.

He gave a slight smile as a loud convoy truck filled with artillery shells rumbled by. Beauty had once been a girl's bosom rising under a lace blouse. The smell of her hair. But that was a world far away.

Riley saw a mud-spattered orderly jog up to Captain Tomkins with a message. The captain's face gave nothing away as he read the order and snapped it back into his pouch.

"Spencer, Norton, Cotting!" Tomkins called. Riley shifted his rifle over his shoulder and beat to the captain. Sydney Norton, a beefy, ginger-haired lieutenant huffed over from his platoon, his breath visible in the cold. Private Cotting, the smallest of the three, fell in beside him.

Tomkins' posture was parade-ground perfect, his feet shoulder width apart. They saluted him.

"Lieutenants Norton and Spencer, it's time to earn your lieutenant's badge. We've spotted a party of Boche setting up a signal trench. Only four men right now, but if we let it linger, there will be a hundred come tomorrow. I need it dismantled posthaste and I want their transmitter. You'll capture it and meet up with the rest of the battalion three miles due east of this road for the night's billets. There's a barn up this road tended by a Belgian farmer."

Riley brightened. Not an open field covered by machine guns. This was progress.

"Spencer, what day were you commissioned?"

"October tenth, sir."

"Norton?"

"October fourteenth, sir."

"Then Spencer, you're the ranking officer."

"Yes sir!" said Riley, brightening.

"But sir!" protested Norton. "He's part German."

Riley looked sharply at Norton. He'd not liked him in training camp and he didn't like him any more now.

"So is the king," said Tomkins. "Cotting, I'll ask—"

"Spencer nearly shot a man at rifle practice, sir," interrupted Norton. Riley saw young Cotting blanch. Tompkins glared at Norton, then turned to him.

"Spencer, is this true? Have you shot one of your own men?"

"Not since training camp, sir," said Riley, frosted at Norton's protest.

"Do you plan to shoot any more of the king's subjects?"

"Just Norton, sir."

Tomkins frowned. "I'd urge you not to. I'm told he's the best shot in the company." The captain turned to Norton. "Spencer will command this mission. He is both an officer and a son of a Member of Parliament and I do not doubt his patriotism. Do you understand?"

"Yes sir!" said Norton, his face reddening to the color of his hair. Riley glanced sideways at him, thinking what a joy it would be to order Norton to step lively through the mud.

"Private Cotting, your age," demanded the captain.

"Eighteen, sir," said the slight boy, his voice nearly cracking to soprano. His face was white and thin; his rifle might weigh as much as he.

"I'm your captain, not the recruiting office. Your age."

The boy puffed his chest and held his head high. "Fourteen, sir."

The captain's lips tightened. He leaned down, his hands on his knees. As Riley stared ahead, he heard the captain's voice soften. "Paul, this is not a test of your courage. I know you have the heart of an Englishman and not one of my men would say different. But this is a test of your head and I expect you to keep yours. I'm counting on it because I've good use for a smart lad like you."

Cotting brightened. "Yes sir!" Tomkins stepped back.

"I'd send out a party of seven if I had the men, but we don't. So it's to be the three of you." He turned to face the south and pointed to the horizon. "The orderly who brought us this information has run the mud between here and there. It's molasses. You'll slip, you'll get dirtied. But as hard as it is, you mustn't dawdle. If their snipers are out you'll be sitting ducks until you reach the wood. I want you to hand your packs, shovels, canteens, coats, everything except your ammunition, grenades, and rifles to the quartermaster. You need to be light on your feet and running should keep you warm."

Tomkins waved his hand and the quartermaster, all grizzled in khaki, with his gut bulging over his belt, huffed over to take the packs.

As Riley took off his coat a fresh blast of wind took his breath away. He quickly unbuckled his heavy tool belt and handed it over. From his pocket he pulled out a flask.

"Permission for a bracing drink, sir?" he asked.

"Dear Lord, yes," said Tomkins. Riley took a pull of scotch and offered the flask to Norton.

"I drink beer," said Norton. Cotting, looking up at Norton, refused. Riley shrugged, replaced the cap, and handed it to the quartermaster half-full. He brushed some falling snowflakes from his eyelashes, feeling inexplicably chastened. Beer, nothing. He probably preferred grog.

"One more thing, men," said Tomkins. "There was a fight in that wood a couple months ago and you won't like what you find there. But the dead can only hurt you if you decide to let them into your mind." He looked back at Spencer. "March directly into the trees and when you get to a stream follow it east to a clearing. There you will find your Germans. If you hurry you should come out all right."

"Sir?" asked Riley.

"Speak."

"Do we take prisoners?"

"Prisoners or casualties, either one," said Tompkins matter-of-factly. "We don't want them back in the German army. If you can, get the signal corps member alive. He might know German intelligence codes. But don't stop for burial. If you do, you could join them. Others will come looking for them. Are we clear?"

"Yes sir," the three said.

"And when you fight, Cotting, you will fight hammer-and-tongs."

"Yes sir," said the boy.

"Lieutenants, your men are watching you. They want to have confidence in their lieutenants and this is your chance to show them why they should. I am counting on you to come back and inspire them with tales of bravery, but not of heroics. Am I clear?"

"Yes sir," they said. Riley wished he could get moving. He was cold.

"Then to king and country."

"King and country!" replied the men.

"Dismissed." Tomkins jogged back up the wet ditch to the front of the line. Riley turned to Norton and nodded as the north wind began to pick up again. Norton pretended not to notice.

"Due south," Norton pointed, and then began to march.

"South," echoed Riley, who had to pick up a bright pace to catch up with his subordinates as they headed toward the blackened wood.

CHAPTER TWENTY-SIX

THE MENIN ROAD

December 14, 1914

SEVEN HOURS EARLIER

L ieutenant Wils Brandl sat in the dank shambles of his crowded billet in a corner of Belgium he cared never to see again. He used a makeshift stool, wrote by candlelight, and shivered in his soaked boots, field gray short coat, mud-spattered trousers, and wet wool overcoat. Water pooled at his feet and dripped through the slats above him. The wind gusted through the cracks of the old barn's plastered walls. He needed rest, but he had just finished three days of signal duty in the trenches and refused to sleep until he'd written to Helen.

His breath came in steady puffs, visible in the candlelight. His cracked, sore hands were still caked in clay, although he'd washed them twice. They stuck to the thin pages as he wrote, forcing him to rewrite constantly. But he hurried along with his letter: he was exhausted and a dawn raid was always a risk. A Victoria Cross by breakfast, the khaki soldiers were fond of saying. The only thing that seemed to stop them was the fact that British shell manufacturers were a fat and poor lot, something for which the German army often gave fervent thanks. Their list of blessings typically stopped there.

Second Army, VII Corps
13th Division, 25th Brigade
16th Uhlans

Dearest Helen,

I have just left three days of duty, and am writing before I fall to sleep. Writing you is the only joy out here, and I'll not delay it further.

There isn't much more to tell about the war. We've no cover from the cold or wet. Water fills the ruts we've dug & we're forced to crouch along the edges of the trenches on sandbags or in the cold mud. If you stand up straight you're likely to get your head blown off or cause someone else to get theirs hit. We fix our wires, listen, & wait until we're allowed to leave.

I call to you in whispers from the fields. I reach out again & again grasping for anything that will bring me close to you. I listen in the lunatic winds and in the aftermath of shells. I must believe that you listen for me too.

There is little else to listen for. The music of symphonies, cathedrals, drawing rooms, your voice, is all fading. I now listen for the difference between a shell (sounds like a freight train and if you hear one you had better run in a different direction) & a rifle bullet (if you hear it, it's already hit someone, so no need to move). My skills at shooting are seldom used, but when I do shoot, I hit. I hate that it's so, but if I didn't, I'd not be writing you now.

The news this week is that the regiment has been assigned a Roman Catholic priest—the one who swam in the mud! Our Lutheran pastor died in the mêlée that killed Lieutenant Heinsel, although heaven knows it wasn't because they were at the front of the line. The British had just lobbed a random shell behind our lines.

I like the new fellow although he is the pope's man. I

have written to assure my mother that I won't take to
worshiping the pope unless the pope calls off the war.
In fact, I've decided I will worship just about anyone or
anything who can accomplish this.

This priest seems to be able to shoot better than any of
us (if pressed), crawls along the trench lines to
minister to those who fall, & gives mercifully short
sermons. He is quick to grant absolution both in town
& in the trench, except in cases of severe drunkenness,
where the chastisement tends to be more about
sharing than abstention. Father Rupert is his name & I
hope he will be around for a while, though there has
been some grumbling from the Lutherans—

Wils was interrupted by a splash outside. Three men in the crowded
room looked up at the open doorway. He glanced quickly through the
cracks in the wall's plaster out into the half-light. Nothing else.

It is lighting, and I must go. Dawn is a dangerous time
out here, even for those who are off-duty.

> All my love,
> Wils

He picked the letter up and kissed it, saying a silent prayer that it
would reach her. Last week's mail orderly had been shelled along with
his mail pouch, destroying their letters. Wils put it in his pocket to drop
in the mail basket after he awoke.

His hands shook with fatigue as he reached for the candle to blow
it out. His back hurt, as did his shoulders. He would sleep first, clean up,
and then he'd write his mother. He needed a new set of boots. The soles
had started to rot off this pair after only two days trench duty and he'd
be damned if he'd be invalided for failure to take care of his feet.

Straw was scattered along the floor of the barn, soaking up the
mud. Several soldiers had left for duty and a space beckoned. He put

down a blanket, anxious to close his eyes, which were scratchy and burning with fatigue.

"Brandl!" He heard the bark of Captain Grimber. "New posting for you today."

Wils turned with a blank expression. His head was in a fog. The gaunt captain, his face unshaven, towered in the doorway. "Sir, I just returned."

"We've no more men who can help at present. A truck is ready to take you to a wood due northwest by five miles. There you will establish radio contact in a new position. If we wait there's a risk that the British will find it."

"Sir, I've just come back from three days' duty."

"We've no other men available. The truck leaves in five minutes," said Grimber.

"Sir, twenty minutes. Please," Wils pleaded.

"Sorry, Brandl. Five."

He'd sleep on the truck, Wils thought. Perhaps it would get stuck in the mud, and he could catch up on his rest.

As the captain turned to go, an orderly ran up to the door, a servant of Major Beumel assigned to the Second Army. He was broad-shouldered and clean, a member of Saxony's aristocracy. But so was everyone else, thought Wils. They handed out titles to every child they'd produced.

"Lieutenant Brandl!" he barked.

Wils saw Captain Grimber stop suddenly. The men around him did not waken. "What is the meaning of this?" the captain asked.

"Major Beumel would like the lieutenant to re-string the telegraph wire at the front. A row of sandbags fell backwards, breaking the lines we just established. The major says it's urgent."

Grimber frowned, the muscle in his cheek twitching. "I need him to go north."

"The major needs him for trench duty."

"What would the major, then, recommend regarding the wires at Ypres?"

The orderly looked haughtily at Grimber. "Someone else. Possibly yourself," he said with the arrogance of one assuming the manners of his own superior officer.

Grimber crossed his arms in front of himself, the gray tunic drawn across his wiry frame. "You can't have Brandl. He's had no sleep." Wils felt he might smile, but that would have required energy. Only a few seconds ago Grimber cared nothing for his fatigue.

"Brandl," said Grimber, "back to the front lines. I'll wake Schmitt and put him on the truck. He can barely tie his own shoes, let alone string the wire." A shadow passed across his face. "When you return we're marching to Fromelles, just south of here. You'll need to be ready to leave."

"Fromelles? To fight the Indian regiments?" asked Wils, his stomach giving a lurch. Colonials were often overeager to prove they were better than their British overlords.

"No. The Indians moved farther south. We'll face more British. Seems the French told the British to punch through just south of Ypres."

And with that, Grimber turned on his heel. Wils wearily shuffled out into the cold, wet gray of dawn. The rain was turning to snow as the temperature fell. His head throbbed in pain.

As they marched toward the first set of trenches, Wils saw a mail basket and dropped his letter to Helen in it.

"Will the mail run today?" asked Wils.

"No. A shell got the last boy and buried him along with three sacks of mail. Headquarters should send another mail transport next week."

"You didn't dig out the letters?"

The boy shrugged as they moved past men unloading a massive flat of shells. "You wouldn't wish to touch those parcels even if they were from the King of England calling off the war."

[CHAPTER TWENTY-SEVEN]

NEAR YPRES

December 14, 1914

1:00 P.M.

R iley Spencer, Sydney Norton, and Paul Cotting slogged through the muddy plain as the noise of the convoy receded. In the distance, crows perched on islands of snow and picked through the waterlogged fields. Riley was hot. German blood, indeed. He knew who the bad apple was. It was Sydney Norton, the Philistine whose mail was so filled with complaints the censors sent it back to him.

Nothing was ever good enough for Norton, and it hadn't been since they'd first laid eyes on each other at training camp. Norton complained constantly about the dirt and the generals and even about the boxes Princess Mary had sent for the soldiers' Christmas. He didn't work half as hard as the other men at digging. He whined about his feet getting wet and his hat being made of cloth—the same conditions they all lived with. His older brother had been killed at the Marne and you'd have thought that he was the only casualty of the entire war. In fact he'd complained, and complained, and complained some more about bleak privation until no one in the regiment liked him. The only thing you could trust about Sydney was that he'd be first in line for free cigarettes.

Well, thought Riley, that wasn't exactly fair. You could trust his aim. It was flawless. The fact that this hulking, lazy jackass could be so gifted was a sign that the gods had truly abandoned their senses.

"How are you doing, Paul?" asked Riley. The boy's cheeks were pink with exertion.

"Just fine, sir."

"Where are you from?"

"Salisbury, sir."

Riley smiled. "I once knew a girl in Salisbury."

"Really?"

"Sally Gimble. Do you know her?"

"Can't say as I do."

"Do you have a girl back in Salisbury?" asked Riley.

He shook his head. "Just my mum, and six sisters."

"Six sisters! Well, when the war is over I expect you to invite me over so that I can tell them about your bravery."

"There it is," whispered Norton suddenly, pointing to the woods, rising from the field a quarter mile ahead. It was the first thing he'd said since they'd begun walking. Riley looked at him harshly. Such a know-it-all prig. He'd like the opportunity to cuff that man.

But that lesson would have to wait. Riley frowned as they drew closer. It looked like no wood he'd known. The firs and pines had been snapped like cornstalks, their splintered trunks broken. Leafless dark branches reached for the sky like the dry bones of hands, stopping well short of heaven. Other trees lay on their sides, uprooted from shelling. The cross section of one of the trunks was taller than Cotting. The craters left were filled with chalky water, some with thin crusts of ice forming at the sides or floating in the middle. Large piles of blue clay offset the deep scars. On the ground were the forms of the dead, both men and animals, bloated and dark. Shrapnel littered the ground around them. And it smelled like sulphur, spoiled eggs, and much worse.

Cotting's eyes widened. "No," he began muttering, walking backward.

"Stop it, Cotting," said Norton. A branch fell and splashed into a puddle. They looked up and froze.

"Sydney's right," whispered Riley. "You'll be fine."

Cotting shuddered and didn't speak. The look he gave Riley, along with the sick smell of wet decay, made Riley want to retch too.

It was only Norton's presence that bolstered his stomach.

"Mr. Norton, would you please come here," Riley called over to him. Norton stepped a few paces closer.

"We don't have typhus," said Riley. Norton's eyes narrowed. "There may be snipers, so we'll move quickly using the trees as our cover. When we spot the soldiers, I say we hold fire until we know how many there are and then set up our positions."

"Bayonets?" asked Cotting.

"Not until we need them." The bayonets added a good pound of weight and foot of length to the end of the rifle.

Norton wore a bemused expression.

"Yes?" asked Riley testily.

"Safety gear on, sir?" asked Norton. Cotting gave a nervous laugh.

Riley's eyes narrowed. He knew how to deal with this man's arrogance.

"Norton," said Riley, "I've learned all about the safety latches on the Enfield rifle."

"Glad to hear it, sir," he said with a smirk.

"Your mother taught me whilst I shaved her back," he said with cold contempt.

Paul Cotting's eyes widened. Norton's face flushed bright red with anger. "You will regret that," Norton muttered.

Riley moved closer to Norton's face and squinted. "I swear on your dead brother's unburied corpse that if you so much as look at me the wrong way from now on I will report you. You may be the best shot in the regiment, but there is not one man here who calls you 'friend' and a lack of friends, you will find, can make for a very nasty turn of events on a field of battle. Do you have anything else to say, Mr. Norton, to your ranking officer?"

Norton looked ahead and said nothing.

"If I ever hear about the rifle incident again you will be sorry."

Riley saw Norton's fists clench, but the pathetic man kept silent. Spencer ignored his look and walked confidently in front of him, taking care not to slip in the mud. That would look terrifically poor given what had just transpired.

Riley turned into the broken wood. They followed carefully, crouching behind stumps and moving silently from tree to tree, looking to the left and right, listening for the sound of the German party.

Norton's sharp eyes saw the stream first. "There," he whispered. The creek had overflowed its banks, mixing the mud even deeper. They now moved as softly as possible, wading in mud up to their knees. Their rifles they held up out of the bog.

After an hour of picking their way down the swollen stream, Riley heard a German voice. Out in the clearing he could make out the enemy soldiers working—digging, talking, smoking. But it wasn't four men. It was fifteen. Riley motioned Cotting and Norton closer.

"Time for bayonets on and safety latches off," instructed Riley. "I'm going in. I can understand them, which is, Norton, of some use to the king today." Riley adjusted his gear and picked his way carefully through the trees. A soldier was barking out orders about digging—the same Riley had heard in his own training camp. A young man with short black hair was busy testing a transmitter. Two guards, not much older than Cotting it would seem, were carelessly smoking their cigarettes, their guns resting beside them on the ground. The other soldiers were digging hurriedly, their rifles behind them with their lieutenant, who also busied himself with a shovel.

Those men thought they were alone in a still wood. No one stood watch. It was all quite lucky for him personally but a shocking display of disrespect to the king of England's troops. This ignorance was what mandatory conscription got you, he thought disgustedly. Riley crept back to Norton and Cotting.

He placed Norton on the left, behind a tree from which he could shoot three of them easily. He (Riley) and Cotting would take the middle and right sides of their thin line.

"When you hear me start shooting, then you fire off as many shots as possible. If we fire from three different angles we'll make it look like we're a much bigger force than we are. Norton, you take out the man holding the transmitter. Paul, there's only one man with his hand on a pistol and you're to shoot him if Norton misses. The others have rifles at rest. If they get a chance to pick them up, then we'll be outnumbered."

"What happens then?" asked Cotting anxiously.

"We keep shooting," said Norton matter-of-factly. "We either kill them or they run away. There are no other options."

"All right, then." The young man had turned green, but nodded dutifully and moved into his position behind the scarred trunk of a large tree.

The daylight was fading as Riley looked over at Norton, poised ready to shoot. Riley hoisted his rifle to his shoulder and put his cold, wet finger in the trigger. He looked down the barrel at the strip of men digging and talking. These men would as sure kill him as blink. He stepped back, only to land in a hole. His ankle wrenched as he fell. His finger, tangled in the trigger, shot off the gun.

Riley heard the Germans yell as he leapt back up, his ankle burning in pain. He turned to see Norton firing with an icy coolness, men falling before his deadly accuracy. Cotting, it seemed, was either firing into the dusky sky or the mud. The Germans picked up their rifles, returning the compliment.

Riley aimed carefully, winging one firing in Cotting's direction. Norton's rifle barked, and another man went down. Suddenly a cry rose from the trench and the line gave way. The Germans began running back, including one with the transmitter. Riley stepped out and began to run after them, his ankle burning. Before he could take a third step the soldier with the transmitter slumped down, killed by Norton. In less than two minutes, it was over.

Riley hobbled over beyond the shallow trench. Littering the ground were shovels and kits, the rifles of the dead. The signal corps member lay dead beside his radio. He looked so young and fair, thought Riley, as Cotting picked up the small box. In the dusky gloom he saw Norton running to each of the German dead, bending over them, obviously proud of his quick and deadly work. And he should be. He'd killed five.

"Let's get back to camp, men. Good job, Norton. Sorry about the slip."

The muscles in Norton's jaws tensed and his eyes shouted reproach.

"Mr. Norton, you have something you wish to say?"

He remained silent.

"I said I was sorry about my slip," said Riley.

"Ten escaped. We could have captured them if you'd not given us away."

Riley's shoulders sagged. "Our objective was to get the transmitter."

"You cost me a Victoria Cross," snapped Norton.

"What?" asked Riley incredulously, as blood rose to his cheeks. "What army would give you a VC for merely doing your job? You picked them off because you were hidden and provisioned and they were sitting ducks. No one gets the Victoria Cross for that. Really, Norton, the several weeks for which I've the misfortune to know you I thought you would have at least understood your place."

Norton's expression became uglier and angrier. But Riley refused to censor himself. Norton was a rebel and needed to be caged. Next thing you knew he'd be telling the men it was evidence of oppression by the wealthy class. Well, the simple fact was that Norton needed to be oppressed no matter what his station in life, and Riley was delighted to do it.

Norton turned toward the woods and began walking back, angering Riley even further. Cotting, ecstatic to be alive, ran to catch up with the ginger-haired giant.

"How did you learn to shoot like that?" Riley heard the awestruck young boy ask. Riley began to hobble along, trying to catch up.

The snow fell sparsely but the temperature dropped. Despite the action, Riley was colder now and wished to be back in billets. He ignored Norton the rest of the trip back, and the only occasional chatter came from Paul. Riley's ankle felt less pain the more he walked on it. He was thankful that it wasn't broken. The infantry didn't seem to care one way or the other.

The sun had long since set by the time they made it to the crude company headquarters along the supply road near Ypres. But it never really got dark in the war zone. Flares, shelling, the lights of trucks, men working at all hours kept things a dull gray.

An adjutant directed them toward a small shambles of a house where Tomkins billeted with a Belgian family.

A farmer in a patched overcoat admitted them to the cramped parlor through a stout door that barely survived on its top hinge. Riley caught a glimpse of what appeared to be the man's wife and baby huddled in a side room by a stove. The warmth of the house drained what energy Riley had left. He wished to make his report and be done with Norton and Cotting.

The captain sat in the parlor at a small table filling out paperwork. The table and chair seemed pathetically wobbly under Tomkins' muscular build, as if he could break them both by merely pressing too hard with his fountain pen.

Tomkins looked up from his desk blankly, as if he'd forgotten who the three were. "Where are your kits and coats?"

"With your quartermaster, sir," said Riley. Tompkins' brow furrowed.

"You have a report for me?"

"Sir," said Riley, "we secured the transmitter at the edge of the wood as you ordered. Five German casualties, all shot by Lieutenant Norton, including the signal corps member. Ten infantry escaped."

Tomkins face brightened. He now seemed to recall the mission. "Three against fifteen?"

"Yes sir," responded Riley. He took a deep breath. "I regret to inform you that I discharged my weapon unadvisedly before the fight commenced, alerting the enemy to our presence. I have reason to believe we could have captured all of them had they not been so alerted. I stand responsible for my mistake."

The captain shrugged. "Well, better luck next time. But three against fifteen. You won't hear me cursing you for that. I let nearly one thousand run away when we stormed the castle at Gheluvelt. The good thing is that the Germans no longer have their position."

"Yes sir," said Riley, surprised at his good fortune. Norton would be miffed at that news, of course, but that was just his cross to bear. And not a Victoria Cross. What rubbish came out of that man's mouth.

After a few more questions the captain gave them leave to go to their evening billets, the farmhouse next door. He dismissed them and they turned to walk away.

"Stop!" said Tomkins suddenly. The three halted. "What's that sound?"

"Sound, sir?" asked Riley.

"Take one step back."

They did as ordered and turned to face Tomkins. Riley heard a faint jingle.

"Lieutenant Norton, what is that around your neck?" demanded the captain, his face white-hot in anger. He walked over to Norton and stood in front of him, his forehead two inches from the giant's nose.

He swiftly grabbed a chain around Norton's neck, pulling it out from under his shirt. On it were several identification disks.

"What are these? Did you take souvenirs from the dead?"

The captain let out a string of explosive profanity that Riley was certain young Cotting had never heard.

". . . These were once men! You are the King's Soldier and the King's Soldiers do not desecrate the dead, Lieutenant Norton! Doing so inflames the enemy and lends credence to their claims that we are the same barbarians as they. Do you understand?" he shouted. "Do you understand?"

They heard a clatter from the other side of the house. "Bollocks! I can't believe you did this," said Tomkins. "Will you ever do it again?"

"Sir no sir!" said Norton. His face had splotched white.

"Spencer!" said Tomkins.

"Yes sir!"

"You are to write this incident up and assign Norton a fitting punishment for this disreputable behavior. This makes every Wiltshire look bad."

"Yes sir!" said Riley.

Tomkins now closed in on Riley. "How is it that you failed to notice a fellow officer desecrating the dead?"

"I don't know, sir."

"You will learn to watch more carefully next time."

"Yes sir!"

"Norton, I am turning these over to headquarters. And God help me, if you are ever caught doing this again you will be broken by a court-martial. Are you clear?"

"Yes sir."

"Leave me, then," he snapped, turning on his heel.

Captain Tomkins did not look at them again as they filed out, but instead returned to his tiny desk and tablet, shaking his head in silence.

[CHAPTER TWENTY-EIGHT]

THE FROMELLES ROAD

December 25, 1914

C hristmas had come to the Western Front, although from the look of the fields in the wet gray dawn, there was not much to celebrate. For days there'd been rumors of a truce to bury the dead, but the rumors had proved false. The orders were as usual: stand guard, protect the wires, and shoot on sight. Brook no mercy with the enemy, even if he is flying a white flag: it is a trick and you will receive no mercy at his hands once you're captured. On this last point there was ample evidence. Corpses littered the soaked field between the trenches. Most were just shot. Mutilation would occur only if you were captured—a random cycle of now-personal revenge occurring when an officer's back was turned. It had been this way since Belgium. The stories of torture were bone-chilling, and Wils Brandl had seen enough to know that more than a few of the tales were true.

He flicked a louse crawling up his sleeve into a large puddle at his feet in a front-line trench. He was covered tip to toe in mud except, he supposed, for the inside of his mouth.

He should have been back in the communications trench, fighting for a solid duck boarding plank with another officer. But instead he'd been shuffled off to stand in a large heap of silt and coffee-colored water that these Westphalians considered a trench.

He was to guard and repair several thin wires that transmitted news from the forward positions back to headquarters. They'd been

snapped only a half dozen times by jackboots more intent on gossip-
ing about an unannounced truce near Bois Grenier than shoring up
the walls with sandbags. Captain Grimber had thought that if an officer was posted by the wires, the enlisted men would stop tripping on
them. Instead, they tripped over him too while dragging a Christmas
tree to the fire bay. It was the height of folly, thought Wils, who, to keep
his head from being shot off, had to squat uncomfortably in the shallow trench for the better part of the shift.

The Kaiser had sent a few trees to make the trenches seem more
hospitable, along with copies of the Bible and *Thus Spake Zarathustra.*
Wils wished the men would chop off the branches to create a bridge
over the more egregious water holes that punctuated their flooring.
But the men did not. They were trying to signal to the other side by setting candles on the tree's branches for Christmas. They still believed in
the holiday.

In some ways it made sense. As there was no order to who got
killed out here, why not attribute the good luck of living to God, the
Ghost of Things Yet to Come, the Angel of Mons, or anything one might
see while standing on the verge of Jordan under heavy enemy fire? It
was a lovely thought, but in contradiction to the events of the past three
weeks. The French had been banging on the British to blow through the
German positions south of Ypres. The British had tried at Wytschaete
and at La Boutillerie, which was why Wils was now sitting in the
trenches across from this ruddy hamlet making certain that the problems that had occurred with these transmissions last week did not
recur. The move had delayed his mail once again. He'd had only two letters from Helen, and knew there were bound to be more.

And such a letter, he thought, as a smile broke through the dirt
that caked his face. She told him of a half dozen nothings—her return to
class, Copeland thundering on about the use of the passive voice—not
because they were important, but to amuse him. She'd included a lock
of her hair, which he had carefully placed in his wallet, and wrote softly
about their time together in the woods.

A flare shrieked overhead toward them. He closed his eyes and listened for the shell. It hit farther down the line. He scanned the trench.

After the blast two men sat back up and again tried to tie candles to the tree's limbs—a nice sniper target. It was good for them all that in the moist air the candles kept going out.

It would be so different with Helen, he thought, as he checked the new wires again. They would live in a clean house with a large study and windows that stretched from the top of high ceilings to the floor, with chairs and desks for only the two of them. She would be his companion for eternity. They would laugh, and sing, and write, and kiss, and make love all the day long, one day becoming the next without end. He saw another flare, this time headed toward the British. He'd not have to move for that.

He looked down at his boots, submerged in mud. It was only time until he saw her again.

After another hour of sporadic firing a sentry splashed up. He crouched at the fire-step and lifted a periscope to view the battlefield, then closed it and shook his head.

"Anything out there?" Wils asked.

"Yes," said the sentry in a weary voice. "One of ours. A soldier from down the line with a Christmas tree."

"A suicide?"

"The men say there's a truce."

They heard the crack of a gunshot, and Wils shook his head, sorry to have been right.

The sentry shrugged, left his periscope and turned back along the narrow corridor, nearly slipping in the mud on the wires.

Wils crawled over to the fire-step and peered through the periscope, over the parapet. It was lighter now—bright gray, to be exact. He didn't see the man, but something hanging on a broken tree caught his eye. He checked again. The tree stood, and an electric torch hung from its branches. He smiled. God bless that boy. He has his Christmas now.

The sentry returned with another splash. Father Rupert stepped quickly behind him, a look of concern on his wide, florid face.

"Another soldier gone up," huffed Rupert.

"Dead?" asked Wils.

"Not yet," said the sentry. He lifted the periscope and pointed to the right.

Wils took a look. His heart began to race. "I give him twenty seconds."

"Fifteen," countered the sentry, pulling out his watch.

"Eight," said Father Rupert glumly. "Tell me it's not Konrad," the priest said as they watched the seconds tick off.

"No, Father," said the sentry. "One of the Saxons. They've been drinking since midnight." Twenty seconds passed.

"What are they waiting for?" said the sentry. "Get it over with."

"A drunken suicide," Rupert mumbled, crossing himself. His jowls sagged as he shook his head. "What a waste." The priest sat down beside Wils in the narrow trench, sinking into the mud, seemingly oblivious to the cold and damp. "Wilhelm, what brings you to disreputable parts such as these?"

"Watching communications wires break."

From a distance they suddenly heard a voice—a song. Wils shook his head as the deep baritone voice rang through the dawn. The startled sentry took another look.

"Seventy-three seconds. They're not shooting," the stunned sentry said.

Wils couldn't believe his ears.

He took the periscope from the sentry and looked over the top of the trench to the area where the sentry had pointed. He saw the dim outline of a figure walking steadily toward the British line. How he'd made it past the barbed wire, Wils had no idea. His voice cut like a knife across the gloom of no-man's-land, slowly silencing the murmur of men on either side of the divide.

Stille Nacht, heilige Nacht,
Alles schläft, einsam wacht
Nur das traute hochheilige Paar.
Holder Knabe im lockigen Haar,
Schlaf in himmlischer Ruh!
Schlaf in himmlischer Ruh!

The song ended. Still no shots. Wils shook his head and gave the periscope back to the sentry.

After a pause, the German sang the song again. Wils heard Father Rupert, his head bowed, murmuring a prayer and saw him crossing himself. The three waited for the silencing crack of a rifle.

"Now, your turn, Tommy! You sing," shouted the soldier in broken English. Wils winced, waiting for the shot.

"He's almost to the other side!" said the sentry. "They'll take him prisoner and hack off his ears."

"Another look," demanded Wils. The sentry stood back as Wils took the periscope again and looked up over the trench.

As the soldier went farther toward the British lines, again, palms outstretched, Wils suddenly dropped the periscope and peered out with his own eyes. The lone figure repeated his offer. A flare went off overhead and Father Rupert jerked Wils back.

"Don't get yourself killed." The priest's face looked ashen.

In the distance, a British response exploded across the lines:

Silent night, holy night.
Shepherds quake at the sight
Glories stream from heaven a-far
Heavenly hosts sing alleluia
Christ, the Savior, is born!
Christ, the Savior, is born!

"Mein Gott im Himmel!" said Father Rupert, his eyes bulging. "A miracle!" He pulled out a flask and screwed off the top. "To our Savior's health, men!" he said, taking a drink, then offering one to Wils and the sentry.

"Hear, hear, Father!" said the sentry, downing a gulp. Wils took a draught. The schnapps felt like fire in his throat.

Suddenly the narrow trench was filled with many men, rushing to the crumbling mud wall, trampling his precious telegraph wires into the ground.

"Truce! Truce! Truce!" they yelled.

Wils stood with Rupert, in amazed disbelief. The war—lowly enlisted men were calling off the war!

"Go!" yelled Rupert to Wils, stuffing the flask into his coat pocket. The priest fashioned his corpulent hands into a stirrup to help push Wils over the parapet. He demanded a hand of help himself once they were up, from both Wils and the sentry.

They rose to the field, as men of both sides flowed past. He looked around the desolation. Before him were acres of severed barbed wire and shrapnel, shards of trees cracked as if they'd been matchsticks. Ancient stone houses had been shelled into piles of mud. Corpses of men and animals lay scattered everywhere.

And among the devastation stood the living—walking and running through no-man's-land. They were shaking hands, stunned—as if the calamity could be called off by a small mutiny of soldiers. As though the hostilities were theirs to stop. His eyes stung as the chorus of voices rang up from the hell around him, lifting him out of the ruin.

What was this? He was aboveground breathing the sulphurous air, free for at least a moment from Prussian order. Free of the rats and lice, the freezing water, the waiting—the boredom of waiting to be killed.

He looked at the waves of men—at least a thousand—wandering in the field and wondered what in God's name he was supposed to do with this temporary freedom. The songs became a tumult around him. He heard laughter—what business did laughter have in anyone's throat that day?

He gave a shiver. He walked a few more paces as the song lifted again, and then fell to his knees in the mud, breathing the rotten air as deeply as he possibly could. Dear God, what if it were over? What if he'd actually go home alive to Helen?

And kneeling there he joined in the chorus of voices singing. He was above the ground and he would sing with the angel who'd brought them there—a simple ransom he'd pay for a reprieve.

After a while he stood up, laughing himself. Perhaps he'd been wrong about this stretch of Hell. He'd thought that kindness had left that world—that it had burned, dissolved, and blown away like so much ash on a cold north wind.

To be wrong. He shook his head. What would he give to be wrong.

∝✠✠∝

AT THAT MOMENT a small British soldier with a cleft palate walked up to Wils.

"Fritz! Trade you some bully beef for chocolate," he said with a lisp.

Wils looked down at his empty hands. "I've nothing with me." The young boy's eyes widened.

"Yes, I speak English."

"So did every German cabdriver in London," retorted the young boy, giving him a cautious glance.

Wils shrugged. The young man's wrapped legs were already sinking in the mud. A thought came to him.

"I'll give you my belt buckle if you know how to get me to Lieutenant Rhyland Spencer. Have you ever heard of him?"

The young soldier squinted at him and shook his head. "Where's he from, Fritz?"

"London."

"That don't narrow the field," he said, shifting in the mud.

"He went to Harvard. In Boston. The United States."

"Nah, never heard of him," the soldier said dismissively. "But, hey, Fritz! Got an electric torch? Trade you my beef for one."

Wils shook his head. "It's back at the trench."

"How 'bout I get it next time we're over there?"

"Right," said Wils nervously, looking around to find another soldier. "See you later, Tommy," he said and turned to walk away.

"Fritz!" the soldier called back. "I'd check up the road there," he said, pointing west. "I heard there was some ambulance drivers from Harvard come to help us out."

"Thanks!" said Wils, his face brightening.

Riley! He turned and started moving toward the road as fast as he could. He'd no idea how long this cease-fire would last.

He found a northbound road and had begun to walk its deeply ridged, soggy ruts when a truck of laughing British and German soldiers drove by. He waved them to stop, but they passed him by without looking back, splashing him in their haste.

Minutes later he heard an ambulance. Wils waved madly at it and yelled as loud as his hoarse voice would allow. It stopped.

"I'm looking for a British soldier and a Harvard man," called Wils up to the driver. "Name's Riley Spencer. Do you know him?"

The grizzled driver looked down from the car. "I don't know any Spencer, but I know some Harvard folks just past La Boutillerie. I can take you to them but you've got to promise to keep your eyes closed. It's one thing to be on the field back there, but up here they may not take it as well. Hop in."

"Thanks, Tommy!" he said with a grin. But as he opened the door, he gagged at a foul odor. He got into his seat and turned back to see the back laden with decomposing bodies.

"Been waiting to get our men," he presently said as they bumped their way toward north. Wils held tightly to the door.

"Where'd you learn English?" the driver asked after hitting a particularly nasty crater.

"Harvard."

"I knew a guy from Harvard once. He was a jerk."

Wils nodded. "Some are."

After a few miles of soft road, the ambulance came to a quick halt outside a white tent with a red cross on it. Men with stretchers and a chaplain in black bands emerged from the tent.

Wils climbed down from the truck, and thanked the driver, who pointed him to a garage shop nearby.

"Hey, Fritz, do you know a Friedrich Kriesler?" asked the driver.

Wils shook his head. The driver shrugged. "Met him in London. Was a waiter at the Savoy." He shrugged. "Good fellow. Well, if you're back by noon, I got my second run out to pick up more poor lads, or, er, what's left of 'em, and I'll run you back," he said matter-of-factly before motoring away through the puddles.

Wils checked his new pocket watch—two hours. He turned quickly and walked across the road to a roadside stand of round stones and weather-beaten boards. A large flag with a red cross was sadly draped between two boards, creating a doorway for Wils to enter.

One man stood in overalls soiled by big patches of black oil. Another wore a khaki jumpsuit, his white armband sporting a red cross. They seemed to be arguing over who was going to get under the vehicle. Surprised by the field gray uniform, they looked up bewildered. Wils held up both his hands.

"Harvard," said Wils.

"Yes. And you?" asked one in denim overalls cautiously. He had a flat Midwestern accent and a dirty blond hair.

"I'm class of '15. Wilhelm Brandl. There's a truce for the day on the front. I'm looking for Riley Spencer—a cousin of mine."

"You're a '15? Shouldn't you be studying for exams?"

"Why start now?"

The midwesterner gave a lopsided grin. "Who did you say you were?"

"Spencer's cousin. Wils Brandl."

He looked at him cautiously. "Spencer's just up the road a bit. I saw him last week. You can walk it from here. In fact, if Mike here can work on the ambulance, I'll take you myself. I haven't had much luck talking with the Boche. I've been too busy cleaning up after him. It's worse than living at Grays."

"You lived at Grays?" asked Wils.

"Indeed. Where were you?"

"Beck."

"Beck Hall! We've got a prince here!" said the man, his look softening. He wiped his hands on a dirty rag.

"Grays—do you know Jackson Vaughn?"

The young man's eyes widened. "The rich boy who went crazy after his girl left him? He's trying to fly planes now. Don't know how that's going to work out."

"That's Jackson," said Wils.

The young man nodded and extended his dirty hand. "Bill Wimmer, Chicago. Class of '16. I'll take you to Riley, but put on this armband," he said, handing him a white cloth with a red cross on it. "They won't bother you."

Wils nodded. "I can't stay long. My ride leaves soon."

"We'll walk fast. Good to meet another Harvard man. Dark times, these are," said one from behind the wheel of the car. The others nodded in agreement.

So Brandl and Wimmer began walking along the cold, bombed-out road for another half mile to Riley Spencer's regiment. They spoke of little of importance and found themselves laughing at times. And in their laughter, they savored the rare quiet of the day, as they did not know when the next lull would come.

[CHAPTER TWENTY-NINE]

REUNION

December 25, 1914

R iley, a writing board perched in his lap, reached over to pull the kettle off the small open fire on the brazier near his feet. He poured hot water into his teacup, smelled it, and made a face. The lemon acid had barely covered the stench of the water.

He rubbed his hands together and took up his pencil again.

2nd Wiltshire Regiment
2nd Battalion, 7th Division, 21st Brigade
British Expeditionary Force

Dear Edith,

How I was saddened to read your latest letter. It grieves me that you have been worried. But Edith, you must not chastise me so for not writing more often. It means nothing regarding my affection but that nearly every hour is scheduled with soldierly duties.

Riley looked up and frowned. He'd never met a woman who actually believed that. Women jumped to the conclusion that if you didn't write it showed a lack of interest in them and was just cause to analyze you for all sorts of moral faults. In his case, when he didn't write they were right to be suspicious about him. But there were many other innocent, overworked lads who were abused on this account, and it was just not right. He felt strongly about that.

Yet even though he knew his first paragraph would be ignored, he still felt he had to write it as a formality. He'd write it and she'd ignore it. Nature's way with a wife, he guessed.

He stopped again to give a laugh at the thought. A wife! A woman whose job was to satisfy him every night! How ridiculous that he was away at war. This way he had the duties of the relationship but none of its benefits. There had once been a time when he'd consider this arrangement the very definition of hell.

It was a fine arrangement for a day such as this, however. Just fine. All the nostalgia for lazy days rowing along the Charles River—the wind to your back and the sun bright on your face—could not change the lice or the mud or the shells exploding in the foggy night sky. Good to have a family behind to send you things, keep you in their prayers, and to return to.

His mind ached to think of something female. Something other than the mind-numbing marching, firing, cleaning, digging, reporting, and endless talk of duty and courage at the front.

What had become of soft lips and flushed cheeks? He closed his eyes and tilted his head back. The thought gave way to memories of perfumes, of long ringlets and lace shirts. Of dancing with Helen in August. Of racing through the park in a red car.

He thought of the acres of time he'd spent by himself, sculling silently along the Charles River, free to come and go as he pleased. At Harvard the only danger had been that too many of his admirers would attend the same dance. Not sniper fire from an unseen man. What a fool he'd been not to savor it more.

He continued:

> —When we're not in the trenches, they have us up at
> six, parading until eight. We then have a full slog of it
> working on trenching and musketry. The afternoon is
> spent parading, drilling, and studying the laws of war.
> They don't feed us until eight and we must be in our

billets by ten. In between that and our constant
moving about we've little time for writing, and you
know I've never been a good writer. Still I do not wish
to grieve you and will try to do better.

Thank you for the biscuits! The men and I ate your
shortbread to the last crumb, and blessed your kind
heart for them. You are a princess, they say, and the
men might elevate you to angel if you were to send
another tin and this time include chocolate, lemon
drops, and bismuth soda pills. Good brandy would also
be appreciated as we find our flasks constantly empty.
Your packages, dear wife, are *most appreciated!*
(However, as you see, my address has changed yet
again to the above. Edith, I must ask that next time
you not write anything else in the address line. The
censors will return it to you, or worse, eat the biscuits
themselves!)

But you can at least know where I am in very specific
terms—and you will laugh when you learn. Your
husband is literally billeted in a pig sty—luxury
compared to the men at the front. I sit with straw at
my feet to sop up the mud. (The dikes were all broken
in the last battle, and now we often sit in a cold
mud stew, without a useful rock between here and
Hamburg.) But don't think of this as complaining.
The British spirit is indomitable. We'll win this one,
and about that there is no doubt.

He thought about his predicament further, then continued:

Captain Tomkins continues to be a true find. I'm lucky
to serve under him. Yesterday the captain set up a
revolver shooting contest in which we were to shoot a
tin of bully beef from varying distances. I placed a

solid third and I was encouraged to hear that there are
two others at least as good as me because I won't be
able to take out all the Germans by myself. Placing
second was the captain himself. A lieutenant by the
name of Sydney Norton won the competition. He
seemed to wish to make it a personal duel with me,
but I'd have none of it. Sydney is a designated
sharpshooter and, unfortunately, a professional
complainer. We all have reason to complain but it does
no good. We must make the best of it, rain or shine.
(There's more of the former these days.) I am glad that
I have four days more seniority than he does or I'd
have to answer to him, which would be bloody awful.
He is a nasty sort, who went a bit unhinged when his
brother died at the Marne.

Instead of worrying about me I'd encourage you to go
out and buy something for our baby. Worry will only
do yourself harm and won't help me or our child.
What will help me are items on the attached list, and
perhaps a good pair of wader boots. Anything else will
be too difficult to carry in the trenches.

> Yours,
> Riley

He gave a half laugh reviewing that last paragraph. Something for
baby! There were people in this world who had the luxury of thinking
of new life.

He heard a retching noise nearby. He looked over to see young
Cotting, bent over and convulsing.

"Private Cotting!" Riley barked. The boy couldn't eat an apple
without becoming ill.

The young boy's watery brown eyes looked mournfully at him.
Riley spied a pile of chocolate wrappers nearby.

"Did you eat the entire box of chocolates?"

"Three boxes, actually. Traded the other men for the tobacco," nodded Cotting, holding his stomach.

Riley stood up and went over to him. He hated to see anything look this pathetic, especially in front of the other men.

"Cotting, would you like to take my place and rest?"

"Can't. Stomach hurts awful. Need to stay here." The boy's eyelids fluttered.

"Now, man, steel yourself."

The boy whirled around and retched again. Riley rolled his eyes. "Have you tried the bismuth tablets?" he asked. Paul's breath smelled terrible, and that was saying something, as everything out in that war-torn land smelled terrible.

Cotting shook his head.

"Paul! You've got to learn to take care of yourself." Riley went over to his kit, pulled out three pills, and handed them to Cotting. "Chew these. They'll settle your stomach right nice. Ask your mum to send you some in her next package. A big bottle will help you digest all the Princess Mary chocolates you can get your hands on."

The boy ate the chalky pills. He made a face and then, in a few more seconds, he returned to his natural color.

"That worked quite nice, guv'nor," said Cotting, then toddled off.

"Glad to be of service." Riley wished he could leave too. But he was behind in his letter writing and now had to face a more difficult, more painful letter.

He sat down and pulled the writing board up closer.

Dear Edith,

In the event of my death I have been instructed to write to you to make certain that you know my final wishes.

He shook his head and threw it into the fire. This letter business was all so damn awkward.

Riley thought for a few more minutes, then picked up his pencil and started again.

> Christmas, 1914
>
> Dear Helen,
>
> In death it is said that we only wish to hear that God loves us. But that is not the case for me. I wished to hear that you loved me, and this is not to be.
>
> But I wished for so much out of this beautiful life and much was granted to me. I got more than I ever deserved and fully enjoyed what I had. At times like these, when the end feels very near, I know that it was enough.

"Lieutenant!" a cracking voice called to him.

Riley looked up. It was Paul Cotting again.

"What, Cotting?"

"A truce! A truce on the front!" he called.

"Good. Let's go home," said Riley, not moving.

"It's not that kind of truce—not official-like. Just everybody seems to have stopped fighting at the front for Christmas. We're meeting the Huns in no-man's-land for some sport and Christian burials. Want to come?"

Riley shook his head and sighed. "The captain said I couldn't do anything until I wrote my farewell letter."

Cotting wrinkled his nose. "Now that's the Christmas spirit."

Riley smiled. "As I would be the one dying I would think she should be writing me."

"So you can't come?"

"No." Riley scowled. "This will take a while. Have fun with the Boche, Cotting."

> I married Edith. I will become a straight and honest husband and father. I will do my duty because that's what you would have me do.

It was refreshing in my life to find someone unjaded, whose principles and sharp tongue showed that one could be expected to meet higher ideals.

And that, for me, made all the difference.

"RILEY!"

"What now, Cotting?" he snapped.

Riley looked up. A Red Cross officer in a German uniform advanced. He squinted, then slowly moved his writing desk aside and reached for his rifle, not taking his eyes off the man. A German shouldn't be this far across no-man's-land. The soldier was covered in mud, his glasses dirty. He reached for his helmet—the helmet of an uhlan, no less—and removed it to reveal a shock of blond hair.

"Wils?" he whispered, squinting. "Wils? Is that you?" He stood up suddenly. "Good Lord, Brandl! You look awful!" Riley yelled, grabbing his cousin and hugging him fiercely. "I had no idea where you were. I can't believe you're here! Sit down and tell me all about it. Oh, God, Wils, I've missed you! You wouldn't believe the trouble I get into without you."

As he welcomed Wils into his small corner of France, he noticed how thin his cousin had become. Wils' eyes were hollow, his face was dirty, and his hands shook. Riley sat him down at the edge of the warm brazier and opened as much food as he had, urging Wils to eat with him.

Riley gave him some water to wash his hands of the clay, and then a cup of hot tea and a tin of beef, as he listened to his cousin explain what had happened at the front and how he'd come to Riley's camp.

"How are your feet?" asked Riley. "Do you need to warm them up?"

"Feet? Oh, yes. Some days are better than others. I try to keep them dry. The rain last week made it difficult."

"We lost three companies because of trench foot," said Riley.

"Now we have to pull double duty until we get replacements." He shook his head. "I never want to set foot in a field again." Riley pulled his head closer to Wils. "And our general has a nasty habit of referring to the enemy as the French."

Wils grinned. "Do you think it's better over where I am? Our generals think we should already be in Paris and the fact that we're not means we should just work harder."

"Well, by the way mine talk, we'll be in Berlin by the Kaiser's birthday."

"January?" said Wils, rolling his eyes. "I think our army's supposed to be in London by then. I'll say hello to the king for you."

"Tell my mother to send more food," said Riley. He frowned as Wils pulled a new watch from his pocket and checked it.

"Riley, I can't stay long. I'm sorry. There was a break in the fighting. I didn't think I could find you, but I asked and they said you were here. I wanted to see you again."

Riley looked at his cousin's haggard face. "You're cold. Would you like my coat?"

"No thanks, Riley. It just does me good to know you're all right."

"Have you heard from Helen?"

Wils eyes lit up. "I got a letter from her last week. Thank God for that. It's so difficult to get mail unless it's the government sending sausage and Christmas trees. She is quite well."

"Well, please tell Helen I'm a married man now, honest as the day is long."

Wils looked at him carefully. "The child—"

"Should come in February. Hope you'll be at the christening." He was not ashamed.

"Of course."

"Wils, is something wrong?"

Wils looked down. "I hadn't told you yet, but I am married myself."

Riley forced the smile to remain on his face. "Congratulations!" He reached out mechanically to clap Wils on the shoulder as one should do in these instances, and as he did his letters, on the writing board beside him, fell to the ground. He picked them up quickly before Wils could see.

"When did you marry?"

"Before we left. I was hoping to get your blessing."

Riley swallowed hard. "Wils, I've long been over Helen. I saw she had eyes only for you, and wished then and there that you two would be as happy as you could be. You have my most heartfelt and warm wishes." He saw a flicker in Wils' eyes.

"Now, Wils, you and Helen had better get on with things, as my firstborn will tower over your children by the time you get around to having them. Your wife—is she doing well?" The word hurt to say.

"She said she was getting along. Her work in class was coming to an end. She said she missed us all frightfully. And Riley, I believe she always will hold a soft spot for a British rake."

"A woman of fine taste."

Wils paused, then looked back toward the path from which he came. "I've got to go back. Give Edith my best love."

"Don't go!" Riley protested. "You just got here."

"The truce won't last. I have to get back."

"Wait! I've an idea. Get a pass and let's meet next month."

"What?"

"Let's meet next month," repeated Riley.

"I'm not up for being shot by a firing squad for desertion."

Riley raised his hands. "No. You won't. On the Kaiser's birthday, I'll get a pass to go with the ambulance corps to bury the dead. Do they give passes for that for your side?"

"Yes."

"Well, you get a pass to move a little north along your lines," said Riley.

Wils seemed to mull over the plan. "That's the way we drove today. The lines aren't solid. We passed the ruins of an old stone farmhouse just outside of a wood. It's by a new cemetery—about a hundred small crosses. I could get there, and so could you."

"Eleven hundred?"

"I'll try," said Wils, looking down at his soggy boots. "But if you get me killed, Riley—"

"I won't. Helen would murder me. And German machine gun fire is easier to deal with than her temper."

"Gunfire is more direct," agreed Wils.

"Shells have less shrapnel," answered Riley. "Mum is so worried about you, Wils. She always liked you better than me."

Wils laughed. "I've no doubt why. But I must go now, Riley. My ride is about to leave." He took a few steps and turned. "What if we take Ypres before we meet?"

"The Germans take Ypres? Good Lord, Wils! That would be out of character for the Hun." He shook his head. "I mean, what if wishes were our wives' kisses?"

Wils' face softened. "What I wouldn't give for one."

"Me too," said Riley, more somberly. He got up and walked back with Wils to the ambulance, leaving his pages unfinished by the fire.

But beside the tent, near where Riley and Wils had been sitting, a pair of eyes followed them disapprovingly. Norton took careful note of the young German's face, and the easy camaraderie he enjoyed with a soldier of the king.

He fingered the trigger of a pistol in his belt. Spencer was no soldier of the king. He was a German in the wrong uniform.

It was said Spencer had gotten a girl pregnant and that he'd bedded many more. He had a wife, and yet he'd said he wanted to meet Cotting's sister. And here he was talking with the enemy, probably about things he ought not to be speaking of. Blood would tell, and someday the captain would be man enough to admit it.

The captain, he thought, shaking his head. He ground his heel into the soft mud. It came up to his ankle. The captain was a hero all right, but not the first one to be blinded by the son of a Member of Parliament.

He looked up again through the gloom. He could shoot both of them right now—he should. But he'd be the one given the court-martial and he wasn't ready yet to stop killing Germans.

Norton's eyes flickered as he stood mumbling to himself.

Filthy. Just filthy. Two Germans before him, and he couldn't shoot either one of them. Not now, at least.

No German should enjoy such a day, thought Norton. Not after killing his brother and leaving him to rot in a field.

[CHAPTER THIRTY]

THE KAISER'S BIRTHDAY

January 27, 1915

It was the dawn of the day of the Kaiser's birthday, and Father Rupert slept in a dirt dugout after a long watch with soldiers near the front. His feet, having been warmed at the brazier, were wrapped in a sandbag to ward off frostbite.

Wils couldn't imagine that anyone could snore that loudly and not be considered an enemy target. He sat across from him on an icy plank, rifling through a package that his mother had sent. On his belt he'd attached his pass for ambulance duty that bitterly frigid day.

A large tin of chocolates had just arrived from home, and he ate them by flashlight. His hands trembled such that it took him two attempts to open the tiny chocolates in the indigo light. He steadied his palms on his lap as he refolded the red waxed-paper wrappers into little squares to pass the time. Dark mud and grease outlined his fingernails, their whites buckled and soft.

His mother had enclosed a card written in her neat cursive hand. His eldest cousin, Manfred, had received another medal. Another cousin, Karl, had just been accepted into the flying academy. Wils' dog, Perg, was adjusting to life with Karl's spaniels and Gretchen, Manfred's ill-tempered cat. The countess sent her love and encouraged him to keep his feet dry and his head down. She was working on a plan to get him a desk job nearer home if the war weren't over by spring.

Wils looked at his own boots, only a month old and in desperate need of repair. He frowned as he placed the tin back in his canvas haversack. There had really been no way around it. The flooded marsh had flowed onto the trench duck boarding and had then frozen solid. No amount of bailing had helped. And as his mother had sent chocolate instead of boots, so he'd just have to wear these today.

He stood up carefully, pulled on his pack, re-checked his canteen, and his day pass. Ambulances were in need of help north of their station. His commander hadn't asked for further details and Wils hadn't offered.

"Rupert, here's chocolate for you," he said, nudging his friend. The priest didn't rouse and Wils placed his haversack in the crook of his arm. Wils took out his own blanket and put it over the man's shoulders, then left, walking north through the trench system.

Wils stepped over sleeping men, quietly flashing his pass to the occasional sentry and keeping his head low. He put on his crawlers to go between trenches. The mud had frozen into black ice, making the path treacherous.

As he made his way up through the back roads, his eyes skimmed the gutted terrain. The land had not changed much since the Christmas truce. There had been no major skirmishes since the last days of October, just steady shelling and often in the wrong direction. The British had an uncanny ability to shoot their own troops by not directing their shells far enough.

Wils checked his compass and walked due northwest, toward the old stone barn in the cemetery.

OUTSIDE OF LA BOUTILLERIE, just west of the British lines, Riley Spencer had little difficulty securing a day's pass once word had spread that he was using the time to help the ambulance corps and to requisition chocolate and coffee.

"Spencer, here's a fiver for chocolate," called Norton. "My French lass wants some."

Riley looked suspiciously at Norton. The privation of the trenches had not whittled away an inch of Norton's girth. How the man had any girls at all was beyond him. He seemed to grow more idiotic by the day.

Riley took the money as Norton scowled. Under that withering stare, Riley calmly adjusted his leg puttees. Norton had become such a damned nuisance, always looking over his shoulder. During all of January he'd seemed to become even more embittered. Riley wished to have never laid eyes on the disagreeable man, let alone have had to have the misfortune of commanding him and punishing him when they'd first met.

At least the other men were much better suited to the camaraderie of the field. He'd taken great pains to make his men's lives better— he supplemented their rations from his own pocket, visited the hospital, and helped with the heavy work even after he'd worked a full day on his own. It seemed to make a difference to the enlisted men that he noticed and would struggle with them. He was a hero last week when he'd taken a forward position in a mêlée that led to the capture of twelve Germans. His men returned uninjured and even Captain Tomkins looked impressed.

He felt for his pass in his pocket, and then pulled on his overcoat.

"I'm off to Italy, Captain Tomkins," he called. The captain, writing a letter in a small field chair, looked up, his face taut with strain. "Sir, I'm joking. I'll be back before nightfall."

"I've had enough of your jokes. If you're not back by seventeen hundred you'd better be dead. I'll not write your parents that I lost track of you in the countryside. They are already put out with us for taking five months to topple the Kaiser."

Riley nodded and waved his pass.

"Seventeen hundred!" boomed Captain Tomkins.

SINCE CHRISTMAS, Riley had gone over every regulation and detail regarding his visit. He had marshaled his arguments for its legality and practiced a number of convincing stories if it looked like the truth would not suffice. In the end, they were at war. He met German soldiers on nearly every mission. He just didn't share drink with them.

He would be happy to see Wils. His cousin was resilient, but it was the resiliency of the civilized, not of the soldier. At Christmas he was thin and his eyes had a hollow look. He'd be glad to know Wils was still among the living.

Riley had thought of capturing him on this visit and taking him back to England for safekeeping. Wils would be hot at the idea of it. But then again, Wils would be alive. Riley's father would be sure to get him put in a comfortable prison in England—not the Tower or anything like it. He'd resolved to talk with Wils about the plan.

And then there was Helen. She didn't care for him, but she'd care more if she knew he'd checked on Wils. Maybe she'd forgive him for being such a cad.

Riley hitched a ride on the back of an open ambulance truck to a desiccated village to the northeast. The battle lines were not yet contiguous across the Western Front, and this area had been quiet since October. The village housed fewer than a hundred people, but with the army nearby and billets scarce, the town did a booming business.

Riley jumped off of the tailgate and thanked the driver. He crossed the road to a chemist who also sold coffee, tea, pastries, and other foodstuffs. He left a list with the shopkeeper's wife and said he'd return for his items by evening. The ambulance would pick him up there in time to be back at camp by curfew with a load of men re-fit for duty.

Riley walked along the iced ruts in the road, turning east into the rising sun. An open path led to a wood. He turned to see that no one was around, and began to walk down the road, his rifle over his shoulder, revolver in hand.

The trees nearest the village had thick black-gray trunks and tall empty canvasses. The trees had littered the ground below with a thick carpet of dead wet leaves and twigs. When the wind picked up, branches creaked in its wake, causing debris to fall to the ground like rain. He pushed through the brush, stooping below slender growths that occasionally would snap back in his face. But he made quick progress.

As he moved farther into the wood the ground grew softer. Nearly every step into the mud filled immediately with water. The water table was full—a lesson everyone trenching on the Western Front knew all too well. He walked with care, not wishing to lose a boot in the icy waters or trip on a submerged root.

The marsh led to a swollen creek, which chilled him as he waded across, holding his rifle high. On the other side a thick swath of wood was cut down into a wide path heading southwest as far as he could see. An ancient oak showed axe marks deep in its trunk. The path pointed toward Paris.

He stopped to survey the area. He heard nothing except the sounds of the trees creaking in the wind, water burbling down the stream, and the occasional fall of twigs.

He walked another twenty yards to the east and found an outcropping of gray rock, dirtied with mud. Mounds of dead brown moss lay scraped away from its base as if many men had crossed here. He scrambled up for a look.

This was where the war had been, a cemetery of a hundred new crosses to prove it. He saw a row of shallow trenches, now abandoned. Metal debris littered the plain. A horse's body lay rotting near the end of one of the trenches, abandoned in either pursuit or flight. The line had been given up for a stronger line farther southeast. Hills rolled through the field, patchy with dead grasses unharvested by the planter and bent by the weight of the winter's ice. A few small cattle shelters punctuated the rolling hills, most near collapse. He spied the abandoned stone farmhouse, beside which the road led. It was quiet, and there looked to be nothing around.

The wind suddenly picked up and he heard a crash behind him. Riley turned quickly and held up his revolver, scanning the wood for an intruder. But all was quiet again. He saw nothing. It was probably an abandoned farm animal slipping on ice. He gave a sigh of relief and carefully made his way down the outcropping to the field.

A gentle slope led up to the abandoned farmhouse. The dwelling had been encircled by two sets of fences: one of wood at the hill's base and one, near the top, of stone. Just inside the stone fence a large tree grew, its branches nearly touching the broken roof of the old house. In between the fences were scattered piles of debris—a cord of tree branches, stacked as if someone would come for them someday; rusted rolls of barbed wire sinking into the mud; an old plow. Across the road from the farm lay the field of crosses.

The field was quiet, something Riley was not used to after the past few weeks of rumbling engines. He checked his pocket watch. Almost eleven hundred.

He walked over the iced grass. It provided little cover, but it was preferable to the open road. The openness of the farmhouse made him uneasy. He looked behind him and saw nothing. He passed the wooden ring of fencing at the base of the hill. As he walked through, a length of wire stretched out from the post caught his leg.

Damn, he thought, looking at it. A small red stain welled through the wool puttees at his calf. It was a scratch he'd need to tend to when he got back.

Halfway up the hill he saw the damage to the farmhouse clearly. A fire had blackened the barn's masonry and destroyed a portion of its roof. The wooden door swung open on its hinges.

He suddenly heard the crack of a bullet hit a fencepost behind him. The wood splintered. Instinctively, Riley threw himself on the ground, flattened and desperate to find more cover than the grasses. Blood pounded in his ears.

He looked around searching for the sniper. A stack of tree limbs was piled a few yards ahead. His breaths came short as he quickly crawled behind them, the wet mud seeping through his clothes.

Riley heard another rifle crack, and covered his head with his arms. A bullet hit the top of the tree limb farther up the hill and clattered loudly into the stone wall. He heard another shot shatter one of the branches. Suddenly pain seized his side. His jacket had ripped over his rib cage.

Dazed, he lay back. He was bleeding.

Damnation, Riley thought, as he tried to stanch the flow of blood. What sniper had gone all balls-up in the middle of this sodding field? His side felt as if it were on fire.

He got back on his knees. As he pulled his head up, he nearly fainted. "Come on, Riley Spencer. You're not done yet." He raised his pistol.

The sound of heavy footsteps came up the hill. He could hear a man panting. Riley pulled the safety, his hand trembling. The red hair of Lieutenant Norton was visible. "Firing on the king's officer!" Riley raged, his throat on fire. He raised the pistol to Norton's face.

Norton knocked the pistol from Riley's hand as if it were a cigarette. "The Kaiser's officer, you traitor."

Riley could barely see. Norton was on him, grabbing for his throat, choking him as he yanked at his identification disk. Pain shot through Riley's chest.

"This is for my brother's death, you German—"

But as Norton raged, a crack rang out. Norton snapped back, shot through the forehead. Riley moaned, his legs trapped under Norton's weight. His hand was wet, covered in his own blood.

"Riley!"

"Father?"

"Riley! It's Wils!" he said, pushing Norton off his cousin.

Wils looked down at Riley. His face was ashen, and his jacket was stained with a dark glaze.

"Are you hurt?" Wils asked, his heart racing. "What? What's this . . . " His voice trailed off. A fury passed over Wils and he turned his pistol on Norton's corpse, firing into it until the chamber was spent.

Wils knelt beside his cousin under the gray sky. "Riley! You have to wake up."

"Hit," he said, nearly inaudibly. Then he gave a wet cough.

Wils pulled out his morphine pills from his pocket and pressed one between his cousin's lips. It bubbled up in his mouth, mixed with blood. He held his own flask up to Riley's mouth. Riley took a sip and grimaced.

"Is this what water tastes like without gin?" he whispered. Wils gave a laugh and wiped warm tears from his face.

Wils took off his own coat. The cold hit his chest like a hammer. He stripped Riley of his jacket and shirt, wrapping him up in the German's coat. Blood was everywhere. "Riley, they will think you're one of ours and get out of the way. Now, I'm going to carry you to the dressing station. It's going to hurt."

"Not to Germany" he said, fading.

"Riley! Wake up!" said Wils as he dug through Riley's kit. He found Riley's pass, and some letters, which he stuffed in his pockets. He stood up and looked around, spying the identification disk in Norton's hand. He grabbed it swiftly and put it in his pocket.

"He's out there," said Riley.

"Who?"

"Norton. Hates me."

"He won't hurt you now." Riley gasped as Wils lifted him. Wils bolted up the hill, hauling his cousin back toward the German lines. He no longer heard noise, felt cold or pain. He saw nothing but the path that would take him to the first dressing station he could find.

"*Achtung!* Casualty!" he started calling. "Where is the dressing station?"

Some soldiers stepped aside, others he stepped over. An attack had begun, and soldiers were filing into the narrow trench corridors.

Wils raced on, heaving for breath as he ran.

He found an advance dressing station and put Riley on a stretcher. Spying a nurse in faded whites, smoking a cigarette on the edge of the tent, he ran to her, grabbing her arm. He reached inside his tunic for a paper and waved it in her face.

"Nurse, the patient is the Kaiser's cousin, as am I. Should he lose one more drop of blood, you will be held to pay!"

She blanched, tossed her cigarette aside, and ran to a doctor, who hustled them into the chaotic station. More German casualties were arriving. Two orderlies carried in an officer, setting him down with a thump and running out for more. The nurse pushed the officer aside to find a cot for Riley. She checked his vital signs. He had turned a pasty white, and his lips had a bluish tinge.

Wils held his cousin's hands and tried to warm them.

A surgeon ran over, short and balding, with round black-rimmed spectacles. "Table six! *Schnell!*" he called. Two burly men carried Riley's bed into the crude operating room. Wils sat down outside the tent, cold and shivering. The nurse brought him a blanket.

He was there for more than an hour. When the operation was over, the doctors came out and spoke in hushed voices as they moved Riley into recovery. Wils sat by him throughout the night, holding his hand, singing old songs to his friend, and praying.

But despite the efforts of the German surgeons, Riley could not be saved. Little by little, the breath wafting from his body into the frigid January air grew lighter and more still. After midnight, he never regained consciousness.

As the indigo night began to fade, it was clear that there was no more hope for Riley Cabot Spencer. Wils was with him in the early dawn, when he drew his last breath.

He kissed his cousin's forehead and closed the eyelids on the green eyes that had caused so many hearts to smile. He borrowed a comb, brushing aside the brown hair Riley had tended so carefully. Wils then stepped back, and put his hands to his face, bursting into tears.

After a few minutes he collected himself, tired, white-faced, and shaken. A young orderly, not more than sixteen, came to him with Riley's personal effects—his own bloody jacket. Wils could hardly speak about the burial arrangements. But the young man was patient and kind, and assured Wils that the remains would be interred as directed.

That afternoon, Wils walked slowly back to camp, mute, not bothering to notice the swarms of men moving about the post. Each muddy step was an effort.

Father Rupert immediately gave up his board to Wils, who grunted thanks. Captain Grimber yelled at him for returning late and promised him another month of wiring detail.

THE CAPTAIN'S THREATS were useless against the force that was Wils' mother. Three days later Wils received a cable. Countess von Lützow had asked the general in charge of his sector to move Wils from the front lines to Berlin. Her telegram was followed within twenty-four hours by an order from headquarters granting Wils a transfer, in three weeks, to begin flight support training. Father Rupert read it and said he would miss him. Wils wasn't certain that the rest of his company felt the same, but overall, they'd tolerated him well enough. Those who didn't were typically too drunk to bother him.

That evening Wils was assigned a forward position to roll wire across a stream to an observation post where they'd lost radio contact. This was the third time Wils had strung that particular wire; the last two lines had snapped under bombardment. Wils said nothing as he waited. He would be glad to be rid of the trenches.

He leaned against the wall of sandbags, listening to the soft mutterings of Father Rupert playing cards with a soldier in the dugout nearest him. After midnight, a rifleman tapped his shoulder. "It's time," he said gruffly. "I've been sent to cover you."

They peered over the edge of the trench. The dark made for decent cover, but the moon was full and motion would be detected. He'd not heard much fire in his sector that night, though. He took a deep breath, pulled out his flask, and emptied it of schnapps. He adjusted his crawlers and followed his guard into the icy field.

He had little problem making out the machine gun on the other side of a narrow stream. The bodies of the squad responsible for the gun littered the ground.

The young soldier's rifle was ready, and his head darted in all directions to cover Wils. He made good progress and quickly got across the stream to the observation post.

A crack rang out over Wils' head. He looked up to see his guard shot, fallen facedown in the shallow stream. As he turned, he suddenly came face-to-face with a pack of British soldiers armed with grenades.

One exploded to his right. Wils was hit with such force, he fell back across the water, his head resting on the muddy bank. He dropped the wire as he fell, one arm in the stream.

His hand went numb as he gasped for breath. In the dark he heard the rumble of feet around him and the staccato crack of rifles. The British turned and fled. Boots and men began pounding from behind him, running over the stream and disappearing beyond the bank.

But the noise began to fade. He was vaguely aware of Father

Rupert praying above him. As his eyes dimmed, he thought of Helen and his mother, of Riley, and of his little dog, Perg, running madly around his house.

The water from the stream welled around him, tickling the edge of his nose. In the darkness his face twitched in a half smile. Perhaps this was the crystal stream that flowed from the throne of God, come to take him home.

[CHAPTER THIRTY-ONE]

LONGWORTH HALL

Cambridge, Massachusetts
MARCH 1915

O n a frosty day in early March, Helen walked into the main entrance of Longworth Hall, back from morning classes. She looked to the counter. She had patiently lived through so many achingly dull moments that the mail had become the most wonderful moment of any day. Even if there was no note, there was always the hope that one would come tomorrow. She read each one a thousand times if once.

And today there was a letter. Just one.

The girl behind the counter gave her the mail—a thin letter bearing the address of the Spencers in London.

The Spencers had never written, she thought, picking it up nervously. She swallowed hard and walked swiftly to her bedroom, closing the door behind her. She could hear her pulse beating in her ears.

She fumbled with her mittens and jerked off her coat. With trembling hands, she pulled a chair close to the light of the window by the radiator and opened it. Spreading open the two fragile pages, she spied a government signature. Her hand went to her mouth as she read,

COPY

5 March 1915

Dear Mr. and Mrs. Spencer,

I regret to inform you that we lost your son Riley
Cabot Spencer. He went missing on 27 January.
It had been his idea to fire a 21 gun salute in honor
of the Kaiser's birthday. The Germans waved a large
flag each time we missed. Riley, on the 11th shot, was
able to knock the flag down, much to the enthusiasm
of our troops.

It was after that sally that he left on a day's pass to
volunteer with the ambulance corps. When he did not
return by nightfall, we feared the worst.

Riley was immensely popular and a fine soldier. Not
being able to find him inflamed our men, leading to a
victory a week later, when we briefly overran the
German position, breaking in as far east as the
Fromelles Road.

The soldiers who overran the enemy's headquarters
found, just beyond the hospital, a small cemetery. We
assumed it was for German dead. Yet we found a newly
dug grave, with the enclosed identification disk—Riley
Cabot Spencer—draped over a white wooden cross.
The cross read, in English, "Riley Cabot Spencer. Son
of Laughter. 1894-1915."

Officers often bury those from the other side, as death,
we believe, does not distinguish between nations. Yet I
know of few such instances in this war where a British
soldier has been treated with such kindness by the
enemy. Riley inspired such devotion by foe and friend.
He was a gentleman and when he expired, he was
buried as such.

Your son and I arrived to our duty with the 2nd
Wiltshires at the same time in Belgium, and it is my
sad duty to write this letter. Please be assured his

personal items left at the camp will be sent home and
are now in transit. As I had been instructed, I have
informed his wife, Mrs. Edith Spencer. He also asked if
I would pass on to you a request to inform Miss Helen
Brooks about his passing. For your records, her
address is Radcliffe College, Longworth Hall,
Cambridge, Massachusetts, USA.

With my sincerest regrets at our loss, I am

> Yours,
> Capt. Aubrey Tomkins

Riley's parents had also enclosed a letter of their own. They'd
been notified that their nephew, Wilhelm Brandl, had been killed near
the French border. Helen reeled as she read that his body had been
identified and interred near Neuve Chappelle.

ANN HEARD HELEN'S CRY from the next room and ran into her bedroom. She saw the letter on the floor, with its telling government signature. Helen looked up at Ann and gasped for breath.

Ann rushed to Helen's side and pulled her close. She ripped open
Helen's white lace collar, pulling apart her top shirt buttons, allowing
her to breathe. Straining to reach a rocking chair, Ann pulled it over by
the window and struggled to bring Helen into it. And there Ann held
her, rocking gently and soothing her until the bitter sobs grew fainter
and fainter, and then, exhausted, her dear friend fell into a troubled
sleep.

[CHAPTER THIRTY-TWO]

LONGWORTH HALL

October 1915

Dearest Wils,

Today my studies are difficult and tedious and my heart cannot be found in any book. I write and re-write my essays a dozen times, asking you out loud whether or not you'd use this word or that. Ann no longer listens to me. She is still here at school while Peter works for the Navy in Washington, D.C. They've decided to marry once the war is over, a ceremony we shall attend together at Appleton Chapel.

I walked outside this evening and looked up at the night sky. It marks a year since you left; a year since we exchanged our vows. The stars —the Pleiades, the Hyades, Orion—were in the sky when you left and then again in March when you died. They've returned, and you, somewhere in the cold ground, will have seen them too.

This past year my letters have become my uncomfortable comfort. I summon your presence; I kiss your thoughts; I repeat your words. I write to you every day in my mind. I've written to your family and to your uncle in London, and to your school in Prussia, and your pastor, but they all say you have died. So I no longer talk to them, I speak, in my mind, to you.

I fear this is how madness takes hold. We talk to the dead instead of the living. For there are no others living with whom I would wish to speak.

I have heard the news that Jackson Vaughn was killed in a plane crash over France. Perhaps in Heaven he finds the balm he sought here but could not find. I never understood his love for Jenny McGee; I ridiculed it, and now it comes back to haunt me twelve-fold, and will until I see your face again.

I have tried the experiment of living, only I found too late that once we relinquish our books and soft carpets, we have no armor to combat the ravages of separation. I have tried to make my life, even in its details, worthy of the contemplation of my most elevated and critical hour. In this I know I have failed, and I now renounce all philosophy as ideals I cannot attain. I count myself among the poor in the world. For I have fettered myself to a ghost who once walked along the Charles River, and now walks beyond my reach. You were my courage, my strength, the color in my heart.

I strive to live where the claws of fear cannot find me, but I have found no antidote that helps me in these pages or in walking around Walden Pond, should I walk there a thousand times.

They say you are dead. I seem to know this fact. I used to wake up having forgotten it, but I accept that you are no longer alive. But my love for you is not dead. I won't wish it away and in doing so leave your side. You died without me but I will not leave you. I cannot bury you twice.

God loves forever, and so will I. It will be this straw at which I grasp; with arms that clasp the air in reaching for you. I would give my life if only I could see you one more time.

I will not bury you again. So instead I will keep these words from a hymn and bury them in my heart:

> *What language shall I borrow*
> *To thank thee, dearest friend;*
> *For this thy dying sorrow,*
> *Thy pity without end?*
> *O make me thine forever;*
> *And, should I fainting be,*
> *Lord, let me never, never,*
> *Outlive my love to thee.*

PART III: 1932

Harvard

————◆◆◆————

Cambridge, Massachusetts

. . . New England knows
A deeper meaning in the pride
Whose stately architecture shows
How Harvard's children fought and died.
— Christopher Cranch
The Harvard Book

The killing thing in life is a sense of loneliness.
— Harvard Professor Willard Sperry
Rebuilding Our World

CHAPTER THIRTY-THREE

MERRIMACK HILL

October 1932

The Great Depression had not spared the wealthy in Boston. The stock market crash of 1929 sent some of the families into bankruptcy and shoved others, such as the Brookses, to the edge of financial ruin. Two-thirds of their own family's trust had been lost between the collapse of the stock market (a risk they had attempted to mitigate) and the run on several Boston banks (a risk they had failed to predict). The remaining third of the fortune, while substantial, could not support three empty mansions.

Their parents long dead, Peter and Helen sought to sell the houses in New Hampshire and Maine as soon as the extent of the financial crisis had become evident. The taxes on the three estates were too high to pay. To avoid foreclosure on all of their property they decided to sell Merrimack Hill in Lexington along with its seven hundred acres.

It took nearly three years to find a buyer, during which time both Peter and Helen overstretched their finances to pay the property taxes. They'd auctioned off furniture, paintings, rugs, the wine cellar, and even a large number of books for which they had no longer had room.

The price the buyer was willing to pay was a deep discount from what the property was worth. But there was talk in Lexington of pulling down some of the mansions, as no buyers could be found and the cost of repairs and taxes were now out of reach for the owners. Debt was an unsentimental business.

Helen wore her navy jacket, three-quarter skirt, and a silk rose at her throat to pay her final respects at Merrimack Hill. Peter picked her up from Harvard's library, where she worked in the rare books room and drove her out that October Monday.

The sun was bright that day, and the light seemed to make the house diminish. Now that Merrimack Hill was emptied of furniture and paintings, the rooms seemed smaller. Plaster and a fresh coat of paint in each room hid the holes where family portraits, now in storage or auctioned off, had hung. The dark ash patina covering the bricks of the study's fireplace had been scrubbed away, revealing red brick. The books on shelves, once stacked in the alcoves by the old bust of Edmund Burke, were all gone. The models of ships had been given to the Geographic Society as a bequest of her father's will.

The garden had gone to seed. They'd only halfheartedly tended to it since Mr. Brooks' death in 1928 due to a massive heart attack. He'd died six months after they'd lost their mother to stomach cancer.

The study no longer smelled of leather and tobacco. It smelled of nothing.

She heard footsteps echo from the hall.

"Ready, Helen?" asked Peter. She turned to look at him. He looked stouter in his dark suit, now that he was almost forty. Wrinkles lined his eyes, and his hair was thinning. The financial shock of the past few years had given his voice an edge, and he had little patience for sentimentality. Creditors did not accept prior prestige, only bank drafts. "I'll need you to sign these papers. We'll leave them and the key in the mailbox."

She turned her back on the empty rooms and the wild garden. There was no point foot-dragging. It was like when they had buried Father. He had insisted they do it quickly and with little fanfare. She signed the papers and then walked outside.

Helen locked the door, placed the key in the envelope, and walked to the mailbox while he drove the car around. She frowned to find a letter in it, one with several bright stamps and PAR AVION in blue letters. Peter was supposed to have made sure that the mail was being delivered to them, and no longer to this box.

The color drained from her face as she read the address twice. It was from Rhyland Cabot Spencer, Junior, and postmarked September. She nervously opened it.

Highgate, London
September 1, 1932

Dear Miss Brooks,

I am writing in hopes that you might help me as a favor to my father, Rhyland Cabot Spencer, and to my uncle, Wilhelm von Lützow Brandl. My own name is Rhyland Cabot Spencer, Junior, and I am, at present, seventeen years old. I am Rhyland's son and my beloved mother was the Baroness Edith Kinnaird. She died shortly after my birth and I have been raised by my Kinnaird family. They show me every kindness imaginable, and now support me in my efforts to commemorate my father's war service at the Imperial War Museum.

I have recently been asked by members of a committee at the museum to donate a narrative of my father's life and other materials from his war service to the museum. I am most excited to help them and am contacting those who may have known him or recall him with some degree of fondness.

As part of this effort I am going to visit Boston in December, in order to visit my father's college, take some photographs, and speak with a few of his former friends.

My father wrote three letters to my mother while he was at war. In one he referred to you as my uncle Wilhelm's wife. I did not know anything really about my uncle, including that he had married, and by the time I thought to ask there was no one who knew how to contact you. Wils' own mother, my great-aunt, had long since died and their estate had been confiscated and sold by the new government to pay for war reparations. A professor Copeland gave me your name.

Thus I have little to work with. However, if you did know my father, I write to you in hopes that I may pay a call on you when I am in Boston. I am making inquiries here in England to find any of my father's other letters or possessions, and hope, if you have any, that I might persuade you to donate those as well to the war museum's efforts.

I hope that my visit would not rekindle painful emotion. I hope to commemorate the noble service of my father. I feel l have little past, as I never knew my parents, and thus this is an opportunity to learn about a man of whom I have little knowledge. And, as a man of seventeen, I feel it is now my place to do so.

Please let me know if I might call upon you,

> Sincerely,
> Riley Spencer, Jr.

She folded the letter silently. It threatened the frail grip she had on self-composure.

"Did you know Riley Spencer had a son?" she asked Peter as they drove in his black 1929 Cadillac out from Merrimack Hill.

"Riley Spencer," he said, his jowls sagging. "I'm surprised he didn't have a dozen natural sons the way he— Well, he did have any number of liaisons and I cannot assume they were all chaste. He did marry, though, you once said."

"Yes. The baroness." She told him of the contents of the letter and of the expected visit.

"That was his child?"

"Apparently so."

"That liar!" he said, shaking his head. "He denied both the engagement and that the child was his, all in order to try to seduce my sister."

"It wasn't his best moment."

"He was a liar."

"Peter, perhaps he didn't know what made a child. That was Mother's whole point back then."

Peter shook his head. "He was a philanderer of the first rate and can't be surprised if we doubt the dubious contention that he was ignorant of what activities might lead to children."

"He's dead, Peter. Isn't dead enough for you?"

"Ask his son. When Junior finds out the true nature of what we think of his father then he might be sorry he didn't leave the past alone."

"You will say no such thing," she snapped. She turned to look out the window. Peter was just as cross as she. But he had no right to be. It wasn't as if he'd ever cared about the house or Riley and Wils. He'd made fun of her some years past—he thought her marriage to Wils a sham and had told her as much to her face when she'd refused an invitation to a dance or any of the men he and Ann recommended she speak to. He had his future: his wife, a house, and children.

Yet his bitterness came through in caustic talk or a wall of silence. She preferred his silence.

And that is what she got. They drove without another word back to Boston and Beacon Hill, where she now lived. But she was about to get out of the car he cleared his throat.

"One last thing. I know this will do no good, but Ann told me President Lowell just hired a new engineering professor: Robert Brown."

"Robert Brown of Lexington?" She'd not seen him in years.

"Yes. The one who everyone wanted you to marry."

"But he did marry and move to California after the war."

"Ann said his wife died a few years ago, and that President Lowell persuaded him to move back. Ann thought perhaps we should pay a call on him. Unless you wish to sabotage this meeting like you have the others."

She ignored him as she got out of the car.

"Helen, Ann says he was wounded at the Somme, and by his wife's death."

She straightened her shoulders. "I'm certain Robert doesn't believe in second marriages."

"Then he would be a perfect friend for you." He shook his head and without another word, he drove off and she turned to her house on Chestnut Street.

CHESTNUT STREET on Beacon Hill was a good part of Boston for a woman of thirty-four to live by herself. The spinster was a welcome staple in those parts. Helen's town home was situated up near its peak, across from the bustle of the Boston Common, near the State House, and most importantly, close to the Boston Athenaeum, a private library. Proximity to this library had kept her from her brother's mistake of moving onto Commonwealth Avenue, a commodious and straight boulevard designed to look like Paris.

Boston was not Paris. Boston was a city for insiders, the insiders felt, and the concept extended from the private gardens, drawing rooms, libraries, and clubs for the rich to the narrow, twisting, one-way streets. Ample good space was provided for the public weal: a symphony, library, garden, and common, as well as numerous churches and sports venues. Yet the heart of Boston could not be broad avenues attempting to imitate a city known for frivolity. Her father had never understood why Peter and Ann would wish the inconvenience of Commonwealth Avenue, no matter how many crystal chandeliers one could stuff in an Italianate mansion. The whole concept had been implausible since its inception, and he never could quite get out of his bones the feeling that the whole Back Bay venture had changed the tenor of the town toward the commercial and trivial. It was a loss for Boston, and, thus, a loss for mankind.

Her father had relented on her desire to move to Beacon Hill when he was faced with the Back Bay alternative, or worse, near the student tenements in Cambridge. Before his death, he'd made clear that he approved only in that many of the families his family had found so objectionable these past generations had fled to Chestnut Hill, and, as a result, the allure of 10½ Beacon Street, the home of the Boston Athenaeum, could be better understood. In a library members weren't supposed to talk, so his daughter would not be bothered with frivolous social diversions.

She'd spent many days in the Athenaeum's reading room, working, researching, and at times, pretending to read while looking out against the tall bank of windows overlooking the Granary Burying Ground. From her chair she could watch the tree leaves spend the summer and fall on the graves of Paul Revere and John Hancock. In the winter the snow would outline their dark and wet branches. Sometimes they would be encased in ice. The shrill wind was kept out by the length of buildings along the burying ground's two sides, creating a quiet haven in the center of the city. It was hard to believe she was not back in Lexington in her father's old study, looking up from a manuscript and into his garden.

And after she was through she would walk to her house on Chestnut Street. Hers was in the middle of a row of brick town homes that sat across from a nearly identical row of town homes on the other side of the street. They had flat roofs and three narrow floors, black shutters at each window, and doors painted black. Flower boxes were in a few windows, and slender trees punctuated the walks—chestnut, linden, honey locust.

Each evening as she returned she would check for her mail in the polished brass box, unlock her door, and enter into her spotless parlor. She'd walk to her kitchen and sit at a small table, reading her mail while eating the meal she'd picked up at the grocer's on Charles Street—boiled beef, some carrots, an apple, and a glass of milk. She'd retire upstairs to her bedroom, unpinning her dark hair, brushing it out, changing into her nightgown with the long lace cuffs.

Before she went to sleep, she'd often open a drawer beside her nightstand and touch a packet of yellowing letters. It was just a fleeting touch, more a vestige of a prior time than anything else. The addresses, the ink from the censor's marks, the coloring on the stamps had faded.

Wils Brandl was now more a hazy memory than a real person. Touching the letters or just looking at them. At times that touch might calm her. But those occasions were fairly rare. One could not survive on memory.

Or anger. She'd been angry at him as well. They'd had such promise. Her fury had lasted a few years, during which time any number of suitors Ann and Peter suggested were unthinkable. She was too busy screaming at Wils in her mind about why he'd left for some noble goal that only left him dead. Over time her anger became lethargy. She was tempted at points by the young men in her path, but she never had the energy to risk her heart again. Peter said she was a keen saboteur. She didn't care.

But she had no solution, and so she fell back on habit. One could be faithful. Fidelity showed character.

Her isolation hadn't happened overnight. It set in through the years. She kept to the path she knew. After all, it was an honorable path. She'd made a promise before God to love her husband forever—and it was a promise she intended to keep.

Die Liebe welche Gott geweiht,
Die belibet bis in Ewigkeit.
The love which God consecrates abides for eternity.

[CHAPTER THIRTY-FOUR]

HOLLIS HALL

The next morning, during a break in her work at the library, Helen walked across the Yard, buffeted by a brisk wind under a bright sun. She pulled her hat farther down around her ears while brittle leaves scurried ahead of her as if in a game of hopscotch. She hoped to find the old man of Hollis 15 before he left for his lunch.

As Helen walked up the flights of steps to his room, she wondered just how the aged professor could make this climb several times a day. At the top, she was out of breath. She took off her wool topcoat and draped it over her arm before knocking on the door.

A shuffling came from inside. Professor Copeland, a tiny man, now stooped with age, opened it. He stood before her in an oversized tweed suit, and his face wore a sour look.

"Yes?" he said. His spectacles were so thick, they resembled fish-bowls, and magnified the sagging skin on his cheeks.

"Professor Copeland, I'm Helen Brooks."

He paused but didn't open the door farther. "You're from the library, aren't you?"

"Yes. But I've come to see you about a different matter. A museum is collecting letters."

"I have no appointment at nine fifty-five. Come back when you have scheduled with my secretary," he said with a cough, and began to close the door.

"But, sir, I need to speak with you."

"You can't have my books. I got an extension. They're not over-due. Please remove your foot from my door!"

"It's not about books. It's about Riley Spencer and Wils Brandl."

He stopped. "Who?"

"Riley Spencer, a British student, and Wils Brandl," she said, taking her foot from the door. "The German."

He gave her a careful look. "I knew Wils. Come back at ten o'clock, punctually," he said, closing the door abruptly in her face.

Helen raised her hand to pound on the door once again, but then she caught herself. After seventeen years, she could wait another five minutes. Still, she indulged in a few hard and bitter thoughts about the eccentric old baggage as she sat down on a chipped wooden chair outside his door. How he'd survived all these years at Harvard, she had no idea.

When ten o'clock chimed, Professor Copeland came back and opened the door promptly.

"Ah! Miss Brooks! Please come in," he offered, and ushered her in. The bright sun illuminated the room, adding a golden touch to the yellowing piles of students' papers on his massive desk. On the floor rested stacks of books, their overdue notices crumpled beside them.

"I'm having these carted to the library tomorrow," he said nonchalantly, offering her a seat on his sofa. "Please sit down." A cut-glass decanter with the word "Scotch" around its elegant neck rested on the table. It was nearly empty.

"I'm late on congratulating you on your promotion. I hear you were made the Boylston Chair and Emeritus."

Copeland looked at her and rubbed his eyes under his spectacles. "Emeritus is awful. Only when I'm about to die does Lowell make me the Boylston Professor of Rhetoric and Oratory and then he turns me emeritus! He never appreciated what I did for Harvard," he muttered. "But what is it about the German boy, Miss Brooks? I've not much life left in me. Please don't make me use it waiting for you to get to the point."

Helen stiffened. She was no longer some young student to be bullied. "I'm here about Wilhelm Brandl and Riley Spencer. Riley's son is looking for letters of his for a collection for the Imperial War Museum and he said that you wrote to him saying I might have some of Riley's letters. But I don't and thought that—did Riley or Wils Brandl send you any from the war?"

"Brandl? Spencer? I don't think so. I sent him to you."

"I just found out yesterday that he's collecting information for a museum. I'd never heard from him, and I'd never checked with you to see if either Riley's or Wils Brandl's letters were in your famous collection. Could you check?"

"Certainly. But I'm quite sure I've nothing. I would have remembered a letter from a German boy. It would have been my only one."

"But you received so many letters. The collection—"

"Is my greatest pride," he interrupted. "I know every letter in it." He said nothing more, but sat as if in deep thought, or perhaps light sleep.

After a few moments of silence, he spoke suddenly, causing her to jump. "You know, Miss Brooks, most professors around here who did receive correspondence from Germans burned the letters. At the time it was what the young men wanted. Things were not good for Germans during those days."

"Did you burn any?"

"I said I don't think I received any," he said snappishly. "Have you tried Kuno Francke? Countess Brandl gave a lot of money to his German Museum, as I recall," he said getting up and slowly shuffling over to a shabby old trunk in the corner shadow.

"Professor Francke's dead."

Copeland turned and gave her a hard look. "I know that, but his papers may be with your own library. Perhaps you should consider that before rattling creaky old professors like me. Ah!" he said, lifting out a large red volume. "Here's the first one."

Helen went to his side to help him carry the volumes. She noticed how much weight he'd lost. His outstretched arms seemed frail under the bulk of his ill-fitting jacket. He had always been a dandy and she was sorry to see him looking so aged. She took the volume and two others like it to the table, moved the decanter to the mantel, and then sat down.

He walked over to the sofa. "This book has the earliest letters," he

said, sitting beside her. He opened its pages slowly, and a smile flickered across his face. "These letters I received before I knew what I was
doing. I don't recall throwing any correspondence out, but there was a
lot going on. I was grading piles of papers every day so that young men
could get their marks before they left."

He continued turning the pages slowly. She pursed her lips, feeling impatient. Now that the book was in front of her, she wished he
would flip faster.

Copeland grumbled. "Here, Helen, read this one." He looked at
her. "It's short, Miss Brooks. You'll not miss any appointments on its
behalf."

> Barnwell Abbey
> Somerset
> February 27, 1915
>
> Dear Copeland:
>
> I am home for a few days leave, a welcome change
> from whipping a part of Kitchener's New Army into
> shape. For I am now a Lieutenant in the Duke of
> Wellington's West Riding Regiment. When we shall get
> to the front, no one knows. We hope before long to do
> our share in reducing the Germans to sanity.
>
> I was deeply touched by your note. I know what it
> means for you to take quill in hand. I hope when the
> day of stress comes, I shall prove worthy of your
> remembrance and of Harvard.
>
> > Ever yours,
> > J. T. Murray

The last line caught her off guard. It was good to see the fusty old
man had a heart.

Her face lit up at seeing the old dry bones smile. He was genuinely
happy sitting by her explaining the details of each letter and turning

the pages. She'd heard that many flocked to him and that this had been a happy table they shared. The memories stayed with him—not so far away—in the growing shadows of his mind.

There were many more pages in the volume. Some were newspaper clippings, others came from students in training in America, reporting from the front, or those painting in Europe. At one point his eyes lit on a telegram and his face darkened. Saddened, he looked away.

"I sent that telegram after we lost Billy Meeker," he said gruffly, turning the page.

Toward the back of the final volume they opened, she found a folded note put into the book. It was signed "Harvard." She looked up at Copeland. "Lionel Harvard?"

"The only Harvard to attend Harvard," he said with a nod. "Did you know him?"

She shook her head, then opened the letter carefully. It was a copy of a letter sent to Lionel's wife, Mary. She'd read a similar one.

COPY

17 Battn. Grenadier Guards
B.E. Force.
1st April. 1918

Dear Mrs. Harvard,

It is with feelings of very deepest regret that I write to offer you my sincerest condolences in your great and irreparable loss.

Although I had only been commanding the Battalion three weeks, I had already formed the highest opinion of your husband as a soldier, and had given him command of a Company.

His quiet manner, competence, and gallantry in action were beyond all praise, and I feel I have lost a friend, and also one of the very best Officers in my battalion.

We have buried him in the French Civilian Cemetery in Boisleux-au-Mont, and I have had a white enamel wooden Cross erected so that his last resting place may remain sacred until such time as a more lasting memorial can be put up.

He was killed during the morning of 30th March by a German minderwefer, and died instantaneously. The Battalion was in front line, and was very heavily attacked by the Germans, and his whole Company suffered very heavy casualties.

His personal belongings and kit are now on their way home, but I am afraid they may take some time in transit.

I hope you will allow me again to express to you my own personal sorrow at his death, and my grief for you.

Yours sincerely,

GORT

She closed the letter slowly and put it back in its envelope. "It was such an awful time."

"Yes, it was," he said, sitting back in his seat. His face was pale again. "A ghastly business."

"Did Mrs. Harvard give you the letter?"

"No. The Harvard War Records Department did."

"That's not possible. Harvard doesn't keep any pieces of personal correspondence."

He shrugged. "I guess you're wrong on this account. I found it in the folder. Perhaps they requested it from England. You know, perhaps they can request Wils' or Riley's information as well. You should look into it."

"I have, no fewer than ten times," she said quietly, getting up to replace the books.

"Oh. Sorry to hear that. So Riley had a son?"

She nodded.

"He was the one with the bad reputation?"

"I hardly think that's relevant."

"It will be when his son finds out. But what about Wils? You know," he said, sitting up, "I'm not surprised you are here. I too have become interested in his case—along with the other German students who died in battle."

"I was Wils' wife."

His eyes widened briefly behind his thick glasses. "Then you must also be interested in the church that President Lowell is building. The one that will honor Riley but exclude Wils."

"I'm not," she said. "I do not involve myself in political matters." She was disappointed. There were no letters from Wils here. It was a dead end. He had nothing.

He gave a cough. "I would think that the people who knew Brandl might want to lift a finger and do something about his memory." He paused and glared at her. "You know, people with considerable family influence."

She shook her head. "I can't change President Lowell's mind. Many have tried."

"You haven't tried. And here you are—the wife of a German student. You would make a difference. Your mother would have relished this challenge."

She looked at him blankly. "She's not here to take up the matter."

"Her daughter is."

She shook her head. "Forgive me, Professor, but why do you care?"

"How could I not? It shouldn't surprise you that when I find something unjust about one of my students I am willing to speak my mind about it."

Helen was taken aback. She not considered that anyone really cared about Wils except her. It was such a fruitless mission.

"I meant no disrespect. But I have loved and lost and it is too painful to lose again on this account. I prefer to let Harvard do what it wishes to do and to memorialize who they wish to in whatever building they build. The president and the college rarely change their minds on these matters. Look at the exclusion of the rebels from Memorial Hall. You'd have him commemorate those who fought for the Kaiser and not for Robert E. Lee?"

Copeland sat up in his chair, engaged. He seemed to think he might persuade her. "That was not our fight, and if it were we'd never win it. But your husband, and the others—they were honorable men too. And this is a church as a memorial. It would be wrong to exclude them in a church no matter how despicable I found the Kaiser and his warmongering."

She shook her head. "Professor, even if I had the time—"

"What better use of your time could you have?"

"For a useless task?"

"You could withhold your family's largesse."

"We have no largesse," she said. He sat back, stunned for a moment.

"I'm sorry to hear that. A number of families lost all in the crash."

"We didn't lose all. But we've no financial leverage with the president." She looked down at her wristwatch, a gesture he caught.

"Miss Brooks, have you remarried?"

"I don't believe in second marriages."

"But yet you come seeking letters from your dead husband. It speaks of a lasting fear and hurt."

"It's a lasting love."

"I disagree. May I ask what you do when not working in the rare books room at the library?"

"I read."

He frowned. "A friend of mine around here says that 'the killing thing in life is a sense of loneliness.'"

"I am not lonely."

"Glad to hear it, Miss Brooks, but I don't believe it and I think you are lying."

"What are you saying?" She frowned.

He sat back as she glared at him. Above his head was a portrait of an ugly Spanish peasant. He looked good by comparison, she thought.

Perhaps that's why he had it there.

"I think you're here because you've absorbed some wrongheaded thinking about what you owe the dead."

She said nothing.

He sat up, his eyes lighting. "I'm not saying it's wrong, Miss Brooks. I love our students too. Lowell loves them too. We're trying to make them immortal by writing their names in gold and marble in a monument. And we're encountering the same problem as you. We're trying to mix the sacred and the mortal. We can't make these men immortal any more than you can make your love for your husband immortal."

"I can love my husband as long as I wish to."

"Not without injury to yourself. And we can't make men immortal on this campus without injury to our community—you see it in the way the protests are so angry about whether or not to include the Germans in the church memorial. Such love," he sighed, "becomes its own form of idolatry. I've seen it not under a hundred times in books and poems."

"I beg your pardon," she said, bristling at the thought. "Religion urges us to love as God loves."

"But you are not God."

"I didn't say I was."

"Then when you try to love as God loves—or when we do," he said, leaning toward her, "you forget your duty. I think you'd use your time to make use of the opportunities that present themselves instead of fretting about something which makes you timid, and cowardly, and doesn't help anyone else. As that seems fairly useless to me, so I shall put you to work."

"Sir, my father counseled me to reject political debate. And it stood him well—"

"My dear friend Jonathan Brooks doted on and coddled his daughter. You would have been better off following your mother's lead."

"You don't know me."

He sighed, sitting back in his chair. He looked out the window. "You have come to my door a thousand times in other forms, Miss Brooks. I know what a dead dream looks like. You may fool others, but you can't fool me. I saw your face after the unsinkable ship sank, and after the war, and now after the crash. We have had some dark days around here and I know because I wasn't too timid to talk to students who came to my door and exhort them to find new dreams."

Helen caught her breath, unable to reply. "I thought you might have a letter," she said, her throat dry.

"You know, Miss Brooks, I am glad you will be on my side in this matter. I've been barking like a seal about the memorial, yet you never managed to swing by before. But I'm glad you did today. Your mother would be proud. She'd not let a golden opportunity to help others learn the meaning of 'equal before God' pass her by. That's not like any Windship woman this city has seen. Ever. Your family would be appalled."

"My mother was arrested many times for her work."

"Those arrests pleased her immensely."

"Harvard's church is not my cause."

"What would be, then? Finding letters of nearly twenty years ago? How is that worthy of your entitled heritage?"

"I've never been talked to like this—"

"What would you say to Wils if you could see him?"

"What?"

"What would you tell him? That you were sorry he died? My guess is that he is too. How would that help?

"Put this misguided sense of love away. I've seen enough of your type, Miss Brooks, to know that there is nothing that the Boston woman cannot accomplish. You possess these mythical qualities of tenacity for social justice, yet when I ask you, you can give me no example of what you do with your time other than look for letters. Am I incorrect? Am I incorrect to suppose that you may have spent too much time in sentimental grief? What happened to Thoreau's admonition, 'One world at a time, brother, one world at a time'?"

"Thoreau is not my philosopher."

Copeland's eyes widened. "Things are bad, I see. You should have come to me before. You must pick up a pen and write to the president."

She gave him a fierce look. "I know my duty."

"Then do it. I want you to go write—no, talk—on behalf of your dead husband, to President Lowell and change the nature of this memorial he's got it in his head to build. He needs to hear from people other than angry students and ancient professors."

"It won't do any good," she said, exasperated.

"How do you know that? You're a Brooks. And I guess you were a Brandl once too. Why did you not change your name to his?"

"I had no signed wedding certificate," she said.

He nodded. "Then let this be your tribute to your marriage. It's at least some use of your life beyond that of your own edification."

As he stood up she opened her mouth to protest.

"No, please, say no more. I know your brother, Peter, and what you've had to overcome. But I liked your husband, Wils, and thought him talented. Tell me what President Lowell says, and then," he said, ushering her to the door, "perhaps you'll join us among the living."

She bristled as she walked out the door.

SHE WALKED the long way to her office in the library, by the new church.

The sun was much brighter than her mood and the October air chill and crisp. Workmen were stringing paper lanterns across mature trees that had burst into their autumn color. Students ambled along the broad sidewalks, their dogs and friends in tow. At the base of the unfinished Memorial Church building, electricians wired spotlights to the four spare pillars of its south porch. A delegation assembled not far from them, pointing in different directions. They were most likely preparing for Sunday's service to raise money for the church's completion. It was a service she would not attend.

It was no secret that President Lowell had wished to tear down Appleton Chapel from the minute he had become president. He was said to have cringed every time he was forced to walk by the pile of light-colored sandstone bricks. He found it neither Gothic nor Roman, but Byzantine in both concept and execution.

Lowell had taken years to raise funds for the new church, and now it was near completion. Its white steeple stretched high above a red-brick stem. Arched windows had been set in its walls. Sheets hung in their hollows until the glass could be purchased to put in their place. Tarpaulins covered portions of the church roof, and the stocky column legs of the west portico were rolled and tied into a neat bundle by University Hall.

The project had been immersed in controversy from its start. The Congregationalists and Unitarians tried to convince themselves it was just going to be a fancy meetinghouse for social work. The architects and alumni worried that it would be a lump of limestone, compounding the architectural mistakes that led to "the oppressive mass of Widener" Library. Catholics objected to a Protestant church.

But the central problem was the war memorial. Students protested that the war dead would have preferred free beer. Those who'd funded the John Singer Sargent murals in Widener Library were irate that their memorial would get second billing to Lowell's church. Lowell clashed with faculty and students over the idea of including the German students in the church.

And this was the reason Helen had closed her eyes to the debate and turned her attention away from the building across the Yard. Until today.

Copeland's faith surprised her. He actually believed she could move this mountain. She'd consider it.

The old goat had been wrong, of course, about all the other things.

CHAPTER THIRTY-FIVE

UNIVERSITY HALL

Two weeks later, Helen heard a car's horn blare from in front of her window one early workday morning. She looked out from the heavy white curtains in her parlor. It was Peter, in his dark topcoat with a wool hat, waving to her from the driver's seat of his car. He idled its engine in the middle of Chestnut Street. She frowned, opened her door, and called to him.

"Civilized people knock."

"Get your coat!" he called over the noise of the car's engine. "We've an appointment."

"With whom?"

"No time to discuss. Can't you see I'm in the middle of the road? Get in!" She reached inside the foyer for her coat, lunch bag, purse, and the keys. She locked the brass door behind her as a car pulled up behind Peter. There was no room to maneuver in the narrow street, as cars were parked on either side of the town homes all the way back down Beacon Hill. The driver put his head out the car window and gave her a look of moral opprobrium as she walked to Peter's car. She hurried. At least the man behind them didn't blow his horn too, she thought. She would hear about Peter's flare-up from the neighbors.

When she got in, she noticed Peter's cheeks were flushed. He looked almost happy. Or, if Peter could look happy, this is what she'd imagined it would look like.

"Peter, where are we going?" she asked, closing the car door.

"We have an eight o'clock appointment this morning with President Lowell."

"What?"

"Indeed!" he said, smiling triumphantly. He gingerly inched out into the Beacon Street traffic. A full grin came to her brother's lips, one she'd not seen for quite some time.

"Yes, Helen. I ran into Professor Copeland last week in the Yard when taking Ann to one of those interminable Phillips Brooks House advisory meetings. He asked how you were doing."

"He didn't—"

"Oh, but he did," said Peter in rapid, clipped speech. "And he and I decided, dear sister, that it was time for you to make peace with your past. And so I'm driving you today to a meeting with President Lowell that Ann arranged so that you might make a case for your husband to be included in Memorial Church."

"Merciful heavens!"

"That's exactly the point you'll make to the president: forgiveness, not judgment." He nodded. "Now I realize I've not been the most supportive brother—"

"—You're driving me where?"

He looked over at her. "You look fine. Your hair is neat and your dress appropriate."

"You had no right! I'm not prepared."

Peter turned onto the Massachusetts Avenue bridge.

"Yes, you are. In the backseat you will find a dossier the Reverend Willard Sperry and I compiled on the lives of the Germans who are to be excluded. They all have references of good character and they all— now this is important—died before America entered the war. They did not fight our men."

"Reverend Sperry?"

"Yes, he said to wish you well and that he and the faculty of the Divinity School would lift you up at a prayer service this morning."

"The Divinity School faculty? You talked with Dean Sperry?"

"Oh, we did more than talk. The group of us—Ann invited some of the more fair-minded donors—"

"What? Who?"

"I don't recall. A few members of the Harvard Corporation and, you know, donors. There was a group from the library as well. They are very concerned about you over there."

"Why?"

He pulled along Quincy Street to the Yard's wrought-iron gate and idled the engine.

"I know I've made fun of your marriage to Wils, but in between the death of Mother and Father, and selling Merrimack Hill, I—well, Ann has helped me see that even though I don't understand your grief, I do want you to laugh again. I want us to be happy. Perhaps if you laugh, then I will be able to as well."

She saw in his eyes the same pain that she had seen in her own mirror. But before his stoic reserve could melt, he turned to the backseat and picked up a folder.

"It's time for you to breathe fresh air," he said. "Take this research and know that your many friends are pulling for you."

"I've many friends?" she said, blinking back tears. "I thought I was alone."

"More friends than you'd ever know. So does Wils."

She shook her head. "I didn't know anyone knew."

"Everyone knows."

"I'm mortified."

"Don't be. Even though we're all a bit afraid of you, we do love you."

She looked down at her lap.

"Now, Helen, remember Mother. She'd have President Lowell in tears. You don't need tears, just acknowledgment that your husband should be commemorated as well if the soldiers of World War I are to be honored. Forgiveness in a church is preferred to judgment. You'll do fine and I will catch up with you after work today."

She nodded, took the folder, and got out of the car. She watched from the sidewalk as her brother drove off.

The sheaf of papers was labeled clearly and annotated in his handwriting. It must have taken him hours.

Such was the face of kindness that day that touched her as she walked under the elm trees to the cold gray stone building that was University Hall.

THE ELM TREES under which Helen walked were of particular significance to her conversation that morning.

The trees were the subject of a bitter fight and loss for President Abbott Lawrence Lowell's power in the early years of his presidency. There were those who said it was good they got him while he was young, as his neck had only become stiffer with age.

In 1909 the leopard moth had attacked the American elms. The pests laid larvae in the branches of the ancient elms—destroying trees that were more than 300 years old. While the Harvard arborists hacked away at the branches trying to prevent the larvae's spread, President Lowell ordered the planting of oaks amongst the elms in the Yard.

It was a fine solution, he believed, planting a different variety of trees, so no one moth or beetle could destroy the Yard. This was simple fact. The red oak grew fast and its canopy was high enough to provide an unimpeded view across the Yard. And that should have been that.

But he'd not reckoned with the pull of sentimental precedent among the older generation; the claim that all seemed to have on running Harvard; or the desire of those among the faculty and administration to trip him up. When the venerable Class Day Elm fell in 1911, the replanting issue ignited into a firestorm.

President Lowell deigned to convene a committee, but assumed that the replanting would continue. Powerful alumni had other ideas. The American elms, the alumni decreed, were to be replaced with large, live American elms, science be damned. And if King Lowell sought to replace their elms with other trees, they would repot him.

President Lowell responded that the plan made no sense. The moths would eat the new trees just as they had the last ones. It didn't matter. They offered to fund the replanting; and they asked President Lowell not to meddle further with the heart and soul of Harvard.

In 1914, President Lowell begrudgingly ordered the planting of large American elms to replace the lost elms in the Yard, negotiating only the inclusion of a few English elms—variety for the leopard moth's diet, he grumbled. It didn't matter that a half century later history would prove him right, when Dutch elm disease would invade the campus, killing more than four hundred of the seven hundred elms.

It was the first fight he'd lost, and it taught him a great deal about working with Harvard's factions. He vowed that though he would lose again in the future, such losses would be rare and they would not be splashed across the pages of the *Harvard Crimson*.

PRESIDENT LOWELL'S suite of offices sat at the top of the steps of the suspended granite staircase on the south side of University Hall. Helen gave her name to the gray-haired, gray-suited secretary and was told to take a seat in the waiting room. She did as asked, sitting under a large oil painting of an American elm. The brass plate read "With High Regards from the Harvard Alumni Association."

At eight o'clock a clock chimed. The secretary returned to the waiting room and ushered her through a tall arched door that was recessed into the thick wall separating those waiting from the president's office.

The room was spacious, as befitted a man whose employees called its officeholder "President" and the man in Washington, D.C., "Mr. Hoover." Tall windows on two sides allowed full morning light to filter through the room, creating warmth not found in the waiting room of the upper hall. Priceless portraits hung on the walls, below which university treasures were displayed in antique cabinets that framed a sitting area at one side of the room. The other portion of the office was devoted to a large walnut desk. It was uncluttered, save for a fountain pen, a fat folder, and two scrolls of architectural blueprints secured with a length of black ribbon. The Persian carpet on which she was standing was rumored to be worth more than the entire Divinity School.

President Lowell had held his office since 1909, and now, in the twenty-third year of his presidency, he'd heard complaints about everything from students' marks, the back-biting faculty, the flow of the Charles River, and many other issues in which it was clear that not all parties would ever be pleased with any outcome. For a university president in his twenty-third year, nothing was new under the sun.

President Lowell was seated at the desk, reviewing a sheaf of papers, and didn't look up as they entered.

"President Lowell," said his secretary in a loud voice. "Miss Helen Brooks is here to see you."

"What? Oh, come in!" he said, his large mustache spreading over his wide face in a perfunctory smile. He pushed back his chair from his desk, stood and adjusted his wool jacket, then walked over to her, offering a large, beefy hand in greeting. He asked her to sit at a nearby table at which there were two chairs, each carved with the new Harvard crest. She sat, placing the folder Peter had given her on the table and grasping the handle of her purse in her lap.

"I'll have to ask you to speak loudly, Miss Brooks. I've become a little deaf in one ear." He leaned toward her with a conspiratorial whisper. "Well, actually it's both ears. I never thought I should live to be a decrepit old man. And, if I had just been a decrepit young man I should be used to it by now!" he said with a chuckle.

"For all your activity, you would hardly know that age even affected you," she said clearly. "I see you inspecting the Memorial Church each day."

"Yes, I do. Coffee?"

"No thank you," said Helen.

"That's all, then, Miss Pebbles." The secretary turned, her steps muffled on the thick carpet. Helen heard the door close.

He gave a slight cough and shifted in his seat. "Miss Brooks, my secretary tells me that you have some concerns about the fate of those young German soldiers we are not going to put up in the Memorial Room of the new chapel. It's a very popular subject these days."

"I do." She nodded. "One was my husband."

"Who?"

"Wilhelm Brandl."

He swallowed. "Wils Brandl," he repeated. He thought for a moment. "Yes," he said nodding. "I have heard about him. A promising student, by all accounts."

"That's true."

He looked away and began to speak. "This isn't easy. The fate of those who died was heroic. We have to go through a life that is much more continuous and complex." As he looked back at her, his eyes seemed tired. "Sometimes I envy them.

"I am not one to look for controversy and I know how to make the honorable compromise. But I must be clear. I am the caretaker of a serious legacy: the memories of hundreds of Harvard men who have died in a noble cause. It's an important matter."

Helen straightened. "I can't agree with a decision to divide friend from friend in a *church*. A church is a place of reconciliation." As she spoke, her voice became almost confident.

"Whatever a church is, Miss Brooks, it is definitely not a place to commemorate unworthy causes. And a war memorial without a moral is worthless. This is the exact point some members of the Brooks family made after the Civil War when they sought to exclude the rebels from Memorial Hall. I'm certain there were a number of Confederate widows with your point of view, yet the Brooks family prevailed. Are you saying that your family was wrong to do that?"

She'd not thought of that. "Perhaps it's time we reconciled."

He gave a snort. "I don't think Harvard will ever forgive the rebels. In fact, I agree with your grandparents. We try to encourage people to do the right thing at a school and in church. We cannot, and certainly not in a church, equate dying for a cause that was right with dying for a cause that was wrong. This is a place to learn the correct code of conduct, not just any code of conduct."

"But, sir, the German student soldiers died before the United States entered the war." She held up her sheaf of papers.

He shook his head. "They were part of the German army that attacked a neutral country. Should we ask the Belgian orphans how they feel about this action? Yes, indeed," he continued. "The Germans were wrong and our allies lost a generation of men for their mistakes.

Our halls were emptied of men in a way that hadn't happened since the sixteen hundreds in the Indian Wars."

"You need not lecture me on that account," she said, her eyes flashing with anger. She put the papers back on the table. "But if you build this memorial to one side in a church where all sinners kneel, then you build a memorial to human frailty. Honoring only one side will set your judgment in stone as long as the memorial exists."

He looked surprised that she was arguing. His face grew stern.

She swallowed hard. "As I recall, Yale included the rebels in their war monument."

"Has Yale ever been our standard?" he asked derisively.

She tried again. "Memorial Hall is a political monument to a triumph. Harvard chose not to forgive but to rejoice in its victory. If you make the hall a religious place I believe that fair-minded people would be right to say all should be included."

"I'm building a place to show our people that we value fidelity to just causes and that we will be faithful to those who were faithful to us. I don't mean to sound callous because I'd really like to persuade you. Let the Germans create for themselves their own memorial at their own universities. Built into the room is a clear statement that this room was for the people who fought with our allies. In fact, our donors gave money such that the Allied war dead would be honored. I cannot go back now and change the terms on them."

"So now the donors are the reason for what we're doing?"

President Lowell sat upright, tall and proud. "Miss Brooks, I am sorry you lost your husband," he said.

"President Lowell, my argument is not made out of some kind of wounded sentiment."

"Well, it actually is. Otherwise, it's the same argument I've heard already from the others." He caught himself, and then continued in a softer voice. "It doesn't make it easier that if I had counseled our German students back in 1914 that I would have told them to fight for what their conscience dictated. But it's difficult to separate the men from their country's mission, and that mission was wrong, even if in retrospect."

His back straightened in the chair. She looked at his hard eyes, and she knew she had lost him.

"But wasn't it found to be wrong because they lost the war? Because they were not strong enough to win?"

Lowell shook his head. "It was wrong because their cause killed millions and mutilated their own country. I will not change my path to support the idea that it doesn't matter what side you fight for. I don't accept that, not even in a church where all are presumed equal before God. If I were God I would not look to the killing of a generation of men kindly. And to my regret, that means that I cannot grant the request that you and many others have made that Wils Brandl be memorialized with the others. I am not against the boys, just their Kaiser's cause. And I have made the argument to Dean Sperry, the entire Phillips Brooks House, and some 300 petitioners this past spring. Your Mr. Brandl has some powerful friends on campus," he said with a kind smile. "But the matter is settled."

Helen looked down at her feet. What would she tell Peter or Copeland? That she had walked away? She looked up at the president. "My mother once told me a matter is only settled when the opposition walks away."

He gave a wan smile and they looked at each other in the bright morning light for a moment. And then, with nothing left to say, President Lowell and Helen Brooks exchanged a few pleasant words about the weather and the new forthcoming edition of Milton's verses before the clock chimed the half hour. He stood up and, with all courtesy, ushered her out of his office.

As she walked out of University Hall, instead of turning to the library, she went the other way, to the church. She stepped with purpose around the boarded walks, ignoring the call of the workmen that the church was closed to the public.

She was an officer of Harvard by virtue of her employment in the library. And she was part Windship, after all. Their rules didn't apply to her. She wanted to see the tomb.

[CHAPTER THIRTY-SIX]

THE MEMORIAL CHURCH

The church was bright and cold inside. Helen opened the door and walked down the central aisle, careful to avoid the workmen's debris. Bags of plaster, some open and dusty, littered the floor. Scrap wood lay in a heap, near scattered sawhorses and piles of dirty cloths. Paint cans were stacked by a tall scaffolding, and brushes soaked in open jars of pungent turpentine. The tarpaulins in the window wafted to the wind's dictate, blowing to the central aisle of the church. She could hear workmen's saws and hammers outside.

The wide aisle was flanked by rows of pews on either side. To the north, Helen saw a line of seven tall columns and window frames. To the west, she saw the outlines of a balcony above the doors. To the south, another set of seven columns had been put in place, rising into the arched ceiling.

She looked to the side, where large doors were closed before what she thought must be the Memorial Room. She took a deep breath, went through the dust and around the scaffolding, and opened the door.

A solitary bare bulb strung from the ceiling hung down into the dark room. As her eyes adjusted, she saw against a wall a heavy statue, a woman carved in marble mourning a lost Crusader who lay in her arms. His feet were not crossed—a sign that he'd not reached Jerusalem.

She swallowed, catching her breath. She was not one for crying at gravestones.

Around the top of the walls was an inscription she could barely make out:

While a bright future beckoned they freely gave their lives and fondest hopes for us and our allies that we might learn from them courage in peace to spend our lives making a better world for others.

She stepped back against the wall, and stumbled over a stack of travertine panels yet to be installed. She knelt down to press her hands into the grooves of the names.

There they were.

Child upon child of Harvard who had died in the Great War, their names carved by class year into the panels and gilded with bronze. There were so many names.

She looked up at the north wall, where several classes had already had their names set in place. It was there she saw them.

The Class of 1915: Riley Cabot Spencer. Jackson Marion Vaughn. She looked to the later classes. No Wils. No Germans at all.

As she looked around the memorial, her anger was overpowered by a silent grief. After seventeen years, her losses were there, facing her. This was no home for her. Her heart had been crushed and broken and she'd found that all the king's horses and all the king's men could not put it back together again.

In the dim light of the Memorial Room, she stood up, dusted off her skirt, and said a short prayer to whoever might be listening. She walked out the south porch, to the surprise of some workmen, who moved a pair of sawhorses so that she might pass.

New dreams, she thought. It was time for new dreams.

As SHE WALKED to the library, images of her mother standing before City Hall came to her mind. The newspapers. An idea began to form that perhaps publicity wasn't always a bad thing. Newspaper pressure had certainly helped her mother's cause. Perhaps it would here too.

No, she thought, shaking her head. It wouldn't. It had been in the papers before and caused no such change in policy.

She pursed her lips, arguing the case with herself. The president's reputation had been badly tarnished by his stance in the Sacco-Vanzetti anarchy trial and it was beginning to be said, in some circles, that the president had not outwitted his enemies, but outlived his friends. Perhaps at this late date, pressure could be brought to bear on him such that he would bend.

But who could affect him? The back room was where the Harvard Corporation sat, the only ones with real influence over the president at Harvard, and she could not influence that table.

She shook her head as she began to walk to her office at the library. Some yards down the broad path, she saw a sign tacked to a freestanding bulletin board. "Copeland in the Yard at Sever Hall. Introduction by President Lowell. Seating limited to first five hundred." She stood looking at the flyer and her eyes widened. She turned toward Hollis Hall.

She walked up the steps to Professor Copeland's door and knocked.

"I've no appointment at nine twenty—" came a thin voice from behind the door.

"Professor Copeland," she called in a loud voice, "it's Helen Brooks."

"Have you found your courage?"

"I spoke with President Lowell and he has denied the Germans inclusion in the war memorial."

The heavy wooden door squeaked open on its hinges a crack. She saw one of his eyes blink at her from behind his thick glasses.

"But I've a plan," she continued. "It requires that you humiliate the president."

The door opened immediately, and he bade her come in.

[CHAPTER THIRTY-SEVEN]

THE LOWELL LECTURE HALL

November 1932

O n an evening in early November, Professor Copeland puttered over to Sever Hall. His assistant, Thomas, a thin young man with a mop of brown curls, walked in tow with his water glass and book. As they passed in the shadow of Memorial Church, looking to Sever Hall's brick arches, they saw an unusually large group assembling. They made an attempt to wade through the crowd, but the throng of students hanging from the stairways, sliding down the banisters, and otherwise cluttering its floors prevented them.

"Thomas, you see what all the ruckus is about. I'll wait outside," Copeland said, sitting down on a step. It was too loud inside.

Young Thomas came back a few minutes later, his face ruddy. "The crowd—they're waiting for you," he said breathlessly.

Copeland's face brightened.

"Not knowing if you'd die or something and this would be your last reading."

Copeland's eyebrows fell, but he checked himself upon seeing President Lowell coming up the path, his hair flowing out from under a black fedora.

"Copeland!" called the president with a smile and a wave. The balding Copeland had long been jealous of Lowell's thick gray hair. He didn't deserve all that hair.

"So I hear this may be the last one," said the president in greeting.

"I can't get into the classroom," he said loudly.

"What? Oh, yes, I see," he said, looking through the glass around the doors at the crowd in Sever. "No problem. Just move it to my lecture hall."

"The new lecture hall?" Copeland said, raising his eyebrows. "I read in Sever Hall," he said stiffly.

"Is there a problem?" asked Lowell, bowing his head to hear Copeland over the voices of the students pouring from the hall.

"I read in Sever Hall," he repeated into President Lowell's good ear.

"Now, now, Charles, I know it's not like old times. But they want to hear you. Come on, now, we'll walk over there together."

"Boy!" Lowell beckoned to Thomas. "Go tell the students that they will see Mr. Copeland at the new lecture hall."

As Lowell turned, Copeland said quietly, "Thomas, make sure Miss Brooks knows about the new room." And he left to accompany the president to the clean, shiny, newfangled lecture hall.

THE NEW HALL was located beyond both the Memorial Church and the large Victorian Memorial Hall, to the north of campus. Built in Lowell's favorite Georgian brick, it looked like an elegant box on the corner of Kirkland and Essex Streets, and sat nearly one thousand students.

By the time Helen arrived at the new location, the president had already begun his introductory remarks—a eulogy of sorts.

She entered the room from the back. Copeland, she saw, was still fiddling with his lamp and his water glass. Lowell concluded his remarks and went to sit in the front of the room, his hand cupped behind his good ear. The room was filled, except for several seats around the president. Students did not wish to get too close, it seemed. Nasty rumors always floated about regarding how presidents randomly expelled students for all sorts of odd reasons.

She caught Copeland's eye. He nodded at her, peering above the rims of his spectacles.

"Lock the door against the latecomers!" he said. The student ushers promptly got up to do his bidding.

"Wait!" came a voice. Helen turned to see her brother and Ann enter, followed by four elderly men. Helen's heart gave a leap: they were four of Harvard's richest donors and their fortunes were known to have weathered the crash. She glanced quickly at President Lowell, who gave a surprised look and stood up, beckoning them to come and sit beside him in the reserved section. Copeland nodded in their direction.

"Any others?'"

There was silence.

"Then lock the doors!" And the students did so.

"You should all know the rules by now," said Copeland. "I will give you two minutes to do all the coughing, sneezing, and chewing you wish, but then I require total and complete silence. Total and complete. Anyone who wishes to cough, sneeze, hack, or in any other way disturb thy neighbor may leave through the window."

A general murmur went through the crowd as they took this to be their cue to talk, cough, sneeze, hack, and otherwise disturb their neighbors. But at the end of the allotted time, the laughter quieted and all eyes focused on Copeland.

Helen saw him survey the crowd, excited. She thought he looked ten years younger.

And with that the reading began. He read selections from Chaucer, from Balzac, and Dickens. He read Shakespeare and Marlowe, verses from Longfellow and passages from Thoreau. Two hours flew by.

"This will be my last reading for the evening."

The students began to protest. "Be quiet and you just might learn!" he called, taking a drink. There was silence again.

"We've had a lot of talk on campus about war recently. You here have grown up without one. You don't know the price we've paid. Tonight's last reading is from the Old Testament."

Helen sat back in a corner of the room, taking it all in. It was different from the first time he'd read to her—seventeen years ago. Now he was shrunken and stooped, his checkered jacket hanging loose on his frame. His voice was still clear, though chiseled with age and wear.

His story began quietly, in the Golden Age of Israel, when King David ruled the land. Copeland started where all the trouble began, when Absalom, King David's son, decided to wage war against his father. She heard his voice grow stronger as he read of Absalom's rebellion:

> And there came a messenger to David, saying, the hearts of the men of Israel are after Absalom.
>
> And David said unto all his servants that were with him at Jerusalem, Arise, and let us flee; for we shall not else escape from Absalom: make speed to depart, lest he overtake us suddenly, and bring evil upon us, and smite the city with the edge of the sword.

She looked at Lowell, who shifted in his seat. I hope he falls out of it, she thought uncharitably. As Copeland continued and Absalom was killed by David's captain, the audience was silent, caught up in the ancient feud.

Copeland looked up. Lowell was glowering now, his face almost pink, sensing what was next. No students were moving, no noise was heard.

> And the king said to young Cushi, Is the young man Absalom safe? And Cushi answered, The enemies of my lord the king, and all that rise against thee to do thee hurt, be as that young man is.
>
> And the king was much moved, and went up to the chamber over the gate, and wept: and as he went, thus he said, O my son Absalom, my son, my son Absalom! Would God that I had died for thee, O Absalom, my son, my son!

The professor paused, closed his Bible, and looked up at his audience. President Lowell sat back in his seat, crossing his arms before his chest.

"That ends the reading for tonight," said Copeland, "With one exception. I beg of your attention for another moment," he said, holding up his hand to the audience. "Patience, please." He pulled a page from his coat pocket.

"In 1914 I had a student who wrote poetry. He wrote some damned awful stuff. But before he left for war, for his last assignment, he turned in one of the most beautiful poems I've seen from a student. I'd like to read it tonight."

Copeland gave a cough. "Oh, yes, he was a German by the name of Wils Brandl. But we're all friends tonight."

He caught Helen Brooks, in the back, her lips parted in surprise.

A Prayer
by Wilhelm von Lützow Brandl

Is this how a spirit dies? On a dark
August day under the guns of strangers
Our children drown in the blood of a world
Not we but our fathers made. We die for
Thoughts we don't think, and for men we don't love.
Luther's God, build your fortress round our hearts
Until our souls are welcomed back to earth.
Grant the gift of Spring to a broken race.

As Copeland read, tears fell down her cheeks. When he finished, the room burst into applause. President Lowell turned to survey the room, looking as if he'd just had a drink of vinegar.

A thin young man stood up. "The Germans—they were ours, sir," he said, looking directly at President Lowell. Another student stood up. "Ours, sir."

Another stood up, followed by row upon row, until the entire room stood—including Peter, Ann, and the donors—each one claiming the dispossessed.

"They were once ours," said Helen, standing, surveying the room.

She swallowed, hard. They had come and stood up for Wils, a boy they'd never known. She felt the calm assurance that they would prevail. A smile came to her lips. Winning was fun.

She left the room before it was over. Its air had become suffocating to her. She went to the door, unbolted it, and walked out into the cool night air. The air hit with a refreshing gust, chilled and clean.

She began to walk slowly back to the Yard. She wasn't in a rush. She wasn't angry. She just needed a bit more space.

Perhaps Wils really had been a better poet than she. Maybe. Possibly. Her face broke into a grin, thinking how outraged he would be that this was a question that required pondering.

IT WAS NOT MUCH LATER, when, on a cold day in late December, and with little fanfare, a plaque was found on the wall of the new church, outside the confines of the Memorial Room.

> *Harvard has not forgotten her sons who under opposite standards gave their lives for their country, 1914-1918: Wilhelm Brandl, Fritz Daur, Konrad Delbruck, Kurt Peters, Max Schneider.*

Few could read it, however, for it was engraved in Latin.

[CHAPTER THIRTY-EIGHT]

THE MEMORIAL CHURCH

Christmas Eve

It was Christmastime once again in Boston, and colored electric lights decorated the storefronts. Despite the toll of the Depression, money was still found for windows to be hung with holly wreaths and stair railings to be draped in boughs of fir and pine. Helen had managed a red ribbon on her front door.

The morning of December 24, she was called from her coffee and toast by a knock at her front door. She walked to the door and was surprised to see Robert Brown standing there, in a dark suit and topcoat, with a copy of the day's newspaper. He was tall and thin, with wrinkles beginning at the edge of his brown eyes. His hair was dark, yet, as she got closer to him, she saw much silver in it. His cane and limp, she had heard, were souvenirs from the Battle of the Somme.

"Robert!" she exclaimed, pleased to see him. She'd tried to meet him in the past few weeks, but his calendar had been quite crowded. "Please come in!" she offered.

He didn't move, but rested on the cane while holding up the front page of the newspaper. "I see you made the news, Miss Brooks," he said with a smile. His breath came in white puffs. His cheeks were red.

"What?" she asked, puzzled. She stepped outside to take a closer look at the paper. The cold hit her hard, biting through her wool sweater and snapping at her legs. She crossed her arms in front of her.

The photo in the paper was of the new memorial. Its caption read,

*The Harvard compromise memorial plaque, above,
was supported by Rev. Sperry, Prof. Copeland, and
Librarian Helen Brooks. Students from the Phillips
Brooks House gathered to protest the compromise
Monday as "too little" and "a memorial to division."*

"Too little! Those students should be grateful they—"

"Your mother would be proud," he interrupted. "And I walked over here on a cold day to tell you. You got yourself involved in politics and prevailed."

"I've become my mother!"

"I certainly hope so," he said with a smile. "Your father loved her." He folded the paper and put it under his arm. "My mother had said that the passion of the Brooks family died with your mother. I'm glad to see it didn't. I was given hope."

Her eyes stung in the wind. "Hope?" she frowned. "For me?"

"No. For me. She is what you should have been all along. I'm glad to see people return to their old selves. That's all I came to say."

"Would you come in for some coffee?" she asked. "It's freezing out here." He took a quick look at his watch. "Robert," she said softly, "I'll not keep you long."

He gave a little laugh. "Perhaps another day."

"You prefer to stand on my porch in the cold but not come inside."

"Yes." They stood in silence for a moment. He cleared his throat. "Well, I'll admit I need to speak with you about another issue. It's an invitation for the Christmas Eve service tonight, at that new church you're so fond of. Of late I have found it useful to have old friends around at Christmas. It's one of the few times of year, since Jane died, when I actually look forward to something." A fragile smile crept to his lips.

She looked at him carefully. "Robert, do you think God cares for the dead?"

He thought for a moment. "I do."

She took a deep breath. "I've not thought much about Christmas since the war. I thought it a farce," she said. "Perhaps it's time I held it in higher esteem."

"I should say so."

They stood in silence a moment more, the chill of the shaded street setting into their bones.

Suddenly Robert's eyes brightened. "Did you hear about Caroline?"

Helen shook her head.

"She's now to become Caroline Peabody Adams Hilliard Faulks." His eyes turned merry.

"Robert," she said, stifling a laugh, "I'll admit I'm grateful to be rid of Caroline."

He looked at her. "You were not in Caroline's league. She had power over us all."

"Now she can have power over Mr. Faulks." She smiled. "Do you remember—"

She heard the telephone ring in her kitchen. "Wait," she said hurriedly. "Please don't go, Robert. And get in out of the cold," she insisted, beckoning him in as she went to pick up the phone.

Riley Spencer Junior was in town. He arranged to come by. Helen put down the phone and steadied herself.

"Robert. Riley Spencer's son is coming over."

He stared blankly then suddenly frowned. "That name." His eyes suddenly opened. "The dance before you went to Radcliffe! And the car at the Harvest Festival. I wanted to do some fairly awful things to that young man," he said.

She gave a half laugh. "He probably would have deserved them, too. But he married and died in the war. His son is looking to create a past."

"And you're part of that?"

"Briefly."

He looked at his shoes and nodded. "I'll leave you to your visit. I'll be over at my house," he said. "Perhaps we shall go together later this evening?"

She looked at Robert and smiled. She remembered his friendship so many years before in Lexington.

"I'd enjoy it. We could discuss your mother's plans for your life."

He suddenly brightened. "I'll need an ally in that battle. You know, she always did approve of you. You had better watch out."

Helen took a deep breath as they walked together out into the cold December air. She had always approved of Robert Brown. She waved at him, watching him leave. The tap of his cane seemed almost energetic.

ON MOST DAYS the white parlor saw no one, yet today she had two male visitors, neither a blood relative. Her neighbors on Chestnut Street thought this might be the year's Christmas miracle, and resolved after the holidays to converse among themselves about the odd goings-on at Helen Brooks' house.

At the appointed time a young man had arrived at her doorstep. He was a good bit taller than his father, but had the same brilliant green eyes. His teeth were a bit large, perhaps his mother's doing, but his smile was quick and kind. He seemed at ease with an adult, projecting the confidence of a remarkably untroubled life. Since he'd had such rough beginnings, she could only think it reflected well on his Kinnaird grandparents.

"Miss Brooks, I've only a half hour before I'm to catch the train to New York, and I wished to come by to speak." His voice was his father's. She could barely contain her smile as she invited him in.

As he spoke of his family, she felt a burden lift from her shoulders. She had long thought she was the only one who cared to recall the lives of these cousins. But here was another generation who would know, and would wish to learn of the young men. She no longer felt alone. It was the touch of cool water on the tongue of the thirsty.

They talked quickly, and she learned much. Riley was entering a military academy in England. His German relatives in Prussia had been devastated by the war. The Brandl estate had been overrun and looted, and Wils' mother had been placed in an asylum, where she'd died shortly after the war. The toll of the war and the depression had been difficult, but he'd a faith that things would right themselves.

"I am quite thankful for any news that you might provide me about my parents such that I could place it with the museum."

She looked at him carefully. "I didn't know your mother."

He beamed. "She was a beautiful woman. I think it was heartbreak that led to her death. She adored my father, and it was so clear that he loved her too. If I can only find that in my life, I would think it complete."

She looked at him carefully. He knew little. "And who else will you visit while you are here?"

"I saw a few professors and the Memorial Room. I'm off now to see Mr. Morris Rabin in New York. I had a hard time finding my father's friends, but it seemed time to give it a try."

She related to him what she could—the story of her courtship with Wils, of Riley avenging him, and how he'd promised to marry Edith in their last meeting.

As the time drew near for him to leave, he reached into a scarred leather satchel and brought out a folder. "Miss Brooks, I have something for you that recently came into my possession. It is of such a personal nature that I could not send it by post." She looked up quizzically at him.

"I was given two letters before I left England. Apparently my uncle Wils was with my father at the time of his death. When Uncle Wils died, the letters were retrieved by a priest, a Father Rupert, who was subsequently killed by a British soldier. By an odd coincidence, when the Imperial War Museum called a meeting to request donations for their collections, I attended, as did a man who had letters which, we both acknowledge, belong to you. They were opened when they came into my possession and I have them here now.

"I'll let you read these in private; I know you must wish to." He looked down at his watch. "I am sorry but I must be off. I've an invitation and my train leaves soon."

She saw Riley, and not his son, as he smiled and gave a quick nod of his head to depart.

SHE SAT in a stuffed high-back chair in the pristine parlor looking at the envelopes on the table—one thin and one thick. It had been so long since she'd had one. She picked up a thin, brittle envelope. It was addressed to her and in Wils' handwriting.

From Riley to Helen. I received this on the battlefield. I found him and buried him.

> Madam,
>
> I beg to inform you of my marriage to my dearest Edith Kinnaird. We have of late received the joyous news announcing an upcoming birth and are delighted with the news. I understand congratulations are in order for you as well, on your marriage to my dear cousin. I pray that we will all meet again at the christening of our much-expected child and in the meantime, wish you all grace and Godspeed.
>
> With joy,
> Riley

Behind the letter was a yellowed, wrinkled newspaper page: the kiss from the Petition Drive, so many years ago.

Helen blinked back tears. It was all lies. But she understood. This was Riley's gift to his unborn child. Well done, she thought.

And so it was that she picked up the second envelope. It was different from the others—bulky. And the handwriting was Wils'.

As she opened it a yellowed satin ribbon fell out, with her pearl ring on it. She broke into fresh tears.

> My wife,
>
> At Harvard we were asked to find our futures, and you were mine. You gave me everything. In my death I

have asked my mother to provide for you as my equal and her sole heir.

For the past few weeks I have seen the hollow faces of those who have lost loved ones, and I am reminded of how I felt when Max died. He wrote me a letter—a gift of absolution and well wishes. It released me, and was, in death, the kindest thing he could have done.

I have asked Father Rupert to include your ring in this letter. It is a wondrous pearl—one I kissed many times while waiting for life—and eventually, while waiting for my death. Yet I never wish it to become the pearl of great price, for which you sold everything. I pray your life will be as beautiful as the time you gave me.

When you feel a warm breeze cross your lips, know that it is from the gate left opened for you to the golden fields of God. There I once again will await the pleasure of your company. Let us learn to laugh again.

I loved you. And now, my dearest Helen, I release you.

Wils

Helen Windship Brooks didn't know how one changed, but after reading his letter, she no longer felt seventeen, crushed beneath the weight of grief, in her cold room at Longworth Hall. She felt as Wils had walked through her, and his spirit, cold and eternal, had left again, for another place. Apparently he'd said his good-bye to her years before. She'd just not known it until now.

She sat back and inhaled deeply, looking at the letter.

She wanted to kiss his letter. She closed her eyes and held it to her. In her mind she saw his laughing smile.

She blew her nose, put the letter down, and laughed in her tears.

The lightness felt good, and refreshing. It felt as if at that moment she was free to write a hundred bad plays, to visit all sorts of unknown places, and to— to—, well, to do whatever she decided she was going to do. Instead of a very empty glass, her portion, perhaps, was full.

Her shoulders shook, and, after a while, she found herself giving a good sigh. They were gone.

She picked up the phone. "Morris Rabin of Brooklyn, New York. Yes, I'll wait."

She sighed. It was time to make new plans. It was time to begin anew.

"Hello, Morris. This is Helen Brooks. Yes, it has been too long. Much too long. I hear that young Spencer will be there in a few hours and before he gets there I will need you to rewrite a bit of history. It's about Riley's women."

"Women? What women? Were there any others beside Edith?"

"Exactly," she said. "He loved her deeply and welcomed the news of his son."

"That's the truth as I remember it and no one can tell me different," came his reply.

A GENTLE SNOW fell outside that Christmas Eve, dusting Harvard Yard in a white blanket. The muddied prints in the grass, the dull gray of the library's steps, and the grime of the streets disappeared under a fresh, quiet field of white. The snow was undisturbed as Robert and Helen drove up to the church. The students had left for Christmas, and, except for those attending the evening service, Harvard Yard was deserted.

Robert pulled his car into the Yard, close to the church. As the bell tolled for the service, Helen walked with him slowly up the church steps, careful that he not slip. As they reached the top he removed his hat, offered Helen his arm, and together they entered the church vestibule. The ushers handed them a program and a small candle.

Tonight the church was warm. Candles lit the arched window above the oak screen, beyond the choir. The windows along the north and south walls were decorated with holly and lit with candles. Outside, the snow fell silently onto bare tree limbs.

The high white wood pews were hung with boughs of green and

red velvet ribbons, hemming in the hundreds of congregants who packed the church that evening. Twelve tall white columns, topped with elaborate carvings of eagles and rams, lions and lambs, reached to the arched ceiling. She looked behind her to see the clock squarely opposite an ornate pulpit. As the organist began to play, the choir filed in behind the altar's wood-and-gold screen, their faces barely visible. Student ushers in dark suits lit altar candles held in flourishes of iron filigree. A gilt eagle, wings outstretched, held a large Bible.

The choir sang "Adeste Fideles" as vergers led the Reverend Sperry and President Lowell in a processional down the long aisle for the evening's service of carols and scriptures. It was a lovely church, and a lovely service.

At the behest of the students of the Phillips Brooks House, the choir's final song that Christmas Eve was "Silent Night," sung in both German and English. The students, still unhappy that they had to compromise with two memorials, thought the song should commemorate the Christmas truce during the first year of the Great War.

As the lights dimmed in the church, the robed choir emerged from behind the altar and filed into the church's aisles. They took a flame from the altar and passed the candle's flame from person to person, illuminating the dark room with flecks of light. Their candles cast friendly shadows in the December darkness. The light multiplied amidst the music of the congregation, a soprano voice soaring in a beautifully measured descant.

At the very last verse, Helen felt a draft from the Memorial Room—a sharp gust that extinguished her candle's flame. She looked over at the room, and then quietly slipped out from her pew to enter the marbled hall. Soft lamplight illuminated the walls and the names of the dead that surrounded her. As before, the marble tomb of the fallen Crusader was cold and silent.

She saw that the door to the south porch had been propped open. As she went to close it, she spied in the distance a young boy and his dog running in the snow away from the church, and into the dark of the night. She watched them leave, and then closed the door to the night air.

They were gone, returned to their immutable field of play. The war was over.

She walked back to the pew and stood beside Robert as the members of the congregation bowed their heads for the benediction. Reverend Sperry stood, and in the candlelight of the church, held up his hands in blessing. He released them to the Christmas night, saying,

"As the Psalmist wrote,

'Surely, goodness and mercy shall follow me, all the days of my life,
and I shall dwell in the house of the Lord forever.'
And now may God's blessings flow to you
this Christmas night,
and forever.
Amen."

AFTERWORD

H ARVARD 1914 began as a story about the building of Harvard's Memorial Church. It is ultimately a story of abandonment and reconciliation. A young woman who seems to have it all has been abandoned by her activist mother, and by her father, who thinks she's a book. War takes the rest. She needs a new imagination to build a bridge between the past and the future.

I found at Harvard that unusual imagination built into its very walls. To include both sides of a horrific war in the same memorial takes courage and vision beyond our abilities. Yet there are places, including Harvard's Memorial Church, where reconciliation occurs in stone. And there are others—such as Harvard's Memorial Hall, not two hundred yards from the church—where it does not.

This is a work of fiction, yet it has some basis in fact. In 1991 Harvard University's Reverend Peter J. Gomes delivered a sermon entitled "The Courage to Remember."* It points to a path to restore connection. Here is a portion of what he said:

> Over on the North Wall, in the far back is a plaque in
> Latin, which most of you will be unable to read. In
> translation it says this, "Harvard University has not
> forgotten its sons, who under opposite colors also gave
> their lives in the Great War." And then there are listed
> four German members of the University who died in
> the service of the Kaiser in the First World War. This
> is one of the more extraordinary memorials in this

church. You will notice that it is separated by a vast
acreage from the memorial to the war dead of the first
War in the Memorial Room. This was a controversial
matter in 1932 when this church was built. And the
University authorities said that they could not in good
conscience include the war dead of the enemy in the
same place as the war dead of the Allies. And it was my
predecessor, the Chairman of the Board of Preachers,
Willard Sperry, who with his colleagues said this is
wrong. "We cannot contravene the President and
Fellows of Harvard College, who are we against them?"
But we could improve upon their narrow vision and
in this church we shall remember them. And we did
and we do and there they are. A reminder of the fact
that humanity transcends the sides and there are no
victors ultimately; there are only those to be
commended to God.

This sermon became the basis for *Harvard 1914,* a book about loving
enemies.

But that is not the end of the actual memorial's story.

In 2001, Rev. Gomes dedicated a memorial plaque to three women
from Radcliffe College, Harvard's sister institution. The women, Lucy
Fletcher, Ruth Holden, and Helen Homans, died in World War I as
nurses to soldiers in Russia and France. Their lives were honored publicly in the *Radcliffe Quarterly* in 1918. Because Harvard and Radcliffe
were separate institutions, women were honored at Radcliffe, and
men in the Harvard student memorial. Two years after Radcliffe for-
mally merged with Harvard, these women were honored in Memorial
Church.

Finally, I would like to publicly thank Rev. Gomes for what his
work meant for me. I enjoyed reading his sermons long past my gradu-
ation date at Harvard. I use my last few words here to reprint a portion
of a benediction that he delivered to Harvard seniors, but that is appli-
cable to us all:

Go out there, then, with courage, grace, and imagination. We give you our love—a word not used much around here, and saved for your very last moments—and we commend you to the love of one another and to the greater love of a loving God. This now, at last, is the best that we can do for you. This is the best that there is and it is yours, so go for it, for God's sake, and for your own. Amen.

Allegra Jordan

---

* Peter Gomes, "The Courage to Remember," November 10, 1991. Copyright President and Fellows of Harvard University.

ACKNOWLEDGMENTS

THIS BOOK IS A SIMPLE LOVE STORY. But not just any kind of love. It's a love that points to a new imagination in the midst of a violent, broken world.

There was a time in my life when I needed a new imagination. During that time this manuscript sat in a drawer for six years. Through the love and help of the following people, the manuscript found its way into the world:

I thank Nancy McMillen and Jan McInroy for their impeccable design and editing skills, and their encouragement of my mind and heart; my writing partner Jack Getman; the librarians at Harvard University, the Imperial War Museum, and the Harry Ransom Center at the University of Texas at Austin. Thanks to Jonathan Jordan and Philip Bobbitt for insight or review of WWI military matters. I thank my friends who provided encouragement and advice: Hendey Hostetter, Paresh and Eliza Shah, Adrian and Yun Soo Vermeule, Debora Spar, Eve Kushner, Mark Peterson, Terri LeClercq, Stefanie Griffith, Robin Swift, Liesl Ward Harris, Virginia Wise, Bunny Ellerin, Annie Dingus, Amy Carr, John Finley IV, Stan McGee, Alex Albright, Linda Werlein, Brenda Bennett, Kathy Bradley, Chris Brady, Andrea Brown, Reed Brozen, The Lucky Ladies' Lunch Club, the Writers' League of Texas, Oscar Dantzler, Trisha Kenneally, Jerry Alena, Joyce Gabriel, Steve Klein, Grace Hobbs, Dorothy Leonard, Bob David, Darriel Harris, the Duke Youth Chapel group, Amy Gutman, Claudia Groeber, Michelle Wachs, and a prayer group led by Fay Chandler and Ildiko Szabo. I thank those who helped me learn what it means to flourish: Everdith Landrau, Wyatt McSpadden, Ray Barfield, Esther Acolatse, Mary Ann Andrus, Willie Jennings, Jeremy Begbie, Jim Thomas, Malcolm Guite, Angelina Atyam, Yoko Sato, Emmanuel Katongole, Chris Rice, Jo Bailey Wells, Richard Hays, Sr. Peter-Paul, Sr. Mathias, Charlotte Awino, Richie Jean Sherrod Jackson, Henrietta Smith, Stephen Gunter, Judith Heyhoe, and Rex Miller. I thank all of my teachers. I honor my large Southern family and my small Northern family; I treasure the memory of my late father, Malcolm Jordan; and I send love to my wonderful immediate family. I welcome Theodore's family, especially Alex, Valya, Dan, and Colie. Finally, I wish to thank my partner, Theodore, and my sons for their love and support. Ted, Alex, and Michael, you are my *anam caras.*

A portion of the royalties from this book will go to support the work of Epiphany School, a tuition-free school in Dorchester, Massachusetts. The school was co-founded by John H. Finley IV, whose own grandfather mentored a generation of Harvard students by focusing on the good in people and urging them to excellence.

ALLEGRA JORDAN grew up in rural Alabama in
the wake of the civil rights movement. She is
an honors graduate of Harvard Business School
and Samford University. Jordan has written
best-selling cases for Harvard and published
UT Law, the award-winning magazine of the
University of Texas School of Law. She serves on
the board of the Southern Documentary Fund
and is the founder of Innovation Abbey. Jordan
lives in North Carolina with her two sons and her
dog, Belvedere. *Harvard 1914* is her first novel.

PHOTOGRAPH BY REX MILLER

Made in the USA
Lexington, KY
11 January 2013